To
Bubbs
Xmas 1974
Myrt & Ray

Also by Harriette Simpson Arnow

THE WEEDKILLER'S DAUGHTER
(1970)

THE FLOWERING OF THE CUMBERLAND
(1963)

SEEDTIME ON THE CUMBERLAND
(1960)

THE DOLLMAKER
(1954)

HUNTER'S HORN
(1949)

MOUNTAIN PATH
(1936)
(as Harriette Simpson)

The Kentucky Trace

THE KENTUCKY TRACE

A Novel of the American Revolution

Harriette Simpson Arnow

Alfred A. Knopf

NEW YORK · 1974

This Is a Borzoi Book
Published by Alfred A. Knopf, Inc.

Copyright © 1974 by Harriette Simpson Arnow
All rights reserved under International
and Pan-American Copyright Conventions.
Published in the United States
by Alfred A. Knopf, Inc., New York,
and simultaneously in Canada by
Random House of Canada Limited, Toronto.
Distributed by Random House, Inc., New York.

Library of Congress Cataloging in Publication Data

Arnow, Harriette Louisa (Simpson) Date
The Kentucky trace; a novel of the American Revolution.

I.   Title.
PZ3.A7654Ke [PS3501.R64]   813'.5'2   73–20748
ISBN 0–394–48990–X

Manufactured in the United States of America
First Edition

The
Kentucky
Trace

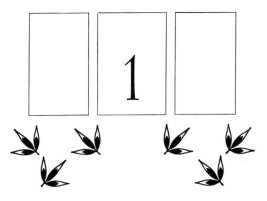

The wind died to a whisper, the pine-knot torches blown down to embers revived, and Leslie could again hear the about-to-die pray for the already dead: "—do thou give them rest there in the land of the living, in thy kingdom, in the delight of Paradise."

The English officer stood tall on the tailgate of the wagon, taller-seeming than when they had ridden through the woods together. It was the rope around his neck made him hold his head so high, the hangman's knot under one ear; his arms tied behind his back made him stand straight—or did he stand tall because he wanted to show these bastards he was not afraid to die?

The why didn't matter. Tall or short and a Tory into the bargain, the captain was a man, too much of a man to be hanged by anybody. These villains wanted him dead so he could never testify in court to their thievery.

The captain was going to die; the boy lieutenant was already dead because this rebel, William David Leslie Collins, had let himself and prisoners be tricked and captured by a gang of horse thieves and brigands. Prisoners was right but it sounded wrong; in their few days together, the men had seemed more his companions than captured enemies.

Lost, their long wandering had brought them and their

worn-out horses, hungry as themselves, to his campfire. He reckoned they'd followed the scent of frying ham. He felt the rawhide ties tighten on his wrists. He was making fists again. Looking back was no good.

He looked at the driver of the wagon, a black man captured with the wagon and team of mules. His face was clear as he bent to firm up the chock under a wagon wheel; was that tears or rain on his cheeks?

The outflung hand against his knee seemed heavier now. The boy couldn't take it away. He lay as his angry murderers had dumped him, angry because he had cheated them of what they had wanted to do. He had on the tailgate of the wagon stood straight as the man there now. The scoundrel called Zach who appeared to be the leader had looked him over, laughing a little. "You're a pretty young thing to be in the King's army. No beard on your chin. You're not worth a piss aginst the wind, you little son-of-a-bitchen mama's darlen, but you'll swing anyhow."

The boy had looked out and away as if he were alone and could see beyond the black gulch below, where in the quiet a sapling sobbed out the pain of its drowning in the risen creek. The boy was still looking ahead when he said loud and clear: "I pledge allegiance to His Majesty King George III of England."

Then, as if he were running through the woods and found a little brook to cross, and because he was so filled with life and youth, he had given a great leap that sent him over the gulch and above the sobbing tree. The rope brought him back, no longer a leaping boy, but a struggling puppet, heels striking the tailgate Zach had jerked up. Darkness was spreading over one pant leg.

"The heathern's gone and killed hissef and pissed in his pants to boot," somebody yelled.

Zach had cursed the speaker. There'd been too much slack in the rope; if it had been short enough to make him stand on his toes, the boy couldn't have jumped. Tighten it up for the next man.

They had.

"There is one glory of the sun, and another glory of the stars; for one star differeth from . . ."

The voice of the officer, the rain, and the sobbing sapling—a sawyer, a boatman would call it—were buried in a wailing gust of wind that brought the flambeaux down to glowing embers swaying on the lower limbs of the old white oak. "A fine hanging tree," one of his captors had called it.

Leslie was glad that while the boy was still swinging a wind like this had come to blow down the torches. Nobody could watch or hear his death struggles. It had seemed a long while he'd swung in the wind. Was he dying, struggling for breath all that time, longer-seeming than any man he'd seen hanged? But then he'd never watched one die. The leap ought to have broken his neck. Could a man feel pain with a broken neck?

The villains had at last with oaths and obscenities cut him down and dumped him in such a way that one of his hands had fallen on Leslie's knee.

He lifted his head to search the sky. Rain fell into his eyes and rawhide tightened on his throat. Neither star nor shape of cloud. Nothing but the blackness of a rainy October night in the dark of the moon. He dropped his head.

The wind roared as it shook the oak, screamed in the gulch below him, ran cold fingers up his back as if it planned to pluck him off the bluff and fling him down onto the rocks he couldn't see.

Under the screams of the wind as it fought the rock walls below were rustlings and whispers. The rustles came from the stiff, cold leaves of what sounded to be a sycamore, so tall its top was almost level with the bluff edge. The whispers were the voices of a hemlock, tall and close, else he wouldn't hear it.

A hemlock would be kind to him when he jumped into it. If he could jump, and he wouldn't jump without the captain—unless they'd already hanged him.

He was wasting the darkness. His captors had tied his ankles together with about a handspan of rawhide between, then brought the long strip up and around his neck. The three sons of bitches working on him had pulled so hard on the rawhide

5

he'd had to squat or have his wind choked off; squatted to their satisfaction, his wrists were then tied together behind his back with enough rawhide left to tie his wrists to the knotted loop about his ankles.

Soon as they'd left him to prepare for the hangings, he'd dropped to his knees to slacken the rawhide enough that he could look around. In a short time he had seen what he thought might help; now in the darkness he kneed his way to a loose sandrock, small enough to get between his tied-together ankles. The sandrock, worn though it was, could still fray the rawhide when he pushed it back and forth with his fingers.

The wind quieted.

"That it may please thee to strengthen such as do stand, and comfort the weakhearted." The voice was calm, quiet as the wind; under and around it Leslie could hear the rain on the rocks and last year's leaves, hiss of the flambeaux under the drops, and in the gulch the drowning sapling sobbed and gurgled.

There was again light; he could see the boy. The hand on Leslie's knee had fallen onto the wet leaves when he'd gone for the sandrock. The boy looked lonesome and cold, rain falling into his bulged-out eyes. Leslie wished he could at least cover his face.

". . . and comfort the weakhearted." The captain had quoted that. Leslie Collins had been weakhearted, else he would have killed the captain and the boy when they came upon him. It were kinder had he done so. He hadn't. There were some who'd call him traitor to the cause; but then maybe he'd feel a traitor to mankind if in the woods he'd killed two men only because they'd worn the uniform of the enemy. They'd come with no white flag, only a polite request for directions to the headquarters of Major Patrick Ferguson.

No need to ask on which side they were. They had worn the uniforms of English officers. He ought to know; he'd made enough red coats grow redder. He told them what he'd heard: there had been a battle at a place called Kings Mountain; Ferguson was dead; his troops dead, wounded, or captured.

They'd taken the news like the men they were; but you

could see the sorrow and the disappointment in the captain's eyes.

He'd stayed awake half the night, hoping to hear the good news of their sneaking away, and so save him the trouble and the shame of turning them over to some trustworthy man like John Sevier, who'd put them on parole. But he hadn't any idea of the whereabouts of Sevier then, shortly after the Battle of Kings Mountain.

". . . and prosper all their consultations to the advancement of thy glory, the good of Thy Church, the safety, honour, and welfare of our Sovereign and his Kingdom; that all things may be so ordered and . . ."

Another surge of wind scattered the captain's prayer and blew down the pine-knot flames. Leslie tried again to find the sky, but the boundless, shapeless blackness remained unchanged. It didn't matter. He knew where he was. Had the night been clear with stars, he would have seen the long wall of Clinch Mountain cutting off the bottom of the northern sky from east to west. And in between was Holston River, for he was on a branch of Reedy Creek that emptied into the Holston two or three miles away.

He straked his ankle ties over the sandstone, and wished he'd turned back to Marion's camp. It would have been a long trek for the captain and the lieutenant and their tired horses, but no farther than the long hard journey to their miserable deaths. Trouble was that Marion and his men in Loyalist country were hungry half the time, forage as they could. Anyhow Marion didn't have any prisoners.

They'd have been better off as prisoners from the beginning of their trip. Trouble had been in the saddle with them all the way. Over their first breakfast together, he learned from the captain they'd started out from Charles Town with guides, Loyalists, and so not worth a tinker's damn.

According to the captain, it wasn't noon when they got within sight of a tavern. The guides claimed it was time to rest and bait the horses; the scoundrels hadn't said so, but it was also the tavern's day for rum fustian. The guides had gone

7

overboard with rum fustian. The officers, after getting directions from the taverner, had gone on alone to hunt Ferguson's head-quarters as neither guide had been in shape to travel.

While listening to the captain's story, Leslie had collected words to tell the officers they would have to consider themselves his prisoners. Instead he'd told them he was paroling them to go where they wished, except, no different from other parolees, they could no longer be active in the war.

The officers had thanked him for the parole, but continued to ride with him. They were well armed. Leslie figured they could at least have tried to take him prisoner. It could be the captain was too much the gentleman to try to harm a man who'd saved him from starvation, or were they afraid of Leslie Collins? It was neither, he decided. The officers were prisoners, not of him, but of the rough country and the mountains they could see ahead. He misdoubted if they could have found their way back to Charles Town. It didn't matter. They had a friendly peaceable ride together.

He strained to hear the captain's voice below the wind. The voice reminded him of his father's saying the same words at morning prayers when he'd lately learned from a ship's captain that Parliament was in session. The two voices ought not to sound the same. His father was at least a fourth-generation Virginian; his people had come when Cromwell tried to make over England. Yet his father had always considered himself, his wife, and his children as loyal English subjects.

And why should he want to hear his father's voice? Never at home in his father's house, he'd run away for his first longish trip when he was seven years old. That time they were glad to have him back and for several times after. Running away from that public school in England to which his father and his older brothers had gone was a horse of a different color. That had pretty well cut father-mother-son relationships. He was nobody's son and nobody's brother any more.

He worked until the wind quieted and the flambeaux flared again. "And may our great leader, Major Patrick Ferguson, taken from us on the field of battle rest . . ."

He'd be damned if he'd listen to prayers for that son of a

bitch. Mean as Tarleton. " 'Oh where are you going, my pretty maid?' 'I'm come to Camden battlefield to help the wounded, sir,' she said."

He'd never learned her name. To look at her had been enough—then. A beautiful filly with hair the color and brightness of the inside of a freshly opened chestnut bur, and her eyelashes long and black when she shuttered her dark blue eyes. And what a fine figure she'd made riding on a spirited stallion.

She was a good sight to see on that battlefield at Camden. The place was like something out of Revelation when it was over and he could take time for a look. Tarleton's dragoons had mowed down the panicked rebels like wheat. The men were lost with no leader. Their cowardly General Gates had run away; he had fleet horses; they had none.

Some of the women come to help had shivered and cried when they saw the sea of wounded men and bloody dead. Others had knelt over their own. She had never wavered, but began at once to carry water to the wounded able to drink. He had lost her in the fog. Where was she now? Safe at home? Or had Tarleton's gang burned out her people?

He was making fists again when he ought to be straking the rawhide over the stone. That pretty chestnut filly at Camden hadn't stopped his heart, but one of the enemy had. His line, what little there was of it left, was retreating, hacked to death, shot to death, trampled to pulp under the hooves of the chargers. All he could do was load and fire, no time for patching or measuring powder, but don't waste the priming powder; prick her touch hole, spit a couple of balls down her muzzle, draw a bead, quick, and fire. Plenty of heads above the red coats to aim at. He'd had a bead on one of Tarleton's officers riding high and sitting proud, bending only slightly as he swung his saber toward a fleeing rebel's neck. Leslie saw his face; shifted his aim, saw blood spurt from the shattered arm as the saber fell to the ground. He reckoned he'd wonder forever if his bullet had caused his brother Percy to lose his arm, or made a wound that went into gangrene and killed him.

He had expected Percy to take the King's side, but not under a commander evil as Tarleton. He had supposed he was

9

somewhere far from South Carolina, maybe with his other brother, Francis, whom he'd seen near Philadelphia with an outfit under Howe. And where was his father? He'd be a red-hot Loyalist.

"Man that is born of woman hath but a short time to live, and is full of misery. He cometh up and is cut down like a flower."

He hadn't noticed the hush in the wind. He'd frayed the tie so long it ought to be thinner now. That one tie cut would loosen his neck. He could then stand up and be a man, have a good chance to save the captain. Untied or no, he'd go over the cliff before he'd be hanged like a thief.

"O spare me a little, that I may recover my strength; before I go hence, and be no more seen."

The captain ought to pray for wind, darkness, and weak rawhide; there was no rawhide in the Book of Common Prayer; howsoever, he was saying a good deal not in the prayer book, and what was there, he'd mixed around.

The few flambeaux that had survived the wind and rain had flamed up, but so little light was coming his way he continued to strake the thong. And how was Kate making out? Hungry? Had the villains offered her nothing but raw pumpkin, the only thing they'd tried to feed him? Near the foot of the ridge they'd dragged her away while there was still light enough to see how she struggled to get to him. The very devil himself wouldn't treat that good and beautiful Chickasaw running woods mare that could make sixty miles a day where the going was good the way these blackguards had.

In a way Kate was luckier than the mules. They'd been beaten and forced to pull the wagon up the steep rocky ridge while a handful of his captors had walked ahead to cut brush and roll out rocks to make a road of sorts. He and the English officers had walked behind, hands tied, firelocks touching their backs.

The driver had quarreled all the way; they were killing his master's mules and ruining his wagon, he'd said. He'd tried to hold the mules back when, after reaching the place, Zach had ordered him to back the wagon until the lowered tailgate was over the bluff edge. They'd beaten him, but not into complete obedience.

"We brought nothing into this world, and it is certain we can carry nothing out, the Lord gave and the Lord hath taken away."

The captain was wandering in and out and all around the prayer book. "Lord, I beseech thee: Let my cry for him come near before thee."

Leslie looked at the captain; he didn't think that prayer had a *for him*. That was for the boy.

He held the rawhide still above the stone. He thought he'd heard the faint sound of a body slipping through wet brush. He wasn't certain; his captors, eager for the hanging, were grumbling at the delay, but the captain was going strong, now in the Litany: "Remember not, Lord, our offences, nor the offences of our forefathers; neither take thou vengeance of our . . ."

Leslie straked the rawhide again while the once familiar words rolled on. Looking straight in front of him, he watched the off mule step away from the wagon tongue until he like the lead mule stood almost at a right angle to the wagon. The black man still had a rein on each, but had unhooked the trace chains to better his chance of not losing wagon and team over the bluff. This would give the captain a few more minutes of life. It would take a while to get both mules back over the traces and hooked in; unchocking the wheels would also take time.

He saw the off mule's ears from being lazy drooping go straight up. That mule had heard something. Leslie shut his eyes, held his breath, and listened. He soon heard, from the woods on his side of the wagon, a limb breaking; soft as if it were rotten; a man or some big animal had stepped on it. He heard nothing more though the mule's ears were still up.

His captors were too drunk on stolen rum and brandy to notice anything except the length of the captain's prayer. Grumbling and curses were coming from under a low-limbed pine where most had taken shelter from the rain.

The sandrock was telling on the thong, so thin by now he thought he could break it with his hands—if his hands were free. His ankles would have to do it, but tied close together as they were, he couldn't get much leverage. He'd be better able to spread his legs if he squatted.

He was teetering on his toes, ankles touching, wondering why it was so hard for a man to keep his balance when he squatted with his hands behind his back, when more wind swooped over the ridge. Nothing to see but darkness. His ankles were touching; his balance was slightly better. Gathering all the strength he could muster, he jumped upward, only a few inches, but high enough that his feet cleared the ground and he could give a quick jerking-apart of his ankles.

The thong broke more easily than he had expected. His legs flew wide; the loop around his neck held, and he fell backward, head landing on the lip of the gulch.

He had a moment's thinking he would roll over the bluff, nothing to catch hold of with his tied-together hands. Then, he knew he wouldn't. He would live and again go west of the Illinois. He wouldn't turn back when in sight of the mountains as he had last time. He would go into and over those mountains, higher and wilder than any here, their tops always white with snow. And in that white snow world there'd be no fear of killing his father or his other brother before he recognized them in the heat of battle. He'd wait till the rebellion was won; some were calling the war a revolution. The name didn't matter, only sticking till the victory.

Rain was falling in his face, but he lay a moment to enjoy stretching and waving his freed legs. The discomfort of lying on his tied-together wrists kept reminding him to kneel again and get to work on that tie. Anyway, the wind was moving on, flambeaux reviving.

He was in a good way of working on his wrist tie when he heard Zach yell to the mule driver: "Pull the wagon out from under this bastard; he's already prayed too long."

". . . assist our prayers that we make before thee in all our trouble and adversities, whensoever they oppress us; and graciously hear us, that those evils, which the . . ."

The Litany was lost in a blast of curses. Zach had noticed the mules were standing at right angles to their unhooked trace chains; he cursed the driver and threatened him with death by slow fire if he didn't get the team hooked up in a hurry.

The black man didn't move. "This team is already skittery. Less'n you want em to run clean away, you'd better hook em up while I hold their heads."

Zach swore. The captain prayed. Neither the mules nor their driver moved. The off mule was almost parallel to Leslie. He studied the mule's flank, and thought about what he'd learned of mules down around New Orleans. He searched out his captors; those he could see were paying him no mind.

He soon saw what he wanted; a fairly long branch, but small enough he could handle it with his fingers. Ankles free, he quickly reached it by shuffling on his knees. Still kneeling, he straddled the bigger end, felt it with his fingers, then took another look at his captors. Most stood near the tailgate of the wagon, eager for the hanging as cur dogs for raw meat. Two were pushing on the lead mule; Zach stood by the off mule's head as he cursed and pummeled the black man. However, he soon began beating the mule instead of the man.

Hands on stick, Leslie moved within reaching distance of the off mule's flank. He saw Zach's legs on the other side of the mule's belly, then looked at the mule's ears; they were laid back. The big beast gave no sign he'd heard when Zach promised: "I'm goen after that trace chain on the wrong side a you, then beat you with it till blood runs out your asshole."

Leslie spread his knees and picked up the stick. Zach started to walk around the mule. He soon stepped into the right spot, not too close, but within good reaching distance of the animal's heels. Leslie, his stick at the ready, punched the mule's flank.

The mule let fly with both heels. Zach's body shot up and away. A pistol, gold coins, a watch, a bottle of brandy, and last a hunting knife still in its sheath showered from his pockets. Leslie kept his glance on the knife. Poor as the light was, he recognized the sheath and handle as belonging to the knife his captors had taken from him.

"Lighten our darkness, we beseech thee, O Lord; and by thy great mercy defend us from . . ."

The voice was drowned in a rising racket of oaths and

13

yells. Most were too drunk to understand at once what had happened to Zach. The more sober ones didn't care: two were name-calling each other as they scuffled over the watch; another ran stooping to pick up the scattered coins.

Nobody was going for the hunting knife, fallen into a huckleberry bush on the cliff edge. Leslie looked around, then kneed the few paces to the bush. Stout and close growing, it held the knife until he could pick it up with his teeth. He had the knife handle clamped between the heels of his shoepacs, wrist tie sawing down on the blade, when somebody bawled: "Zach's bad hurt from a mule kick. It's that nigger's fault. Let's git him."

Leslie cursed and pushed harder on the wrist tie. He wouldn't let them kill the black man for something he had done. He wouldn't let them kill him for any reason. His wrists came apart. He started to spring up and fell sidewise into the huckleberry bush. The loop around his neck was still wound around one wrist.

Freed in a trice, he sprang up knife in hand. The gang had converged on the driver, or where he had been. He was yelling from the woods like an embattled Shawnee, and must have got in some good licks for somebody yelled: "You've bloodied a white man, so we'll skin you alive, real slow, inch by inch."

A little runt of a man held up a pistol, the silver inlay of its stock twinkling in the light. Stolen, Leslie figured; it was almost as fine as his father's dueling pistols.

The little ruffian held it about four fingers from the lead mule's head as he called into the woods: "I just recollected: we don't aim to kill you, but sell you to the Chickamauga, or maybe down below Natchez where they'll work you to death in the sugar cane. But I do aim to kill your precious mules."

The mule driver leaped out of the brush larruping the spare brake pole. He was coatless, hatless, shirt and breeches torn, one eye swollen shut, blood trickling over his head and face. The man with the pistol jumped clear of the whistling pole; too angry to remember they'd planned to sell the black man, he tried to get a bead on his head.

The pistol leaped as if alive. The would-be murderer staggered against the wagon as the crash came, sounded like a tree falling about fifty paces back in the woods. The frightened mules snorted, kicked, fought the reins. ". . . and may he know neither sorrow nor pain and all . . ." Down below the sappling sobbed out the pain of its drowning; the creek talked to the rocks; the driver talked to the mules; that was all.

The hangmen were stopped in their tracks and stood with soundless tongues like the dead.

Leslie figured the bullet had come from a rifled barreled gun in the hands of an overmountain man. He'd heard it was the overmountain men who with their long rifles had defeated Ferguson at Kings Mountain. The shot could have come from one on his way home. No man in a hurry to be home from the battle would climb up to this desert—except to do some villainy.

He'd had to believe that old scared-to-death tavern keeper in North Carolina. The man hadn't fought at Kings Mountain, but was glad to hear the rebels had won. One evening a bunch had passed his place with a long line of Loyalist prisoners. They'd encamped close by. The old man had gone to the encampment. He'd wanted to tell the overmountain men how glad he was Ferguson's men couldn't steal and plunder any more; it was pitiful what they had done to the country.

He could still hear the tavern keeper's voice, shrilled up with terror: "An you know the first thing I saw when I got within seein distance? Why, a captured soldier swingen from a limb, and oh God was he haven a hard struggle choken to death. An the next in line beggen to be shot stead a hanged. And then I saw three corpses. They'd been hung, from their looks. I left. I didn't want to see no more."

Leslie wouldn't believe until he'd heard much the same story from another man who'd said one bunch of overmountain men had hanged thirty Loyalists.

All that meant they'd hang the captain in a hurry—if they could get their hands on him.

He realized he'd forgotten to get back on his knees. It didn't matter. The commotion had kept anybody from noticing. He dropped down, sheathed his knife, buried it in the fold of his hunting shirt, then shuffled back to the bluff edge. There, he lingered a moment by the boy, then went along the jagged edge of the cliff in the direction of the wagon's tailgate.

He had to be certain of the exact location of the hemlock. Going slowly, looking into the gulch, he at last made out, about fifteen feet from the bluff and five below, a spire blacker than any rock around it.

"Yea, though I walk through the valley of the shadow of death, I will fear no evil; for Thou art with me. . . ."

Leslie tried to catch the captain's glance. Failed; the man was looking into eternity. Anyhow, it was too soon. That black spire could be a jag of rock or a dead tree. He wouldn't be actually certain it was a hemlock until the black spire swayed and sounded right in the next gust of wind. They wouldn't stand on the very edge, but a few paces back so as to have room for a running jump; either on or below the low ledge back from the shelving rock would be a good place.

Half hidden behind a scrub pine, he could see none of his captors except Zach, who lay where the mule had kicked him. The others were hidden in the brush or under the wagon. That didn't mean they couldn't see him, but he reckoned it was about the best time he'd have to get ready for the jump.

He clamped his hat between his knees, found the horn comb in a hunting shirt pocket, and began to comb and tie up the strands of wet hair that had been straggling across his eyes, getting into his mouth, and tickling his throat. Hair tied back in a deerskin thong, he pulled his hat as low on his head as it would go. He was now about ready to jump—except for the captain now on another psalm.

He had cut an armful of pine boughs and was laying them over the boy when the wind struck. He hurried through the darkness back to the shelving rock and dropped on his stomach, head over the bluff edge, the better to see and hear that black spire. He could see little, but plainly heard its moaning sighs. A hemlock all right.

He and the captain could jump in the next time of darkness. There was still a chance to get him to John Sevier, who'd do the right thing and parole him. He found the tailgate of the wagon and sprang over. "I am weary of crying; my throat is dry; my sight faileth—. What the devil?—Oh, Mr. Collins. Sorry. However did you get loose?"

"A sandrock and a mule kick. I'll explain later," Leslie whispered as he worked on the captain's wrist ties. He continued to whisper, outlining his plan of escape, as he struggled with the knots, afraid of cutting the captain's wrists if he used his knife in the dark.

Hands free, the captain gripped Leslie's hand. "You're a brave man, and a good one. Jump if you will, but I'll stay here."

Leslie didn't answer. Somehow, he'd have to get the man to change his mind. Knife ready, he felt above the captain's head for the hanging rope, then grabbed it. He was thinking of how he could change the captain's mind when a bullet sang above his head. A length of rope fell across the captain's shoulder as a rifle sounded from across the ridge top.

Leslie and the captain automatically dropped flat into the wagon bed. Save for the frightened mules and the driver's soothing talk, all was silence. The captain stared up at the rope end, cleanly cut by the bullet as if done with a sharp knife. His glance continued on the rope while Leslie whispered the merits of his plan, ending with: "I got you into this mess. I mean to get you out."

The captain shook his head. "I was all for going to help that liar save his packhorse. I should not have permitted Lieutenant Wyatt to come with us. He might have . . . I intend to stay with him."

Leslie heard the sorrow in the man's voice and said nothing; no amount of talk could change his feeling.

"Anyway, I believe hanging is out for me." The captain's whisper sounded as if one way or the other it didn't matter. "Had that marksman meant for me to die, he would have shot me instead of the rope. Only military men could perform such feats of marksmanship. And in no civilized country on earth does the military hang prisoners of war."

"The overmountain rebels are not military men," Leslie whispered back. He was wondering if he should tell of the Loyalist prisoners of war hanged by some rebels when the cap-

17

tain whispered: "Getting away might be a good idea for you. Even if the marksmen in the woods are rebels, would they know you for one? I have wondered how in this war men know when they are meeting friend or foe, at least in the back parts where nobody wears a uniform."

"It's not simple," Leslie answered. He'd stayed too long. He'd talked too much. Somebody would be hearing his whispers, if they hadn't already. The captain would never leave the boy to come with him. They wished each other well, and Leslie slid off the tailgate.

Nobody but Zach was in sight. The others kept quiet and hidden as a covey of quail under the shadow of a hawk in the sky.

The silence was soon broken by one of the thieves. "This shooten iron here she's primed and charged. Any man that won't foller me is a yaller-hided coward."

A hat rose above a low branch of the bushy pine, stopped while the voice ran on: "We're cowards to hide here all night on account a some drunk fools passen by fired two shots. Let's git about the hangens." The hat had risen high enough any fool could see it was on a stick, no head under it.

A mule stamped restlessly with a jangling of harness. The captain had recollected more of the Litany. "—Mercifully assist our prayers that we make before Thee in all our trouble and adversities, whensoever. . . ."

The empty hat continued to beg some fool to waste powder and ball on it. Nobody did. The owner, after a long wait, grabbed it, slapped it on his head, jumped away from the wagon, and yelled: "The drunks are gone. We're nothen but a bunch of old squaws."

Leslie reckoned the man had never known an "old squaw"; whatever courage was, squaws had it. He was watching the man, thinking of a squaw met in the Illinois, when a button leaped from the shoulder of the man's stolen military coat. The shot came from a direction different from either of the others; the sound, the fear-crazed mules, and the silence of his captors were all the same, except for the man who'd lost a button. "I'm kilt," he said, and slid to the ground.

". . . and grant that in all our troubles we may put our whole trust and confidence in thy mercy, and evermore. . . ."

It was a fine thing to hear so much of the Litany, but for once Leslie wished the captain would be quiet. One of the mules was braying.

What did a mule say when it brayed, and why would he say it now? Leslie left off cutting pine boughs to put an ear to the ground, but the devil himself could have heard nothing for the distant roar of a gale coming his way; the wind was out of the southwest, must now be hitting the lower end of Clinch Mountain. He put a finger in one ear, and soon heard with the ear on the ground a sound out of tune with the traveling wind. He thought it was the click of a horseshoe on rock.

The oak boughs creaked and cried as the wind struck. Dead leaves, rotten limbs, and twigs flew over him as he tried to keep the pine boughs over the dead boy. The wind screamed in the gulch, and roared in the higher hills, but through it all he could hear the whisper of the hemlock.

The wind moved on to the next mountain; as it quieted both mules brayed. This time a voice answered. "I'm comen, boys." Sounds of horseshoes over the rocks grew clearer, closer, and soon the voice again. "What in God's name are you all doen away up here? The mules all right?"

"The mules and me we're still alive, Colonel, suh," the driver answered.

Leslie wondered on the colonel's voice. There was in it no tiredness, no weariness of war and blood as it ordered: "Sergeant Grimes, take a party to the left, and you, Sergeant Snowder, go in the other direction with your men, just in case."

"No case. Where we've not got em surrounded the bluff has." The tired drawl came from less than ten paces back in the woods, and was hardly finished before the man on horseback ordered more lights.

Back in the woods a rifled barreled firelock made the sputtering blast of a gun with her touchhole plugged and powder-sprinkled tow in the priming pan. The tow flamed. Leslie could make out hand shapes lighting fat pine splinters.

The light grew until he could see the colonel's mount, a

good-sized roan gelding, a credit to the man who rode him. Rigged out in a long cape and a fancy blue and gold uniform— must have once been an officer in the muster—he had the well-fed look of a man just come from a good dinner with plenty of fine wine. So far, he had appeared to see nothing but his mules.

"Almighty God, Father of all mercies, we thine unworthy servants do give thee most humble and hearty thanks for—"

The voice ended in a choking gasp. Leslie whirled to see what was happening to the captain. A man in a dark hunting shirt was in the wagon untying the hangman's knot which the captain, though his hands were free, had not bothered to take off. Leslie wished he could see the man's face; dressed in shoe-pacs, leggings, and buckskin breeches almost covered by the long shirt, he could be a hunter or overmountain settler known to him.

Others were showing themselves; in their dark rain-drenched clothes that showed the spareness of their bodies, they were a scraggly lot until you looked at their long rifles, walnut or rock-maple stocks gleaming in the light as did their sets of polished powder horns, many banded with silver. These were the men who'd killed Ferguson and routed his army at Kings Mountain.

The colonel was, between oaths, telling the world that his was the finest mule team in the whole country, and about the only one. Spanish mules, he'd paid a fortune for them down below Natchez, and he was going to see that every last man who'd tried to steal them was hanged. "George, how in the hell did you manage to get into this mess?"

"Why, the first trouble, suh, was you picked the wrong mountain. The one you rode up had nothen but peace."

"Tell me what I told you to tell."

"I'm tryen to git on—suh. About a dozen men come. I didn't like their looks. First thing, they told me my master had been kilt, and that afore he died he'd left word for me to go with them. I knowed that was a lie, less'n you'd fell off your horse."

George was silent while his master cursed him for hinting *he* could fall off a horse.

Leslie cursed himself in whispers, and turned away. The black man had acted with more discretion than Leslie Collins.

Had he been wary as he ought, that young lieutenant wouldn't be dead and the captain waiting to be hanged. He ought to have known that butter-tongued stranger was up to some meanness when he came begging for help to get his packhorse out of the gulch into which he had fallen. Fool-like, he'd let the officers come with him down into the gulch where a dozen hidden brigands waited.

Rain was again falling into the dead boy's eyes. The hard wind had carried away the shingling of pine boughs. Leslie ran about to pick them up. Nobody appeared to notice him. Even the captain, now in the wagon seat, was silent.

One of the brigands called to the colonel, "You're not letten that damned Tory go without bein hung, are you?"

The colonel interrupted a low-voiced conversation with another outlaw to tell the would-be hangman to shut up. He added: "You fool, he's an officer in the King's army. We're hangin jist the Loyalist prisoners."

Another voice came from out the darkness. "My mess ain't hanged any kind a prisoners. And moreover we're not aimen to."

Leslie wanted to shout: The captain is in safe hands. He'll be treated right. He remained silent. Four overmountain men were picking up the boy.

"An what a you all aimen to do with that corpse?" the colonel asked when the men walked past him with their burden.

"Straighten him out and lay him in the wagon," one of them answered as he moved on.

The colonel swore. "You're acten without my orders. Leave him be. The mules won't like the smell a blood."

The men walked on as if they had not heard.

Leslie remained on the bluff edge where he and the boy had been together. Its emptiness made him lonesome. He didn't know why. A dead man was no company. And the young lieutenant he'd met in the woods and who'd wrinkled his nose at the first taste of persimmons was dead. He had laughed, asking: "Do the settlers actually make pies out of these?"

It hadn't been a fair trial; too early in the fall for enough frost to take the pucker out of persimmons. The boy couldn't know that. Seventeen, fresh out of school and England, proud of his new ensigncy, he couldn't know anything of this country or of pain or war or how it felt to kill a man with whom you had no quarrel.

The colonel was roaring and cursing again, his glance fixed on the little man who'd threatened George with a pistol. Next to the blood from his wounded hand, the most noticeable thing about him was his wig, a flowing mane of brown curls over his ears down to his shoulders. He squirmed and fidgeted under the colonel's gaze like a man covered with seed ticks.

The colonel, finished with his long look, nodded, then in his official voice commanded Sergeant Grimes, "Bring up a detail of four men." They came after a while. "Two a you hold him, while you other two git one on either side his wig and pull it up and off."

The prisoner flung both arms around his head as the men started to do as directed. Unable to fend them off, he was soon screaming in pain as the wig parted from his scalp.

Leslie looked once. That was enough. The wig must have been fastened on with some kind of strong sticking stuff; pieces of bloody scalp were coming with it. One side of the wig was already lifted enough to show what the colonel had suspected— the red, lately healed scar where his right ear had been sliced off. He'd lost his ear because he'd been caught with a stolen horse; his first offense, otherwise he would have been hanged. Why torture him so? He was no worse than the rest of the gang; all were horse thieves, robbers, and murderers.

The colonel, so kind to his mules, seemed to enjoy watching the torture. "Squeal on," he said. "That won't keep you from hangen."

He next ordered the sergeants to have their men strip the captives of all boots and other clothing that looked to have been stolen. One man began a whimpering explanation of how they had no other clothes except what they wore, and anyhow not all they wore had been stolen. "You've got the skin you was born in, coveren enough till sunrise when you'll all swing."

Leslie saw with something like satisfaction that the tired overmountain men went about the work of stripping in a half-hearted fashion; mostly they were taking only hats and military coats, leaving breeches and boots.

The colonel was roaring again. He had stumbled over Zach. "Git up fore I shoot you up. Quit tryen to hide. One mule kick couldn't lay out a tough bastard like you."

Zach let out a gurgling moan, and slowly like a dying buffalo lifted his head. The best Leslie could tell in the poor light, the man didn't have a face left. The heel calk of one iron shoe had caught him across the bridge of his nose. The rest of his face below was a bloody, tooth-and-bone-spattered mess. He hadn't meant or expected a mule kick to do all that. Kinder to have killed him at once, but he couldn't with neither knife nor gun, that is before the rest of the gang closed in on him.

"God works his will in wondrous ways. For you it was the hind leg of a mule. But you're goen to walk down this mountain so come sunup you'll be dancen at the end of a rope."

That damned colonel was happy saying that; prostituting the Holy Writ into the bargain. He shivered. Did he shiver because the rain was cold or because his jump wasn't many minutes away? The captain was out of the brigands' hands. Why didn't he jump now? As good a time as any. No, he wasn't where he aimed to be.

Zach's inhuman sounds were what made him shiver. No. He had seen worse faces in Indian warfare. Even at Camden; faces hacked and trampled to pulp, heads with no bodies. Even that brave girl had lost color, but she'd kept on giving water to the wounded.

Was she married? What had made him think her a filly? One thing, she wasn't running around looking into the faces of the dead and the wounded to find her man. Maybe he'd been killed in another battle. She wouldn't stay a widow long.

The colonel was ordering George to move the wagon: "—jist enough the mules can git used to the dark." Leslie felt somebody was looking at him. He turned and saw the captain twisted around on the wagon seat, face turned in his direction. The captain waved. Leslie waved back, then watched the darkness swallow him and the dead boy as the wagon lumbered away. He soon heard it stop as the colonel had directed.

The colonel was occupied with his line of prisoners. Tied together at the ankles with ties only long enough for short steps, they were having a struggle to get dying Zach up and tied on the end of the line. Leslie saw that the main reason for their clumsiness was each man's wrists were looped together on one long rope, the hanging rope he reckoned. He cursed under his breath. Why couldn't that foul-mouthed poppycock of a so-called colonel let a man die in peace? Each time Zach tried to lift his head, blood that looked to be spotted with teeth and pieces of bone gushed out to enlarge the pool around him. And when his head dropped the colonel punched him with his bayonet.

The colonel was getting impatient. "I swear by the twelve apostles and ever hair on Esau's belly, I'll skin the lot of you alive, if you don't git that man up and tied. You all pullen to-gether'ull be better than a big pine top at holden back my wagon on that steep rocky downhill where my mules is liable to try to run away. And if you don't pull back hard you'll ever last one be skinned alive when they do run away."

Leslie walked along the cliff edge. He had caused the mule to do that to Zach. He ought to have to look at that smashed face the rest of his life.

He was staring into the darkness beyond the gulf when oaths began pouring out of the colonel like dung from a foundered hog. George was not to start up the wagon. There was one more prisoner loose on the bluff edge.

Leslie heard the hemlock whisper he was in the right place.

2

"Take off your hat and let's have a look. You three men over there doen nothen, bring up some torches."

Leslie remained motionless. He'd fixed his hat low and tight to protect his eyes when he jumped; he didn't aim to change it. The colonel stood on the low ledge above the shelving rock where he stood.

Light washed over him; the rounded mound of pale silk waistcoat in front of him took on the pale shine of a frog's belly.

"How do you call yourself?"

"By my name."

"And what in hell is your name?"

"Collins."

"Collins? I've heard that name somewhere, but I don't know as I'm acquainted with a Collins. Where's your home?"

"Over the mountain."

"What mountain?"

"Clinch."

"You don't sound like a backhill man. Another Tidewater Loyalist run to the backwoods, huh?"

Leslie clenched his fists and gazed at the glimmering mound of belly. The "colonel" had put on too much weight for his fancy muster uniform.

"How long you been gone from home?"

And what business of his was that? What was home any-how? "I left sometime in late spring."

"It's October now, the twelfth day. And what was you up to all these months?"

"Worken."

"So you've not been helpen in this great war. What was you worken at?"

"Surveyen." Lying was crawling; he was crawling. He had surveyed a big boundary of land in western Pennsylvania for a company that aimed to burn all that fine timber into charcoal to run the iron furnaces they were building. In these gone-wild-for-western-lands times nobody—royalist or Continental—cared which side a surveyor was on, long as his work was correct and honest. He'd finished that Pennsylvania job in July, learned what he could learn, and started back to Marion's camp in South Carolina.

On the way he'd scouted the country for Marion and got into the battle at Camden. He didn't aim to let anything slip about scouting for Marion; he didn't trust this man.

"Answer me. I've asked you twice which side you was on at Kings Mountain."

"Neither." He had known and reported the whereabouts of Ferguson, but hadn't known there was to be a battle. His gaze wandered past the belly to the pistols in their handsome holders, all atwinkle like the hilt of his sword. "A froggie would a wooing go. And he did ri-i-ide, sword and pistols by his side." That wasn't right. His black mammy's froggie had a sword and buckler. What was a buckler? His mammy didn't know. His father wore a sword sometimes, but never a buckler. One day he'd recited a bit about the froggie to his father, then asked what was a buckler.

"An ancient form of shield," his father had answered, and added: "I trust you will never repeat that stupid rhyme again. It is unfit for an Englishman."

"Damn you. Answer my question. Did you or did you not give aid an comfort to the enemy? My captives tell me they found you in the woods with them two English officers, and you hadn't tried to disarm them for they still had their weapons."

The cockadoodle had taken the word of horse thieves and murderers. Leslie clenched his fists, then thought of the English officers. Their cool politeness had never cracked, not even when they'd asked to be shot instead of hanged. No, the captain's voice had kind of choked off when he begged for the boy's life.

"I cain't, in the face a what my other prisoners tell me, believe your Tory buddy they was about to hang. He claimed you'd captured him and that infidel that killed hissef, an you was bringen them in when my other prisoners surrounded you all. Now, I figger you wasn't tryen to bring in prisoners, but given aid an comfort to the enemy."

"They're not my enemies." He would not stoop to this jackanapes by trying to explain how the officers had happened to be his prisoners. Furthermore, a prisoner was in a sense no longer an enemy.

"And what did you do for your Tory friends?"

"Same as I'd do for anybody I found in the woods, misguided and without provisions."

"And so you took it upon yourself to—"

"You're gitten Leslie Collins all wrong."

The familiar voice came from an irregular line of dark hunting shirts a few feet behind the colonel. He swore, whirled around, and called the speaker a foul name before he commanded: "The man who interrupted me step forward."

"I spoke." The words came from a tall man, his face so covered with beard and long black hair straggling from under a broad-brimmed black hat, Leslie could make out little but a nose. That and the voice were enough.

They belonged to Isaac Huffacre, his teacher in the woods and on the rivers. Must be close to ten years since they'd first met in Montreal, and had traveled together to Detroit and on to the Illinois. Not much past seventeen, Leslie had known little except what he'd learned in school. That hadn't helped much in the woods. Isaac had educated him.

He'd be happy to shake his hand. Maybe now he wouldn't jump.

The colonel had forgotten Isaac. On turning to find the source of interruption, his glance had fallen on Sergeant Grimes

27

who, with four men, had been ordered to guard the prisoners. He cursed Grimes until the air was blue. Breath back, he tried questioning the sergeant; but when the questions brought no answers, he at last turned back to Isaac. "Well? I'm waiten."

"I'm waiten, too," Isaac answered.

"I'm waiten for you to apologize for breaken into my questionen of a prisoner. Didn't anybody ever tell you to salute a superior?"

"Salute? Where's the superior?"

"I asked why you interrupted."

"I spoke because you're not asken questions but are mostly name-callen. You're not treaten him right!"

"And how in hell do you treat a man not doen his part in this war?"

"However you treat yourself. You never saw Kings Mountain. Supposen Leslie Collins did feed two British officers. In most places prisoners of war get fed; and I don't like given ours nothen but raw punkin. But you, you're given a heap more mind to your mules; said you knowed they was hungry. What about us men? We've had no supper."

The colonel had been repeating: "That will do."

Isaac heard the last one. "Law no, what I've said won't do. I've hardly started. Wheresoever you was back in the fall a 1774, nobody saw you on the Point Pleasant campaign. Leslie Collins was there. I was with him. I'd never seen and never will see a better scout and braver soldier, and him so young."

Leslie wished Isaac hadn't brought that up. Something he didn't like to remember. He'd done his part in the battle, kill or be killed, keep the man beside you from being hit. Coming back through the woods, he'd had the thought that he had killed a good many Shawnee, men of whom he knew nothing except whatever meanness they'd done hadn't been done to him. The Shawnee, he figured, had died not for their sins but for the land that belonged to them.

In spite of the colonel's commands to be silent, Isaac went on. He'd finished telling how Leslie had saved a forted station besieged by "a powerful army of Chickamauga," and was detailing Leslie's great deeds on Clark's campaigns, when another voice begged: "Please, Isaac, let me put a word in."

Isaac hushed, and the other voice came on, calm and easy as if the owner heard none of the colonel's commands and threats. He didn't know Leslie Collins, but he did know Collins had walked from the Battle of Camden while he let the wounded use his horses. One of the wounded men had been his brother-in-law, so he knew the fact for certain.

"Shut up. He didn't fight at Camden." The colonel's voice was giving out.

"How do you know? You wasn't there," somebody said.

Leslie felt a light finger of wind on his cheek. He listened for the hemlock, but could hear only human voices.

Oblivious to the colonel's threats of hanging for mutiny, Sergeant Grimes was having his say: "—an you've been riden and we've been walken because you ordered us to sneak up this hill on foot, and all the time it was your mules and your wagon, not Tories you claimed you was after. We took a short cut up the hill. We aim to take it back. Walken that roundabout way to guard prisoners, then back and around to our horses would take us till midnight. You guard your prisoners."

Anger was hot on the colonel when he at last turned back to Leslie. "Taken all these lies I've had to listen to fer the gospel truth, you've still got Tory leanens; but mostly you're a yellow-bellied coward, spraddled out like a man tryen to cross a river on two horses, aimen to stay with the one that gits over. I'm aimen to—"

At the word *coward* Leslie had stepped back. He came forward with all he had; a right to that frog's belly, a left to stop that mouth.

The colonel was down, rain in his face. Leslie staggered; nobody had hit him. He was a coward; too rattled to turn and take a running jump from the bluff edge. Jump so there'll be plenty of you to catch on that tree. If it is a tree and not a bush.

Plenty maybe for the buzzards. Don't forget the buzzards. You'll never climb and cross the western mountains with your eyes picked out by buzzards.

There would be no buzzards—yet. Trees had always been kind to him; kinder than men. He was in his father's house, not long graduated from the nursery to a room of his own, but not from pinafores. He had run away to watch a boat unload at his father's dock on the lower Rappahannock that bordered the family plantation. He had been sent to his room after a good talking to for the crime of going to a forbidden place; no tea for him; nothing till morning. He wouldn't have minded the loss of tea, except he'd heard there was to be for the children a special treat of Bath buns. And what was a Bath bun?

He'd sat on his window sill and talked to the big wild cherry tree, so close that when the wind was high one of its branches tapped the window. That night the tree promised it wouldn't let the limb he could reach break before he could swing down to a bigger one. He'd asked no promise of a safe return. He could get help from the kitchen or the stables.

The tree had kept its promise, but the hemlock had promised nothing. He was leaping, arms outspread. There was a second's exaltation. He was an eagle swooping over craggy mountains.

Where was the hemlock top? He wasn't a bird, or a man, but a spent rock, a rock thrown high and now plummeting a thousand miles down through empty dark. Hemlock needles brushed his face and hands, but with each grab they went down like loose feathers. One hand caught a needled branch, but it, too, slid away. Too small.

Flailing with arms and legs, his fall became a slide head foremost. One shoulder struck a good-sized limb and stayed him long enough he could hook a leg over the limb above. The limb let his leg slide off, but not before he'd grabbed the bigger branch under his shoulder. He hung a moment, spread-eagled upside down on the limb.

He righted himself and sat a moment on the bending limb. He reckoned he'd jumped clean over the top of the hemlock to land on the side away from the bluff. He could see nothing, but the creek sounded directly below him. He worked his way along the limb to the trunk, bigger than he had thought. He patted the trunk and thanked the tree for catching him. Somewhere above a drooping branch sluiced rain onto his head. He didn't move. He was warm inside. Isaac and overmountain men he didn't know had stood up for him. The captain had not exactly lied for him, just hadn't told the whole truth of his capture. The world was a good place—for Leslie Collins, not for the dead lieutenant or Zach. He had been lucky; his hat was on his head and his knife under the double fold of his hunting shirt.

He was beginning to feel the damp through the back of his woolen hunting shirt and on one leg of his leather breeches, but his feet and legs up to his knees were warm and dry in their woolen stockings under leggings and shoepacs. He could thank Isaac for dry feet.

He'd been wearing deerskin moccasins with holes in the soles when he'd first met Isaac Huffacre. They'd encamped together that night, and it was then Isaac had lectured him on "Proper Footgear in the Woods." Leslie could still hear him: "Deerskin's no good for moccasins. It soaks up water like a dried apple. It won't last. And you oughtn't to be wearen moccasins; they're too low and light. You need shoepacs. And you ought to always carry extra footgear leather into the woods. Now, hold out your foot."

Isaac had measured the foot with the palm of one hand and fingers of the other, then brought out a roll of tanned elk skin and gone to work. Shoepacs, Leslie had learned, were made much like moccasins—a seam in the back and gathered over the instep, the whole put together with leather whangs; but shoepacs had higher tops than moccasins, coming well above the ankle so as to cover the lower edges of his leggings. Also different from moccasins, shoepacs had an insert over the instep and were double soled.

He was quietly working his way to the ground when he saw, high on the bluff across the creek, a curious band of quivering light that made the rock look as if it instead of the light moved. Made a man think of the strange lights in the old ghost tales, lights that warned people they were about to die. Fox-fire in the woods on a rainy night was a pretty sight, but fox-fire didn't glow on bare rock.

He had heard no sound of humankind since jumping, but

that light came from flambeaux above him on the cliff. Somebody was trying to find him. Who wanted him? He'd heard no order from the colonel. He tried to look straight overhead; the hemlock branches let nothing through but the glow of the lights above him. He crawled out on a limb until he could make out an arm holding a torch over the cliff edge. He moved back to the hemlock trunk; if he could see them they might be able to see him.

He wished he could hear the colonel. Two little licks ought not to keep him quiet so long. He shouldn't have hit him in the belly, a soft-bellied man unsuited to fighting with anything but his tongue. A bite and gouge fight would have been better; no risk of killing the bastard, just let him come out of it with one eye hanging down his cheek.

He turned to watch a light going along the bluff edge toward the head of the creek. Another flambeau came to help the first. They moved on together until they picked out the top of a mighty sycamore, taller than the hemlock. Its top looked to be less than six feet below the cliff edge.

He watched one of the torches above the sycamore begin a slow fall, then stop on a ledge eight or ten feet from the bluff top and behind the upper limbs of the sycamore. It flamed there, lighting a way out for him, he thought. A man could climb the sycamore until he was level with the ledge, then swing out to it —provided the sycamore limb didn't break.

The pine knot on the ledge was still flaming when another fell on the downcreek side. The flame died as it fell, but the embers glowed bright enough to let him see it disappear in thick creek fog. Fog so thick down there nobody could see him on the ground. Staying close to the big trunk, he went down the hemlock, a kind and friendly tree with many limbs, some so close to the ground he could hang on to find a footing on the steep, slippery creek bank.

He was on the ground when Isaac bellowed as if he wanted all the world to hear: "We've been looken, thrown over torches the whole time you've been out. He's dead. No man could jump onto them rocks and live. Whyn't you take a look down?"

So the colonel had revived, but couldn't give loud orders.

He could still give them, though. Somebody almost directly above him spoke with the same unusual loudness as Isaac: "If you say so, why I can look a little while longer. But I've already seen a bloody rock."

Torches fell on either side of the hemlock; others were flung out to land in the creek. Standing on the ground with his back to the hemlock trunk, he was under the fog; he could see the torches begin their falls, hear them sometimes strike rocks or hiss in the creek water, but not the way to a sycamore limb he could reach; too many torches died on the way down and the fog was too thick.

It didn't matter. He'd make out. He laughed to himself as he felt his way along the hemlock bough. The torches had been flung over to show him the way out, not to find him. Isaac, the old coot, had read his trail easy as a hound dog on warm fox scent. He knew why he'd jumped where. Lights had fallen all around, but never into the hemlock.

The sycamore was up the creek. The sound of the creek was louder upwater than down; must be a fall up there past the turning of the cliff. Below him was the drowning sapling. He must walk away from that sound and toward the other.

He felt until he found a hemlock bough on the upcreek side of the trunk. Holding with one hand, he used the limb to guide him along a rocky bench so steep and rain-slippery he now and then had to throw all his weight on the limb to keep his footing. Brush and briars clawed at him and tried to drag off his hat.

He stopped when he reached the tip of the hemlock limb. No more torches were coming over; glows from the few that had landed flaming were dead in the wet fog. Isaac and the others were gone. They'd given him more than enough help.

He stood in the dark and thought of sycamores he had known: they didn't grow in one certain way; hemlocks always had branches close to the ground; sometimes sycamores did and sometimes they didn't; this sycamore would act like any other tree growing close to a bluff: it wouldn't put out big limbs on the bluff side where there was never much light and no room for a limb to stretch out. And anyhow sycamores liked to hang

33

their limbs above creeks and rivers. The best thing to do was go straight on to the trunk, then start hunting for a limb on the creek side.

He left the tip of the hemlock limb, and slipping, sliding, sometimes falling, often crawling, he got on, guided by the sounds behind him, ahead, and below. He found the trunk without too much trouble, but it seemed forever that he circled the tree hunting a limb, and when he jumped to feel above him, he usually lost his footing.

He was working his way along the edge of the creek when in front of him he felt a rock wall almost as tall as he. He continued to hunt with his hands until he learned it was no wall, but a big rock fallen some time or other from the cliff. He swung onto it, found firm footing, and stood up.

William David Leslie Collins was a lucky man. Not quite shoulder high above the rock was a big limb holding out its hand to him. Working his way along the limb then climbing the tree was quick and easy. He found the ledge by the smell of the burned-out pine knot, so close he could reach out and touch it. The small high branch he was on made a cracking noise to say it wasn't hickory and so couldn't hold him much longer. He let loose of the limb, swayed and teetered an instant, then flung himself toward the ledge. He landed hands on the ledge, legs dangling. He swung his body up, but ended stretched full length on the ledge, one leg still dangling, face on the rock.

He righted himself after a while, and with both hands on the wall at his back, catwalked toward the sound of the waterfall. He thought he was nearing the turning of the cliff when the ledge narrowed until the outer edge of his forward foot had nothing under it. It would widen up ahead; this was the way out; Isaac wouldn't have flung so many torches near the turning if it hadn't been the way out. He moved on, no longer picking up his feet, but pushing out to feel before he shifted his weight. He tried to hurry. He heard the roar of wind, distant as yet, but it would soon be trying to knock him off the cliff.

The wind hit while he was shifting his weight. He figured he'd reached the turn. He pushed a foot out for another step. It swung in air. He brought it back to feel below; air again. He reached with one hand high as he could; nothing but a sandstone wall.

A hard wind shrieked up the gulch as he lifted his other hand for a feel. He needed all he had to hang on to the rock wall while the wind whipped round the cliff corner to suck or push him off the rock. It was an evil wind; he could feel the coldness of it through his wet clothes, numbing him into stiffness so he would fall.

It seemed a long while he had to stand and take whatever the wind offered, rain in his face or a dead tree branch flung hard against him. A lull came at last, and after getting back some of his breath taken by the wind, he catwalked back the way he had come. He cursed himself in whispers. He'd misread Isaac's torches; the ones on the upcreek side of the sycamore had been meant to show him the ledge petered out in that direction. He had scarcely glanced at the torches on the downcreek side of the hemlock.

The ledge was again wide enough for his feet; the hemlock top was just below him; he could smell it and hear it. He went on for a short distance and stopped; the ledge was steepening. He took another step and his forehead struck stone. He stepped back to explore with his hands and found a ledge of rock, maybe a foot thick stuck three or four feet out over nothing. He'd swung up and over higher things. The creek on the rocks below him was telling him what would happen to him if he didn't have a good purchase on the ledge above while his feet trod the air. He'd have to reach out, swing high and wide, else his legs would come under the overhang instead of on top.

He drew a deep breath, put both hands on the stone, and swung out and up to land with less than half of him on the ledge above. The dangling leg and the half of his belly resting on air seemed uncommonly heavy. He bore down with one elbow, clawed with his hands, and slowly worked himself inch by inch over the rock until his clawing hand got a hold on a tough little huckleberry bush.

Up, he lay stomach downward, heaving. He was getting

old; a little climb like this oughtn't to take all his strength and breath, or maybe the two days of nothing to eat but raw pumpkin had something to do with it.

He thought of Kate waiting for him, and turned over. The rain had stopped, the wind was quiet, and glory be he could see the sky. Most of it hidden by rolls and sheets of flying cloud, but still a sky where a man might find a star. He never found a star, but standing, he could make out the deeper blackness of tree trunks.

He wanted to get on; this was near the spot where the boy had leaped into eternity, and the air was foul with the smell of blood. He found brush still bent from the wagon's standing so long over it, and followed its trail.

The way down and around was a long one, but he had no trouble following the wagon trail marked by bent and broken brush with now and then a small stump still oozing sap. And for most of the way he had the smell of Zach's blood.

Coming up with a gun at his back, he had memorized the road after they'd taken Kate away. He had reached the place far down the hillside where water ran across the wagon trace when he stopped to listen, certain he had heard somebody singing. Nothing but the wind in some faraway mountain. He shook his head over his foolishness and hurried on as fast as the road and the dark would let him. Kate was hidden somewhere in the brush around the next turn.

He rounded the sharp bend, saw first the glimmer of rock on the low bluff above him, then, less than a mile away, paled by a thin fog, the glow of campfires and torches. The poor devils who'd been tricked by the colonel were just now getting ready for mess. No need to think of them as poor devils. Somebody down there was happy. That singing he'd heard hadn't come from the wind, but by men bawling out about somebody's true love. The tired men he'd seen, still hungry, were not the singers, he reckoned. There were too many lights for that small detachment. Most of the campers would be other Kings Mountain men on their way home. He stood a moment to watch and listen, but mostly to wonder on Zach and the captain. The boy was dead; no wonder there.

There'd been a wild magnolia by the road at the place where they'd taken Kate away; no matter how dark, any man would know a wild magnolia from the feel of its leaves, long as his arm. The glow from the campfire picked out the trunk of the magnolia. Past it, he was in pure dark.

He was moving slowly, feeling out trampled brush when he heard the angry neigh of a horse. That would be the good-looking stallion ridden by the captain. The proud beast had, no different from Kate, disliked his new masters. He'd also had to bear the further indignity of being turned into a packhorse; they'd loaded him with a turn of shelled corn.

Leslie was hurrying toward the sound, wondering on his own and the lieutenant's mount, a gelding, when something smooth and cool touched his neck. He jumped away, then at once reached out to give a gentle pat. Nothing but a horse's nose, and it belonged to a smart mare, for along with horse and leather he smelled corn and heard teeth grinding. His hand moved on to the horse's back where he found only girthing instead of saddle and blanket. These were under her belly.

Cleo, his good packhorse, was up to her usual tricks. She was a smart girl. Her back was uncommonly dry for a mare supposed to have stood for hours in the rain. In straightening her bridle, he found it entangled with twigs and leaves. Young, but meek-seeming as a broken-down plow horse, nobody had taken the trouble to tie her securely to a good stout sapling. Instead, the thief had done a slovenly job of fastening her to a bush. It had been easy for her to chew free, then snuggle under some kind of wide-limbed, close-topped tree, most likely a beech.

One of her tricks, common to many horses, was to suck in a big bellyful of wind soon as her packsaddle was ready to be cinched. She'd hold all that wind until the girth was tightly buckled. Then she'd go back to her normal size, so that after traveling less than a mile, the saddle would be slipping sidewise or already under her belly. He had more or less cured the trouble by leaning back and pulling until she could no longer hold her breath; he also had her wear a crupper.

He flung the bridle over Cleo's head and walked on toward where he'd heard the stallion. Cleo followed, wanting more

37

corn. Eager as he was to get to Kate, he took pity on the stallion, uncomfortable with his head tied too high on a close rein, hungry and maddened by the smell of corn he couldn't reach. He'd managed to free himself of the sack, unbalanced when they'd hung it with no ties across his saddle. In falling, the sack had burst, and corn was everywhere except in his mouth.

With the stallion loosened and feeding on corn, Leslie hurried to Kate, who already knew he was there and was nickering her heart out because he hadn't come first to her. Whoever had tied her up ought to be hanged; head too tight and high; worse, she was carrying the load they'd put on her. She'd have the beginnings of a saddle sore standing so long under a heavy load with her blanket soaking wet. He loosened, fed, and unsaddled her, then turned to the others making a great racket as they demanded corn and freedom.

He didn't free them, but loosened their reins and gave each some corn. Six in addition to his own: three mares, the stallion, and two geldings as he remembered. He turned to Cleo as soon as the others were fed; she had followed, nudging his backsides, on all the trips he'd made from horse to corn and back again. The following wasn't for love, but with the hope he'd get that packsaddle from under her belly. Served her right. Still, he freed her from the saddle and load, then tied her up. She was already on the way to foundering herself on the stolen corn.

Cleo's blanket was dry enough to give both her and Kate a rubdown; then, what would either mare do for a blanket? He remembered he was hungry, and he ought to be hunting around to learn what, if anything, the thieves had left him. He went first to Kate's saddlebags, and from the right one took a leather pouch. He hefted it, smiled. Today was his lucky day. The bag was as heavy as ever.

He loosened the drawstring and pulled out a round wooden box with a tightly fitting cover lifted by a small round knob. He turned the box over, felt the smooth bottom, then shook it, and heard the clink of gold. He had been paid in guineas for his summer's surveying. His captors had found too much high living in the colonel's wagon and elsewhere to bother with a salt-box that smelled of maple sugar and parched corn. And rightly so; above the false bottom the box was filled with the mixture he had pounded together. He helped himself to a mouthful with the horn spoon on top, and, still chewing, began the search for the rest of his goods.

On one of the geldings he found his sextant and other surveying equipment; on another a rifled gun that from the heft and the flying wild goose carved into the stock, he knew for his Ruthie. Search over the other strange horses yielded his powder horns, shot pouch, and single bullet mold, but powder and ball were gone. He didn't find his second-best breeches and coat or the good white linen ruffled shirt he hadn't worn; his flour and ham were also missing as was the small jug of brandy he always carried in the woods.

Such losses didn't matter. The high-living thieves had left enough bacon, meal, tea, and coffee for the ride home, along with a small bag of shelled corn for the mares. He found the elegant prayer book his mother had sent to him on his twentieth birthday, not knowing her schoolboy son was no longer in England. The thieves, he reckoned, were not much on prayer. He wasn't either. He wished he were on speaking terms with God; he'd thank him for his safe deliverance. He had not properly thanked anybody, anything, not even the good little huckleberry bush that had helped him up the cliff.

He took another bite of parched corn with maple sugar, then put the box away. Time to get going. The horses had finished the bit of corn he'd given them and were now more restless than ever. He'd saddle Cleo first; she would wait for Kate. And what would he do for dry saddle blankets? He was giving Cleo's feet a quick going-over, when he gave a low whistle. He'd just remembered he had a wife born Sadie Mehitabel Hawkins, daughter of a South Carolina tavern keeper. She'd ordered him when he left in early June to bring back a pattern of heavy woolen, scarlet cloth. Every other woman, she had said, could wear a scarlet cloak. She didn't have one because he wouldn't keep sheep to grow wool for her to spin and dye and weave.

He hadn't planned to buy any such thing, but had run into a widow woman in need of money with a blanket-wide web of scarlet woolen she wanted to sell.

Satisfied that Cleo didn't have a loose shoe, he again went into her pack. The cloth was there, and thanks to Cleo's bad habit, still dry. He stretched a length from nose to extended arm, hooked in his thumb to hold it as he brought it back to his nose to make another fold.

The cloth was strong and heavy, but his knife slashed through the folds with no trouble. He wasn't certain in the dark his cuts were straight, but by folding each cut piece he had two big thick saddle blankets. Cleo and Kate needed the cloth worse than Sadie. Red or any bright color was dangerous to wear in the Indian hunting grounds where they lived. Furthermore, Sadie with her orange-red hair, freckles, and pale blue eyes would look worse than usual in red. The girl he'd met on Camden battlefield could wear a scarlet cloak; she could wear anything and still be pretty.

Home, he'd have to hide all the cloth in the barn where she wouldn't be likely to find it. Sooner or later she would; then he'd have a hot time. Well, not much hotter than usual; she'd gone after him hammer and tongs soon as she'd learned he was going off to survey before the corn was laid by. Now it would be the same thing over because he'd been gone so long, and had brought neither cloth for her cloak pattern nor a "pretty" for her little boy she claimed was his.

Kate and Cleo saddled to the tune of his angry thoughts, he untied them, then hurried to untie the others, taking care to leave no dangling bridle rein. All made for the corn he'd left by the stallion. He untied the stallion last, and holding his rein, grabbed the sack of corn from under the mouths of the hungry horses, careful to hold it with the good end of the sack down, and mounted the stallion.

"I'm expecting all of you to follow me and get back to your rightful owners," he told them, and headed through the pitch-black woods toward the road. The stallion wanted to go every place except back to the road. Leslie figured he remembered how the rogues had treated him there. Kate acted up worse than his mount. Already in a pet because she'd had to stand for hours in the rain under a heavy load, she was now furious that her master had picked a strange horse to ride instead of her. In spite of the dark and the trees and brush that came between, she tried to keep abreast of the stallion; once she brushed hard against his leg. He cursed, then smiled; it was something out of the common in his life to be loved too well.

The stallion, he decided, was a rebel at heart. He behaved better when they'd rounded the hillside, and the songs of the bivouacking soldiers came clearly: one group was singing a bawdy song, while another sang "War and Washington"; he'd first heard that one in Pennsylvania.

He reached the place where campfire light made a glittering on the wet rocks. He dismounted and poured the remainder of the corn from one side to the other of a big flat rock. He waited to count the horses; all were there. He wished he could turn around and take the lot to Marion; his men were always in need of good horsestock. No, he couldn't do that; the four not ridden by the English officers could have been stolen from rebels.

He mounted Kate and, leading Cleo, rode down the hill. His way crossed a creek, then became a road of sorts through the encampment. Torch lights let him see on either side, though in the low thin fog shapes were blurred, but song, talk, and laughter came more clearly.

He stopped Kate and searched among the shapes. He wished he could ride among the fires until he found Isaac; with him there might be other men he knew. He'd squat by their fire and listen to the talk. He'd learn what was happening to the captain, whether Zach got over the hill alive, and whether the boy would get a decent funeral. He'd also like to learn the truth about Kings Mountain: had the victors hanged all their prisoners?

Searching through the lights for a silhouette that could belong to Isaac or the English captain, he saw a line of men. They stood still and close together. Captives. Were they, too, waiting for the choice: stand on a wagon tailgate with a rope around your neck and pledge allegiance to the rebel cause or be hanged.

Had they already hanged his father? Would they hang a man of his standing, or only confiscate all his goods and drive him and his mother out of the country with nothing except the clothes they wore?

He rose in the saddle and called: "Horses loose nigh the creek. Horses loose and saddled."

He rode on.

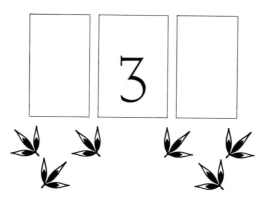

The early sun was sending long yellow rays into the pines above, but the narrow creek valley was buried in a cold, foggy twilight. He checked Kate; she knew home with her stable and Beau the fine stallion were less than two miles up the creek; but this was no place for fast traveling.

The creek valley was so narrow there was scarcely room between rock ledges and creek water for the trail. Worse, the rocks underfoot were slippery with their covering of yellow-red mud. Last year the mud had been mostly black with washed-away topsoil; this year yellow-red; next year redder as the hard rains gouged out the plowed-up soil of his hillside cornfields down to the clay and rock bones of the earth. His fields. This creek would never again run clear and clean as when he and Sadie had settled here less than two years ago.

He cursed Sadie, her corn that went mostly into her still to come out as whiskey to sell now for cash or keep for the "by then" when they'd have a tavern "like Papa." Sadie lived in the by then; some day there'd be a big road up the creek valley by their place with crowds of passersby stopping in; by then if they saved and worked and built a tavern "finer than Papa's" they'd be somebody. That last was kind of pitiful: the only way to be a somebody was to be born a somebody. Sadie didn't know that.

Yellow-hided, weak-kneed, he had come to the place at the

43

insistence of Sadie and her parents. They owned the land and were deeding it to Sadie as part of her dowry; she must go live on it.

He hadn't seen the sense of moving to this out-of-the-way hole in Clinch Mountain. He loved rough backwoods, but not for farming. He owned a lot of land as he was often paid with as much as a third of the boundary he surveyed. Any parcel of it was better for farming than Sadie's. He hadn't understood her real reason for moving until about six months after their marriage; they'd have no neighbors here—or so she'd thought—and so nobody around could know how long she'd been married.

He dismounted, led Kate up a steep rocky bank around a waterfall, waited until he saw that Cleo with a light pack was making the climb with no trouble, then remounted. Past the waterfall, the valley widened and the creek became a shallow, sluggish stream bordered by swampy soil filled with willows and lush weeds.

Kate was hurrying along when she stopped so suddenly Leslie swayed in the saddle. He couldn't get her to go on in spite of sweet talk and reassuring pats. She kept trying to back off. He dismounted. She never acted this way without good reason.

He walked ahead, looking carefully on either side the trace until he saw, half-hidden in swamp grass and weeds, the bleached rib cage of some large animal. Long since picked clean by buzzards, bleached by sun and rain, the skeleton had been there a long while, but not when he left home. Jumping from hummock to hummock of grass, he got far enough to see a horn sticking out of the water. It belonged to one of the two cows Sadie had brought with her.

Snake bite, he guessed. He'd told the woman when she'd started driving the cows down here because the higher woods were too dried up for grazing that the swamp was dangerous with water moccasins. He was glad it wasn't one of his horses she'd put down here while he was gone, but why in thunder hadn't Jethro buried the animal?

He forgot his vexation over the unburied cow when, past a clump of willows, he could look up and see what the few people who knew about it called Collins Place. He was ashamed to have his name tied to it.

The two-story log house with kitchen in back sat on a rolling piece of hillside with a fairly level bench below and another above; everything dull brown and gray, for the sun came late to the valley and left early. Riding on, he kept glancing now and then at the house. Its ugliness struck him afresh; no porch, or tree, or shrub, or flower, no blade of grass, only the raw red earth, a lake of mud when wet and dusty in dry times from the scratchings of Sadie's chickens.

Where were the chickens? The dogs ought to be running down to meet him. They'd cried when he left, but they'd cry harder on a surveying trip when they wanted to hunt and he had to survey. Nothing moved, not even smoke from the kitchen chimney. The only sound was the faint rustle of what sounded to be dry leaves. He looked across the rail fence he rode past and stopped with an oath. October almost half gone, and the fodder not stripped; the rustle of the shattered leaves was what he'd heard. Ruined now; all the goodness gone from what little hadn't blown away. Fodder was the only winter forage he had for his horsestock in this godforsaken place.

He hurried Kate to the barn. Jethro would have stripped that fodder if he'd been able. Could be he was crippled or even killed out alone felling big trees on orders from Sadie. She wanted more land cleared for corn.

She had made field hands out of his two blacks. Angela, a slip of a girl brought up in his father's house to be a lady's maid, was sent by his mother as a wedding gift. Jethro, born with a gift for horses, had by the time he was twenty-one risen from stable boy to overseer of the family's riding and carriage horses. They were about the same age, and when Leslie was twenty-one, Jethro had been given him.

He stopped in front of the barn. Head-high stickweeds had flowered and gone to seed across the hall. He trampled his way through and unsaddled the mares. The log barn smelled of nothing but wood, no barn smell left.

Horses fed, he ran to the house, but took time on the way to look into Jethro's cabin. Empty of anything alive except a spider building a web above the empty bed.

He hurried on to open the closest door to his house, the kitchen. Big table, little table, chairs, not even a kettle on the fireplace crane. He looked at the ashes, no need to feel them; there was a crusted spot where drops of a hard rain had got down the chimney when the fire was out. He turned to the loom in a corner of the big room. The cloth had been cut away to leave the warp hanging free.

He opened a door that led through a double thickness of log wall and into what Sadie called "the big house." The name had always irked him; the rooms were big enough, but only four, two below and two above. He had hoped the room next the kitchen could in time become a dining room. Sadie had made a flax manufactory out of it, but today it was empty of flax as well as spinning wheels, flax break, and hackles.

He climbed the ladder that served as stairway to the rooms above. The bed was still in their sleeping room; that was all; even the bed cord of good hempen rope was gone. The windows were curtainless. Sadie was a great one for curtains, bright ones of cloth never meant for curtains; he had hated the red and yellow things. The other upstairs room was empty. Sadie's boy and Angela had slept there.

He hurried down to what Sadie called "the front house." The wall above and by the outside door was empty; his rifles, pistols, shot pouches, and powder horns had hung there. Everything gone except the big bed in one corner, a cupboard in another, a chest of drawers, and by the bed a small table, bare of its customary cloth; but on it still the golden glow of scrolls and flourishes in gold that said Holy Bible on the fine leather, binding gold-edged pages.

Indians? Would Indians kill a cow, carry off everything else, and leave him the one thing he didn't want? He had written his parents of his marriage to Sadie Hawkins, daughter of a South Carolina tavern keeper. He hadn't told them it was a fourth-class tavern, unfrequented by gentlemen because it was no place for gentlemen. They must have found out for themselves, and more. His mother had sent the big family Bible, new. It had come with Angela, the horse she rode, and another horse loaded with a variety of gifts.

Horses? He was running around the hillside to the one field in which he had tried to grow grass and clover. The big field was filled with head-high weeds and sprouts. That was because no horse had grazed there for weeks, maybe months. He didn't go hunting them. Standing by the upper bars, he could see most of the sloping field. Empty. Thistles and wild asters grew in the remains of old horse manure close to the bars. No fresh.

He looked at his shadow; a long way from noon. Kate oughtn't to be too tired to take the five miles or so to the Weavers', his closest neighbors and good friends.

He had saddled Kate when Cleo let it be known she wanted to come, too. He let her; she no more than Kate needed a rest. He had spent two days ambling home, and had camped less than two miles away last night. And anyhow, tired or no, this dead place would be lonesome for a lone mare.

The Weavers had been living in another creek valley down and around the mountain when Sadie settled on *her* land; but she hadn't known it. The families visited back and forth; if anybody knew what had happened, the Weavers would.

Weaver's Place was better than his own, with a grassy door-yard and a porch with vines and flowers. Now, the marigolds and bachelor's-buttons were weed-grown and withered; everything from barns to wash shed was silent with the empty look of his own. Still, he dismounted and knocked on the front door. He might as well have banged on a tomb for all the answer he got. The only sounds came from the wind higher on the mountain and a nearby field of corn where ungathered fodder blades whispered like his own.

Riding away, past a row of Indian peach trees by the barn lane, he stopped Kate, and pulled down a peach tree limb. He had glimpsed hanging there the shine of bright hair touched by the sun. He shook his head after a close look and rode on. Sadie's hair shone like fire in the sun—when it had a fresh washing—but the two long hairs on the peach tree bough were

47

bright yellow; must belong to a man with a yellow wig; a woman wouldn't be apt to be tall enough in the saddle for her head to hit that limb; and anyhow a woman would keep her hair tied up and covered when riding.

He'd come this far; might as well ride the two or three miles to Siler's Place. He didn't get out of the saddle when he reached it. He didn't want to knock on another door and the only answer be the echo from an empty house. He could see light through the cracks of the dripped-out ash hopper.

A short time after his marriage, Amos Weaver had come in the night to tell of a Cherokee war party headed in their direction; a boy from Scott's Station had brought the word. Everybody was advised to bring guns, ammunition, and horsestock down to Scott's, the closest forted station, and it about twenty miles away over rough going.

He had gone as directed. He had ever hated the forted life, and Scott's Station was worse than the usual run of stations: too crowded, walls too low, spread over too much territory, but the station wasn't as bad as old man Scott. Scott claimed he had received "the call"—whatever that was—to preach; tongue full of his brand of religion, the rest of him pure devil. He'd worked three wives to death, and was going strong on the fourth. Leslie and Sadie had stayed at Scott's for about two weeks.

Could be another Indian scare. Sadie was most likely there now having the time of her life. He'd ride over in the morning; there and back was more than Kate could do in one day considering how much she'd already traveled.

He'd go back to his place and search for the keg of powder and a big gourd of French priming powder he kept in the barn loft, a safe dry place with no fire close by. And were the kegs of whiskey still in the hole Sadie had made Jethro dig for them while they waited for the "by then"?

The liquor didn't matter, only maybe money. Powder was another matter. He'd made what loading powder he had, but here he couldn't make more; there were in these parts no caves with niter dirt to make saltpeter. As for priming powder, he'd never tried to make it.

The days were shortening fast, but with the sun not much past noon, there'd be plenty of time to ride back, make his searches while the mares rested, then ride eight or ten miles in the direction of Scott's Station. He'd rather camp in the woods than stay in Sadie's empty house.

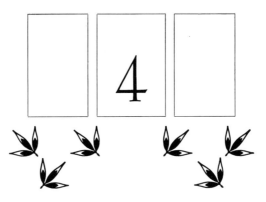

Another fine day to ride through the woods; leaves coloring up on the higher hills, but still green in the valleys. He'd enjoy the ride more if the swing and jounce of his powder horns didn't constantly remind him they were empty, along with his bullet pouch. His long search yesterday had yielded no powder, lead, sulphur, or whiskey; all gone like the meat in the smokehouse.

He stopped Kate. They were now on a flank of the mountain almost directly above Scott's Station. The nigh way was straight down over ledges and through woods. Too steep for Kate and Cleo, but he could manage it, and save a ride of two or three miles to the road and around past the front of the station. The mares could use the rest.

He tied Kate with a loose rein, told Cleo to stay close to her, and started down. The going was more a slide than a walk until he came to a path. He had followed it into a little vale, thick with fern, when from the corner of his eye he saw a white thing leap behind a beech trunk. He stopped to wait for a better look.

Dark hair showed itself on one side of the beech, and a child's voice said: "I thought you was some Indian."

"I won't hurt you," he said, when a small girl, after giving him a long look, peeping round the beech, slowly came out of hiding, her gaze on his face.

"I'm hunten my horses and a bright-headed woman with a boy baby, old enough to walk some, but not talken much."

"There's a lot a women with babies down at Paw's place." She was now looking at a pile of ferns by the path. "I reckon that's about all I can carry this time. They're about all I can find to—to cover his grave." She started crying, softly as if afraid of being heard, but the crying didn't hinder her from piling fern into her gathered-up pinafore skirt.

"You're getten a mighty big load. Couldn't I take some?" Leslie offered.

"I thank you kindly, but I can manage these." She turned to him. "Please, could you cut some boughs off that pretty pine over there? They'd look nice, and they're soft. I couldn't break any off. Uncle Matthew liked the pine—it's white pine—like that in Granpa's yard."

Matthew? Matthew? Could it be the one they'd called Matt? He was too young to die, hardly more than a boy. He looked from the pine she'd pointed out back to the child. "Matthew Saufley?"

She nodded, and said between sobs: "They killed him at Kings Mountain."

He swore under his breath as he unsheathed his knife and went to the sapling. White pine as she had said, and scarce in these parts. He cut the boughs she'd bent down and no more.

Quick as he was at the cutting, by the time he had sheathed his knife and turned around with the pine boughs on his shoulder, she had vanished. He didn't catch up with her until, after crossing a footlog over the creek, he found her struggling to get herself and fern over a ten-rail fence.

He swung her over, fern and all; then, not forgetting the pine boughs, vaulted. He landed on the edge of a good-sized cornfield; the untopped stalks were too high to see across, but, different from his corn, the fodder had been pulled, so that he could see down the rows.

He walked on, looking down the long rows with the hope of seeing the fort or a house at the end, or the child. She must have gone to the graveyard. As he remembered, it was on a bare knoll. They'd put a man, and a woman in the family way, there

51

as soon as they could after the Cherokee had withdrawn. Lonesome-looking and ugly; no fit place for Matt Saufley; he didn't belong in any graveyard; so young, so alive, and brave with it.

He switched to a corn row going crosswise of the one he'd been on, and after a short walk saw a picket fence past the end, and beyond it a big double log house, the wood bright-looking and unweathered. The Cherokee had burned the older house. Yard and porch were filled with women and children. They looked to be dressed in their best. He wished he'd worn better clothes to Matthew's burial.

The corn row had ended, and he was nearing the muted sounds of women's and children's voices when a child screamed: "Indians." Women and children ran into the house. He stopped, looked in every direction, saw no sign of an Indian, and walked on around a picket fence and through a gate.

He was going up the porch steps when a long sapling of a boy slid off the roof and jumped in front of him. "He's no Indian. Recollect what we heared about Leslie Collins last night. It's him." He had grabbed Leslie's hand. "I sure do want to shake the hand of a man who's done what you've done."

Leslie, wondering what he had done other than run away, joined in the shake. The boy had grown about two feet in the less than two years since he'd seen him. He was Jimmy Scott; that would make him a nephew of Matthew Saufley. "I'm hunten my horsestock and my wife," Leslie told him, "but I am sorry to come dressed the way I am when there's a burial."

"Burial? Whose?" Jimmy asked.

"There'll be no buryen, no funeral, not for that blackguard. And why have you come with a hat on your head to dissicrate a house a mournen?" Old Scott had come to the doorway.

Leslie answered the old man in as civil a tone as he could muster. "I am looking for my horsestock and other lost property. Have you seen a red-headed woman with—" He jumped back. The old fool had grabbed up a rifle and was using the barrel to beat the pine boughs across his shoulder as he screeched:

"Tory, Tory, upholder of that popish faith. Git. Git from my sight with your cursed pine boughs, emblems of the antichrist and his upholders. A son an—"

Jimmy had jumped in front of him. "You're three sheets to the wind, Paw. Git back into—"

"And who do you think shot the son that come forth from these loins? That nephew I took to my bosom and—"

"Rightly speaking, you've got no bosom, Paw." Jimmy grabbed the rifle barrel, and in trying to take the gun from the drunken man, jerked him onto the porch.

Now in the sunlight a man could see the glitter of his silver knee and shoe buckles and in between the shine of silk stockings; more twinkles came from the silver buttons on his fine black coat with a gold watch chain that sparkled brighter than the satin weskit.

Still hanging on to the rifle, he tried to aim it at Leslie as he yelled: "Matthew Lucas Saufley is dead to me and mine, dead, dead, buried alive and gone to perdition. And what do you think Matthew wore in his hat when he sent that fatal bullet into my son? Git goen, you Tory swine. May you and all your England sink, yea even as did Sodom and Gomorrah."

A woman's voice came from beyond the doorway. "And may you remember, Paw, 'Be kind to the stranger within thy gates.'" A comely young woman in a white flounced apron worked her way through the gaggle of children blocking the doorway, and came to within handshaking distance of Leslie as Jimmy lifted the pine boughs from his shoulder.

"Law, you're no stranger. You're Leslie Collins. Nobody can ever forget how you saved this station."

"Give the credit to my horse, and anyhow I was just one of several men," he told her, taking off his hat, shaking her hand. This woman, he'd just realized, was Miss Nancy, old Scott's fourth wife. She sure was holding up well, prettier with a little more meat on her bones, and a nicer, fuller bosom than when he'd seen her the other time.

She turned from him to look across a horse pasture. Leslie followed her glance to see the bare knoll that held the graveyard; and among the gravestones was the moving whiteness of the small girl as she brought up her fern. Miss Nancy turned to Jimmy. "Paw hurt you?"

"Lord, no. I punched him in the belly with the stock."

"Your paw," she said as if her husband, still quarreling and trying to aim the rifle, were out of hearing, "has with his wild talk got your little sister thinken Matthew is dead. Could you go set her straight?"

"Yes, maam," and Jimmy ran toward the graveyard, pine boughs jouncing on his shoulder.

Miss Nancy turned back to Leslie. In spite of the prodding gun barrel which she now and then grabbed, he told his business and asked his questions.

She shook her head. "We heard everybody up your way had moved to the Cumberland settlements. But ask my father. He's over at the fort. He might know."

The rifle barrel was in his belly. Miss Nancy knocked it away as her husband roared: "Don't go nigh that fort. Be gone by the nighest way. I want none a mine to have intercourse with you. Take one step toward that fort an I'll consume you with fire and lead, yea even as Moses consumed the burnen bush."

Leslie turned and started for the fort as Miss Nancy said: "There you go sinnen agin, Paw, misquoten the Bible to serve your end. Moses didn't consume the burnen bush. —Mr. Collins, you be sure to come back in a few minutes; tell my father I said he was to come, too."

He walked on, listening to Miss Nancy: "Paw, you know you couldn't hit a buffalo if it had its head through the yard gate. But God works his will in wondrous ways. He could maybe let you shoot an unloaded gun with no primen in the pan."

Halfway to the fort, Leslie met Jimmy's grandfather, John Saufley, a good many years younger than his son-in-law. They shook hands, John Saufley explaining he'd heard of Leslie's trouble from one of the little shavers who'd been listening in the doorway. He apologized for the behavior of his son-in-law. "He wasn't too stoned to know what he was sayen."

They were walking back toward the house as Miss Nancy had directed when John smiled. "Have any burnen in your ears last night? Isaac Huffacre stopped in at our place, mostly I reckon to find out if we'd seen you. He said you was all right, at least you could still ride. I laughed till I cried when he told how you'd laid that bantycock of a Lister Marcum low."

So that was the reason for Jimmy's praise. Aloud, he hoped he hadn't given the man a bad hurt.

"He'd been better off in the end if you laid him out with a blow to his windpipe so he couldn't talk for a month," John said, and talked on of Lister Marcum as they walked along. "First, he owned a big hill-and-valley farm somewhere in the lower Yadkin country. In spite of the fact that he was well-to-do, an officer in the muster, he had never lifted a finger to help in the rebellion, and the Tories had never bothered *him*.

"So there was already considerable suspicion of him. The men he'd tricked to go on the hunt of his wagon had been mad as fire when they got to the encampment; and so were the rest when they heard the tale. Well, pretty soon he came riding in, cursing out the men because they hadn't walked with the prisoners as he'd ordered. The wagon got in with two poor devils dead on the end of the line, skinned alive on the rocks coming down the mountain. The big one on the end had already been half dead from a mule kick, and had dragged down the little man tied next to him on the line.

"Somebody said the same thing ought to be done to the colonel; he'd killed two men and lied into the bargain. Another feller said, tar and feather him first. They'd got the tar on, but since they couldn't find any feathers, they was plannen to roll him in horse shit when Isaac left. He's on his way to Natchez.

"Oh, no. That English captain got good treatment. They was aimen to turn him over to Sevier for parole. And before Isaac left, some prisoners was diggen a grave for the lieutenant. The only prisoners the Kings Mountain rebels hanged were Loyalists back at Bickerstaff's old fields. Some said they'd picked out about fifty to hang, but had just got through nine or ten when John Sevier rode up and stopped the hangens—there's a good man.

"Sorry you have to walk so slow to keep abreast a me, but I've never been much good at walken since that fool Braddock led us spank into an ambush, and I got my knee laid open by a spear with an Iroquois on the other end."

He sighed. "War. There's been nothen but wars since and wars before I was born."

55

"Maybe," Leslie said, hoping to comfort the man, "this war will be the last."

Saufley shook his head. "Supposen the rebels lose. They'll try again. Supposen they win? How can they ever stick together in one nation? They'll be jarren and fighten around over slavery, trade, and a lot of other things. Right now the East don't want the West, and the North is a different world from the South. And they've got Spain on their doorstep. But supposen they do clean out Spain, kill every Indian, plow up every acre a ground from the Atlantic to the Pacific? They'll still have their wars."

Leslie disagreed, but was wishing he could say something to make the man feel better, when a young girl ran up to them. "Miss Nancy said give you all these." She held out two clean towels and a bar of yellow soap.

They took her offering, thanked her, and walked on around the picket fence. Back of it, the preacher's kitchen yard looked to be filled with women and girls busy around cook fires that from the smells were baking, boiling, and roasting a variety of foods. The women and girls were all good looking, but none so pretty as—

"Collins, man, kindly put your eyes with your feet."

He stopped in time not to bump a girl, grown but not yet womanish, carrying two big pails of water. "Let me," he begged, and grabbed the pails.

"Why thank you," she said, startled as a bird.

"Just show me where to put it." He'd hoped she'd walk abreast of him. The spring path was wide enough, but she walked ahead to the water bench on the back porch. He could look at her again when he'd set the buckets down.

"I thank you kindly, sir," she said, blushing.

She was even prettier when she blushed. "You're welcome," he said. He was wishing he could think of more to say when a swarm of small children, all thirsty, surrounded her and the pails.

He hurried back to Mr. Saufley who stopped when he came. "I got off the trace back there talken about war and never got it straight about your wife. All I know is, she and your horse-stock is missen, an you think maybe the Indians got her. Anything else bothered?"

56

The spring path, twisting now around a hillside, was long enough for Leslie, beginning with the cow's skeleton, to tell how things were when he reached home.

"And you had two grown blacks and two good dogs with your wife?" the older man asked when he had finished.

Leslie nodded. "I had good young, honest help, a man and a woman. They wouldn't run away. I know they wouldn't."

"But you found no sign of a struggle; no dead dogs? And nobody had tried to burn the house?"

"No."

Saufley shook his head. "I don't know. When every Indian nation, north and south, has picked up the hatchet for England, a man can expect the worst anyplace any time. On the other hand, a band a Chickamauga—they're the worst—wouldn't be apt to go way up to your place when there's plenty more closer. Anyhow, I've seen homes where they've come in on a lone woman with children. You've seen such places, too, set on fire most a the time."

"I know," Leslie said. They had reached the log springhouse, shaded by a tall poplar, and built over a fine stream of water that gushed from under the rocky hillside above. A few feet below the springhouse a length of hollowed-out cedar carried a big stream of water to the poplar wash trough so that it was always overflowing with clean cold water.

The place was aswarm with small boys; some up a sycamore down by the horse trough, three trying to wash while others tried to dunk them in the trough. Seeing men ready to wash, the boys quickly finished.

Leslie had washed and was clubbing up his hair when Saufley said: "But you have to recollect, man, not all the mean wickedness in these parts is done by Indians. Maybe more is done by evil white men."

Leslie nodded, and wished for a change of subject.

"The reason nothen was left at Weaver's Place is they've been gone since back in July, early July. Not long before they left, a party on their way to Weaver's Place stopped here. Most were his kin; they was headed for the Cumberland settlements at French Lick. But there was a yellow-headed woman, no kin of anybody around here. She had a packhorse man with three horses loaded with her plunder, black help, and the fanciest guide I've ever laid eyes on. She was aiming for Detroit—I don't think she had any notion of the troubles she'd have in trying to get there. Said her man was there. Tory, I reckon; he'd have to be, liven in a British fort."

"And you think Weaver went with his kin?"

"I'm pretty certain. A few days after that party passed through, he was down to sell me the corn in his field, offered it for almost nothen; and to tell me and my wife good-bye. My notion is your wife went with them."

"I don't think she'd just up and leave, take everything."

"You're wiser than Solomon. He kept his wives under close watch. Anyhow, this moven's like a fever; one catches it; all around him come down."

They were walking back when a catbird called a few feet behind them. Saufley didn't look around as he said: "Pretty good, Jimmy. You've almost got it."

The boy ran up to walk beside them. "Mr. Collins, it sure was good a you not to tell that soused old fool the pine boughs belonged to Cissy. When he's got the Timothies he's a little worse than common. I ought to a took my fist to his snout when he was mistreaten you. Him, usen Holy Writ as the excuse for a bender."

"Jimmy, you oughtn't to talk disrespectful of your father. And what's this about Cissy?"

"Him helpen make me wasn't my doen. And, Granpa, you know all this talk about his dear son's mortal wound is a great big lie, and he's got no proof that Matt shot him, and his wound is straight across his fat butt, not in his gut. The women and girls are titteren theirselves sick over that wound. How would you like to have a half brother with a bullet scrape across his backsides? I'll never live it down. I'll wish forever you all had let me go to that battle."

"You're too young for such," Saufley told him.

"I'm older than some a John Sevier's boys that went." He was silent only a moment before starting again on his father.

"This mornen the roosters had hardly stopped crowen before he was quoten Paul to Timothy: 'Take a little wine for thy stomach's sake.' The only wine he knows is whiskey."

Saufley shook his head, and reminded Jimmy he hadn't yet told of Cissy's trouble.

"Well, I reckon it started because Cissy didn't know the rebels at Kings Mountain stuck slips a paper in their hatbands so they'd know one another. With paper so hard to come by, where do you reckon they got enough pieces for over a thousand men? Anyhow, the Tories wore pine twigs in their hats so they could tell one another." He hurried with the rest of the story that ended with: "So, like Aunt-mama Nancy told me I took her to Granma's. It was a happy place; Granma was singen and maken honey bread when we went in. Mr. Collins, you can tarry awhile with us, at least all night."

Leslie thanked him for the invitation, but declined. He had two mares waiting for him about a mile up the mountain. He thought the best thing for him to do was get them and ride back a way different from the one he had come. He wanted to hunt as much as he could for horse sign. He figured his might have got out of the pasture; somebody could have left the bars down.

Saufley nodded to his plan, but urged him to stay at least for the night; his wife would enjoy having him.

"Your horsestock could be in the woods," Jimmy agreed. "Howsomever there's plenty a horse thieves around. I'm goen to ride, maybe all the way to the Nolichucky, and norate the word about missen horsestock. I'd sooner be away from here than not when that celebration comes on tonight."

"It's a far piece for you or anybody to go alone in these times. I'll go with you, if I can make certain somebody's spenden the night at our place. I don't want to leave your granma without a grown man around."

A half-grown girl dashed by on her way to the springhouse. Jimmy ran after her; to help bring milk for dinner, he said.

Saufley nodded backwards. "No whiskers on his chin, but he's already runnen after girls. He's my oldest grandchild, born to my first child, Mary. Cissy was her next child that lived; the

59

six others in between died in the bornen. Mary died when Cissy was born. My wife found a wet nurse and they pulled the baby through."

He was silent until a passing child was out of hearing range. "Why a girl like Mary just turned fifteen would take up with an old widower like Scott I never could know. My wife thought she took him out a pity. We lived in western Pennsylvania then. He come through with a preacher, mighty religious, stayed with us, and told pitiful tales about his little motherless children and how he'd loved his two dead wives. First thing we knew, he had beguiled Mary into runnen away with him. I hunted him up, aimen to beat him into sausage meat. I found them, had him tolled off from Mary a good ways, and had him down, bloody as a stuck pig, when Mary heard his screamen and come runnen. I figured she was already in the family way, and stopped. Back home my wife said the best thing to do was to move close to Mary."

He walked on in dour silence until Leslie said: "At least your daughter, Miss Nancy, seems to be holden her own."

"And more. She married him so she could take better care of her dead sister's children."

The dinner horn blew as they neared the house. Leslie wished he didn't have to waste time in eating, but there was no way to get out of going to the table. In these parts if you were at a man's house close to mealtime, and he and his wife didn't invite you to eat they were uncivil no-goods; it was even more uncivil for you not to accept.

The long puncheon table on the back porch was surrounded by boys when Mr. Saufley, at Miss Nancy's direction, took the place at the head of the table; "Paw," who ordinarily sat there, had passed out. Everybody stood in respectful silence while Saufley asked a blessing, then prayed for the safe reunion of the visitor and his wife.

Prayer finished, Leslie looked at what was before him. The linen tablecloth was freshly ironed, the pewter shone, and further down the table, the trenchers used by the smaller boys looked to be of polished walnut. He didn't think he'd ever sat at a table so heaped with food, several kinds of meat and game, pickled beets and a variety of vegetables. A long trestle against the wall was loaded with cakes, pies, sweet breads, and conserves. The only vacant space was in front of Mr. Saufley.

They were scarcely seated when Miss Nancy called from the porch steps: "Don't run in front of us, anybody."

She and another woman were bringing up a great charger that held the mightiest pie Leslie had ever seen; the lid was big as a cart wheel, and the walls at least two handspans high. He thought it an uncommonly big Shropshire Christmas pie such as he had seen in London until the woman helping carry it said, as she helped place it before Mr. Saufley: "Here's my sea pie. I hope it's good."

Saufley edged back as if afraid the walls would break to send a flood of hot meat and gravy over him. "I know it'll be fine eaten, but don't you want to keep it for the victory celebration tonight when your man's home?"

"Oh, no. There's another one baken out there about as big. I want you and the company and the boys—four are mine—to have this one. It'll hold up while you dish it out. I put a bushel a flour in the crust." She smiled. "And my pie crust's not famous for tenderness."

Saufley got up, cut a hole in the lid, and fished out a chunk of venison and a quail. "Eat hearty," he said as he served Leslie. "The women have been boilen and baken and fryen and mixen and stirren since they got word a the victory. Some have brought in horse loads of cooked victuals, and all their men but ourselves either comen back from Kings Mountain or gone to meet the ones comen home."

Jimmy, sitting across from Leslie, said he figured the men would do their celebrating before they got home; all they'd want would be more from their jugs.

Saufley, struggling to get out in one piece the half of a young turkey, turned on his grandson. "Such talk's not fitten around these women and little ones. They'll all know it soon enough."

The hungry boys were sending up their trenchers, and Saufley gave each a big serving, but when finished, with a chunk of venison on his own plate, the pie looked about as big as ever.

61

Girls came round to serve coffee, tea, sweet milk or buttermilk, while others passed a variety of hot breads, bowls of butter, and platters and bowls of a number of things that included green beans cooked with lots of bacon, turkey with stuffing, and a sliced baked ham.

The girl he'd met carrying water was serving cabbage slaw; he didn't care for slaw, but he took some so they could look at each other when he thanked her. The slaw like the other food he ate tasted good.

Miss Nancy was all over, making certain nobody lacked anything, that cups and glasses were kept filled, empty bowls refilled, and that the shoo-fly girls let no fly get close. She saw that Leslie's plate was empty and hurried over. "Mr. Collins, you've just nibbled; if you're tired of meat and vegetables have some cake and pie. I'll declare you're leaner than when you was here last time."

"Don't fault him for his leanness," Saufley said. "He's made that way, like I am. People have been tryen to fatten me up since I was born, an never done a lick a good. But do have some cake or pie; else the womenfolks will feel hurt."

Miss Nancy urged the persimmon pie upon him as being uncommonly good. "Do the settlers actually make pies out of these?" came back along with the choking-to-death boy. He declined it, and though he already felt stuffed, he did manage a piece of gingercake.

Cake finished, Leslie noticed the smaller boys were leaving the table. Jimmy had also finished, but appeared to be waiting for him. He got up. He knew that in places like this when a big dinner was served to a good deal of company, the table had to be cleared, dishes washed, and a second table set up for the women and girls.

Outside, he tried to thank Jimmy and Mr. Saufley who had followed for their hospitality and plans to spread word of his missing horsestock and wife. No more than any man would do, Saufley said, and furthermore they were returning only a small part of the favor Leslie had done them in saving the fort less than two years ago. And couldn't Leslie spend the night with them? His wife would be mighty glad to see him again.

"Why, there'll be plenty a room here; no need to go up to Papa's place." Miss Nancy was coming up.

Leslie declined both offers with thanks. "I'm in a hurry to get back and do some more searchen. Could be there's a letter I overlooked."

They understood at last, and it was time to say good-bye. Jimmy and Miss Nancy had disappeared. He shook hands with Mr. Saufley, and was asking him to tell the others good-bye for him when Miss Nancy hurried up with a half-bushel split basket on her arm. "I do wish you'd stay the night," she told him, "but if you can't here's a little snack for your supper."

He didn't want to carry that heavy basket up the hill to Kate, but he thanked her for it and the good dinner.

He had turned to go when Mr. Saufley said: "If it's Jim you're looken around for, he's gone for horses. You didn't think we'd let you walk up that mountain to your mount when we've got more than enough to carry you there." He looked at his shadow. "At the best, you'll be dark getten home."

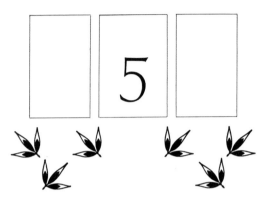

Sunlight was still aslant the higher western slopes, but the valley was thick with twilight by the time he reached his barnyard. He dismounted to let down the drawbars. He let an end of each pole down, but continued to stand.

He would, he reckoned, look through the house again; he might yet find a letter. No, he wouldn't. Ought he then to strike out for French Lick on the Cumberland? Sadie could have gone on a long visit to her mother away over in South Carolina. He shook his head. He'd thought of that before. Mr. Saufley had thought she might have gone off on a long visit. Sadie might do that, but she was too eager "to get ahead in the world" to take the help with her and leave the place go to rack and ruin. She'd leave Jethro and Angela to work.

Could be she was a captive in some Indian town, maybe north, maybe south. Bad, but it wouldn't be of her own doing like going off without a word to the Cumberland settlements with help and horsestock she'd stolen from him.

He had to believe that or Indians. He wouldn't believe she'd taken his goods and gone off with another man; the one who'd fathered her child might have come back.

He'd trail them down and . . . Kate's head was over his shoulder. Lacking a human neck, he'd twisted and pulled on her bridle rein until she was almost on top of him. And why was he holding her anyhow? She would stand. He was letting Sadie drive him out of his mind.

He patted Kate on the shoulder, and walked on to the barn. Unsaddling Cleo, he found the basket of food Jimmy had tied on her packsaddle. He hadn't wanted the food; he didn't want it now. They pitied him down there; he was to them what he was wherever he went—a stranger. No, he didn't feel a stranger in the woods or among Marion's men. He would like to forget Sadie and go back to the partisans.

He'd planned to stay home only two or three weeks, then return with what Marion needed most—horses and gunpowder. He wouldn't go back empty-handed. Right now he must get some corn to shell and parch for his trip; wherever he went he ought to have parched corn for traveling along even if he couldn't mix it with maple sugar. There had been a good deal left from last spring's making, but like everything else it was gone now.

He had taken an armload of corn ears from the crib, and was coming back through the barn hall when his foot struck Miss Nancy's forgotten basket. He stopped. Some woman or women had worked hard to cook the victuals in it. He could at least carry it to the house.

Corn and gift of food on the kitchen floor, he found, in spite of the heavy twilight, firewood that when split would do for torches; and glory be, an ax was in its usual place by the house wall. Dry hickory wasn't as good as fat pine, but it would have to do—provided he could get a light with no powder or dry tow. He did have a flint in his gunlock. He could strike that against the ax, and maybe get a light. He went into the black kitchen and rummaged in the woodbox until he found a few splinters of fat pine dropped from long-since-used kindling.

Ax and flint worked together to make sparks; the split pine caught them and made a small flame, but big enough to light hickory splinters; more splinters lighted the small foresticks he laid in the fireplace, and when that fire was burning well he lit his torches.

The room he hated most was "the front room." He would go there first and be done with it. Standing in the center, his torch left the corners and walls in heavy shadow. He hesitated, then took a step toward the corner that held a bed. The golden scrolls of Holy Bible rolled toward him through the darkness. Nothing beside or below them.

Cursing, he went back to the kitchen, and the past. Three or four months after he'd written home of his marriage, and while he and Sadie were still camping out in this unfinished house, here had come his wedding gifts: Angela, her mount, a packhorse, one hundred guineas in a leather bag, some other goods including silver from a few relatives, and that big family Bible. Considering his father's lands and goods, his mother's dower, the wedding gifts were not exactly generous; still, they were more than he had expected from parents who had long since despaired of him for "throwing your young life away" and "not living up to your birth."

In spite of all that, he had hoped for a letter in return for the one he had written of his marriage. There had been only a brief note from his mother: she had given the usual congratulation and wish for happiness, hoped Angela would serve her new mistress well, hoped he was in health, and said that in "these times" she was extremely busy with almost no time for writing letters. He had flung that polite note to a stranger into the fire.

The time she'd spent on the fine new family Bible was more than enough to have written a long letter with news of the family and the war in Virginia. She'd written in the Family History section of the Bible his maternal and paternal ancestors for five generations back, coming on down to his and Sadie's marriage, August 7, 1778; below this were blank lines to be filled with the names and birth dates of his and Sadie's children.

Angela had been brought by a guide strange to him about the time fall was turning into winter, late October he thought. The guide had also brought a letter from a man who offered high pay for surveying a boundary of land near Harrod's Station in Kentucky.

Leslie had been restless, eager to get back into the rebellion or take one of the surveying jobs he'd already been offered. He hadn't gone because he didn't want to leave Sadie with only Jethro and no woman around; she'd told him around two months after their marriage she thought she was in the family way. He had left to survey two or three days after Angela's coming.

He hadn't quite finished platting the boundary of land when he got the news that "Hair Buyer" Hamilton had recaptured Vincennes, and that Clark, still at Kaskaskia, needed more men to recapture Vincennes. Leslie left his work as soon as he heard the news; he'd gone once to fight Lord Henry Hamilton's Indians, and he would go again.

It was a nasty trip, wading miles of icy water, sometimes breast deep, but when Clark once again held Vincennes, and Leslie could go back to his work, then home, he'd had a proud feeling of victory.

The first thing he'd seen in his house was Sadie's mother in the kitchen bossing Angela. The first thing he'd heard above the old woman's tongue was the strong yowl of a baby in the next room. Speechless, he'd gone in to find Sadie sitting by the fire as she changed the yowling, kicking baby on her lap. She had looked at him, tried to smile, couldn't meet his glance, and looked at the fire as she spoke her piece: "He's come a way too soon. Maw said she thought it was caused by my haven to—"

He'd wanted no more of her lies and left the house.

There was no need to count months on his fingers; gestation for a woman was the same as for a cow. This was March; wondering on how Sadie was making out, and worried over the war in the South, he had hurried to finish the survey and then home as soon as Vincennes with Hamilton was retaken. It was less than eight months since he'd first slept with Sadie; and that baby wasn't new. He'd thought Sadie uncommonly thickset for a young woman.

He never did learn the child's birth date, but stray remarks from Sadie when she was off guard made him reasonably certain the borning had been in the Christmas season.

Several months later when he picked up the Bible, it had fallen open at Family History. He noticed new writing under Births. Unwilling to believe what he read, he'd carried the book to the door for better light. The writing didn't change: Joseph Hawkins Watson Collins, May 7, 1779.

He cursed the writer for the lie put into his Bible; done to make a bastard his child for anybody who didn't know the truth. The child was not newly born when he'd first seen it in March. Would he want anybody to know the truth; that William David Leslie Collins had let himself be tricked into becoming the world's greatest cuckold?

He glanced at the fire; almost out, and giving too little light for him to see if the corn he'd shelled for parching was all good grains or had chaffy kernels from the ends. He was letting one half-drunken night at a tavern ruin every minute of his life.

He got up. Now, while the fire was low, would be a good time to get out that wedding gift of guineas. Angered by a gift of English gold instead of a letter, he'd thought he'd never spend it. His father, a Loyalist he was certain, had heard his youngest son was a rebel, and so had not written one line, but flung him some money as if he'd been a pauper.

Much as he hated money given in such fashion, he'd better take it with him. He didn't know what was ahead. Angela had turned the money over to him while Uncle Tom Tiller was building the kitchen chimney. He'd bided his time until everybody was out of the house; the mortar was still fresh on an inside round near the beginnings of the arch. He'd pulled out a good-sized rock, chipped a piece off the back end to leave room for the sack of money, slid the money in, put the rock back, and smoothed the mortar so nobody would notice.

He lighted a splinter, stuck his head into the chimney, and looked at the rock; the mortar around it was cracked as if somebody had been fooling with it. Why? Nobody knew money was behind it; Sadie didn't know he had received a gift of money.

The big rock came out so easily with his first hard pull he staggered with the weight of it. He lowered it to the hearth, then reached into the hole for his bag of money. His hand, searching all around the empty square, touched nothing but rock. He lighted another splinter and looked to find nothing but an empty hole.

He gave up after a second look and heaved the rock back into place. He'd get along without the guineas he hadn't wanted, but how could they be stolen when nobody knew they were there?

In walking away from the chimney to get wood for the fire, the slight roll of two floor puncheons annoyed him as usual. The floor had been laid firm and solid, in spite of Sadie's objections. She had wanted a "cellar hole" near the kitchen hearth where she could hide if Indians attacked. He had told her a hole under the house floor would make a good roasting oven for her if Indians should come; they'd burn the house after taking all the plunder they wanted.

He'd come in one day to see why Jethro hadn't come to help lay rails for the horse pasture. He'd found him head-deep in a big hole through and under the kitchen floor. He was digging and shoveling under Sadie's direction while Angela, also under her direction, was raking the rocks and dirt off the kitchen floor and dumping them behind the house to make more mess.

Sadie had got so mad she'd lost her tongue for a minute when he took Jethro off the job, and stayed quarreling mad while he left the open hole for weeks.

The hole, he reckoned, was empty as always; it was too much trouble to get into and out of to be used for a cellar as Sadie had planned. Still, it might be a good thing to take a look. He heaved; the puncheon rolled on its side as he had fixed it to do. He lighted a torch and looked down; the hole was better than half-filled with flax straw. Why, he wondered, and swung himself down.

One foot landed on what felt to be the top of a crock. He went down all the way to hunt through the flax straw. The crock he'd touched was full of maple sugar. That was only the beginning; the flax straw covered enough edibles to keep a lone man for months. Better than food were the certificates of ownership for his help, and the deeds with plot maps of the lands he had earned through surveying. All were still as he had left them, wrapped in hog bladders to protect them from the damp. He found no powder, but his sulphur was there. Soon as he got into the saltpeter-cave country he could make powder.

Among other foods, he found some roasted coffee, ground

69

and ready for use. The smell of it made him hungry. He found a pot, put in enough coffee for several cups, and set it in the edge of the fire where it would come to a slow steep and not a quick boil. That would ruin it.

He shelled corn until the coffee smell grew strong and he could hear the little hissing thumps it made to say it was getting ready to boil. He pulled the pot out on the hearth, then went for the basket he'd flung down by the door. Might as well have a look at what Miss Nancy had given him. Smelled like cheese; he hadn't had any in a long while.

He carried the basket to the hearth. Miss Nancy had a curious notion of what a "snack" was. She'd put in half a roast young turkey, slices of beef and ham, a meat pie, little tarts, a loaf of bread—salt-rising from the smell, the cheese, a round of butter with a dogwood flower molded into the top, and, best of all, beaten biscuit to fill the empty crannies. He hadn't thought anybody in these parts had ever heard of a beaten biscuit.

He finished his supper with a drink from one of the two jugs of whiskey he'd found in Sadie's "cellar hole."

He whistled as he shelled the last of the corn, and, still whistling, banked the fire, put out the torches, and went down through the dark to the barn. He'd rather sleep in a saddle blanket in the loft above his horses than in the empty house.

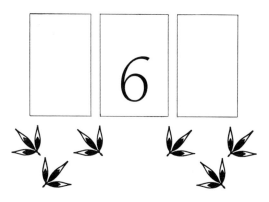

6

The sun was halfway to noon, and he was making no better time than yesterday or the day before. This was the beginning of his fifth day out, and he'd come only around a hundred miles, but this trace ought not to be measured in miles. Up and over Clinch Mountain; Clinch River to swim, Powell Mountain, Powell River, up and down over rocky-bottomed, steep-walled creeks, places so steep a man wondered why the horses didn't fall backwards. The long pull up to Cumberland Gap, down and down into the flat land near the river, mud shank-deep on the mares, then Cumberland River to swim.

More creeks, more up-and-down going, until here he was off the main Kentucky Trace, twelve or fifteen miles west of Flat Lick on an Indian trail he had been on before. And as so often during the trip, he was leading Kate above a steeply falling creek with bluffs on either side.

Making certain he was on Weaver's old trail had cost him time. He'd picked up the trail at Weaver's Place and had followed it easily to the old Hunter's Trace. Once he'd reached that, Weaver's trail was lost most of the time in mud and rock, or under the tracks of the many horses, cows, hogs, sheep, and people who'd followed the trace since Weaver's party had gone over it months before.

He knew the tracks of Weaver's horses and he knew those

of his own, but for all his searching he'd never found a track that belonged to one of his horses. This east-west trail crossed Rock-castle River near where it emptied into the Cumberland, then went on to meet a north-southwest trail that led to the Cumberland settlements. He knew he was on the right trace; he'd found a clear print of a shoe belonging to Weaver's big sorrel.

He was stopped now by a track he'd been seeing since first finding it at Weaver's Place. Here, it was not only headed in the wrong direction, but the toe calk had gone in uncommonly deep as if the horse had been running. Only a fool or a man dead drunk would gallop his horse along this rocky creek bank. Well, a man scared might, or a riderless runaway horse.

"Come on, Kate. I've wasted enough time," and he started up the path.

The only part of Kate that moved was her head, which she tossed. Another rattlesnake? He looked ahead, down toward the creek, up the hillside to find nothing out of the ordinary. He looked at her. She said a bad smell was coming down the creek. He sniffed; nothing but cool air moving down the creek valley to bring the smell of hemlock and clean white water.

He shook his head over Kate, left her, and walked on. He had followed the trace around a jutting ledge of rock when a big-toothed skull smiled up at him. The rib cage and other bones had slid down the hillside. A leg bone, half-hidden by a dirty boot, burst by the swelling rot of flesh, was all that marked the skeleton as having belonged to a man. His skull had been so thoroughly cleaned by buzzards, wolves, and weather there was no telling whether he'd been scalped.

He walked on; the creek bank above offered a more gentle slope. He climbed it. The Warriors' Path was only about fifteen miles to the east; if Indians instead of white men had ambushed Weaver's party, they would have done it on this, the eastern side of the creek.

He had angled several paces up the hillside when a bee whizzed past him, then another. What could bees want here in the deep woods where in late October there were no flowers? He watched and followed other bees as they flew by, until he saw

72

all were lighting on the trunk of a young hickory at a spot about head high from the ground.

Careful neither to crush nor alarm them, he put a gloved forefinger through the center of the cluster; he felt a small hole, no bigger than his little finger, if that big, but clean and round as if made with an auger. There was a slant to the hole as if the auger had angled toward the ground a bit. The hole hadn't been made by a boring auger, but by a bullet from a large-bore, rifled barreled gun.

Weaver had such a firearm. The slight slant to the bullet hole indicated the ball hadn't come from low down by the creek but from the bank on the other side. The bees were beginning to say that if he didn't move on they'd all sting him. They wanted the hickory sap; it wasn't as sweet as that from sugar maples, but sweet enough some overmountain families made syrup of it.

He kept his finger in the hole long enough to sight down and across the creek, trying to give his outstretched arms the same slant as the hole.

Closely grown hemlocks shut out everything on the other side of the creek except the upper branches of a big sycamore. Keeping in line with the hole, he had crossed the creek, and was working his way up the steep bank when he came to a head-high bluff. Sticking over it was a horse's hoof with holes left by nails in a ripped-off shoe.

He felt a moment's relief. Weaver's party had won the skirmish. Indians hadn't taken the time to get the shoes off the dead horse; mostly their war parties traveled on foot, and anyhow their horses would not have been shod. His joy died when he remembered white men could have done the ambushing.

He climbed the low bluff to find the horse's skeleton stretched on the outer edge of a level spot. Bits of hide and tail the buzzards hadn't wanted were scattered about to give the faint stink of carrion Kate had smelled.

The thin layer of earth behind the skeleton still had a trampled look as if a good many feet, knees, elbows, and bodies had struggled there. He saw several dark spots and splotches;

blood stains he figured, from the horse and the people behind it; the men had used the horse as a breastwork. They'd been hard pressed; the small spots where powder had been spilled meant they'd primed and charged in a great hurry, and sent a lot of bullets. Looking out toward the creek, he saw tree trunks scarred by bullets and small branches with cutoff ends.

He went to the big sycamore he'd seen from across the creek. Weaver's party had certainly had the luck; the sycamore grew about fifteen paces back of the dead horse but to the left so that it was out of the direct line of fire. The trunk was at least ten feet in diameter with a big hollow opening on the back. The women and children had taken refuge there; on the always dry dirt of the floor he could make out the prints of children's feet, and seeds of the choke cherries they'd been eating.

He looked higher; that yellow-headed woman still hadn't tied up her hair; a few strands were caught on a rough spot near the outer edge of the hollow. He shook his head. He'd followed many trails, one marked by buzzards, but this was the first where he'd got help from hair. He'd found it caught in tree branches and on briars; the first time he'd been puzzled until he remembered the "yellow-headed woman" mentioned by Mr. Saufley.

A short distance past the sycamore, the ground steepened into what was little better than a bare bluff. Curls of dead moss and horseshoe scrapes on steeply sloping sandstone told how horses had failed to hold their footing and tried again. Several small dead pines and huckleberry bushes dried and uprooted told how people had pulled themselves up the ridge side.

He thought at least one had been wounded. Here and there a rock or clump of lichen was streaked with old blood, washed in the rain, dried in the sun, but still blood. Stepping back he could see, higher on the bluff, places where earth and rocks had been gouged down to blackness by struggling horses. Nothing had grown again to cover the earth wounds, for that black stuff was the beginning of a coal bank, and nothing would grow on coal. Rotten near the surface, a coal bank would give way under a climbing horse to send him sliding back.

Be damned if he'd make his mares go up that bluff. He

hadn't been ambushed. The Indian trail went by the easiest way out; down to the creek, then up it through a low water gap to the top of the ridge; on the ridge top he'd turn left and sooner or later cross Weaver's trail.

Kate and Cleo were where he had left them. Cleo when in the woods followed him more closely than a dog. It was only necessary to lead Kate in a wide circuit on the side of the creek away from the dead horse.

He'd made longer and more wearisome bypasses, but the sun was straight overhead before they reached the top of the pine ridge. The thick layer of pine needles showed no sign of travelers, but riding as close to the western edge of the bluff as possible, he soon saw a break in the bluff where trampled and broken brush said somebody had gone that way quite a while ago.

Certain he was on the trail, he unsaddled the horses for their noon rest, and as there was nothing to graze on, gave each a small feed of corn. He sat on a sunny rock and ate the last of Miss Nancy's beaten biscuit with her butter and cheese he had saved for his journey. Finished, he lay back to study the sky.

At first glance it looked clear blue, but high and faint in the west were the beginnings of mares'-tails. They meant rain; no sooner than late tomorrow, maybe the day after.

He watched a hawk cut holes in the sky. He hadn't seen a hawk in what seemed a long while. Settlers shot them when they could and set out traps for them soon as they saw the shadow of one. Hunters didn't like them either, but here in what he'd heard hunters call "the brush" he doubted if there'd ever been a load of skins taken out; and as for settlers, they'd never come to a place where the valleys had only rocky creeks for floors and the only level land was poor soil on the ridge tops.

Rough as it was, the country still had a mighty stand of timber; ridges covered with tall pine, big hemlock down near the creeks, and on the ridge sides, sometimes in the valleys, were maples, chestnut, hickory, sweet gum, oak, and the finest poplar he had ever seen, their trunks often twice as thick as he was tall. There wasn't much fall color yet, except in black gum bush; their leaves were red as blood.

He resaddled the mares, and, in spite of Kate's angry

75

protests, put the sack of feed corn across her saddle. He had never before taken a long trip into rough unsettled country with only one packhorse. He had brought little provender for himself—even without powder and ball he could, if need be, catch fish in a basket and eat chestnuts—but without corn, the mares would starve in this desert with nothing to graze on. Their corn and his food made an uncommonly big pack for Cleo. He spared her whenever he led Kate by giving Kate more than half her load; but spoiled Kate would never admit it was the fair thing to do.

He was nearing the next creek down when he found the remains of three half-faced camps, but no sign of a cook fire. They'd been afraid Indians would see the firelight. He reckoned he was still on the trail; there was enough bare earth on the other side of the creek to show the track of Weaver's roan mare.

The next valley over was deep in twilight by the time he reached it, and when he had struggled to the ridge top above, only the afterglow was left above a long band of gray cloud. Time to stop. He put Kate's saddle on a high, tablelike sandstone under a pine, then, standing on the stone, hung Cleo's pack with most of his provisions as high on a limb as he could reach.

Horses fed and rubbed down, he ate his supper of parched corn and maple sugar pounded together. The afterglow had faded before he finished, but the band of cloud climbing slowly up the sky left most of it free for stars; the evening star would be the first to show. He stood on the high rock and watched until it came, and then he saw the new moon, low and pale above the band of cloud. He watched until it was lost in the cloud. He went to sleep, head on Kate's saddle, the rock at his back, face to the east, pine boughs above him, while on the next hill over two angry wildcats called each other names.

He awakened in the beginnings of first light. He had had a good sleep; the best in a long while. He hadn't seen or heard the swinging boy, nor had his brother come to shake the bloody stump of an arm in his face.

The light grew strong enough for him to see, close in front of him, the black outline of a good-sized rock. Why hadn't he noticed the rock last night? Plenty of light to see it when he came.

It didn't matter. The cloudy day was too far away to give light enough to find the trail. He'd go back to sleep. As he started to turn over, Cleo snorted. The rock shape moved, took on the outline of a bear, a Goliath of a bear.

The first wild creature, except squirrels, he'd seen since leaving home. He wanted to reach out and pat it, but did not. He remembered the man he'd seen a few years back who'd been in a fight with a bear up on Poor Fork of the Cumberland. The man had let his priming get damp; his rifle wouldn't fire; he'd had to use his knife. The bear had maimed him for life in the minute or so it took him to knife the beast's throat.

Still, this bear gave him a good feeling. A few, at least, were left. Living miles from any trace or hunting ground, the bear had never seen a man, heard a gun, or smelled powder. He came closer, then stopped as if debating. He'd smelled the maple sugar hanging in the pine bough or maybe the ham and bacon. Leslie was wondering how he'd go about getting it when Cleo reared and let out a thundering neigh that would have done justice to a stallion.

The bear stopped and appeared to be considering the situation. Cleo neighed again and reared until she looked to be standing on her tail; sixteen hands high, front legs chopping the air, she was a fearsome sight. He'd wager the poor bear had never seen a horse, but the beast took time for a long look before he walked away, dignified as a county judge.

Leslie reached out his right hand. Yes, he'd done it again; set up two sets of crossed sticks and on them laid his rifle handy to his right hand. One of the first things he'd learned in the woods was to keep a rifle, loaded and primed, within quick reach at all times. He laughed and got up; at least he'd learned one lesson well: he kept his rifle in reach even when he had neither powder nor ball.

He breakfasted on cold corn cakes, ham, and maple sugar. Horses fed, saddled, and ready to go, he laid a fair-sized chunk of maple sugar on his sleeping rock; the bear ought to find it before some varmint grabbed it.

He found the trail with no trouble by the horse, cow, and human manure, bleached by the weather and scattered by birds, but still dung. Travel was about the same as the day before, and that about the worst he'd ever known. Compared to Powell, Roan, and other mountains he'd traveled over, these he now crossed were only hills and ridges. Trouble was, they were so steep it was a wonder how anything could grow on them. Most were crowned with bluffs too high and steep for a man, let alone a horse, to climb. This meant sidehill walking, slipping and sliding, on and on until a break could be found in the wall. And when he wasn't going sidehill or up and down, he was crossing or walking up a swift creek with a slippery, rocky bottom.

He'd given the mares their noon rest and climbed out of another creek when the rain started. It came with a slow, straight dropping that said the clouds were full and had all the time in the world to empty themselves. He had always loved the rain, especially in deep woods where it sharpened the smells of hemlock and pine, dead leaves, and the ground itself. The sounds, too, were good, but now he wished it had held off awhile; the mares were having even more trouble holding their footing on rocks and leaves slippery in the rain.

Rain. Rain when he'd been captured and caused the boy to be hanged and Zach to die a horrible death; rain when he'd gone on Clark's campaigns to the Illinois; rain when he'd got back to South Carolina looking like a beggar, ashamed of his appearance. That was why he'd gone to that third-rate tavern. Rain on the laurel leaves in the slick he walked by sounded much the way it had on the roof boards of the tavern when he'd got into Sadie for the first time.

Cozy; warmed by the liquor high in his blood, warmed by Sadie. He hadn't thought much about her; from the free and easy way she'd acted, he'd taken her for just another woman hanging around a third-class tavern; there not to earn her living as a chambermaid but by accommodating any man in need of a woman.

Why hadn't he knocked Pap down when he'd barged in with a blunderbuss? How had Sadie's father known she was in bed with him? The old devil waving the firearm, declaring Leslie had "deflowered his virgin daughter," had roused the whole tavern. And the fat old mama right behind him alarming all creation with her squalls. Leslie was certain the flower had lost a lot of its petals before it got to him. He said so. At that the old man threatened to blow out his brains. Leslie had grabbed his rifle and told him to go ahead. He wouldn't. He'd wanted a live son-in-law for his woodscolt grandchild.

That hadn't all come through, not that night when he was half asleep still feeling his liquor. Otherwise, he would have knocked the old man flat and gone to his friends, the backhills. Why hadn't he anyway? Suppose the woman he'd slept with was the innkeeper's daughter? She was still a hungry-bottomed whore.

He'd been married on the morning after the night, no banns published, but a preacher, or so they'd claimed, and a wedding dinner very big for such short notice. The most he remembered of that day was that somebody was always handing him liquor. Had he or had he not been too liquored up to know he was putting himself on the barrelhead for what could be hell on earth the rest of his life?

No sooner was he married than Sadie's parents let out their plans for him and Sadie; they were to settle on a tract of land given Sadie as part of her dowry. Sadie had been as eager as her parents to go live on that out-of-the-way creek running off Clinch Mountain. He'd wondered why she wanted to live there until he'd come home to find her with a baby. Why hadn't he left her then? That would have been letting the world know he was a cuckold, had been since the day he'd married. He was a coward or he'd never have gone through with that marriage.

And why was he on this wild goose chase now? He ought to have turned back soon as he picked up the trail south of Weaver's and found no sign of any horse his own.

He checked Kate, going at a good clip along a pine ridge. Cleo was several paces behind, coming more slowly. How long had he been on this ridge anyhow, and when had he last looked for the trail? He had either lost it or Weaver was going west by a few degrees south when he ought to be headed northwest to cross the Rockcastle and get on the Cumberland settlement

79

trace. If he kept in this direction a few more miles, he'd have to cross the Cumberland again where it made a long north-south loop, then again to get on the right trace.

He tried to see beyond the ridge, but the trunks of big pines, black in the rain, stood out for a little space, then nothing but fog and mist. The rainy sky was either on top of the hills or fog from the creek valleys had risen to their tops. It didn't matter; since leaving Cumberland Gap about all he'd been able to see from the top of one ridge or hill was the top of the next.

He rode on, easy riding; the sounds of rain on the dead pine needles on the ground and the living ones above were nice to hear. There was no wind, but overhead the pines, as always, talked among themselves, quietly, with no angry roars.

He had ridden for what seemed a long while along the ridge when he again stopped Kate. He'd heard something that was neither rain nor pine talk. Horses still, the sound came clearly, a low but steady roar that didn't belong to any beast or any tree in any wind he'd ever heard. He listened a moment longer, and rode on, shaking his head over the ignorance of William David Leslie Collins.

That roar came from the Falls of the Cumberland. He'd never been there, but he'd heard the river was easily forded just above the falls; the man who'd been there had also said the ford was godawful hard to get to.

Weaver or somebody with him knew the country; they were keeping clear of the Indian trail, but they'd picked a hard way to go. He figured that past the falls they'd made a beeline for Price's Station, only in this country a man couldn't travel in a beeline; and in between they'd have to ford the Big South Fork, but after that the going would be easier, and at Price's they could get help in crossing the Cumberland again to get on the French Lick Trace.

Twilight was graying the fog before he reached a gap in the ridge and started down. The lower he went, the thicker the dark. He had hoped to get up the next mountain, but in order to do that he'd have to cross a creek at the bottom of this one. He couldn't hear above the rain any sound of running water; that could mean the creek was of swimming size; he didn't want to risk the mares in deep water when he couldn't see the next bank through the foggy twilight.

Might as well encamp, but first he'd have to find a proper site. He'd need the shelter of a half-faced camp on this rainy night. He was crossing a narrow bench of fairly level land when he saw the irregular mass of roots that belonged to a good-sized, half-dead ash blown down in a storm. He was thinking the fallen trunk would make a good back for a half-faced camp, when, on coming closer, he saw that somebody before him had had the same notion. Must have been Weaver's party. They'd built a big, stout one, and it was still in fair shape. The two forked saplings stood straight, and held the roof pole in their high crotches. The smaller poles that stretched from the roof pole to the top of the waist-high log had been laid close together, then layered with hemlock boughs; and as the roof was steeply slanting, he found the ground quite dry when he stepped inside. There was a laurel slick close by, and from it he cut enough laurel to lay over some leaks in the roof, and to mend the two walls made of tree branches and little leafy poles stuck into the ground.

The shelter was so big he fed the mares inside. He found near the open front a spot with enough earth and loose rock he could dig a cookhole. Easy enough to find wood he could shave fine to catch the spark from his flint and hatchet, and more wood for the fire. The pot he'd set at the back to catch the drip had, by the time he had a fire going, caught enough water for tea and corn pones.

Water heating, fire making coals, he unpacked. The three most important articles—corn, sulphur, and stockings—were still dry. There wasn't much danger of the sulphur getting wet; he'd put it in two tallow-dipped gourds. His stockings with extra leggings and shoepacs were dry in his saddlebags, but the corn traveled on Cleo under a bearskin, grease side up; only a lower edge was dampish where creek water had splashed.

He stripped, hung his wet clothing in the roof to dry, then scalded meal for corn pones. These he wrapped in wet leaves and buried in the coals. Work around the fire had dried him off enough to get into dry clothing. He didn't ordinarily worry about keeping any part of himself dry except his feet, on wet days changing stockings at noon. Isaac Huffacre had taught him something he'd always practiced: never travel with wet feet; each day a man must put on clean dry stockings, otherwise his feet would gall until trying to walk or even ride would become a hellish business.

Dressed, he cut and fried rashers of ham; ham done, he made red-eye gravy. He ate, then built up the fire to dry his clothing. Any Indian within miles would see the glow of his fire high in the fog, but any Indian who wanted him enough to come to this hole in the dark ought to have him.

In spite of the fire, the mares showed no wish to go out into the rain, and were still inside when he'd banked the fire and rolled into his blanket.

He awakened to darkness and the quarreling of ducks on the creek below; sounded to be about a dozen with half saying it was time to rise up and go, the other half saying it was best to bide awhile as it was too dark to travel.

He agreed. According to the ducks it was morning, but he could see nothing. He lay and listened to the ducks and the slow, steady rain until he could see to build up the fire, and his thoughts drove him out of bed.

He set a pot of water on the fire, fed the mares, then went down through the gray first light to hunt the best crossing in the creek. He had almost reached the creek when a pace or two ahead he saw a light spot; another step and he could make out the stump of a fair-sized sapling, the stump freshly cut and cone shaped. Beaver. They had stilled the creek with a dam.

He went silently on to the creek. He hadn't been close to a beaver dam in years; with every man in Christendom wanting a beaver hat, and hunters eager to supply the skins, the beaver hadn't lasted long. They'd hung on in this desert because hunters had never bothered to come here. Getting out with a horse load wouldn't have been worth the trouble—if a man could find a horse load—even before the rebellion when there was trade with England.

He soundlessly stepped into the water and waded out until

he could make out the top of the dam, threatened he guessed by the rising creek. A beaver surfaced and swam to the bank, where a short walk brought him to the freshly cut water maple; he chewed off a mouthful of twigs, returned to the creek with his load, and dived out of sight. The dam was leaking, Leslie figured; if it broke the colony would be at the mercy of the weather and every varmint in the woods.

He watched until the beaver surfaced and went for another load at about the same time a second one came out of the woods dragging a beech limb that looked too big for him.

Leslie wished he could watch all day, but if he were going to camp on the other side of the Cumberland tonight, he'd better be walking up this stream to hunt an easy crossing for the mares.

He found a shallow place with banks not too steep for the mares, and by noon had reached the ford above the falls of the Cumberland with no more trouble in traveling except as they neared the falls, the increasing racket of all that water falling onto rocks below frightened the mares more and more. River reached, they plainly showed they didn't aim to ford it. Leslie decided when he waded in to test the current, the mares had been through deeper water many times, but never swifter; but they were already so scared of the racket of the falls, now not ten paces downstream, the swift water wouldn't make them any worse.

He put half of Cleo's load on Kate; then swimming when the rib-deep water took him off his feet, wading now and then, he led Kate then Cleo across. Finished, he put on dry breeches, stockings, shoepacs, and leggings. A waste of time, he figured; he'd be wet with sweat before he'd climbed the mountain in front of him, but it was good to be dry for a little while.

Once up the mountain, it was soon down again into a valley so steep and narrow, with the interlacing boughs of hemlocks on either side forming low dark tunnels, that a man would have had to crawl through had not the remains of the trace cut by Weaver's party been there. Grown up in bracken and briars, it still made the way much easier.

And it was a fine world: big timber from which wolves howled and wild turkeys called, considerable deer sign, and one glimpse of another bear.

Soon, a little wind came out of the northwest to break up the even gray of the sky and change the rain to windy spatters. These soon stopped, and not long after the sun began to battle the scudding clouds for a place in the sky.

Weaver's trace led to an easy crossing of the South Fork of the Cumberland. This river was not big, but for most of its way it flowed between high cliffs a man couldn't climb, let alone a horse.

Past the South Fork the coal banks disappeared, and hemlock gave way to cedar in the vales. There were fewer pines and more hardwood; the biggest oak, hickory, ash, red cherry, maple, beech, and chestnut he thought he'd ever seen. Finer than the hardwoods were the great poplars, and the prettiest; they alone had lost their lower leaves, but after the fashion of poplars they still wore their yellow upper leaves, and as the late sun struck them, the woods looked to be layered with gold.

He hated to give over the easy riding on the ridge, but it was time to hunt a campsite; only the tips of the poplars down in the valley were catching the sun; everything else below was in twilight. He'd rather camp on the ridge but he'd found no water.

He followed the next water gap he came to down to a creek in a narrow vale where wild grasses and clovers grew around rocks that glimmered gray-white in the twilight. Limestone. That meant he might find a saltpeter works any time now on his way to Price's Station less than half a day's ride away. In limestone country there were usually caves with niter dirt that could be made into saltpeter.

He left the mares by the creek, and after crossing the strip of meadow climbed a short way up a steep hillside to reach the sandstone bluff that walled the vale. He found what he had expected: a row of what the backhill people called rockhouses, house-size holes open to the world, formed, he figured, when softer rock wore out and fell away to leave an overhang of sandstone. Here, as in most, a steady drip from the roof above had made a pot in the floor, always overflowing with clean water.

He fed the mares in one rockhouse, took another for himself. His was convenient for cooking, but no place to sleep in good weather. No breeze, and no sound except the slow drip from the roof. He went to a high flat rock he had seen a few paces below the rockhouse.

Settled into his blankets, the site was better than he had expected; no tree branches between him and the stars. The moon, hidden by a ridge to the west, was too young and pale to dim the stars. They had the sky all to themselves, and God what a skyful. The bluff behind him and the hills that ringed the vale shut out much of the sky, but he could still see more stars than at any time since—when? He fell asleep wondering on the when.

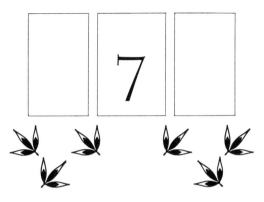

7

His wounded father, tied to a team of rearing, plunging horses, was being dragged to his death down a rocky mountain. Jethro astride one urged the horses on with a long black whip. Leslie screamed: "Jethro! Don't, Jethro, don't." He could hear the crack of Jethro's whip, but not his own voice. He couldn't make a sound.

He knew what he saw and heard wasn't real. Or was it? A nightmare would go away. He came fully awake at last, sitting in his blankets. He remembered the stars and looked overhead. Black as the night the boy had been hanged. People might lie but not the stars. Last night they'd said the night and the day would be clear. He felt his hair, then his blankets. Both damp as his clammy body. Sweat could have dampened him but not the blankets. He was crazy; he was under a heavy creek fog; that was all.

The nightmare was still close. He wished he could get up and be gone, but there was not even the beginning of first light; no sound from any living thing except a screech owl. The ungodly racket it made had probably caused him to have the nightmare, or maybe he'd eaten too many raw chestnuts yesterday, or it could have been the muscadines.

Whatever it was, any suspicion of Jethro wouldn't cause such a dream. He lay down, wrapped himself well in his blankets,

86

and tried to sleep. Wonderings on the fate of his father, doubts and wonderings on Jethro wouldn't go away.

It was wrong of him to have any doubts about Jethro; he felt guilty for having such a dream. He and Jethro had spent their first years together; his black wet nurse had been Jethro's mother. They'd fished together, wrestled, climbed forbidden trees, taken forbidden sails on and swims in the Rappahannock, and grandest of all had been the stolen rides on the family's hunters. Jethro, though he was then so small he had to stand on an empty keg to saddle a horse, had always done the slipping out of a stable or catching in the field, but had seldom gone with Leslie. He was less afraid of his master than his father, head coachman and lord of the stables. Leslie, afraid for Jethro, had given up saddles but not the secret rides.

They'd quit hating girls during the same summer, and it was then Leslie learned he was to be sent away to school, not yet all the way to England where his older brothers were, but far enough there could be no more good times with Jethro. He had gone to his father and asked for Jethro. No, he couldn't take Jethro with him; he was no body servant and never would be; he'd think it foolish to take a boy with the gift for horses Jethro had and try to make a body servant of him.

Leslie hadn't wanted a body servant, just Jethro. At Christmas he had received among other gifts a paper signed and sealed by his father conveying Jethro to William David Leslie Collins when "the said William David Leslie Collins shall have attained the age of twenty-one years."

He became twenty-one. Jethro was his, but he didn't go home to claim his gift. His father, instead of keeping Jethro at Sea Winds until Leslie should come to claim him, had hired him to the owner of a livery stable in South Carolina; his wages were to be paid to Leslie when he showed up.

Jethro had flourished in South Carolina with a good master and good horses, but had been there only around two years when the rebellion began. He and his master were of the same persuasion—on with the rebellion. Soon, a band of Loyalists came and took the horses by force, including the one Leslie's father had given him when he left Sea Winds. In their struggle to keep the horses, Jethro and his master had been badly beaten and knocked about.

As soon as he was able to travel, Jethro had gone to the first detachment of rebels with horses he could find. Happenchance put him under the command of Colonel Andrew Pickens, soon to become a leader in partisan warfare. Whether working as a farrier or riding with a band of raiders, Jethro had done well. Leslie had heard him praised by his fellow soldiers for his courage as well as skill with horses.

He had had to leave the war when Leslie married. Jethro had not been bred to the hard life of a backwoods farmhand, harder still when Leslie was gone and Sadie his task mistress; and though he had never complained or sighed aloud for other days, Leslie felt he'd been loath to leave the rebels.

The thought had come to him when he'd first learned his horsestock was gone that Jethro, tired of Sadie's tongue-lashings, had slipped off to the partisans and taken the horses. He'd been ashamed of such a thought, and cast it away. And why had he dreamed of such evil in Jethro?

No answer came. Nothing to do but wonder and worry, twist and turn while he waited for first light.

It came at last as a graying of the fog on the eastern side of the valley. He lay and watched the fog above the creek change from black to gray-black, and soon the fog whitened and tree trunks showed themselves as black shapes. There was no wind; nothing moved until, after a long watch, he saw a moving blob of darker fog. He sat up the better to make certain the shape belonged to one of his mares.

First light soon whitened into dawn to show several shapes moving in the fog. He stood up as the shapes took form to become a small herd of deer grazing in the wild meadow. Nearer the creek, he saw a bush shake. Elk? They fed on brush. Two shapes at last moved out of the heavier fog by the creek to become elk; one a big buck, the other a doe; both moving up the creek away from the deer as if they scorned the lesser animals.

The buck lifted his head, appeared to sniff the air, then went for another bush nearer the timbered hillside up the creek.

Leslie glanced back at the deer; they were still feeding. He looked from the deer to where he had last seen the elk. They had vanished. He sprang from the rock, and, careful not to step on any twigs that might break or let any rock roll under his feet, he ran down and around the bluff until he was again within sight of the elk. He slipped behind a big sweet gum to watch.

The doe showed herself in a moment, half hidden in a little swag where fern grew higher than her knees. She was feeding on it, but lifting her head at each mouthful to look around. The buck showed himself close behind her. Higher on the hillside as they now were, the fog had thinned into bands and curls that let him see their colors and the fine set of antlers on the buck. Leslie figured he was old enough to know he was in hunting country and what the smell of man meant.

The air was moving down the creek; there was no wind, but the elk had heard him, smelled him, or maybe only thought they had. Neither ran, nor did they exactly hurry or show fright. They just kind of mixed more and more with the timber and brush until there was nothing to see but timber and brush.

He looked down to the creek valley. Empty. Quiet. He felt the foggy chill, and glanced at his feet. As was his habit when in the woods, he had slept with his shoepacs tied about his ankles. He'd taken time to slip them on; that was all. He was a fool to run stark naked just for one more sight of two elk. A few years back not far from here he'd seen herds of a dozen or more; once he'd watched a fight between two bucks.

He was looking back again. His used-to-be was of no more use than Sadie's by then. He had better put his mind on this day, and get a cook fire started.

The day's weather kept the promise of the stars. The smoke from his breakfast fire rose straight and high, and by the time he had decamped and crested his first ridge, the sun was high enough to show a clean blue sky. On such a day with almost no wind, he could see the smoke of a saltpeter cooking fire miles away, and further still the smoke of wood burning into ashes to run the niter dirt leachings through.

It was not yet midmorning when, riding along a ridge, he turned Kate toward the bluff edge and stopped only when she balked at going closer. Leslie thought he had seen a gray-white smudge against the sky. He watched until a veritable tower of smoke shot up and hung over some far place he couldn't see. He figured he could reach it without much trouble—if he wanted to hunt the source of such curious smoke. No saltpeter maker would have a smoke like that either when burning wood for ashes or boiling down a batch of saltpeter. The smoke didn't come from a fire built by an Indian; any squaw or camping-out brave who'd build such a smoky fire would be a disgrace to the tribe and become an outcast.

He turned down the next water gap on the smoke side of the ridge, and followed it down and around to a creek valley. A short ride up the valley brought him opposite the column of thick white smoke that rose out of the trees and brush bordering a high, ragged cliff. The thick growth hid the source of the smoke, but, studying the column, he decided it came from a campfire whose builder had ridden away thinking he had put it out by pouring on water. Only smoldering wet wood could make such a smoke.

The valley was a fine place for camping, much like the one where he'd spent the night, only bigger with a wide meadow and a strip of canebrake. A good place to give the mares a rest; it would soon be noon anyhow.

Mares unsaddled and drinking, he walked up the creek a few steps to a limestone ledge overhanging a deep quiet pool. He stretched out on the stone, put his lips to the water and took a long drink; good water and cold. He lifted his face and looked around. Everything was all right. His hair felt dirty. He ran to Cleo's pack for soap, took off his hunting shirt and hat, and again lying on the stone ledge, soused and soaped his hair. He was rinsing his hair, putting his head deep into the pool, when he heard Cleo scream. He sprang up, turning toward Cleo as he did so. The world wavered through the soapy water in his eyes; soon, instead of Cleo he saw an Indian, not two paces away, loping in his direction.

Leslie made a grab for his knife left in his hunting shirt on the stone. His fingers were closing over it when the Indian caught his wrist. The Indian couldn't hold it, not all the way; his other arm was free; with it and some help from the caught one, he caught the Indian round the waist, and with a great heave tried to fling him into the creek.

The Indian clung like a leech. Leslie stepped on the wet slippery soap he had laid on the ledge. Both went head over heels into the water, the Indian slippery with bear grease on top of Leslie.

Leslie felt the bottom of the pool against his back and wished he'd sooner remembered God's command to Gideon on selecting soldiers; he had lain and lapped water like a dog; worse, he'd dunked his head to wash his hair, and so couldn't watch for danger. He still had his hunting knife. Use it, but where was the Indian?

The Indian grabbed him by the hair and yanked his head above the water when he'd already had his nose out. He shook water from his eyes to see the Indian, back to him as he made for the creek bank. Leslie lifted his knife; he could get him square two rib ridges under his left shoulder blade. That would finish . . . He'd never killed an unarmed man by stabbing him in the back, and this back was young, no dark, leathery look from years of taking the sun. Somewhere he'd looked at an Indian's back like this, only smoother and prettier.

That other back had belonged to an Indian maiden, the prettiest and the kindest—in some ways—he'd ever seen. A *coureur de bois* working west of the Illinois had bought her from her captors for a jug of rum and two knives; Leslie had won her in a *vingt-et-un* game. She'd waited on him like a slave, but when he'd wanted her in bed with him all he'd see was her bare back quaking in a corner. Rape was not his dish, but he'd put up with her until a brave from many moons west had ridden in to buy her back.

He never did give up hope she'd . . . The girl's face vanished when the Indian kicked backward with both heels. Leslie went under again, and surfaced within reach of the ledge. He sprang out, shook back his hair, and saw the Indian stone-still a few feet from the creek. He was young, handsome, and from some tribe strange to Leslie; his hair was neither in braids nor shaved to leave a scalp lock, but swinging long and free like a child's, and there was a trace of childhood in his eyes as he studied Leslie.

Satisfied with what he saw, he drew one hand across his throat, then clasped his hands together and held them over his head.

Leslie didn't know what a hand across the throat meant, but he had learned in the Illinois that clasped hands were a sign of friendship among the Plains Indians who spoke different languages. He clasped his hands and held them up for a quick shake. He wanted to get to Cleo and Kate before they died of fright and anger over what they saw and smelled.

He'd just got a hand on Cleo's neck when a woman called between gasps for breath: "Don't, please don't hurt that boy. He's good."

A black woman ran out of the woods above the meadow and on toward him, a bundle jouncing on her arm. The sight of her when she ran up appeared to soothe the mares, accustomed to black Jethro. Leslie turned to her; as he did so, the Indian standing tall, flexing his shoulder, pointed to him and said: "Meek keeow."

The woman gave a sorrowful headshake: "Oh, honey, he's not a milk cow."

Leslie understood from her slow, split-syllable speech why the Indian pronounced *milk cow* as he did. He looked at her once and turned back to the mares. She brought back a hurtful sight of his childhood. He'd been visiting relatives in Charles Town, and while being driven around had seen a tied-together line of blacks on their way from a slave ship to the auction shed. They'd worn just enough rags to cover their nakedness, but not the whiplash scars; some were so weak, companions had to help them along. Worse in a way were their frightened, wondering stares when they lifted their faces to look at the carriage.

The woman before him could have come fresh from that line: she had a whiplash scar on her upper arm, bare feet, with a short petticoat and waist to hide her nakedness. There was a difference; she could speak his language—after her fashion. He turned to listen as she said:

92

"That Indian boy, he cain't make out what I say, and I don't know what he says. I've been beggen him to hunt that cow."

Leslie nodded. "I reckon he thought you meant a white man."

"A man around would please the missus. She's awful skeered in the wild woods, and looks like that packhorse man won't never come back."

The bundle on her arm wriggled, whimpered, like a young animal dying in a trap. The woman shifted the bundle; the ragged makeshift blanket fell apart to show a small white foot and leg. "I'm mighty glad to see you, but all the white men on earth cain't save this little chap less'n we can git somethen to feed him. I've been given him venison juice and real thin gruel. But now I'm out a meal and he's starven."

"I can give you meal."

She looked at him as if he were Jesus Christ come back to earth. He thought she was going to cry, but recovered enough to thank him. "Gruel can hold him a little while longer, but did anybody ever hear of a baby bein raised all the way on gruel and meat juice? But my mother knowed a woman that raised a baby on cow's milk. And comen here I saw a cow, close. She'd wandered off from her party, Mr. Weaver said. And his wife said she'd be comen fresh one a these days."

"You came with Weaver's party?"

"An with the missus an a lot of other people, all the way from his house to here."

He loathed the asking: "Was there in Weaver's party a red-headed woman with a tow-headed boy close to . . ."—by the Bible he was only a little over a year old, but—"better than eighteen months old?"

She shook her head. "My missus was the only one with bright hair, and she didn't have any little boy—or baby. Anyhow her hair's bright yellow. The rest was goen to a place they called French Lick on the Cumberland River; but the missus, she wasn't goen in that direction. An she got so tired and wore out, she told her packhorse man to leave her here, and come back when the weather got cooler."

The baby was crying again. She rocked him in her arms as

she said: "The little man is starven. That's what ails him. Better than two months old and never a drop of milk."

No saltpeter; no word of his horsestock and Sadie; but he had found the yellow-headed woman, and a baby.

"The Indians killed our guide. I reckon that's why my missus didn't go all the way on," the woman said.

"Indians kill the baby's mother?" he asked.

She turned to look toward the smoke. "I'd better git back to work. I was hangen some clothes I'd washed to dry on the bushes when I heard your horses."

"Your missus too sick to suckle that child?"

The black woman was looking at him again. "Mister, they's real good dry places, rockhouses Mr. Weaver called them, up under them bluffs. Couldn't you please stay one night with us, and use the rest a this day to hunt that cow? She's close."

Leslie finished wringing out his hair as he looked at his shadow. He couldn't make Price's Station this forenoon, but he could ride around awhile cow hunting and get there by sundown—or after. Hunting a cow for milk to save a baby was pure foolishness; he knew nothing of babies, but he'd never heard of one being raised without a mother or a wet nurse. No, he had heard of mare's milk. The baby whimpered.

"I'll try," he said. It was like hitting that fancy colonel. He hadn't planned it beforehand.

This time as the woman thanked him, tears were running down her cheeks. She was choked up when she invited him to stay for dinner; she was cooking a turkey the Indian boy had brought her.

He declined her invitation, told her he had a snack already fixed to eat. He didn't want to waste time waiting for dinner, and anyhow judging from her smoky fire, she'd be no better cook than Sadie.

He looked around for the mares. They'd got over their fright enough to remember cane made for good grazing, and were back deep in the strip of canebrake. Wet as he was from head to toe, he'd better change clothes before he went cow hunting. Going wet when a man didn't have to was a good way to start rheumatism, Isaac Huffacre said.

In turning toward the sycamore with Cleo's pack in its crotch, he saw the Indian, eyes fixed on Kate. He turned to Leslie's glance, nodded back toward Kate while his eyes seemed to say he knew a good horse when he saw one.

Leslie nodded, pointed to what little he could see of Kate's back, then went for Cleo's pack. The Indian stepped in front of him as he reached for it. Enough to give a man the creeps, the way this boy could get around with never a sound. He was holding in both hands a fish that would have weighed better than twelve pounds, a rock bass, Leslie thought, and still flopping. The Indian held the fish higher, closer. A gift he didn't want. He'd have to dig a fire hole, get it hot, build more fire after he put the fish in; make fresh corn cakes to eat with it; all that would leave little time for the cow hunt.

A man had to accept a gift, and certainly from a strange Indian; the fish was more than a gift, a token of friendship. He took the fish and said in Cherokee: "I thank you for the fine fish."

The boy appeared to understand Leslie was grateful for the fish, but said nothing. He had not understood the words. As he gutted the fish, Leslie tried him with the few words of Creek, Choctaw, and Chickasaw he remembered, but no glint of understanding came into the Indian's eyes.

He was trying to remember the Shawnee word for *fish* or *thank you* when he saw on the unwrinkled throat a scar, older than his own, not so red, but made by the same kind of tie used only on prisoners.

Whatever the Indian's nation, they were brothers with the same marks of man's cruelty. The Indian followed as he went to wash the fish in the creek, then walked along it hunting clean, sticky clay mud. He filled the fish with the mud, stuck short sticks through to hold the belly in shape, and covered the fish with mud. He looked around until he saw a maple; he stripped off handfuls of the greenest leaves he could find, doused them in the creek, and plastered them onto the mud until the fish was covered.

He had left the fish to look for a likely cookhole spot when the Indian questioned: "Keeow?" and handed Leslie a small stick.

Puzzled, Leslie looked from the stick to the boy's face. "Keeow?" the Indian repeated, and pointed to the bare strip of sandy earth between them.

The boy was brighter than he; like any sensible person he wanted to know the look of a thing before trying to find it, and since he couldn't understand the language, he wanted a picture.

Leslie quickly sketched in the sand a four-legged beast with a tail and a head. The Indian frowned over it a moment before taking the stick and drawing two horns on the beast's head. He looked at Leslie with a question in his eyes.

Leslie nodded, ashamed of himself; he ought to have put horns on his cow.

The Indian sprang up, smiled, pointed to the bluff then crooked his hand to show they must go over it.

Leslie gave an unhappy nod and picked up Cleo's pack. The Indian had seen a cow all right, but he couldn't ride up the bluff and over; with the Indian as guide—and he appeared to be taking on the job—they might not get back before sundown. Might as well plan to camp in a rockhouse for the night.

He swore as he picked up the meal sack; he'd forgotten to give the black woman meal; now, he'd either have to take it to her and see her cry or fix gruel for the baby himself.

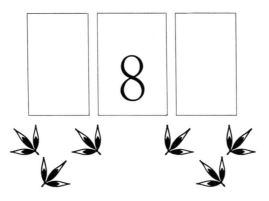

8

He had, Leslie figured, followed the Indian for about five miles of rough going, and through it all they'd done almost no hunting for cow sign. The Indian had covered the ground in a kind of loping walk that never flagged; each time Leslie paused to look for cow sign in what seemed a likely spot, the Indian vanished or got so far ahead he had to run to catch up with him.

They had reached a creek valley with no creek; he guessed it ran underground, but didn't take time to lean above a sinkhole to listen. It didn't matter; no animal would graze in a valley with no water. The Indian had gone up the valley toward a clump of willows; willows meant water. He reached the willows, but saw nothing except a small, sluggish creek sliding over a lip of stone into what looked to be a bottomless sinkhole.

He was wondering if the creek in flood filled the sink and flowed over the valley when from up ahead, he heard: "Meek keeow?"

He found the boy squatted by a pile of fresh cow manure near the creek bank. "Meek keeow," Leslie answered, trying to give the words the same sound as did the black woman. He clapped the Indian on the shoulder; the Indian clapped him, both repeating: "Keeow."

97

Their joy dimmed, then died when they couldn't find the cow. Her tracks disappeared in the creek, and though each walked a bank and searched until the valley was filled with shadows of the hills, they never found the place where the cow had come out of the creek; he reckoned she'd walked out on a rock; flat limestone was plentiful along the creek.

The sun was leaving the ridge tops by the time they'd crested the one above the yellow-headed woman's quarters. Leslie wondered if that quick sketch of a cow he'd made before they started had been enough; and that pile of manure didn't necessarily belong to a cow. What if the boy found a vicious bull and tried to drive him, or came back with a heifer or half-dead ox some mean traveler had turned loose to die? He'd somehow have to explain to him exactly what a cow was. How? He could draw maps to scale, but wasn't very good at pictures.

He heard Kate under the bluff below him. She was in bad trouble; he'd never heard her carry on so. She didn't sound to be in the creek meadow but up on that rocky hillside below the rockhouses. She could be down with a broken leg. The Indian had vanished. He'd find his own way down. He never found the right way, the easy one off the bluff, but with the help of a tree and a grapevine clawing its way up, he clawed his way down the bluff.

He found Kate in a mess of rocks where he figured she'd gone to graze on the fern. There was light enough he could make out a big pale something on her left front leg. He remembered the black woman had said she'd been hanging clothes on the bushes. She must have forgotten some pieces, for Kate looked to be tangled in one. The thing seemed big as a bed sheet; he could feel ruffles, lace, and a long drawstring Kate had managed to wrap around her leg.

He unwound and unwrapped until Kate was free, then flung what he thought was a petticoat over his shoulder, and went for Cleo a few feet away. She was silent, lost in the contemplation of a pale something under a forefoot. Leslie got her off it, and picked up a stiffish garment also with dangling strings. He patted Cleo. "You're smarter than Kate about clothes. She was tryen to get into a petticoat, but you didn't try to put on this corset. If you had, you could have tangled in these stout strings and crippled yourself for life."

He got the mares into the rockhouse next his own, fed them, put the damp, torn articles near his fire now burned to embers; just right for coffee. He put coffee to steep, then hurried off to hunt the Indian.

He went into the first rockhouse he saw with firelight. The black woman was there trying to blow up a no-good fire. She rose when she saw him, and, still short of breath from the long blowing, asked if he'd seen sign of the cow.

He told her they'd found cattle sign, but no cow. He invited her to come sup on the fine fish Little Brother Leaping Fish had given him. "I wanted something to call him by so I named him," he explained.

She only looked doleful as she glanced into the rockhouse shadows behind her fire. "And my little man still with no name . . . I thank you kindly, suh, for the offer of supper. You and the boy go on and eat, but like always I guess he's off in the woods. I'll go down the hill aways where I won't wake the baby and bang a skillet so he'll know it's eaten time. I'll come, too, if I can git away."

From what, he wondered. He understood when seconds after the sound of the skillet was finished, a woman's voice shrilled from around the bluff and slightly above them: "How can you call dinner when I've give you nothing to cook?"

The baby cried from out the darkness. The black woman ran in, dropped the skillet, gave a whispered "Oh Lord," and ran on to the baby. Back with the wriggling bundle, she turned to Leslie. "Please, suh, can you take him?" She nodded upward. "My missus don't like to hear him cry, and anyhow I don't think it's safe or right to leave him back there in the dark." She laid it on his arm and ran.

He undid the blanket—if the piece of dark coarse cloth could be called a blanket—enough to see he'd caught it on its back; the way he reckoned a baby ought to be, but it was screaming like the very devil. The mound of belly Leslie could see under the coarse cloth of its wrapper looked too big for a skinny baby. He plunked it to get the sound of a half-ripe water-

99

melon; must be full of wind. The little cuss was also full of the devil, yowling, waving its fists, and kicking.

He wondered how long the black woman would be gone; if she stayed much longer his coffee would boil and be ruined, Little Brother Leaping Fish come to his rockhouse, find nobody, and be gone again. The baby would cry no harder there than here; furthermore, the little cuss needed food in his belly instead of wind. The black woman had no meal; back in his rockhouse, the gruel he'd set to boil was almost done.

He put his burden belly down over his shoulder and got back to his rockhouse in time to save the coffee on the last part of its I'm-about-to-boil song. And thank God the baby had stopped yowling. He pulled the coffee off the fire, then took from his stack of provisions the remainder of the red cloth he'd bought for Sadie's cloak. He let the baby slide under his elbow, then using his teeth, and a knife in his free hand, cut a length of cloth sufficient for a baby blanket. He eased the baby onto the cloth after spreading it on a clean sandy spot.

He stood up, proud of himself; the baby had gone back to sleep, head to one side, thumb in his mouth. The little cuss was sucking his thumb because he was hungry. Leslie hurried to get the pot of gruel onto a hotter bed of coals, then rummaged among his possessions until he found the smallish, narrow-tipped horn of a heifer. He had planned to cut off enough of the tip to make another powder measurer, but right now the baby needed it worse—if he could scrape it clean, put in holes with his least awl, then boil it awhile to further clean and maybe soften it a bit.

He had cut the horn in half crosswise, put holes in the tip, scraped it well, and had put it to boil, when he felt he was being watched. He looked around to see, dim in the firelight, Little Brother stone still under the overhang as he watched him at woman's work.

They might as well eat, but first he'd better look to the baby's food. Making as little noise as possible, he took the pot of gruel off the fire. He started to set it to cool in the drip pool, remembered that along with meal he'd put in a handful or so of his pounded parched corn–maple sugar mixture to give it flavor. That meant he'd have to strain it, and while it was hot;

cooling, it might thicken. What could he do for a strainer cloth? Part of the petticoat that had almost crippled Kate would make a fine strainer.

Gruel strained and cooling, he dug out the fire hole to find the fish and corn cakes in fairly good shape in spite of their overly long roasting. The clay on the fish had held with no big cracks; he knocked it off; scales and skin came with the outer clay to leave the flesh clean and juicy, while the middle piece of clay brought some of the bone with it.

Little Brother, though he tried hard to eat with dainty slowness to show he wasn't starving, ate everything on his plate and, like Leslie, had a second helping.

Food finished, they were drinking coffee cooled with whiskey when the black woman ran under the overhang. She looked first at the baby, then, whispering, asked Leslie: "Suh, do you know what is caudle—or how to make it?" She held out a nutmeg. "The missus give me this and some oatmeal and a piece a sugared lemon peel—I think it is—said just use half the nutmeg, and she'd put in the wine and sugar."

Caudle? He thought he remembered having caudle as a child getting over an illness. You drank it or sipped it from a spoon, hot. He told her it was a kind of gruel made of oatmeal, sweetened and spiced, then thinned with wine. Cook the lemon peel with it, but put it back on the fire a minute after she'd strained it so she could serve it hot.

His glance happened on the pile of hickory bark he had collected for his morning's fire. He laid two long slabs over her shoulder. "Use this for a good fire," he told her.

She thanked him, said she'd be back for the baby soon as she cooked and served dinner for her missus—she'd sent down a slice of ham and other victuals to cook; and she wanted her caudle after she ate; she ran then, nutmeg clutched in her fist.

That loud-mouthed, yellow-headed woman starving her help didn't need caudle, but he hoped he'd told it right; otherwise the poor wretch would be in trouble. He wondered how the black woman fed the baby. He'd raised a pup from the time it was two days old by letting it suck a piece of cloth stuffed with cornbread and sopped in milk. Maybe a baby could suck thin gruel the same way; the little horn he was boiling to soften for further cleaning would be better, but he'd meant to give it to the black woman to use for toddy; a sip or two of weak sweet toddy would be good for the baby.

He was mixing half a mug of whiskey and maple sugar with an equal amount of water when the baby awakened howling. He laid the horn across the mug, reminded himself to tell the woman she was to weaken a spoonful or so of the mixture with three or four times the amount of water before giving it, then rolled up his sleeves for the attack.

He laid the baby in a clean sandy spot near the fire, and unwrapped the ill-smelling makeshift blanket. Under that was a piece of something that looked to be part of a coarse linen tablecloth with a hole cut in the middle for the baby's head. Under that was nothing but the galled-bottom, sore-bellied baby that had just wet itself.

He jerked off the tablecloth covering, pushed back his hat and considered the remedies he'd brought for possible saddle sores and other horse ailments.

He had whiskey, tar, turpentine, and extra strong lye soap; the brat could use a scrubbing in good lye soap, but it would sting his galled bottom. Whatever he put on that galled bottom, the little son of a bitch would have to be washed first. He glanced at the fire; the pot of water he'd put on for dishes was steaming.

He got the soap he used, laid it and a rag torn from Kate's petticoat by the drip pool, then, carrying the hot water in one hand and the baby in the crook of his other arm, he went to the drip pool. There wasn't enough hot water to make the pool quite lukewarm, but from the way the baby screamed and kicked, a person would think the water had chunks of ice floating in it.

He hushed when Leslie had him dried in one of his towels, and was by the fire, but he still whimpered in a quarrelsome way. Leslie figured a grown man with a galled bottom bad as the baby's would do worse than whimper. The only remedy he had that would help without hurting was the slippery-elm-bark juice and molded-corn salve he always carried with him, but it had an evil smell.

He went for the gourd of gray-black slippery stuff and smeared it on all the galled spots while the baby screamed louder than ever. The smell, he figured, or maybe the stuff was too cold. Rub the red spots with an ear of moldy corn, or just the mold; that, he guessed, was what the Indians had done. Their receipt had been changed away back when it got into a white man's hands. Now, it was a lot of trouble to make: when your corn has plenty of black mold peel some slippery-elm bark, tie it loose in a piece of coarse cloth, then boil it in a lot of water until the water has boiled down and is almost thick enough to scorch; cool it, squeeze everything out of the bark in the strainer cloth, and when the stuff is cool and thick, stir in the mold from the corn.

Finished with the salve, he wrapped the baby in a dry part of the petticoat, and laid him by the fire. His whimpers changed to angry screams. Leslie reckoned he'd either have to listen to the racket or feed him; dinner and caudle for her missus would keep the black woman away for a good while. He listened a minute or so longer, then tore two squares from a clean portion of the giant petticoat and put a piece of corn cake in the center of each to make small soppers.

The baby sucked the gruel-sopped sacks with a right good will for what seemed a long while. It was a messy job, and Leslie was glad when the baby let a gruel sack slip out of his mouth. That meant he'd had all he wanted. He threw the gruel sacks into the fire, wiped the baby's mouth and chin, then beckoned Little Brother forward.

The Indian looked at him, but continued to rub the dirt from an arrowhead he'd picked up somewhere around. Leslie laid the baby down, patted the sand beside it, and again beckoned the boy forward. He next pointed toward the black woman's quarters and flipped the blanket from the baby to show his nakedness. He couldn't think of any other way to tell he must go hunt baby clothing. The Indian got up slowly; plainly he had no mind to do the woman's work he had been watching Leslie do; and to make the job even more distasteful, the baby had started squall-ing as soon as he was laid down.

Little Brother came at last and sat by the baby. Leslie laid the wriggling, squawking bundle across his knees, then ran to the black woman's rockhouse.

She wasn't there, but the pink and white garments he'd noticed before were still hanging around on juts of rock and brush she must have cut. He looked and felt a quantity of what always turned out to be nether garments of that yellow-headed woman; a lot more than any woman needed in the woods. And the baby with nothing, not even the napkin-like clothes Sadie used to "change" her baby when he dirtied himself. On rainy days he'd tried to stay out of the kitchen; the place was filled with baby gear, washed and hung to dry.

Most of the stuff here was dampish to wet, but he did find a dry pair of mammoth drawers with lace and ruffles on the lower legs; split at the crotch, they'd make two long-tailed dresses for the baby. He also found what he took to be a nightdress. Dry, of warm soft cloth, it was big enough for only God knew how many baby napkins and wrappers.

Arms filled with drawers and nightdress, he was hurrying out of the rockhouse when an unpleasant thought checked him. He was a thief, stealing clothes that belonged to somebody else. He shook his head. Marion with no money for buying, and sur-rounded by Loyalists, was always in need of horses. Picking up Loyalist horses at every chance, sneaking them off to Marion's men, was not in the rebel camps considered stealing. It was part of procurement. He was procuring clothes for a naked baby.

Entering his rockhouse he was suddenly worried; he'd left the Indian alone for a good while with a baby he hadn't wanted to touch. And the baby wasn't crying as when he had left him. He hurried over to see him across the Indian's knees, sucking away on the tip of the little horn meant for toddy. The Indian looked up, tapped the horn, and nodded.

Leslie clapped him on the shoulder. He ought to have tried feeding gruel with the horn; looked to be working better than—he'd caught a whiff that didn't come from gruel. No use to look into the horn; the baby was taking the whiskey mixture, and it hadn't been weakened. The mug he'd mixed it in was scarcely half full. He'd put in enough whiskey and maple sugar to do the baby a week or more after it was weakened. He hoped the Indian had drunk it. The baby's head rolled away from the horn; no dribbles, no yowls, instead a sleepy half smile. The horn was empty.

He laid the baby on the ground; it continued to look happy. Maybe it was dying from overdrink. No, its hair was damp with sweat and its lips pinked up from all the work they'd done. He stuck a finger through one of its fists; the hand clung to his finger. Maybe if he thumped its belly then turned it over, it would puke like most other drunks.

He tried. Nothing happened except a small smile. Well, no use to let this happy Indian learn he'd most likely killed the baby. It would have died anyway, but the business made his insides hurt.

Let him die in clean clothes.

He measured and cut and tore, tied on and wrapped until he could stand up and look down on his handiwork. The baby was now wearing a long-tailed dress with tucks, ruffles, and a frill of lace around the neck. This had come from one leg of the drawers. The nice warm wrapper over the dress was part of yellow-head's nightdress.

During the business, the baby had hiccuped twice, his only sounds. Leslie knew nothing of babies, but he thought this one exceptionally fine. In spite of being skinny, he had considerable leg and arm, would make a stringbean of a man; no, more like a ramrod. He'd stand straight and look the world in the face like that English officer, like his father.

He shook his head. The world already had this baby down. He'd be dead by morning, stoned as he was from too much liquor. He heard the black woman's feet, running.

She ran in, gave the baby lying by the fire one quick glance, and hurried on to Leslie. Breathless, she managed to gasp out her thanks for the caudle receipt; the missus said it was all right. She was sorry she'd left the baby so long with him, but she'd have to beg him to keep "our little man" awhile longer, or until she found that nightdress she thought she'd put by her fire to warm for the missus. She stopped for lack of breath, and turned around to study the baby.

One look wasn't enough. She rushed over, stared, then cried: "Lord God in heaven, what'll I do? My missus will kill me. Somebody's cut up her nightdress I was hunten." She looked at the Indian.

Leslie asked: "What is your name?"

"Rachel, suh. I'd better go back to her. The longer she waits, the madder she'll git. But what can I tell her?"

"Don't leave while I am speaken to you, Rachel. And don't throw accusen glances now at our Little Brother. First, I went hunten you to procure clean clothes for the baby. His abhorrent state of filth was a disgrace to mankind and most specifically the female gender. I procured that nightdress and one pair of drawers from her multitudinous collection. I felt I was committing no evil. Whatever the condition of your mistress, this child has the greater need; and unless her nature be hard and cold as a . . ." He shut off *harlot's heart* and substituted, "as the peak of an arctic mountain, she will gladly give of her superfluous possessions to this helpless, unfortunate, naked, and suffering mite of humanity." He stopped, ashamed of having used language ordinarily reserved for mimicking the high and mighty when he wasn't quite sober.

Little Brother was nodding in approval; he would, no different from most Indians, stand stone still and listen all night to an oration whether he understood one word or none. Rachel seemed more mystified than impressed. "Them's fine words, suh, like a sermon, but they won't help me none when the missus finds out she'll get no fresh nightdress tonight." And as if searching for comfort, she pulled away the baby's wrapper to give him a long look. "You've fixed him up mighty nice, but I wish he'd open his eyes." She turned back to Leslie. "The first thing I thought when I seen you was, 'Why, he's got eyes exactly like the baby's, kind a bullet-colored'—I mean a clean gray bullet. I'd better go git it over with."

"Stay here and eat your supper. I'll go tell her I took the articles for the baby."

"Suh, you cain't say that. Please not that."

"Why? It's the truth."

"Say anything you can think up, suh, but not a word about the baby. She don't want me to spend time or anything on him."

"Let him gall, freeze, and starve to death. All right. I won't say a word." He hurried away, cursing the human race. Better to be born a beaver and wind up stretched over some son of a bitch's hat. What could he tell the bitch?

Kate neighed from up ahead as if to chide him for his evil tongue. An instant later the woman shrieked, then yelled: "Get away, you nasty beast."

The gall of that bitch, calling Kate nasty. He ran. She'd scare Kate so she'd jump over the rocks and break a leg. The poor girl was lonesome, mixed up by so many rockhouses when she tried to find him or Cleo. He rounded a bulge in the bluff to come into quivering light that showed Kate. He'd misjudged her; she wasn't thinking about running away. She was pawing, snorting, teeth showing as if she'd bite the very head off that termagant, wherever she was; must be hiding back in the dark part of the rockhouse.

Kate quieted somewhat when he put his hand on her shoulder. "You ought to know I'm not campin here," he told her. It took more talk with love pats to get her turned and headed away from the rockhouse. She was still aquiver when he left her, but he wanted to be finished and done with the yellow-headed woman.

He walked slowly back into the light, arranging in his head what Rachel had told him to say. Still no sign of her, he called: "My mare was here to apologize, and you scared her half to death."

"Scared her? What about me? I hit her over the nose with a stick and the brute charged me." A pinkish blur on the other side of the fire was taking on the shape of a large woman as it came closer.

The shape wasn't all pink; it was crowned with shining yellow hair, undone and flapping around her. Her voice was as ugly as her hair, the words falling hard and sharp, quick as if chopped off with a hatchet; New Englanders talked that way. "Maam, you don't know what Kate's done," he told her when she was close enough he could speak in his ordinary voice. "First, when she was down in the woods hunten fern, she got tangled in and tore a good many of your nether garments. Then she went into Rachel's quarters tryen to find me. There, she chewed"—*would Kate chew cloth like a goat*—"and tramped on and tore your nightdress till . . ."

She yelled: "And that fool Rachel stood and watched."

"Maam, Rachel was up here waiten on you. She'd put the nightdress to warm like you told her."

"She's still to blame, and your horse ought to be better trained. You must pay me or get me exact copies of what she ruined."

"With an embargo on, that won't be easy. I may have to go to Barataria."

"Where's that, my good man?"

So he was her good man; he ought to let her know how good he was. Her voice was lower; if a duck could coo, it would be cooing. She had come closer to stand between him and the fire. She ought to know that standing so, he could see her legs outlined up to her middle under the thin stuff of her dressing gown, the only thing she wore—except perfume. Smelled like a second-rate New Orleans house; a rose would hang its head in shame to smell so; or was it supposed to be rose? Mingling with the flower smell was another odor, faint, but familiar. What?

She was coming closer; her back to the fire, he couldn't make out her face too well, but he could see she was thick-waisted with the beginnings of fat on her belly from the way the pink stuff mounded out. She didn't even have on drawers. "I said where is that place you mentioned."

She was close as she could get, asking for it. He hadn't had a woman since that camp follower he had met on his way home; she was a good rebel, but too tired and put out because Greene had ordered all camp followers to get off the baggage wagons and walk. Then home and no Sadie. One good grab and, big as she was, he could have her back down in that pile of feather beds. She was moving away.

He followed as she said: "Come into the light. There's something I must ask you." Settled on a rock near the fire, she looked up at him. "My good man, I wonder couldn't you take me to—my husband in Detroit. My guide and protector was killed by Indians. My packhorse man wouldn't go on alone. Anyhow, I was too tired to keep on. I—told the packhorse man to come back—in a few weeks. He hasn't come."

She was making up her tale as she went along. Maybe she'd been pretty once, but not now with wrinkles around her mouth and under her fat chin. Her breasts were godalmighty big, but they looked to be tied down. The strange smell was stronger in spite of the perfume; the wine smell on her breath, the bayberry candles, the smells coming from her provender stacked around reminded him of a well-stocked ship chandler's. And the black woman starving.

"Can't you take me to Detroit? You have horses." She moved closer. "If you could just get me to a Kentucky settlement further north, I'd be grateful."

"Sorry, maam, I'm headed south." His knee was touching her thigh. She wasn't backing off. "Would—" Kate nickered; the woman screamed, then called Kate a dirty name.

"Watch your language, maam, when you speak of Kate." He freed the shoulder she'd grabbed in her fright, and ran to the mare.

The woman followed him partway. "You don't think that beast could get me to Detroit?"

"Maam, she won't take a sidesaddle. And anyhow, thousands of braves are out for hair." He didn't answer when she asked what he meant by that. Kate was wanting away from the strange smells, the yapping woman, the firelight, and the candle flames. He led her away. He couldn't take the woman with Kate standing over him, and anyway he wasn't certain he wanted her. Lord, what had got into him? He'd never in his life thought of doing such a thing. Would he if Kate hadn't come along? Would it have been rape with her asking for it, then pretending she didn't want it? He reckoned he would have. No he wouldn't. He'd never known a man black-hearted enough to do such a thing.

The heart didn't have anything to do with it. Cleo down in the creek meadow was letting out a lonesome nicker. Kate answered. He let her go. He hoped they'd settle down and give him a chance to read some in the tracts of Thomas Paine he'd lately bought.

He reached the overhang of his rockhouse, and stopped, struck by the stillness. The Indian was squatting close to the low fire as if he were cold. And cold it was to a man in nothing but a breechclout. Other Indians he had known wore matchcoats—big mantles, often of fur—in cold weather. There was about half of Sadie's red cloth pattern left, also the parts he'd used one day for saddle blankets; they smelled of horse sweat; that was the only dirt.

The black woman was sitting by the cookhole with something in her hand; as he watched she took a quick bite, then another. She was eating corn cakes as if her life depended on the eating. He remembered: "And not a dust a meal left." No wonder she looked like the wrath of God. That bitch with more provisions than she needed was giving Rachel only what she wanted cooked for herself. The black woman had only the game brought in by the Indian. Didn't she know to eat chestnuts?

He must remember to give her some of his meal and flour; he also had maple sugar to spare, and he reckoned he'd better fill that half-empty mug again; he'd give it to Rachel with a strong warning to use it for weak toddy; chances were the baby wouldn't need toddy ever again. If he did waken, he'd have a man-size hangover. If he didn't, Rachel would need strong drink for herself.

He walked away from the light to make water. He wished he could sleep on the ridge top above the rock house; up there he could see more stars, maybe, and study the young moon. It wasn't so young any more, nearing or past its first quarter, bright enough to wash out the paler stars, but from where he stood, he could see only brightness tangled in the trees on the ridge top across the creek. How many days since he'd seen the new moon?

He turned back to his rockhouse. He'd just remembered that on that cow he'd sketched for Little Brother, he'd put no udder, no teats. Tonight he'd draw a cow with a suckling calf. He stopped; if he sketched such a cow, would the boy think all cows had suckling calves, and turn down a good milk cow with a calf already weaned?

He shook his head. Had he tried the boy with French? He was not what the New Englanders called a French-praying Indian, but with the *coureurs de bois* all over the West and the North, many Indians knew a few words of French.

Somewhere out here he'd find a high rock where he could sleep with the stars and waken early to be on his way from these pitiful ones he couldn't help.

9

He rode in fine October weather across wild meadows and over low hills, past familiar places, but had no heart to admire the great trees, most still holding their autumn-colored leaves; nor did he look for deer or elk sign. He gave the mares but little thought. They'd made this trace to Price's Station three mornings ago, and were bringing him back no wiser than when he had gone.

Weaver's party had camped near Price's for a week or so while some of the men built dugouts to take their goods, women, and children under guard down the Cumberland. The other men and older boys had ridden overland to drive the stock.

He'd learned that from old Ezra McFarland, the only man at Price's while Leslie was there. Ezra hadn't heard a word about Sadie Collins; nobody had asked after Leslie Collins; they didn't know Weaver knew him.

He wouldn't go asking again to get another amazed, "Your wife?" like the one from Ezra, a long-time friend. "Law, man," he'd gone on in a hurry, "no wife would go off to a strange settlement with all a man's goods and chattels without letten him know. She's just gone on a long visit to her kin."

Leslie wished he could believe that, but he couldn't see Sadie through Ezra's eyes: after close to thirty years of living on New River with one woman, he still, from the way he talked, thought the sun rose and set in her; in spite of all the time he'd been gone on the long hunts or stayed at Price's, she'd never cuckolded him. She'd never quarreled and picked him to pieces until he'd get so mad he'd have to go to the barn or the woods to keep from hitting, strangling her, anything to silence that tongue. Now, as soon as he got some saltpeter, he'd be going back, and his horsestock had better be there. She'd be there; he was the dog returning to its vomit.

At least Ezra didn't know that. He didn't so much as suspicion that Leslie Collins thought his wife wasn't above running away with another man; mayhap the father of her child had wanted her again. Or did he? The old man was no fool, too kind and polite to let the wrong things show. In his talk he had stayed away from Sadie; he had plenty else to talk about.

Ezra's first greeting had been a hearty handshake with congratulations and praise for knocking out Lister Marcum. Isaac Huffacre had passed by. Leslie, ashamed of what he had done, was glad when Ezra asked soon after: "You see a young lone Indian from a strange nation anywhere in your travels?"

Leslie had described Little Brother Leaping Fish.

Ezra had nodded, and praised the Lord that Leslie hadn't killed him. "We've been afeared some fool would shoot him down like they'd shoot a wolf, for no reason but he's an Indian. Worse, would be for them that had him captured to get him again. They'd burn him at the stake."

Ezra then told what he had heard of the ambush. At the first sign of trouble "that yellow-headed woman's guide and protector, or so she claimed," had turned his horse and started to run. He'd been killed on the spot, and, fallen from the saddle, "his firearm slid kinda under him."

A big Indian had made a grab for the gun, but as he was pulling it from under the dead man, "our little Indian jumped on his head. That big Indian got his hatchet, and had it lifted, but it never come down on our Indian. He jumped clean away, gun and all toward the whites. And just before he got to them, he turned around, bullets singen all about him, and fired off that big gun and killed the big Indian dead on the spot. The firearm was a blunderbuss the fancy man had crammed too full; it knocked the little Indian flat. Weaver dragged him behind a tree.

"And a person would never believe it, but that young Indian done all that with a rawhide tether around his neck, trailen along behind him."

Leslie believed the story—more or less. In an ambush nobody could spare the time or mind to watch exactly what did happen. Children were hidden; wives stood behind their men loading their firearms.

Ezra had been alone for several days and was hungry for talk: he'd talked while they scraped a tanned elk skin, while they rode into the woods for fat pine to make tar, while they slow-burned the tar, and while Leslie washed his clothing in the nearby creek. He'd given his opinions on the rebellion, told of the bad time the Chickamauga and the Creeks were giving the French Lick settlers, and a good deal about "that fool woman with the yellow hair."

The other women in the party blamed the ambush on her. Nobody could keep that woman quiet. Loud-voiced to begin with, she'd squealed and squalled at every little thing, even a measuringworm. It was no wonder a party of what Weaver had thought to be Ottawa had heard her, and planned the ambush.

Ezra didn't know, but from what he'd heard, that woman must be part crazy. They'd camped one night in a rockhouse back across the hills; her packhorse man, a good sort, was aiming to get her from there to the Great Lakes Trail then take her on north to a Kentucky settlement, as far north as he had agreed to go. Well, next morning, she claimed she wasn't able to go on and told the packhorse man to come back in eight or ten weeks.

Weaver hadn't wanted to leave her, but he couldn't budge her, said she acted like she wanted to be rid of him. More than anything he had hated to leave that half-dead black woman with her; with nobody around to watch, that woman would beat and starve her to death. One of the men had said his wife said she was long gone in the family way was what made her so mean. Isaac didn't believe that; no woman, unless she was crazy, would want to be by herself in childbed.

Leslie roused from his long remembering to notice Kate

had quickened her pace, and heavily burdened Cleo was close behind. They hurried because they were looking ahead to that wild meadow with a canebrake on one side where they'd grazed for half a day. "You're both carryen too much weight for fast travelen," he told them. "And don't blame all your load on me. Ezra insisted on given me that elk skin, when I don't need elk skin, two knives for Little Brother, and close to a bushel of meal for Rachel to cook for herself and the baby."

He hushed, ashamed of himself. He was grateful to Ezra; the man had insisted on dividing the little powder he had with him; no more than enough for a dozen rounds, but six rounds for him meant the difference between being armed and unarmed. There was no saltpeter at Price's; most of the men were gone up the Saltpeter Cave Trace to dig niter dirt and make saltpeter; they had sent and would send every ounce they could spare to the hard-pressed settlers at French Lick.

He stopped Kate. Mooning around, he'd let her start over the hill on the same trail they'd made to Price's. Kate tossed her head. She knew she had only to angle down and around this hillside to reach the lower end of the canebrake below the rockhouses where they had camped three nights back.

Leslie had aimed to ride to the end of the ridge to find out if Daniel Strunk had his saltpeter works on the other side. There were already so many men working up the Saltpeter Cave Trace that, according to Ezra, he might do better at Daniel Strunk's diggings: they were located near the mouth of a crooked little creek, not far from where the yellow-headed woman had stopped.

If Ezra was correct, Daniel Strunk was making saltpeter on the other side near the end of this ridge or the next one. The creek below Rachel's rockhouse was as crooked as a crawling snake, and he'd never seen the place where it emptied into the bigger creek.

He didn't aim to ride over there now with all his gear; give Daniel the notion he'd come for a long uninvited visit. A few years back they'd made saltpeter together and been good friends, about as close as any man could get to Daniel. He'd never been the kind anybody would call Dan and slap on the back.

Now, since the 1778 raid on the Overhill Cherokee towns,

Daniel was even more ingrown, at least with white men. He'd been gone when the overmountain raiders killed his Cherokee wife and three small children. One story went that a white man had grabbed the baby by its heels and dashed its brains out against the lodge pole. Some said Daniel had lost his mind from brooding on the deaths.

Kate's disgusted snort told Leslie he must get on in some direction. She wasn't going to stand forever on a hillside where her front feet were lower than her hind ones. Leslie glanced at his shadow; more than enough time to ride on, stow his gear, deliver Ezra's gifts, and come back after midday to ask Daniel about buying or working with him for saltpeter.

He said: "Oh hell," apologized to Kate and rode down the hill. Might as well get the business ahead over with; Rachel would still be crying so hard she couldn't see, even if she had dug a hole and put the baby in the day he left. Unloved, unchristened, dead by the hand of William David Leslie Collins who'd left him alone with an ignorant Indian and a horn of strong toddy.

He was leading Kate down the rocky hillside above the creek valley where he planned to spend the night, when out of the bushes came a howling screech that didn't belong to any human or animal he'd ever heard.

He was trying to quiet Kate in order to investigate—if he left her as she was, she'd gallop down the rocks and break a leg —when an Indian in paint and one feather leaped out of the bushes. Leslie eased his rifle back into its saddle holder. The Indian smiled. He smiled back; a smiling Indian in war paint was a sight to see, and most especially Little Brother Leaping Fish filled with joy and ginger.

He disappeared when he saw what he was doing to Kate.

Kate was glad to be led away from the spot where she'd had the very daylights scared out of her. Cleo was grazing on a clump of fern, unconcerned, as if the Indian were an old friend. They were nearing the creek when Little Brother called from behind a cedar, softly so as not to put more scare into Kate: "Meek keeow, meek keeow." Silence. "La femme boof."

The Indian's words were at first only sounds in Leslie's ears, his mind sick with dread of what he would find up ahead. He and Kate were crossing the creek when he remembered the cow business. Pitiful. A dead baby couldn't use any kind of milk.

Halfway up the rocky slope below his rockhouse, he stopped to listen, pushed back his hat and walked on. That didn't shut out the song rolling out from Rachel's rockhouse, a mournful Watts hymn. Sadie used to sing it over and over until, to keep from losing his mind, he'd go no matter where to get away from it:

> May we this life improve
> To mourn for errors past,
> And live this short revolving day
> As if it were our last.

Planters liked such hymns from their slaves; if a slave thought heaven was at the end of his road, provided he walked it as his owner bade him, he'd behave better. But damn it, even for a slave life ought to be more than a walk through a forest of thorn trees to the by then.

He'd reached his rockhouse. Time to unload, head the mares down to the pasture, then take Rachel Ezra's gift of meal. She'd start crying when she told him of her "little man's" death. He'd been feeling death on his back all day.

The first thing he saw when he reached her rockhouse was the baby's head above her shoulder as she walked around the fire; as her circuit brought her sidewise to him he saw that along with the baby she clasped a bowl of something which she stirred slowly in time to the hymn. Lost in her song, she didn't notice him until he stepped under the overhang and told her good day.

She gave a little squeal, almost dropped the bowl, then her face lighted up like a candle after a long gutter. "I'm so glad you're back. I wanted you to see our baby and the missus has been asken after you."

The missus, always the damned missus. "How's the baby?"

"Finer than he's ever been!" She dropped spoonfuls of batter onto a griddle smoking over a bed of coals. Words rolled out of her like batter off the spoon. The Indian had brought the cow and calf the day Leslie had left, but she could have cried when

117

the baby wouldn't take the cow's milk after she'd skimmed it—babies oughtn't to have too much grease—and boiled it and put in a little maple sugar. She'd had to make his gruel with milk to get milk down him.

"And he's better now than he's ever been. In fact, he took a turn for the better the night you was here. Remember, you had him asleep when I come for him, and for the first time in his life he slept all night. But he was mighty fractious when he did wake up." She noticed his glance had flicked her petticoat. "Looks better, don't it? When you give me that pretty red blanket cloth, I didn't need to use my petticoat tails no more for him. I cut off enough for two little blankets fer him but when you come one was damp; now, I've sewed both back on me."

She squatted, turned one cake, studied it, then carefully turned the other three, explaining as she did so that the missus wanted oat cakes and maple syrup for her late morning snack. The baby began to yowl; she sprang up and started walking again.

"Nameless is spoiled rotten," he told her.

"He cain't help it. They's no place to put him. And please, suh—if you don't mind, I kinda wish you wouldn't call him that. If, if you'll excuse me—but it's like a body was throwen off on him. He cain't help it. I've not got the right to name him, but I sure would like to call him after you—but I don't know any of your names."

"Name him after me? He's not mine to name."

"Excuse me, suh, he is yours. You saved him. He was ready to die when you come along; he was gitten thinner and thinner with nothen but venison juice after I run out a meal. Please, suh, tell me one a your names."

He told her.

She repeated William David Leslie Collins twice, then took off one batch of cakes, regreased the griddle with bacon rind, then put on more cakes, quickly so that Nameless got in only a couple of yowls.

"It's all pretty, but if you don't mind we'll just call him William David till we have the real naming, you know, christenin they call it in my master's church. Then we'll put on the rest."

He backed off. That was his granduncle's name, his god-father. "A child," he told her, "ought to be named after its kin. But—if this baby's father already has sons named after him and his uncles, I reckon it's all right to use my given name. It's handed down from a fine man."

"And he was a fine man, but I'd ruther name the baby after you. So fine looken he was, him tall to begin with, and dressed in his officer's uniform. You know, red and white with a lot a gold braid. He was mighty nice to me. And I think down inside him he was a good man even if he did git the missus—Lord, I hope I've not let the cakes burn."

And so the misbegotten son of a bitch who'd fathered this child and left it to the mercies of a vixen was an officer in the King's army. There was no doubt about it; the yellow-headed woman was its mother. She'd come from Philadelphia. He'd heard that while the British held the town there had been a lot of lalligaggen between British officers and the wealthy women of the town while their own men were either off fighting or making potfuls of gold by trading with the British.

He grew aware that Rachel was looking at him, nose lifted like a hound dog's when the wind brings a strange scent. "Excuse me, suh, but do you smell dried catnip?"

He pulled out the big handful Ezra had stuffed into a side pocket of his hunting shirt. He'd ridden with the smell so long he'd forgotten he carried the stuff. He hadn't wanted it any more than he'd wanted Ezra's long discourse on the wonderful doctor his wife was mixed in with the wonders of catnip; some thought it only for babies, but strong catnip tea was the best thing in the world for a grown person with the ague or a cold. Ezra hadn't sent it to the baby; he didn't know there was a baby —yet; Leslie hadn't told him. He was wondering why he hadn't mentioned the baby, when he saw Rachel was sniffling as she declared him to be the best man in the world; catnip was just the thing for little William David.

He remembered the meal; might as well give it to her now and get this crying business over with. Hadn't anybody ever given her anything?

He picked up the sack and held it in front of her. "Mr.

Ezra McFarland at Price's Station sent this meal for you to cook for yourself and the—William David if he needs it; it's not for the missus."

She took the sack, hugged it and the baby together, and was sobbing out: "Oh, Mister," when a cow bawled just behind him.

A brown straked cow was coming into the rockhouse. She stopped when Leslie jumped in front of her, but tried to get past him when back in the darkness of the rockhouse a calf answered with a hungry wail.

Leslie looked around to see a straked calf loping out of the shadows making for the cow. Rachel nudged him with the baby: "Please, suh, don't let em git together fore I can git to em with a piggin."

He caught the baby with one hand and arm, and grabbed the calf's ear with the other hand, and held on until Rachel had rinsed a piggin and was turning to the cow with a: "Please, suh, mind William David and the oat cakes."

The cakes were smoking; Rachel had reached the cow; he released the calf; the cow at once took off over the hillside, calf struggling to keep up and at the same time get a little milk on the way. Rachel ran after, calling in a low voice: "So-o cow, so-o."

He swore and wished he'd hung on to that calf awhile longer; the cakes didn't matter. Rachel already had enough cooked for a hungry man to breakfast on; and they were for the midforenoon snack of a woman. Still, he turned to the griddle. The baby, quiet while he walked, began crying when he stopped to tend the cakes.

There was considerable batter left in the bowl. While he was putting on more cakes, the baby grabbed a handful of his hair and swung on while the kicked-off blanket fell across the griddle. He saved the blanket from the griddle, but not from a smear of half-cooked batter.

Save for the pull on his hair, the baby behaved while the cakes baked and he could walk. He shook his head over Rachel's troubles as a dairymaid, having to milk whenever the cow took the notion to feed her calf; and that calf liable to step on the baby when Rachel had to leave him to tend to the missus. Didn't she and Little Brother together have sense enough to build a grapevine-sapling calf pen?

He was kneeling to turn the cakes he'd put on when above William David's racket he heard a familiar voice: "Well, well, a man servant. And who might you be, my good man? I didn't get your name the other time we met."

He looked around. She stood in the sunlight at the mouth of the rockhouse, but as she had a long cloak flung over her shoulders there was nothing to see. She came closer while his glance lingered on her breasts, still big, still bound up. He could soon make out a dark spot on the cloth above one breast, like she'd caught a drip from her rockhouse roof.

He hadn't turned the last cake. It wasn't water that wet her dress, but her milk. That cake looked awful pale. Nothing ailed it except he'd already turned it once. That milk wasn't hers to waste; the milk belonged to the baby because she was its mother.

She was smothering him with that loud perfume; and now he knew that other smell, familiar but mixed in with all her provender he couldn't name it before. Camphor; when he was little and had a cold, his old mammy had rubbed his chest with what she called camphor salve. He'd heard it said that women with wet nurses for their babies used camphor to dry up their milk.

"My good man, I asked you your name."

A cake was ready to take up. "King Alfred."

"I've never heard that name before, but it has a pretty sound." She flopped down on a nearby rock. "I'm so weak, and I won't get any stronger until I can get to a place where there's decent food. I've got plenty to cook, but Rachel's so took up with that baby she ruins it all. She's got that batter too thin; cakes'ull be like leather. I'll bet she's off now trying to milk that wild cow. The fool. Thinks she can raise a baby on cow's milk. Such a thing has never been done. Time and again I've ordered her to quit wasting time and, for all I know, food on that baby."

Leslie turned away. He didn't want to look at such a woman.

"My good man, has no one ever taught you to stand and take off your hat in the presence of a lady?"

"Maam, whenever I so much as pass a lady I lift my hat."

He turned and looked until he caught her glance. "What's wrong with you that you can't suckle your own baby?"

Her naturally high color heightened to red, but in a second or so she managed to laugh. "You are trying to make up for your lack of goods and manners by insolence. You know I'm not the mother of that squawking brat."

"He's a fine baby. Milk's drippen out a you."

She looked out and down. "Shit. I've caught a rock drip. You ought to be put in the stocks for talking so to a lost and helpless lady." She took a cake from the plate and ate it with her fingers.

He scraped the last of the batter onto the griddle. Praise God he'd soon be finished; she'd go when he took up the last cake. He didn't mind the baby pulling his hair; the hurt was small; the big worry was his wriggling and kicking. What if he kicked his blanket clean off, and she saw he was wearing clothes cut down from her undergarments? She'd beat Rachel half to death. He stood up, arms wrapped around the baby.

The woman, still eating cakes, was watching him instead of the baby. "I didn't come to you to be insulted," she said, mouth full of cake, "but to ask if in your wanderings you'd met a good-for-nothing packhorse man by the name of John Sawyer. He was supposed to come back for me when the weather cooled down."

Leslie bridled. John Sawyer from all he'd seen and heard was a fearless, dependable guide and packhorse man; according to Ezra, he'd risked his life time and again to take horse loads of powder or saltpeter to the French Lick settlements; a credit to the woman; she'd broken her contract with him.

She sighed heavily. "You don't answer. I suppose you haven't seen him. I can't keep on living here, always afraid of that stinking Indian." She looked at him as if she expected him to say something.

He didn't. He clenched his teeth. Somebody ought to tell her "that stinking Indian" was keeping her in fresh meat; but he reckoned she already knew it.

"You seem to have nothing to do but wander over the country, and you have two horses. Why couldn't you take me at least as far as some Kentucky settlement? That would be closer Detroit."

"I told you once, maam, I couldn't do it."

"Why? I'd pay you well, very well." Her glance traveled over his hunting shirt, an old one and his favorite. "I am sure you can use money. Not Continental Gold."

"New British gold, I reckon." He took up the last of the cakes.

Last cake on, she picked up the plate, smiled at him and said in a voice sweet as her smile: "I have visited you. Now, you must come and visit me."

She was gone; kind of pitiful, a woman trying to use charm and good looks when she didn't have any. William David interrupted with a sound strange for him; he'd never heard anything from him but yowls and squawks. The gurgle of joy came again as he got in an unusually good pull on Leslie's hair.

A pity to put him down when he was so happy, but if he didn't build up Rachel's fire, she wouldn't have anything but ash-covered embers when she got back; and he saw no wood in the rockhouse. He pried open William David's fist and got him out of his hair, then laid him in a clean sandy spot near the burned-down fire. He figured the baby, not yet up to crawling, would be safe to leave for a few minutes; crying wouldn't hurt him for he sure had a loud strong cry.

Leslie ran a short distance around the hillside to where he'd seen some dry, dead oak branches, and was back in a few minutes with a shoulder load of good firewood and a handful of hickory bark. The rockhouse was quiet except for William David's soft gurgles and sucking sounds.

He went for a closer look; looked, dropped his load, and grabbed up the baby. The little devil had somehow got into the fire. Had it been blazing, he would have been burned to death; as it was, he had ashes on his hair and clothes; mouth, cheeks, fists, and toes all black-streaked from sucking the burned-out stick.

He carried him to a drip hole for washing; then shook his head, and went rummaging on the rock shelf where Rachel kept

123

her cooking vessels. Cold water wouldn't get William David clean, but grease might.

He found a kettle of boiled meat, possum he thought; it didn't matter; the stuff was cool enough grease was coming to the top.

He greased William David's black places, wiped grease and dirt away with leaves; regreased, rewiped until he was clean, except for the inside of his mouth, like a wide-open black hole as he screamed; he'd started up when Leslie took his stick away.

He gave up trying to get the black out of his mouth or off his dress, flung him over his shoulder, and managed to hold him there while he fixed the fire, a slow job for one hand.

Fire in good shape, he went outdoors. The day was too fine to waste inside, and anyhow he ought to hunt Rachel. She'd been gone so long, he figured the cow had run away. He had cradled William David in his arms to keep the brush out of his eyes, and was walking under a low-limbed maple when the baby opened his eyes wide to look up into the sunlight-speckled red and yellow leaves. Leslie pulled down a twig and brushed his nose. The baby laughed and reached for it. "You little son of a bitch, little as you are, you like the woods."

William David gave no sign he'd heard. He was studying the leaves. Leslie for the first time got a good look into his eyes. Wide and gray, they made him think of his father's eyes. Not as they were now, hard and cold most of the time, but the way they had looked when his father was a baby. He moved on; he hadn't been around to look at anybody's eyes when his father was a baby. He was letting two women, each with a bastard, drive him straight to bedlam.

He heard Rachel give a weary: "Shoo cow, shoo. I'm not aimen to let you keep your calf the rest a the day."

The sound came from down the creek; she'd followed that mettlesome cow a long way while trying to get a little milk. Hurrying on to help with the calf, he stopped suddenly as he crossed the wild meadow. He had noticed his shadow pointing east by north instead of the opposite direction. The sun was swinging south, and the days shortening fast. Past noon there wasn't enough daylight left to hunt Little Brother, deliver Ezra's gift of two knives, then hunt Daniel Strunk and his saltpeter. And how would he go about explaining to the Indian that a man he'd never seen had sent him the knives? Otherwise, he'd think they'd come from William David Leslie Collins.

He swore. He reckoned that since he might not be able to find Daniel before dark, he'd stay and build the poor fools a calf pen. He didn't want to visit Daniel Strunk after dark; might be bad enough in daylight. He wanted to get the business over with, but building a calf pen out of saplings and grapevines strong enough to keep the calf in and the cow out would take him till dark.

It was a wonder that big heavy calf hadn't already stepped on William David.

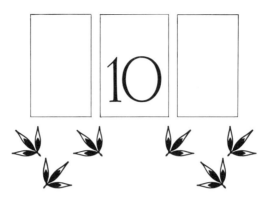

10

Leslie stood on the shoulder of the ridge crest across the creek from his rockhouse. He listened again and took another look down into the next valley, but as before there was nothing to hear and nothing to see except the spires of cedars rising out of the creek fog. The only sign of humankind was the smell of boiling saltpeter coming out of the valley. He knew he was in the right place.

Daniel Strunk could be sleeping late. Leslie shook his head; not this late; sunlight, just touching the higher hill tops when he crested the ridge, was now brightening the sandstone crags across the creek. Furthermore, saltpeter didn't cook itself. He was being a coward as well as a fool; it was too late for any man to be asleep.

He returned his hatchet to its sheath, tucked a small blanket roll under one arm, and with his rifle on one shoulder, a small hickory sapling on the other, he started into the valley.

He didn't think he was afraid of Daniel. It was his feeling of guilt that made him loath to meet the man. He had not been in the raiding party that wiped out Cherokee towns and Daniel's wife and children. Still, he was an overmountain man, a settler on Cherokee hunting ground.

Past the steepest part of the ridge side where the sandstone ended, he could make out dried corn tassels through the thinning fog. They meant he was close to Daniel's garden. He walked on. The saltpeter smell came from his left. Soon, he would find a path between Daniel's garden and his diggings.

He was within sight of the garden fence when a dog snarled, low and ugly. That dog meant business. Leslie was backing against the closest tree with a good-sized trunk when a big yellow-eyed beast sprang on him. Three other dogs leaped from nowhere to join in the attack. One went after his legs, another his fists, one wanted his privates, while Yellow Eyes made for his throat.

Leslie swung the blanket roll around to protect his throat while he kicked and flailed the hickory sapling until it whistled, but no sooner did he knock a dog down than it would be up and at him again. His rifle was charged, but most backhill men would be less liable to shoot a horse thief on sight than the killer of a dog.

He ought to have known: Daniel's dogs had grown up among Indians, and just as dogs raised by borderers fought Indians on sight so did Indian dogs treat whites. He'd be better off in the low-limbed beech behind him, but he'd be damned if he'd let a pack of dogs tree him like a coon.

He swung a fist on Yellow Eyes tearing up the blanket roll in his efforts to reach his throat. He felt teeth through a legging and kicked for all he was worth. He was getting in some good licks with the hickory pole, when a man's voice, close sounding, asked: "Who's trespassen?"

He knocked a dog head over heels with the hickory pole, then directing his voice toward a nearby cedar, answered: "Leslie Collins."

"And who might Leslie Collins be, mistreaten a man's dogs?"

Leslie kicked a black-and-tan cur trying to tear off his leggings, and turned toward the cedar to answer, but instead of cedar greenery, he looked at the muzzle of a rifle sticking out of the tree. "Leslie Collins," he answered. "Recollect, Mr. Daniel Strunk, how we once worked together maken saltpeter?"

There was silence from the cedar until, after what seemed a long while, words came out Leslie thought were commands in

Cherokee given to the dogs. They quieted. The rifle disappeared, and a man stepped from behind the cedar.

Leslie, uncertain of the man before him, didn't move. Daniel had been clean-shaven like other men. This man had a mighty beard, red as Sadie's hair; the mustache above it was black, and peering at him from under a hat were bright blue eyes, brighter than he remembered Daniel's eyes. The rifle reappeared; he'd only taken it off target; now, he swung it up and over his shoulder as he came forward, hand extended.

"The Professor, and I didn't know him. I'm sorry my dogs tried to chew up the man that knocked out Little Punkin—back in North Carolina we used to call him that—till he couldn't talk, then jumped clean away."

Leslie shook hands with him, said he was glad to see him, and tried not to show the praise for a piece of cowardice irked him, and the old nickname reminded him he was a stranger, a loner who maybe ought to have stayed with his own kind. It wasn't so much that he was English from Tidewater, and the hunters and overmountain men were Scots and Scotch-Irish with several Germans, all brought up on the borders and bred to the woods life, but . . .

"Man, you could keep off a pack a wolves and never fire a shot. I don't see any harm my rangers have done you, no blood, nothen but a little tear in your hunten shirt. We'll sew it up soon as we git back."

Wherever "back" was, Daniel seemed in no hurry to get there. He walked to the picket fence that enclosed his garden, motioning Leslie to follow.

Daniel stopped where a lusty cushaw vine had left the garden to climb the fence and crawl along it, bearing big cushaws on the way. He touched an empty stem hanging over the fence. "See that? Growen on it was the biggest cushaw any man has ever seen. I was saven it to take home. Well, late one day when I come out to pick beans it was gone. I was certain no white blackguard could a stole it; my ranger dogs here would a tore him to pieces. And anyhow I could find no sign of man or animal. That cushaw went in the daytime. I know it. I'd seen it that mornen. It went with never a sign nor sound."

He studied Leslie a moment, then after looking around as if he feared eavesdroppers, he came closer to whisper: "Some other curious things have come to pass. Time and again when I'm outside tenden my cook fire, I can feel somebody watchen me, but listen and look as I will, I can never see or hear a thing. And not a sign from the dogs. You know when somethen's not human, not animal, what it's bound to be? A *Utse———ah.*"

The man's whisper had grown so low, Leslie lost the middle of the long word or sentence; he wasn't certain. He had forgotten most of the little Cherokee he had once known. He dredged his memory and decided, with considerable help from Daniel's actions, that the word meant a Cherokee pixie or elf, a supernatural creature, not so evil as a goblin, more given to playing tricks on people than actually harming them. Daniel was expecting him to say something. "I wouldn't see any reason for one of them to bother you."

Daniel laughed. "They don't have to have a reason. It's just their way of haven fun; but it bothers a man. How's the baby over yonder? I reckon you must a camped in its valley. You come from that direction."

Leslie nodded; and surprised by Daniel's knowledge, not to mention his interest, answered with the first thing that came into his head. "Fine, since the Indian brought in a milk cow to feed it."

"I saw the cow—when I was on the ridge top. But what's the matter with its mother that she can't feed it?"

"I got the notion the baby didn't belong to that yellow-headed woman." Leslie couldn't think of any pretty lie that would please the man.

Daniel swore. "So. She's tellen lies into the bargain. That baby is hers. I know the day she had it in early August. I'd tie up a woman like that and make her let the child nurse. My notion is it's a woodscolt. She's come to the backwoods where she could do away with it when she had it." He walked on, glaring at nothing.

Leslie walked beside him.

129

They had gone only a few steps when he gave Leslie's blanket roll a dour glance. "What brings you visiten me, Professor, so early in the day?"

Leslie told him of how he had learned of his saltpeter works, next of his need for saltpeter and that he had been unable to buy any at Price's Station. He finished with: "I thought maybe if you didn't have any to sell, I could work with you for pay in saltpeter."

Daniel answered with a hearty: *"Nah."*

Leslie had more or less expected a rejection, but Daniel needn't be so happy about it. Well, he was happy, too; he'd already decided it was safer to keep on hunting saltpeter than work with Daniel. Ezra down at Price's was only partway right. Daniel wasn't losing his mind; he'd already lost it. He blinked as Daniel continued:

"Be nice to have you around. I remember you as a good worker. I've got no saltpeter to spare now, but will have when I cook off a few batches."

Leslie thanked him. He had remembered *nah* meant yes in Cherokee, and was wondering if Daniel were in the habit of speaking Cherokee when they reached the saltpeter cooker, an uncommonly big, oval-shaped kettle. Leslie looked in to find it better than half filled with simmering saltpeter almost ready to come off the fire. Finished and dried, there'd be at least a hundredweight in this one batch. And Daniel had none to sell!

He picked up the long-handled stirrer and raked it through the mixture. "You must," he told Daniel, "have stayed up all night to get it cooked this thick so early in the forenoon."

"I slept a little off and on. . . . How's that Indian over there where you stopped?"

"All right, I reckon, brings in game and fish to feed the others."

Daniel shook his head. "He'll maybe not be that way long. He ought to move on before some white devil shoots him down for no reason but he's Indian. Or worse, them wicked Shawnee that had him captured will come back hunten him. This time they'll burn him at the stake. But he's got hair on his mind."

Leslie started to say that according to the secondhand account he'd heard at Price's, the boy's captors had been Ottawa, not Shawnee, when he remembered the bitter hatred of the Cherokee for the Shawnee. Daniel was a Cherokee at heart in spite of all that hair. It was a wonder a band of braves hadn't tied him up and pulled out his whiskers one by one. No Indian he'd ever known would tolerate hair on his own face. Daniel was asking a question:

"Don't you reckon that boy's people have been around whites enough they've learned to take scalps?"

Leslie blinked, but got out a: "Maybe so."

"He's got taken hair on his mind, pretty yaller hair. That's why he's hangen around. —I'll swear to God I'm ashamed a myself, fergetten my manners and my beans." He pulled a singing coffee pot from one end of the fire, a kettle from the other, and turned toward the bluff. "Soon as I change the beans and bring out some cups we'll have coffee."

Leslie followed. "Daniel, I can wait on myself. I'll bring out the cups while you—"

"No, you won't." Daniel had whirled around to stand glowering at Leslie. "No man goes into another man's private quarters with no asken."

He appeared to be waiting for an apology or an explanation. Leslie reckoned he ought to say something on the order of: "I was only tryen to help," but be damned if he would. He continued to take Daniel's angry glare and give back one of his own until a grizzled mastiff stuck his head from behind a small cedar by the bluff, and growled.

Daniel spoke more kindly: "I forgot to tell you about the two guard dogs by my place. They'd tear any man to pieces that tried to come in."

Leslie gave the dog a long look, then returned to the cooker. If a man were going to lie, he ought to do a better job than Daniel was doing. That broken-toothed, overfed mastiff couldn't kill a rabbit, let alone a man.

The coffee pot was still quite hot when Daniel returned with two mugs and the kettle of beans which he settled on the fire before pouring coffee. He appeared to have nothing on his mind but beans. Didn't Leslie think it a wonder he still had green beans this late in October, and after he'd already picked and shelled out better than half a bushel of another kind he'd let dry, the little speckled kind, best in the world to cook.

Leslie listened with several *nah*'s and stirred the saltpeter. Daniel, watching him, seemed pleased as he said: "You've not forgot how to do it." He finished his coffee, looked down the hillside, now clear of fog, and got up. "I'd say it was time to put my bread to bake."

He disappeared with a pot of water he'd set to boil, but was back soon with a large dough bowl clasped in one arm, a book and two tracts under the other. He handed the printed matter to Leslie. "Thought you might like somethen to read between stirs. I reckon you've already read *Common Sense,* about everybody has, but Tom Paine has got out these two tracts since."

Leslie had long ago read *Common Sense,* and had the tracts in a saddlebag, but he didn't say so and accepted with thanks. Anything to keep Daniel in a better humor; now, he was whistling while he put the corn cakes to bake.

He still baked bread after the Cherokee fashion: after brushing ashes from a hot flat rock, he laid the pones on it, covered them with a big clay bowl heating by the fire, then built a brisk fire on top of the bowl.

Bread fire burning to his satisfaction, he considered the boiling saltpeter, turned to Leslie, looked him over, then searched the hillside above as if expecting a sally from that direction. He next looked down the hillside, and after long searching looks to right and left, whispered: "I was aimen to leave you for a little snooze I'm so godalmighty sleepy but if you don't want to be by yourself I won't go."

Leslie assured him he didn't mind being alone.

He nodded toward Leslie's rifle. "Keep her handy like you've got her; prick her touchhole and look to your primen. They's no mortal man could kill a *Utse v v liah,* but a shot would let him know you know he's up to meanness. And I'm pretty certain they or somethen or somebody is watchen up there, waiten to do me more meanness."

As Daniel watched, Leslie picked up Ruthie and did as directed, but be damned if he'd waste a speck of the powder

Ezra had insisted he take when he had so little himself on one of Daniel's insane notions.

Satisfied with the state of Leslie's rifle, Daniel advised him to keep a slow fire under the beans, a good hot one over the bread, and let the already low saltpeter cooker fire get lower.

Daniel gone at last, Leslie pushed back his hat. "Oh Lord, to flee or not to flee, that is the question."

Something, he didn't think it was the Lord, said: "Don't be a fool. Sew up the dog tears in your shirt, then finish Little Brother's shoepacs."

He gave the saltpeter a stir, then took from the blanket roll a deerskin pouch in which he kept thread, needles, and his smallest awls. He took off his hunting shirt and had soon whipped together the two tears he found. He'd done a better job than he'd thought keeping off the dogs.

He stirred the saltpeter, then brought out Little Brother's unfinished elk-skin shoepacs. Late yesterday he had found and measured both his and Rachel's footprints, and had worked by firelight on Little Brother's shoepacs. Most of the tedious work was finished: patterns cut, thongs cut, double soles cut, and most of the holes for lacing punched. Only the pleasant part was left; lacing the shoepacs together and watching them take shape.

He settled himself on the windward side of the saltpeter kettle so as to get as little of the smell as possible, but within arm's reach of the stirrer. He worked, and watched the shadows shorten and the twinklings of the creek now bright with sunlight. It was good to feel the sun and smell the cedar and hear the faint whispers of a wind out of the southwest, but in it no threat of rain, no clouds, the sky clean blue above the colored hills. On such a day it was good to be alive—or it ought to be.

He was looking back again. And when he looked back about all he ever saw were his parents and Sadie, mostly Sadie; when he had one little cranny empty in his mind, she would sneak in. Now, it was the wild storm that had blown up as soon as she'd learned he was going away to survey.

"We'd git ahead and be somebody a lot faster if you'd stay home and tend to your farmen. You and your lazy slaves'ull . . ."

He sprang up and began to stir the saltpeter. He was trashy as she; holding her vile lies in his head. His help wasn't lazy; he'd told her that and a lot more until he realized he was shrewish as she and had gone to the barn.

He returned to the shoepacs, finished lacing them, but the goodness was gone from the day. He was losing his mind, already almost as far gone as Daniel. He had begun to feel something was on the hillside above, watching him. Twice, he stood up the better to see all around. The saltpeter cave was behind him; the entrance no more than six paces away; he couldn't see anything much beyond it, but a man in there could watch him; could be Daniel; he hadn't looked sleepy; he wasn't asleep now.

He cursed himself for being a fool. He ought to stay with the saltpeter, almost ready to come off the fire. He was examining the saltpeter stuck to the stirrer when something zinged past his head, close; sounded like an arrow. Reaching for his rifle, he glanced past the cooker to see the feathered butt of an arrow still quivering, head buried in the ground. Rifle at the ready, he studied the hillside above him; the arrow had come from there. Could it be Daniel slipped out some hidden opening and was trying to kill him?

Less than ten paces away, toward the garden, a turkey gobbled. A good gobble, but no turkey would come within a mile of this stinking saltpeter. An Indian who thought a white man didn't know a thing about turkeys; two Indians at least; one up the hillside and the gobbler.

He dropped behind the saltpeter cooker, and, peeping round one end, looked in the direction of the gobble. He saw a sight he had never expected to see: old Yellow Eyes was smiling, wagging his tail for somebody behind a nearby cedar. Yellow Eyes would smile only on an Indian.

He drew a bead on a spot about midsection high and a hand's width from the side of the cedar Yellow Eyes smiled on. The Indian wouldn't try to send an arrow through the thick cedar; if he stood up, the bullet would catch him in the belly; if he squatted, it would hit his head. He was easing a stick of firewood under Ruthie for a rest, when Yellow Eyes, tail still wagging, ran down the hill. And what about his rear? Seemed like he could feel somebody aiming at the back of his head.

He was risking a backward glance when he heard low laughter from still another direction. He stood up as Little Brother leaped from behind a limestone ledge not five paces away.

Horseplay. Leslie managed a fair imitation of a laugh, and put Ruth back on her forked sticks. Little Brother walked past the kettle to retrieve his arrow, a wicked one; flint wedged into split cane and tied with the small tendon of some animal. Satisfied his arrow was undamaged, he returned it to a rabbit-skin quiver on his back. His bow looked stout, and so did the vicious war club dangling by a thong from his wrist. He had either killed a fine buck deer or found a dead one's antlers. He had taken one, chipped off everything except the main stem and the brow antler, and into the angle between the two had wedged and tied a chunk of granite, like his arrowheads shaped by some long-dead Indian.

He might use dead men's weapons, but he'd done his own killing: rabbits for leggings and his quiver; a wolf for shoulder covering. However he'd tanned the hide, he'd left most of the skull in it, so that over his chest, tail and teeth met while eyeless sockets gazed at the beholder.

Leslie shook his head. That young brave now studying the entrance to Daniel's private quarters was nobody's little brother. He could, as Daniel had said, have taking hair on his mind, or had he just come on a—

He grabbed the stirrer. The sound that had interrupted his thoughts was the forgotten saltpeter going *phut, phut.* The stuff was trying to tell him it was about ready to overcook and blow up.

He hurried to drag up the big bowllike cooling trough waiting nearby. Little Brother disappeared to come running back with a long-handled scoop. Leslie took it and began to get the saltpeter out of the kettle and into the trough as quickly as possible. Little Brother used the stirrer to help fill the scoop. He hurried as if he knew the saltpeter had to come off the fire—or else. The moment the kettle was empty, he took the pail of water waiting nearby and hurriedly wet the inside of the kettle, then helped Leslie wash down the smears they hadn't been able to scoop out. He appeared to know that even a thick smear of saltpeter could cause trouble if it got too hot.

Leslie figured the boy had spent many happy hours hidden in a cedar above the bluff, scaring the wits out of Daniel and learning saltpeter cookery. And that was not all he had learned: as soon as they'd dragged the cooling trough back to its customary place, he picked up the emptied cedar pail, and started around the hillside in the direction of the garden. Another pail was half-filled with stale water. Leslie emptied it, and followed the boy to Daniel's spring.

They tarried a few minutes to drink and fill their pails from the fine stream of cold water coming out below a fern-covered limestone ledge. Much to Leslie's surprise, the boy started back with one of the pails; in any Indian tribe he'd ever known, carrying water was strictly woman's work. He reckoned he'd seen Daniel carrying water.

They were nearing the cooker when Little Brother, walking in front, stopped, put down his pail, slid the war-club thong from his wrist, and stood gripping the club. Leslie, looking past the boy, saw Daniel.

He didn't look like a man just come awake as he looked first at Little Brother's face, then at the lifted war club. Leslie downed an impulse to grab Little Brother's arm. Daniel had no weapon, but weapon or no he could finish off the boy—if he could get to him.

Daniel smiled and raised his right hand palm outward, then slowly pushed it forward and back. This, Leslie had learned, was the signal to halt among Plains Indians. Little Brother was taking his time about answering. Daniel waited, both hands by his sides, palms outward to show their emptiness.

Leslie breathed again when Little Brother let the war club slide to the ground, clasped his hands and lifted them above his head to repeat the gesture of good will he had made to Leslie. Daniel made the same gesture, then moved his lifted right hand from right to left.

The boy answered by drawing a hand across his throat. Daniel then came forward, right hand extended and speculation in his eyes. Little Brother did not step forward, but did hold out his hand.

Leslie wiped sweat from his forehead, then carried both pails to the water bench. Daniel was now looking at the cooling saltpeter. "I'm ashamed a myself for oversleepen and letten you do all the work. You've cooked it to a turn, couldn't be better. I thank you. I reckon I'd better, before I set up dinner, start cooken what has already been leached through the ash hopper." He glanced at Leslie. "You can come with me and see the works."

Leslie followed but saw little. Going out of bright sunlight into the cave was like diving into a deep tree-shaded creek. The pale light that came through cracks and holes in the bluff was green-tinged by the leaves it filtered through. He could see Daniel rolling out a keg, and then another. He rolled it to the cooker, and while he and Little Brother poured the leachings into the cooker and built up the fire, Daniel set up dinner. Taking food out of the cook hole, he couldn't see what was happening behind his back.

The two dogs that guarded his private quarters had left their posts to lick Little Brother's hands and knees along with a great wagging of tails. Daniel soon started for his private quarters; the deceitful curs ran around behind him in order to be at their posts when he came.

He returned soon with a crock of honey in the comb and a stack of small flattish baskets finely woven of split cane stalks. These were to serve as plates.

A turkey, fresh from the cookhole, was already steaming on the puncheon table with hominy and a big cushaw baked whole, while a pan of bacon sizzled on the coals. He asked Leslie to carve the turkey while he dressed the cushaw and took up the bread.

Leslie, as he finished a serving of turkey stuffed with chestnuts, thought how nice it would be if Sadie could cook as well as Daniel. Even the cushaw mixed with chopped bacon, a little of the grease, and some maple sugar was uncommonly good. He wished Little Brother would eat more; that would please Daniel; but when the boy wasn't giving Daniel quick, sly glances, he was struggling to eat with the knife and spoon furnished by his host. Leslie, seeing his trouble, ate what he could with his fingers. Daniel did the same.

They ate mostly in silence except for Daniel's attempts to talk with Little Brother. He gave up at last, and during coffee-drinking time told Leslie: "I've tried him in ever Indian nation's tongue I know, even some I know only a few words of, but never got through. You must a tried to talk to him. Have any luck?"

Leslie shook his head. "Well, when I was drawen a cow for him, my second try the night before I went on to Price's, I learned he knew a few words of French, but not enough to be a French-praying Indian. I figured he'd learned the words from French traders or hunters. They're over most of the West. He could have started with a party bound for Detroit or Montreal and been captured on the way."

Daniel gave an absent-minded nod. He had taken out his knitting and was counting stitches.

Leslie went to work on the shoepacs he intended for Little Brother. The small amount of punching and lacing left to do required only a few minutes' work. He held the pair out to the boy sitting nearby.

The boy stared uncomprehending until Leslie pointed to his feet, then his breast. He understood and shook Leslie's hand before putting on his footgear. He was walking about, preening and prancing, when he stopped short. Daniel had come to watch, disapproval in his eyes.

He put down his knitting, left for his private quarters, but returned shortly, bringing with his disapproval a lump of tallow. "Leslie, I don't like to butt in, but it may be many a day before you make another pair a elk-skin shoepacs, and never a one so fine as them. You know elk are mighty scarce; so these ought to be treated right. That means a good greasen with buffler taller fore he wears em."

Leslie started to explain the hide had been well tanned and dressed with bear's oil, but Daniel had already turned to Little Brother. He held out the lump of tallow while explaining with gestures the shoepacs must come off to be greased.

The boy as usual had kept his distance from Daniel and was now on the other side of the cooker. He had backed off another step or so when Daniel came back. Now, with eyes for nothing but the tallow, he edged his way around the cooker until he could touch the tallow.

He took the lump from Daniel, sniffed it, held it, all the while smiling on the greasy lump, happy as if he'd found Swift's silver mine. He turned to Leslie to say something that sounded to be *te ha* with maybe a *p* sound at the beginning. He repeated the sounds as he touched his breechclout. He next waved his arms, turning so as to embrace the land about, then stopped in front of Leslie to repeat the strange word; this time it was a question.

Leslie was wondering how to tell him the buffalo that had been here in the foretime were all dead when Daniel let out a pleased: "*Gha*. The boy knows buffler taller." He nodded to Little Brother and said: "*Nah*."

Daniel at once shook his head. Little Brother was no longer looking at him; his glance was searching the valley.

"Godalmighty, Leslie, I've said the wrong thing. Can you sketch a *used to be* real quick? There's no buffler left around here. The last time I heared of anybody killen one fairly close was last winter when General Daniel Smith killed a few down Cumberland to keep his party from starven. That pore boy, he'll wander forever hunten buffler and them all dead, unless you can . . ."

Leslie had already found a bare spot and was sketching a dead buffalo in the sandy earth. Little Brother, absentmindedly greasing his shoepacs, watched for a moment, then turned away to look up and down the creek.

Daniel, also watching, nodded his approval. "With his head on the ground like that, and his mouth open, he sure looks dead."

Finished with a sketch of the dead, Leslie began to sketch a running buffalo. He planned to nod over the dead one and shake his head over the living. He had the second buffalo almost finished, when Little Brother pointed to the dead one, then went through the motions of aiming and shooting an arrow, throwing a spear, and cutting a throat with his knife. He was skinning the imaginary buffalo when Daniel swore.

"I've dropped three stitches. Looks like any fool could take that dead buffler for a used to be; but he's too full a hunten fever to know up from down. He thinks that dead buffler is one he's aimen to kill." Daniel muttered his way to his private quarters.

He came back with nothing on except a breechclout and old moccasins. He handed Leslie and Little Brother each a breechclout and a pair of battered moccasins. "If you're aimen to work with me in my diggens you must take off your good clothes, else you'll never agin git em clean. Richest dirt I've ever worked and the dustiest."

Leslie wanted to wear nobody's cast-off clothing. He couldn't say that to Daniel, but he could tell him the truth: the breech-clout wasn't big enough to hide half his hair; the moccasins were too big; furthermore he was wearing old clothes. Well, he could strip down to his drawers.

He felt somebody's eyes on his back. He turned to find Little Brother watching him, waiting to see what he would do. If he didn't strip, neither would the boy already sweating under his wolfskin. Leslie stripped and tied on the breechclout. Little Brother did the same after carefully stowing the new shoepacs in a closely grown cedar.

With Little Brother behind him, Leslie followed Daniel into the cave. A band of sunlight brightened the place when Daniel pushed aside a still-green cedar used to cover another entrance—more likely to hide it, Leslie was thinking when Daniel pointed to a barrel by the ash hopper.

"See that? It's full a niter dirt leachens ready to run through the ash hopper, but I don't aim to do it till I put fresh ashes in the hopper. I reckon you've already noticed that my saltpeter leachen vat is about twice too big fer the ash hopper, less'n I could use elm ashes, an they's no elms around."

Leslie nodded and picked up a wooden shovel. An empty sled was waiting by the hopper.

"I don't aim for you to do all the dirty work," Daniel told him, "but you can start fillen the sled while I go harness up Equo."

Leslie was already lifting out a shovelful of soggy, ill-smelling ashes. With help from Little Brother he had filled the sled by the time Daniel got back with Equo, a big-footed, slow-paced gray roan. His slow pace gave time for hunting long grass to reline the hopper; then, it was shovel ashes out of the sled, go to the hopper and shovel more spent ashes into it, then around the hill and out again.

Hopper empty and relined with grass, it was now fresh ashes, light and fluffy, to be shoveled into the sled and out again into the hopper. Next, dip and pour the barrel of niter dirt leachings into the ash hopper, then shovel the spent niter dirt out of the vat and into the sled.

Leslie looked forward to getting out the last shovelful. He'd run to the creek and take a good scrub; his body was crusted with ashes; his ash-filled crotch felt galled; wet niter dirt was clinging to his feet and legs, for nearing the bottom, he'd had to climb into the five-foot-deep vat.

Another shovel ran beside his own. Daniel was back from putting Equo to pasture. Vat empty, Daniel clapped him on the shoulder. "Professor, you sure are a worker. I'll wager that beginnen now, the two of us can crush more than enough niter dirt to fill this vat before dark."

Daniel moved on to the crusher. Leslie followed. The crusher was so long and of such big logs, he wondered how one man could get lumps of niter dirt through it; to make the work even harder, the logs were set so close together, the crushed dirt would come out smaller than grains of wheat.

He was helping Daniel and Little Brother shovel chunks of niter dirt onto the crusher when he saw the contraption had a turning crank at either end. Why, in a one-man outfit? He forgot his wonderings when Daniel stepped to one end and he took the other.

Turning the crushing log when the crusher was filled was like rolling a ton weight over and over to get it up a mountain. There was no stopping. He had to keep up with Daniel. He was making a game of the work, turning faster and faster as he tried to keep up with Little Brother shoveling on for all he was worth. And for a green hand he was worth considerable. Leslie would have enjoyed a round of cursing, but keeping up with Daniel took all the breath he could draw from the dead dusty air of the cave.

He figured he'd been crushing only an hour or so when he began to feel the pull on his back all the way from neck to heels; every muscle was crying for rest—except his arms; they felt as if they were dropping away like dead branches. He needed both hands to turn the crusher, hard to spare one to wipe sweat from his eyes. They smarted with ashes and niter dust worse than his crotch.

The streak of sunlight had long since left the cave floor when Little Brother stopped shoveling. "We've run out a niter dirt," Daniel said when the last chunk was crushed. "And I do believe we've crushed enough to fill the vat twice over. So all we've got to do tonight is fill the vat and get the niter dirt covered with water."

Leslie saw a shovel by the cave entrance and staggered to it, surprised to learn he could still walk. He lingered by the entrance for a breath of clean air. Sunlight aslant the hill tops sent enough light into the darkening valley for him to see his body, covered with ashes and saltpeter dirt, crusted and streaked with sweat.

Daniel was saying behind him: "Soon as we get this vat ready to leach, we'll all go to the creek for a swim. But we mustn't tarry too long; the beans are done and the rest will soon be ready. I aim to have an early supper so you two won't be dark goen back."

Leslie smiled into the twilight. Daniel should be an ambassador for this new nation. Machiavelli himself couldn't have thought of a politer way of telling a visitor he didn't want him around after dark.

11

Leslie, on the way to his second day's work with Daniel, had reached the garden when Yellow Eyes growled and showed himself. Leslie smiled. "Yes. I'm later than yesterday. Daniel told me to be. I tarried on the ridge to split that little hickory pole into four stout laths."

Yellow Eyes sniffed his legs, growled, but made no move to bite. Leslie returned the laths to his shoulder. "Sorry to disappoint you, old boy, but I rubbed my shoepacs and put a few smears on my leggens from the same chunk of tallow Little Brother used. You're maybe smellen his hands."

Seconds later Yellow Eyes was wagging his tail and running past him. Leslie didn't look behind him; he knew that Little Brother, as was his custom, had come out of nowhere to walk several paces to the rear. The three other rangers bounded past to wag their tails around the boy.

Last night when he left, the saltpeter cooker had been full of fresh leachings, thin, and just beginning to boil over a good fire. Now, as he reached the cooker, Leslie saw a brisk fire, the cooker still almost full, but the leachings were beginning to thicken. Daniel was not in sight. He reckoned the man had spent half the night pouring in leachings and tending the fire.

The old mastiff came snarling from behind the cedar with a lively white feist behind him. Leslie slowly backed away from

143

the dogs and stowed his gear in a cedar. He could manage both with no trouble, but he didn't want any racket to rouse Daniel. He'd fly out of his private quarters mean as a stirred-up hornet. The dogs returned to their posts when he made no move to enter Daniel's cave.

Leslie looked at the sunlight on the crags across the creek. Past time to go to work. He could sit quietly and work on Rachel's shoepacs, but he'd already done a deal of work on them while waiting for the day to lengthen. To hell with that. He was tired of pussyfooting around Daniel. He'd better be felling that lightning-struck oak Daniel had said they'd need for ashes. He'd have to find an ax. Yesterday, he'd noticed two, but neither was in sight; could be one in the diggings.

He entered the saltpeter cave, but as the sun was still too low to strike the openings to the outdoors, he could see little until he walked across the cave and took the cut cedar from the other entrance. He at once saw an ax leaning against the cooling trough. He saw the trough was empty.

Daniel, in addition to bringing out and cooking peter beer, had dragged the trough of cooked saltpeter to the crusher, crushed the saltpeter and . . . What had he done with it and all the other batches he'd made?

Leslie picked up the ax and started for the entrance he had uncovered; he ought to replace the cedar covering. Halfway there he stopped to study the floor. The light was in front of him, full on the carpet of dust to show tracks he hadn't noticed when coming in. Made by moccasins, they didn't belong to Daniel, who wore double-soled shoepacs. He had worn old moccasins yesterday at work in the cave, but his foot was bigger, broader.

He'd think them Indian tracks if they were not so deep in the dust. Indians were light-footed—unless they were carrying heavy loads. This Indian had had a load—of saltpeter.

He was seeing things he wasn't supposed to see. He backtracked to where he'd picked up the ax, then, walking backwards he swiped out his tracks to and from the cooker with the head of the ax. He took care to make no marks and leave the other tracks.

Outside on a limestone ledge that left no tracks, he replaced the cedar.

He went round to the proper entrance. Here, there was less dust, and in the dim light he could make out only here and there parts of a track he'd made when he went partway in to find the ax. Still, he walked in to where he'd picked up the ax, then walked out again, swiping out the extra tracks he'd made earlier.

He hurried away, but stopped when, by the garden fence, he could see the half-dead oak up and around the hillside. It could be that when he cut that tree for ashes, he'd be helping make gunpowder for the Cherokee to use against white settlers; old man Saufley and his wife for instance, or that baby over in the rockhouse. No, they wouldn't waste powder and ball on a little mite like that; they'd dash out his brains on a rock, the same way white raiders had killed Daniel's baby.

The Cherokee could get guns and ammunition from the British, but it would be easier to get powder, or at least the makings, from Daniel. A couple of Cherokee braves could load Daniel's saltpeter into a pirogue and take it a long way south going either up the Big South Fork or down the Cumberland. They could, after sinking the pirogue for safekeeping, take a trace, mostly downhill, to the Overhill Cherokee.

Little Brother had seen Cherokee braves around the saltpeter works; that was why he'd been so wary of Daniel. The boy was afraid, and rightly so, of strange Indians. Braves had most likely been hiding yesterday in Daniel's secret quarters while they waited for another load of saltpeter. Daniel wouldn't have cooked all that food yesterday just for himself. Most of it had already been in the cookhole when Leslie came.

He walked on toward the big bur oak. Daniel was an honest man. He had promised him powder. If Daniel didn't keep his promise, he would procure at least enough saltpeter to pay for his work, even if it meant waylaying Cherokee carrying off a load. He still had the six charges of powder Ezra McFarland had given him.

He shook his head and walked on. He could be misjudging Daniel; howsoever he oughtn't to be blamed for helping the Cherokee; he was a Cherokee at heart.

He had reached the oak, and studied her a moment. In spite of a lightning strike at some time or other, she had kept more than half herself alive; a pity to cut her; she might bear acorns for another hundred years.

He decided where the tree should fall and went to work. The tree, though half of her had long since died, had no rot about her; the dead part was iron-hard seasoned oak. Leslie swore, and stopped to hone the ax after the third chop. The ax was already sharp enough. The trouble was himself. Each swing of the ax had brought sharp twinges to his arms, neck, and shoulders, sore and stiff from yesterday's work with the log crusher. He was getting old; twenty-seven wasn't old, but used to be he could do anything all day with the night thrown in and not be sore next day.

Used to be? It didn't seem long since he'd heard his grandparents talk of the "used to be." He'd wondered then if the words meant the same thing as "back then." He shook his head. The used to be was for old men; men so old they had nothing left but the used to be. His wouldn't be much. Right now he ought to be making part of it.

He again attacked the tree; the cut deepened; the seasoned oak either knocked out his twinges or he forgot them in wondering on Daniel. He was swinging back the ax for another stroke when he heard a rock roll in the direction of the garden. He sank the ax into the tree, then stepped around to see.

Daniel was racing toward him, butcher knife in hand. Leslie left the ax in the tree; if Daniel aimed to cut him up with a butcher knife he ought, to be fair, to do his part of the cutting with his hunting knife. Chances were, the man had seen his out-of-place tracks in the saltpeter cave.

Daniel stopped a few feet away. He said: "*Gha*" a couple of times and nodded. He was pleased about something. He came on around the tree, studied Leslie's cut a moment, then clapped him on the shoulder. "And I was thinken you didn't know how to cut a tree so it would fall where you wanted it."

"I've lately learned," Leslie told him, and thought with bitterness of the trees he and Jethro had cut to make way for Sadie's corn.

"Well, you're sure doen a fine job. I didn't know you had come till I was on my way to the spring to wash some ham and heared your ax. I was afraid you'd cut her any old way, and she'd come down to smash my garden fence."

Leslie said nothing. He was wondering how Daniel washed ham with a razor-sharp butcher knife. He wished the man would put it down. Daniel was asking:

"Where's my ranger dogs?"

"Somewhere around with Little Brother, I reckon. He came over the hill with me, then disappeared with your dogs."

"They'll be back. Was the brave still wearen his skins and hunten gear?"

"He had the arms he carried yesterday and a spear into the bargain. And as I remember he wore nothen but his shoepacs and breechclout."

Daniel gave a mournful head shake. "That means he's gone after hair or buffler. I hope it's buffler." He started toward the spring, then stopped. "Come on, now. I'll have breakfast pretty soon. That tree's safe to leave fer a spell; there's no wind."

Leslie started to tell him he'd had breakfast, but changed his mind. He followed, keeping a few steps behind in order to get a good look at Daniel's shoepacs. He saw no sign of saltpeter dust or ashes. He hadn't been into the diggings—yet.

They reached the spring. As Daniel washed the chunk of ham, he used the butcher knife to shave and scrape off some mold on one side. Leslie felt foolish as he filled the water pails and carried them to the puncheon table by the saltpeter cooker.

Daniel, coming up with the ham, stopped only long enough to pull the coffee pot from the coals and apologize for oversleeping while Leslie worked. He was hurrying toward his secret entrance when Leslie stopped him with the suggestion that he pour in more leachings; the kettle was getting a shade low. Daniel agreed. Leslie went into the diggings. It was so dark with the other entrance closed, he had to hunt around a good deal for a carrying pail and thus made a multitude of tracks. He made still more as he dipped up and carried out two pailfuls of leachings. Finished, he figured he'd so tracked up the place,

Daniel would have trouble in telling the new from the old—in case any of the old, out-of-place tracks were left.

Daniel returned with a skillet of ham to fry and a pot of hominy. Leslie cursed himself; he ought to have told Daniel he'd breakfasted before the man had brought out food for two. His head was full of saltpeter going to the Cherokee; he couldn't think of anything else.

Daniel was in a hurry to get back to the tree, and never noticed that Leslie did little more than pretend to eat his hominy and red-eye gravy. They ate and drank their coffee in silence. Leslie made no attempt at conversation. It was one of Daniel's dour days. He was mad at the world, or somebody in it. Walking back to the oak, Leslie learned that one of the culprits was Thomas Paine. Daniel had decided his talk of the rights of men to govern themselves was only for white-skinned men. That meant Indians had no rights.

Leslie disagreed. "I think Paine means all men from Attakullakulla to a slave—after he's freed—will have the right to vote." He'd said the wrong thing.

"Attakullakulla was a traitor to the Cherokee nation," Daniel declared. "He sold the best parts of the Cherokee hunten ground to that Richard Henderson and his gang. But with all his talken he couldn't persuade Draggen Canoe, and Draggen Canoe was right."

They had reached the oak as Daniel began to recite with a mingling of sorrow and anger a Cherokee oration.

Leslie understood enough to know it was Dragging Canoe's speech of dissent at the Treaty of Sycamore Shoals where in 1775 the Cherokee had sold a great boundary of land. He had not heard the treaty making but had heard from others of Dragging Canoe's spirited foretelling of the fate of the Cherokee should they sell their hunting grounds: they would be compelled to seek a retreat in some far-distant wilderness where would at last come "the extinction of the whole race."

Leslie hadn't believed that prophecy then. He believed it now. Nothing would stop the settlers. Sale or no, they would have come anyway. Daniel had finished, and was deciding where they should cut. Leslie praised his delivery and went to work.

Anger drove his ax deep. Daniel admired Dragging Canoe. Now living with a tribe of his own, the Chickamauga, down the Tanase, he could and did kill whites traveling down the river. He also sent his braves against the French Lick settlers.

The oak was not yet down before Daniel said it was time to hone the axes. The axes were sharp enough. He only wanted to quarrel with Thomas Paine: the man ought to have said that in this mighty boundary of land between the oceans there was room for many nations. The Cherokee nation ought to stay where it was. "Recollect the Cherokee are a lot older hands at governen theirselves than you people. Why, your women don't have any kind of voice, but we've got old beloved women in all our councils."

Leslie smiled to himself at the notion of a woman in the Congress or allowing one to vote. He got up. His ax had had enough of the hone.

Daniel wasn't finished with either his ax or his subject. He felt that in this country there should be more than one nation of whites. "You know that a lot of people in Philadelphie and the East don't want this backwoods territory."

Leslie had heard and read such opinions. They galled him.

"And it wasn't your Washington or your Congress that give George Rogers Clark leave to take the Illinois. No, he went to Governor Patrick Henry, and Henry finally got the Virginia Legislature to give Clark a little ammunition."

Leslie nodded, remembering the taste of raw green corn; that was about all they'd had to eat on the overland part of the trip to Kaskaskia; when men walk fifty miles in less than two days there's no time for hunting and cooking.

"And since they don't want you all in the East, you ought to form a nation of your own. John Sevier would make a fine first ruler."

Leslie swung his ax. He had heard such talk from others.

There was no more talk except from the tree. It shivered slightly, then went down with the sad groaning of a great tree unready for death. Leslie pushed back his hat and turned away as the crash came. He thought of the many times he'd heard that sound since he was married. He reckoned he'd be hearing and seeing the same for the rest of his life. Worse were the sounds he couldn't hear and sights he couldn't see that he had caused. He prepared a place for settlers by surveying it. Indians had the right word for a sextant—land stealer.

Daniel was already limbing the tree. He turned to help.

Daniel seemed in a great hurry to get the tree ready for burning into ashes. However, when he finally did decide it was time for their nooning, he took an unusually long one. Daniel was so slow about setting up dinner, Leslie finished Rachel's shoe-pacs on which he had already done a good deal of work in the early morning before time to help Daniel. He realized at last that Daniel was holding up dinner in the hope Little Brother would come.

Dinner eventually served and eaten, table cleared, Daniel took out the stocking he was knitting.

He knit for a few minutes, then turned to Leslie. "Professor, you won't take it hard, will you, if I ask you to be real quiet for the next few minutes? I'm ready to turn the heel of this stocken, and many as I've knit it takes all my mind to turn it right. Once I turned the heel so far it come straight up, and another time it went off sidewise; strangest looken contraption you ever saw."

Leslie, after promising silence, got out the four splits of hickory sapling. He had decided to split each piece twice again. He worked carefully to keep down sounds of splitting that might interrupt Daniel's work. Try as he would, one length came apart with a ripping sound loud enough to cause Daniel to look around.

He returned to his knitting and not long after sprang up with a pleased, "*Gha.* Look, Professor, what a pretty heel I've turned. She'll soon be finished." He paid no mind to Leslie's praise; he was shaking his head over the splits.

"Professor, I don't know what you're tryen to make, but whatever it is, you're old enough to know it's the wrong season for maken hickory wythes. And if it's splits you're tryen to make you ought to know to use a long bolt of white oak like the rest of the whites."

"I'm not exactly tryen to make either."

"Well, what are you maken?"

"A pen, I hope."

Daniel smiled. "I'll bet you're aimen to keep a young coon you've caught. They're easy tamed. I had one once."

"This pen is for a baby."

"You're aimen to put your pore little baby over yonder in a pen like a pig?"

"One of your needles is about to slip out."

Daniel secured his knitting, then asked: "Who takes care a that baby while the black woman's waiten on her vixen? Almost always when I go to yon side the ridge to hunt wintergreen and ratbane, I see the black woman runnen up to that rockhouse or down to the creek, and she's got no baby."

A storm was brewing. Leslie wished he could think of something more soothing to say than the truth. He couldn't. "The baby's not of crawlen size, and can't get around to hurt himself. Rachel, that's the black woman's name, leaves him in a clean sandy spot when . . ."

"Leaves him? All by hisself? Godalmighty. Didn't that fool woman ever learn there's rattlesnakes and copperheads all around here? Late as it is, they're still crawlen, the weather's so warm. Why I killed a rattler, big, with fourteen rattles, a little while back when I was over on that hillside hunten yaupon."

Leslie knew yaupon didn't grow on the limestone sides of low hills, but he nodded as if he'd never heard otherwise. "Rachel has to go when her mistress calls; leaven the baby is not her fault. I think I can make a pen that will keep out snakes."

"But it won't keep out wild hogs; a little drove would gobble that pore baby up in a second. She ought to be carryen it with her all the time in a . . ."

He had lapsed into Cherokee. Leslie caught a word now and then; enough to learn Daniel was quarreling about women who wouldn't work with babies on their backs like Indian women. Daniel continued fractious while they worked, first on the log pile, then cooking off another batch of saltpeter.

Supper was late to begin with, and Daniel's lagging back in the hope Little Brother would come made it later.

The moon, almost to the full, was rising by the time Leslie reached the ridge crest on his way home. He sat on a hump of rock to watch until the moon cleared the tree tops and the ridge became a place of black shadows and white light.

Sitting was good. His load wasn't heavy, but it was cumbersome: Rachel's shoepacs; corn cakes and duck wrapped in hickory leaves, given by Daniel for Little Brother in case he showed up; a nicely tanned deerskin for the baby, also from Daniel; the whole in the biggest split basket Leslie had ever seen, must hold at least six bushels and strong with it.

Daniel had been apologetic when giving it. He'd had it made special, flat-bottomed and big for carrying ashes, but had never used it for that or anything else. A split basket wasn't the thing for a baby, but he figured it was better than nothing. He didn't know how to make the right kind; they were always made by women.

Leslie watched the moon and wondered on the future of the baby. It most likely didn't have a future, at least not one beyond the basket. And did that matter too much? Life wasn't all that good. Why did men live on the earth in the first place? They ruined it. He gathered up his load and walked on. He'd done more than his share of ruination.

He stopped for one more good look at the moon. Now clear of the timber and almost to the full, unsmudged by any feather of cloud or mist, she was fine as the winter moons of the north shining on empty stretches of snow and ice. He watched a short time longer, then shook his head and walked on. A ring had come around her, close and faint, but still a ring. That meant rain. Rachel couldn't carry William David—he must remember to call the baby that—with her in the rain when she went to get cook wood or milk the cow.

He put down his load again after crossing the creek and went hunting his mares. He soon found them in their usual standing sleep under the big sycamore. The moon was not yet high enough to light the valley, but a thorough feeling-over told him they were in good shape.

From the creek he could see the light of a brisk fire coming out of Rachel's rockhouse. She was either working uncommonly late or the baby was sick. He hurried on to find Rachel curled on the sand, feet near the fire, bare toes sticking out from under her petticoat. William David, wrapped in the red woolen cloth, slept between her arms.

He soundlessly put the basket down and went to his rockhouse where he felt in the dark until he found the two pieces of red woolen cloth he'd used for horse blankets, all he had left. He'd planned to keep them for spare saddle blankets, but he'd never ridden with spare blankets and saw no reason to now. They were somewhat stained with horse sweat, but certainly better than nothing.

Back in Rachel's rockhouse he debated covering her with the cloth; she'd sleep warmer; on the other hand there was no hard chill in the air; she might waken while he was covering her and be scared out of her wits. He draped the cloth over the basket, and left to get ready for bed.

Settled on his high rock, he congratulated himself; giving Daniel's gifts and his at the same time had saved him the discomfiture of listening twice to tearful gratitude from Rachel.

He reckoned without Rachel. She waylaid him next morning on his way to work; said she had started to the calf pen. She stood like the guilty on trial as she told of finding the basket she thought he'd left by mistake in her rockhouse; but the basket was so handy for William David, she'd put him in it and carried him with her.

Leslie told her the basket and deerskin were for the baby and who had sent them. The shoepacs were for her to wear now, and she was to sleep under the red cloth.

He tried to stop her usual tearful gratitude by asking after Little Brother. Her answer scarcely checked her tears; she hadn't seen Little Brother in a good while; she hoped he wasn't dead.

William David was making pleasant noises. Leslie took him out of the basket and chucked him lightly under the chin. The baby laughed. Rachel stopped crying as she said:

"Ain't he lively now? Just goen on four months and already tryen to stick his toes in his mouth. I don't know how the other three the missus has got acted when they was his age. I never tended them till they got back from the wet nurse, but I bet they didn't come on any better than he has."

Leslie hurried away after another happy sound from William David. He wanted to be gone from this bitchy place where a black woman was too thankful for a scrap of cloth, and a white one had left three children to chase after a blackguard. At least Daniel would be pleased but shed no tears when he told him how well the basket was serving.

Daniel, already at work when Leslie reached his place, gave him no opportunity to tell of the basket, but asked at once: "Little Brother show up? My ranger dogs got home."

Leslie shook his head.

"Some son-of-a-bitchen Shawnee or white has shot him down on sight. . . ." We've got to clean out the ash hopper and get another run started, but first we ought to git our log piles in a good way of burnen so the rain won't put em out."

Leslie glanced at the sky. Still clear, but the moon wouldn't lie.

Daniel, walking over the hill with him, noticed his glance. "Yes, the sun is shinen, but smoke is fallen down and didn't you hear the rain crows awhile ago?"

Leslie didn't tell him of the ring he'd seen around the moon, but did tell him of the good use to which the basket had been put.

Daniel's only answer was a snort. His ill humor gradually subsided as the log piles burned to his liking and work began to go forward in the cave; by supper time he was singing a Cherokee song. It was a sad song, as if from being angry he had grown sorrowful.

His low spirits hadn't lifted when Leslie returned next morning in a slow drizzle of rain to give the same answer to the same question about Little Brother he'd given the day before.

The rain wasn't heavy enough to bother the burning log piles, or even the cook fires. Work went on as usual. Leslie spent most of the day digging niter dirt; the last of the dug was crushed and leaching in the vat. During the noon rest, he noticed in the west a lighter shade of gray; the rain was moving on.

Not long after the nooning, the black hole in which he was digging grew lighter. He twisted about to see a band of watery sunlight on the cave floor. The rain had stopped. A change in the weather might improve Daniel's disposition.

The change didn't improve his disposition as far as Leslie could tell, but it apparently jogged his memory. During supper he asked: "You recollect Gideon Huccaby?"

Leslie had never heard of the man.

"Well anyhow, I've been meanen to tell you I'm expecten him up from the Cumberland settlements any time now. He'll maybe make powder, at least some, while he's here. I aim to let him have ever speck a saltpeter I can—not fergetten yours. That demon out of hell, McGivillray, half white and callen himself King of the Creeks, is siccen his braves onto the Cumberland settlers. And when they're not taken hair, them mean Shawnee is."

Leslie returned to his rockhouse with a lighter heart; at least some of his work would go to help the besieged settlers; nor would he have to waylay a band of Cherokee to get the powder he had earned.

Daniel didn't ask after Little Brother next morning, but he was as dour as ever, predicting more rain within the next day or so. This kind of sunshine meant more rain. Leslie shook his head as he brought up wood for the cooker. Daniel ought to believe his own words: he'd said Little Brother was not a child but a brave able to take care of himself.

They worked in silence, alternating between crushing the niter dirt Leslie had dug the day before and tending the leaching vat and ash hopper. Around midmorning Daniel directed Leslie to go see how the log piles were burning; more chunks could have burned off and rolled away.

Leslie was heaving a burned-off chunk into the edge of the pile when he glanced through the smoke to see somebody running toward him from the direction of the bigger creek. Out of the smoke he could see it was Little Brother, one fist held carefully in front of him as if it were wounded. Leslie ran to meet him.

He opened his fist to take out a strand of yellow brown hair and said: *"Ptaha."*

Daniel had come running. "I'll be damned. It's out a the belly a one. He's found it caught on a briar."

Little Brother pointed to the big creek, then brought a

cupped hand up and down twice. He next pointed to his shadow, then the western horizon.

"He's tellen us he found that buffler hair, or maybe actually saw one, up the creek yonder, then two hills over. And he wants to go now. We could; that cooken saltpeter won't ruin to leave it all night on a low fire."

Leslie turned back to the boy who had spoken, his words lost in Daniel's voice, listened as he repeated: "Culeeo?" He asked the question again as he walked four fingers over the ground, then pointed to himself.

Leslie said: "Cleo," pointed to the boy, then nodded. He'd given Little Brother leave to ride Cleo, but he'd wager she wouldn't take him.

The boy was off, his running walk faster than common.

"Professor, you'd better start after him, otherwise he'll be off and gone by hisself, maybe to be gored and trampled to death. We'll all ride together. While you're hunten and feeden your horses I'll do the same for Equo, and set up a real early dinner. And bring your sleepen gear. We'll make camp and hunt at first light like in the old days."

Leslie wondered as he hurried up the hill if Little Brother had expected or even wanted him and Daniel to come with him. He had found the buffalo. It was his hunt.

He heard singing, and stopped to look and listen. Daniel stood facing the east, arms uplifted, as he sang a Cherokee hunting prayer.

Leslie went on up the hill. He knew the warriors prayed before killing bear or deer, but he hadn't heard of a prayer for hunting buffalo. If he had a prayer, he'd offer it for the safety of the buffalo; so few were left in these parts.

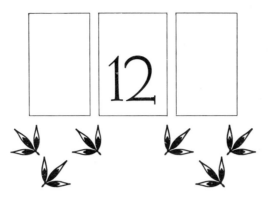

Little Brother rode Cleo as if they'd been raised together. Scorning Leslie's offer of bridle and saddle, he rode bareback with a braided thong to serve as bridle. Daniel gave many *Gha*'s of wonder as he rode up to the saltpeter works and dismounted.

They took only time enough over dinner for Daniel to discuss his plan with Leslie. First, he was taking along plenty of food for supper, and breakfast too, if need be. Buffalo in these parts had been hunted so hard they'd run from the smell of smoke; they knew it meant men or the woods on fire.

He thought he knew the place; up the big creek and over into the next valley four or five miles was one of the finest canebrakes in the country. Used to be buffalo had always fed there, not just for the fine cane, but because there was a salt lick down near the creek about a mile or so from the canebrake. He thought the best thing to do was camp for the night fairly close to the salt lick, but not too close; otherwise the buffalo might take notice. In any case they ought to be on the hunt by first light. If the buffalo didn't come to the lick, they'd have to sneak up to the canebrake and wait above it. A man ought never to go into high cane after buffalo.

The way up the big creek was easy, the rested horses going at a good clip. Daniel might take command of the hunt, but Little Brother led the way on Cleo. Jealous-hearted Kate vented her anger at being forced to follow with all the mean tricks she knew.

Leslie was chary of soothing words. He liked the trip no more than Kate. He thought of a canebrake down the Cumberland near French Lick when he'd been there a few years back; a man could walk through that big canebrake and never touch foot to the ground; he walked on buffalo skulls and bones left by French hunters who'd killed thousands for their tongues and tallow to ship to New Orleans. Now there were no buffalo left for the hungry settlers.

Kate quieted when Little Brother turned from the big creek into a small rocky-bottomed branch bordered by steep tree-covered hillsides below rock walls. There was no place for a horse to walk except in the water over slick rocks that now and then broke off to start higher, like stair steps. Leslie reckoned the sun never shone into this gulch; not much past noon on a sunny day, but still so dark the horses couldn't see where to put their feet under the clear water, and were cautious at being guided. Kate walked as close to Cleo as possible, not with the hope of getting ahead, but for comfort. She was afraid, poor girl.

It seemed they had climbed a long way when up ahead he saw the sky instead of rock walls above the trees. Daniel spoke behind him: "Soon as we come to that water gap up ahead, halt the brave. We ought to hold a parley."

On reaching the gap, Leslie managed to halt Little Brother by calling his name. He then caught Cleo's thong and, in spite of the boy's annoyance, turned her about to face Daniel who repeated most of the advice he'd given at dinner. He did explain that just over this gap was a bigger branch; the salt lick was to their left; the canebrake up the branch or to their right, so they would turn left. They must travel quietly with no talk.

Leslie cursed under his breath when Daniel pointed up the creek and didn't shake his head. At that Little Brother had given Daniel one happy glance, turned Cleo about, and started up the rise.

Kate followed with all the speed she had, but when they crested the gap into a wider valley with easier going, Cleo was galloping down, angling off to the right. Leslie cursed himself; why in God's name hadn't he hung on to Cleo's makeshift bridle until he had her going in the right direction. Kate had gone into a gallop; he ought to check her; she could break a leg; the sidehill was dangerous with rocks and maybe sinkholes; no, it was too high to be in the limestone.

Daniel, forgetful of his orders for silence, yelled with a curse: "You've took the wrong turn." Leslie tried to yell back that he was following Little Brother, but Daniel never heard for alternately calling off Yellow Eyes and the other ranger he'd brought, and cursing them when they didn't obey. Their allegiance gone to Little Brother, they ran with Cleo. Daniel couldn't get close on Equo, a workhorse.

Leslie rode with a lighter heart. Mayhap there'd be no buffalo within sight after all this racket. Still, he followed; a man alone in a canebrake after buffalo didn't usually come out. He'd heard that in the plains west of the Illinois, Indians hunted buffalo on horseback. Little Brother was a Plains Indian, but he must have sense enough to know canebrakes were not for horses when hunting buffalo—or for men either.

The creek valley took a sharp curve to the right and he lost sight of Cleo. Moments later Kate brought him within sight again. Little Brother was standing on Cleo's shoulders looking into the canebrake that filled the valley floor. Leslie saw him nod, slide down into riding position, kick Cleo, and head her down to the cane.

He urged Kate to follow. She ran fast enough, but picked her own course, and entered the cane at a different spot from Cleo. She went a few steps into the wall of cane, higher than her head, and stopped with a snort in mud half to her hocks. Leslie had one glimpse of Little Brother from the waist up, arm lifted, spear aimed. He disappeared in a whirlwind of shaking cane tops.

Leslie rose in the stirrups and saw the back and hump of a running buffalo. No head in sight; that meant he was holding it down for a charge. He cursed, and sprang from the saddle, rifle at the ready. Kate had refused to do anything but try to get out of the cane.

He heard cane stalks crashing behind him now; more, deeper in the canebrake, between snarls and barks from the rangers; but nothing from where he'd last seen the boy. He struggled on, uncertain he was headed in the right direction; cane tops and leaves when he looked up, a wall of cane stalks and leaves in all directions; the sounds were no good as guides; they kept moving. Deeper mud sucked at his shoepacs.

Cane crashed behind him; he didn't look around; the wrong direction. He had to walk toward silence; he could hear nothing from where he'd last seen Little Brother. Where was Daniel with his big rifle? His own little turkey-shooting Ruth wouldn't stop a buffalo unless he could aim at exactly the right spot, and in this cane he couldn't see the right spot.

A few more steps pulling through the mud foot by foot, pushing cane stalks apart so as to get through, and the solid wall gave way to crushed and broken cane, some stalks bright with blood. He was walking on the carpet of broken cane, hurrying to find the end, dreading to see what he must see, and with no mind for his feet, when he tripped over something that moved. A blowing viper he reckoned, but looked down as he swung a leg back to give it a hearty kick. His kick ended in the air; he'd stumbled over Little Brother's sprawled-out leg. The rest of him was lying in the cane, blood over most of him. Dying?

The boy lifted an arm and pointed. Leslie went through a wall of cane to come face to face with a bull buffalo. He was taking aim when, on hearing Daniel's laughter, he saw that the buffalo, though still standing, was closer death than life. The boy's spear had got him in the one right place: on the left side a little below the middle of his back and about a handspan past his shoulder. There, the spear had gone straight to his heart, but to make certain the boy had shot three arrows into his belly, and had somehow managed to cut his throat. Leslie didn't want to watch the fine animal die, and turned away. He had to make water.

He was on his way back to Little Brother when Daniel came out of the cane. No need to wonder where he had been while the boy was killing the bull; he'd been in mire up to his middle and was still dripping mud and water. Leslie suggested they go carry Little Brother out of the cane as he seemed to be too badly hurt to walk.

Daniel shook his head. "This is one a the proudest days in that brave's life, so don't go plaguen him by showen up his weak side. I figger that buffler just kind a sideswiped him with one horn. He's got a good scrape, but if that bull had caught him square, he'd have his guts squshed out."

He stopped to listen to his dogs still snarling and barking. "Leastways, they're still alive. . . . He's maybe got a few ribs broke, but he'll be all right. I recollect once a big son of a bitch spoilen for a fight shoved me hard, I reckon I was standen in his way, against the edge of a tavern bar; one side a my chest hit. Well, it hurt a minute, then I never noticed while I was taken care a that bastard. But next day I was sore on that side a my chest, and it kept hurten along, not too bad, and after a while it stopped. And would you know I had three little humps all in a row; the ribs had been broke and knit back together. . . . He ought to be on his feet by now."

Little Brother, still tottery, was leaving the canebrake when they found him. Each man gave him a congratulatory handshake, but no back slaps. He looked as if a hearty slap on the shoulder would have sent him sprawling.

They were walking with him out of the cane when the crashing, crunching sound of a buffalo running through cane not six paces away to their left stopped both men. Daniel swung the rifle from his shoulder, said: "*Sgeh*," and made no move to hunt down the running buffalo, but continued to look in the direction the beast had gone.

Leslie, watching with him, had decided the word Daniel had just spoken was *listen* in Cherokee, when some distance away, a dog shot above the cane. Daniel let out a mournful "*Gha*," and continued to watch and listen until one of his rangers, tail dragging, came out of the cane. A few minutes later Yellow Eyes came limping in, his hair matted with blood and mud.

"And how does it feel to fly through the air like a bird?"

Daniel asked him. "I hope that little flight teaches you not to tackle any size buffler. The old mama way up the creek somewhere took her time about comen, but she got there."

The dogs listened, then sniffed around to pick up Little Brother's scent. The men followed, and met the boy, skinning knife in hand. They went back to the buffalo, now fallen on his side, eyes glazing with death.

The three of them, all experienced, soon had the hide off; dragging it to the creek to wash out the mud and blood was as tedious as the skinning. Hide weighted down with stones in a fast moving riffle, they went up the creek until they found a pool deep enough for washing. They stripped and scrubbed, both men keeping an eye on the Indian. He looked too weak for safe swimming, but when he got the blood off, Leslie could see, along with scratches and bruises, only one bad wound—the bull's horn had given his chest such a hard scrape a rib or two was showing.

Leslie, still dripping, went for the dry socks and medicine in Kate's saddlebags.

He got the boy to take a good swig of brandy, then poured whiskey into the wound and doused the other scrapes. Whiskey on raw flesh hurt like holy hell, but Little Brother gave no sign he felt it; nor did he sniff at Leslie's doated-corn salve that next went on.

The dogs came up, so meek now they nosed the salve in Leslie's hand and asked to be doctored. The men went over them to find nothing but a small tear on Yellow Eyes and a few cane stabs on both. "It's your feelens that are cut up, not your hides," Daniel told them, "but if Leslie here wants to waste some salve, we'll rub it on."

Salve on the dogs, Daniel turned to Leslie. "You got plenty a liquor?" He shook his head at the brandy Leslie proffered. "I'm not wounded; it's more like my dogs; my insides are all ashake from bein scared to death." He took a long drink, then handed the whiskey jug back to Leslie. "Don't you want a drink? But I don't reckon you was scared. Leastways, you don't act like it."

Leslie drank, then smiled. "You couldn't have been as bad off as I was. I thought we'd all be killed."

Daniel nodded. "You didn't see the buffler up the creek. You didn't see them cows chargen into the canebrake. I thought one was maken for you. I figured you was stuck in the mud; you'd come in on the swampy side. You can't blame your mare. I was runnen in tryen at the same time to get a bead on that bull I was certain was killen our brave when I stepped in a chug hole; when I got out I couldn't see anything but shaken cane. Shooten at what I couldn't see, could a killed you or him. . . . And didn't you think the boy was about to be killed, but you couldn't do a thing?"

Leslie considered. "I thought we'd all be killed or so wounded we couldn't crawl out, and not even the buzzards could find us down in the mud and the cane. I thought about another fool man who went into a canebrake after buffalo, or so it was said. They found him about a week later, barely alive after bein gored and tramped on."

"Nah. I helped bury him; stunk to high heaven; had turned black and yellow before we found him full a maggots. Fools like that ought never to go out by themselves." He laughed. "I knowed a hunter; was a good shot, but didn't know exactly where to hit a buffler. His first shot hurt a big bull just enough to make him crazy mad; he charged before that hunter could reload. That man made for the closest tree, and it was a thorn tree. Lord, was that pore feller a mess when we got him down."

Little Brother, who had been looking at Daniel as if he understood what he said, got up and started for the canebrake.

Leslie took out his hone and began sharpening a knife. Daniel did the same. "I don't think we ought to go rushen in," he said after a moment. "We have to let him know by some means we think it's his carcass to do with as he pleases. And it is. He killed that bull with no help from us."

Leslie nodded in agreement, but wondered if the light would last through a wait and then the work. It seemed hours since he'd seen the sun slipping behind a crag. He looked in the opposite direction and saw sunlight still touching the pines that grew on top of a sandstone bluff high above the valley.

Daniel saw his glance. "It's this shut-in vale makes it seem so late; dark's a long while away, and anyhow there'll be a moon and we'll build a fire. I hope," he added wistfully, "your little brother won't want all the bones. I could set up all night roasten and cracken marrow bones."

Little Brother was more than generous with his kill. He had, when they reached him, cut off the head, ripped out the tongue which he presented to Leslie, then indicated the best part of a buffalo, the hump, was for Daniel. The boy seemed mainly interested in the longer tendons, many of which he had already cut out by the time the men went to him. He also wanted the longer leg bones; this left more than enough marrow bones for the three of them.

The early twilight was thickening into dusk by the time they had cut up the carcass and carried it out of the canebrake. Daniel got a fire going while Leslie took care of the horses. He next went to hunt firewood. Daniel had said they'd need dead hickory to make a hot fire to roast the marrow bones.

He was pulling long scales of bark from a hickory he had found on the hillside when he stopped to watch the last glow fade from a southwestern-facing crag. He thought of the buffalo they'd killed, and the other buffalo, elk, and deer that had used to graze in this snug, high-walled valley where cold winds never came. All dead now; and the little herd they'd found was panicked and leaving the valley. He'd wager there wasn't even a wolf left.

He hadn't planned it. The wolf howl seemed to come from his throat of its own will, a long and lonesome outcrying for the used to be.

An answer came from up the creek, then another from the hillside above him, followed by more howls from the valley and the ridges.

Happiness from the sounds of life eased his sorrow for the dead buffalo.

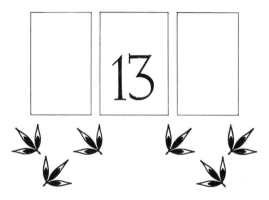

13

Last night while they were roasting and cracking marrow bones, Daniel had predicted more rain. He'd been only partway right; a man could hardly call this wetness rain. It was more like a heavy fog, coming down from the sky, rising from the creeks and the ground to make a wet blanket that hid the world and wet a man inside and out. And he had spent half the day riding in it.

The three of them had, in two trips, leading their horses most of the time, packed out the buffalo head, hide, and meat. Little Brother had already taken Rachel more meat than she could use before it spoiled. Now he was riding up the valley with more.

Leslie cursed himself for the wasted trip and the lie he had told himself. He wasn't riding through the fog to carry meat to where it wasn't needed. He wanted to see William David; most anything could have happened to him in the day and the night since he'd seen the baby. He could be sick.

He shook his head in disgust. Soon, he'd be leaving, never again to see William David. Then what? Would he spend the rest of his life worrying and wondering over a gray-eyed baby who was nothing, absolutely nothing, to him?

William David, according to Rachel, was even finer than

usual. She thanked him for the buffalo beef as heartily as if she didn't already have more than she could use, said she was mighty glad to see him, then cocked her head and said: "Please listen, suh."

He had already heard tinklings and clinkings mixed with sounds from William David, but listened as she directed, then followed her to Daniel's basket on the other side of the fire. William David was having a great time down in the bottom as he grabbed at and kicked two silver spoons dangling within reach from the handle.

"Pore little feller's not got any play pretties so I let him play with the missus's spoons when she forgets and leaves one or two on her tray. And does he ever carry on when she notices she's missen spoons and I have to take em away from him." She gave a sorrowful headshake and looked ready to cry. "He's got nothen, not so much as a name."

"Why, he has a name. You named him after me," Leslie reminded her.

She shook her head. "It's a fine name, suh, but he still has to be named proper accorden to my master's church, christenen they call it. He ought to be treated the same as the other three the missus has got even if we couldn't have a real dinen or reception after we come home from church."

Leslie nodded. "I know he ought to be christened, but insofar as I know there's neither priest, vicar, nor curate in these parts, and no Church of England. William David will have to wait."

"Suh, I know you wasn't brought up a heathen or a New Light. You know William David's waited too long already. You talk so fine. Recollect the first night you was here. You made a speech then. You could be a vicar or even a bishop long enough to christen William David."

Bishop Collins. That would have pleased his father, though he had never thought so high when he'd talked to Leslie of preparing himself for the church. "Pretending that would be a mortal sin," he told Rachel. "Pewter," he added quickly, when instead of crying she bristled for argument, "doesn't have the pretty sound of silver, but I'll bring a pewter mug and spoon for William David to play with when there's no silver."

He had delivered the pewter, borrowed the ax, and, to avoid any more of the bishop business, hurried away to cut firewood. Daniel had said there was no use to come back to work through the little daylight left; the saltpeter and the buffalo hide and meat were all in good shape.

He was several paces past Rachel's overhang when he heard feet in shoes. He hurried on as if he hadn't heard; his luck had held for the past few days; not once had the yellow-headed shrew caught him. Cursing under his breath, he stopped when she called in a honey-dripping voice: "Please."

He waited; the bitch, he reckoned, was fool enough to think a change in tactics would change the shape of things. She came on with a big smile, whispering as if they were conspirators: "I'm so happy to see you're back. I was afraid you'd gone for good. I feel so much safer with a strong, reliable man around. That stinking Indian frightens me."

"He's a man, good and reliable."

She came closer. "How you do tease me. Sir, I hate to bother you, but can't you soften your heart just a wee bit and get me at least to Boonesborough? My guide and protector who was killed said we was to stop there on our way to Detroit."

A mourning dove with honey dripping from its bill could not have cooed more sweetly. "It's not my heart, maam, but my head and my horses. I've only the two mares, same as I told you last time; but supposen you could ride and carry your baby, your help and myself walk, my packhorse couldn't begin to carry half your plunder."

She pouted prettily. "We could leave most of that old stuff behind. I won't need all the victuals I've brought. I have money. I can buy anything I need in Boonesborough."

He spoke with unaccustomed loudness so that Rachel might hear and get the silver spoons away from William David. "Provisions, maam, any kind of food, can't be bought in Boonesborough, not even with all your British gold. The people are bad off, always thirsty, dirty. Men have to go under guard to bring

167

in water for drinken and cooken." William David was screaming; he'd lost his silver, but where was the pewter? Maybe he
was just a smart little son of a bitch, not willing to exchange
silver for pewter.

"And furthermore," he went on, "the people in Boonesborough are starven. The Indians destroyed their crops last year
and won't let them put in any this year. Why, the women, when
they go out to milk the few cows left to them, have to go under
guard to milk. We might get that far with the cow, but if the
baby didn't starve in Boonesborough, he would on the way to
Detroit. You'd be lucky to get through with your scalps, let
alone a cow."

He heard a faint *tink tonk;* William David or maybe Rachel
was pounding the mug with a spoon. The woman was smiling;
in a minute she'd burst out laughing. He turned to go.

"Now, now. Don't run away. I wouldn't blame you after
that great big tale you've just told me. You just don't want to
take me, that's all. And suppose," she went on in her sweetest
voice, "the people in Boonesborough are hungry. It's their fault
they didn't bring provisions. I have plenty. I won't starve. And as
for all your worries over the baby, there won't be any baby."

"But, maam . . ."

"I'll see you again," she cooed as she turned to go.

He swung his ax with vicious strokes into a nearby dead
beech. There were good women in the world, and pretty with it,
like the girl he'd seen at Camden battlefield; but William David
Leslie Collins was forever tangling with the other kind; that
woman and Sadie were worse than whores. A whore was a
whore; she made her living by whoredom; she didn't cuckold
any man. And where were the blackguards that fathered the
bastards the damned bitches bore? They ought to be chained
while they worked like galley slaves to earn money to support
their bastards.

He stopped, ax uplighted. He had wronged Sadie by putting her in the same category as the yellow-headed woman.
That woman wanted to be rid of her baby. All Sadie's trickery
had been for little Watts. He had to have a name and a respect-
able mother. She'd grabbed him for the father because he was a

168

stranger who hadn't known. And he had been a half-drunk, tired-out fool else he would have suspicioned something was up.

One of the first things her old father had asked when he stopped to see about a lodging for the night had been: "Your wife with you?" And he had answered like a fool: "I don't have a wife." That had been enough. Sadie would have made a bid for him had he been the devil himself.

Watts was a tow-headed, pale-eyed dumpling of a baby, slow witted he sometimes thought, but he'd never been around him enough to tell; and anyhow he didn't know anything about babies. It didn't matter. Sadie loved Watts the same as if he'd been as fine a baby as William David. She'd grab him up the minute he cried, suckled him herself, and worked harder than any slave to keep him and everything about him clean.

And what would become of William David?

He swung the ax. There were no answers in the wood, but as he wanted to hit something, somebody, the whole damned world, chopping made him feel better. He worked until it was too dark to see, then, as was his habit, stopped to study the sky before going into his rockhouse.

He hadn't expected anything except the grayness of the fog. Now, he was looking at a handful of pale stars. He listened. The faint sounds of the pine tops in a still foggy world had changed; they were now saying in sharper, louder voices that air too light for a breeze was moving out of the northwest. He was getting old not to have noticed the swing of the air from south by west to northwest. It would be a cold night; most likely the first in a long chain. He wished Little Brother and Rachel had their halves of the buffalo hide.

The hard cold didn't come that night. The hardness was in next day's sky. No matter how pressing the work, he stopped often to look at the sky. He didn't like the way it watched him, smiled at him with the sneering smile of the yellow-headed woman. He didn't think he'd ever seen a sky so blue. Somewhere there had been a great storm to wash every speck of cloud from the sky. Now it smiled on earth and promised something else.

Most of the leaves were still hanging, brightly colored as

they had been for days, but today they had a glittering look. They didn't sound right; that is when they sounded at all. The sky had killed the wind, but the air, unwarmed by the bright sun, seemed to have traveled from ice fields far away.

At supper time Daniel brought out the halves of buffalo hide, handing one each to Leslie and the Indian. "You'll need cover tonight," he said. "That's why I'm given em to you now before they're tanned and softened the way they ought to be."

The three of them together had washed and scraped the hide, then Daniel had taken it into custody saying he could do a better job in his cave. Leslie found the hide surprisingly soft to be only three days off the bull. He praised Daniel's quick work.

Daniel laughed. "I did work hard on it, but you'd never guess how I softened that hide a shade. I folded it over and over and run it through my log crusher over and over."

Leslie shook his head in wonder, then shook it again in wondering how he could make Little Brother understand that he must be the one to present the hide to Rachel. He succeeded with considerable help from Daniel, or thought he had; at least Little Brother left early with both halves.

Leslie awakened next morning with his nose buried in bear-skin. He heard what sounded to be a slow, unsteady, big-dropped, little-dropped rain. It wasn't rain; the hard cold was forcing every chestnut, beech, oak, and hickory that hadn't dropped its mast to do so now. And through and under the thunks and patters of falling big and little nuts was the whisper of falling leaves.

He listened to fall give way to winter and opened his eyes to the glitter of hoarfrost in the pale light of a waning moon. The silvery whiteness covered all things, from the rock on which he lay to the twigs above him.

The moon, not many days past the full, was well on its way down the western side of the sky. Time for the ducks to be getting up. He laughed and pulled on his shoepacs. The ducks, silly as they were, had more sense than he. Yesterday afternoon, they had known that the quieter parts of their little creek would be covered with ice by morning. They had gone on to a bigger creek or any water they knew wouldn't freeze last night. How did they know?

He was wondering on other learnings of birds and animals when he thought of the bee tree he planned to rob. On this cold morning the bees would be too sleepy to bother him if he went early enough. He had figured out a way to get some honey without cutting down the tree and ruining the swarm. The bees were high in the hollow of a big dead chestnut, its first limb at least twenty feet from the ground, and the swarm head-high above that. He couldn't climb to that limb without a rope. He had no rope, but conveniently close was a hickory sapling, easily climbed. He had only to go up it, swing the top to the chestnut limb, lash it there for coming down, and be in the honey business.

He'd banked his fire the night before, and had it rebuilt, corn cakes in the fire hole, and tea drunk by the time moonlight gave way to daylight. He sneaked out one of Rachel's pails, took his kettle, and hurried to the bee tree. The good thing about the old chestnut was it stood on his side of the creek and halfway up the ridge side. Had it been on Daniel's side of the creek, he wouldn't have touched it. He didn't know, but from the way Daniel talked, he considered all the land within the curve of the creek his to do with as he wished, but he wouldn't be apt to claim this bee tree.

Things worked out pretty much as he had planned. Hoarfrost made the hickory slippery to climb, a pail on one arm, a kettle on the other; but the sapling was kind, bending as he wished, not so eager to get away but that he could lash it to the limb with the long thong he'd brought. The bee tree was a fine one, at least for him, but come spring the bees would have to swarm; their hole was so filled with honey they'd soon have no place to live. Now, they were snug asleep in the cold, and never bothered as he cut out great chunks of honey-dripping comb.

Rachel's pail filled, he wondered if he wouldn't do better to climb down a pail at a time than try to climb down that frost-slippery sapling with both arms loaded with honey. Pail in hand, he turned to study the sapling. Little Brother, leaning on the sapling where it met the chestnut limb, reached for the honey.

Leslie hoped, as he handed over the pail, that he showed no surprise at the boy's being close beside him. He hadn't heard a sound. That boy could kill and take a scalp and his victim never know it. He filled his kettle, then pointed to the boy's stomach and mouth; there was plenty of honey left for him and to winter the bees. Little Brother brought up the dried-out rind of the biggest cushaw he'd ever seen. Daniel's. He ought to take it back to him filled with this rich, dark honey.

All the honey he meant to take on the ground, Little Brother politely waiting with it, Leslie lingered on the chestnut limb to look across the valley. Sunlight had traveled halfway down the eastern-facing hillside to touch the hoarfrost on every growing thing and set each twig asparkle; even the rocks looked to be wrapped in polished silver. The pines on the ridge top were smoking, already losing their silver; the sun was taking it away. Soon, it would all be gone, but he had seen it. That was something to keep. The world was a fine place—except for the people in it, including himself.

He straddled the sapling, untied the thong so that the tree could again stand straight and tall, then climbed down. Little Brother left with his cushaw cradled in one arm and Rachel's pail in the other hand. A tidy soul, he had not dirtied his hands with honey as had Leslie.

He was squatting by the creek, cleaning his honey-smeared knife with sand, when some kind of wolf-like animal he didn't see leaped on his shoulders to send him sprawling on his knees and hands. He was springing up, knife ready, when another big beast gave a whimpering cry, leaped on his chest and began licking his ears. Godalmighty, he was losing his mind not to know his own dogs.

Thunder, his young cur that had never had and would never have any sense, named Thunder because he almost never barked, finished one ear and began licking the other. He was no worse than old Cupid, the one who had first leaped on him. Cupid cavorted around him, whining, crying, talking all the happy dog-talk he knew. Leslie petted both dogs, begged them to tell him from where they had come, looked in all directions, listened, but saw and heard nothing out of the ordinary until

Kate nickered, charged out of the lower canebrake, and, with Cleo behind her, disappeared around the creek bend.

Kate had heard something further down the creek he hadn't; must be some or all of his horsestock; maybe his finest, the stallion Beau. He ran after the mares, then stopped. Who had his dogs and horses? A thief or several thieves? He'd better be going for his rifle.

He wished the dogs would hush their love talk. He might hear something. He had run halfway up the hill to his rockhouse when he stopped for another look. This time, he saw coming round the curve of the willow-bordered creek the rich dark gleam of a horse's shoulder. That was his stallion Beau; black, with a shine and sheen no other horse roundabout had.

He continued to watch as horse and rider came into full view. Beau all right, but he didn't know the brigand, for brigand he was, riding high in a fancy Spanish cavalry saddle, stolen like the riding boots with silver spurs and the rest of his gear. The sun had not yet touched the valley but Beau's rider didn't need it to make him shine; everything from his high silk hat to the polished gun boot loaded with a big firearm was all ashine. An unearthly sight, for along with civilian clothing he wore a brace of pistols, a sword by his saddle, and silver-banded powder horns across one shoulder.

He came slowly on, head bowed as if in deep thought, seemingly unmindful of Beau or the two packhorses he led, both the property of William David Leslie Collins. Near the creek crossing, he lifted his head and looked toward the dogs as if searching for something. Leslie saw a dark face; looked again, not believing, then with a cry of "Jethro" ran to him.

Jethro saw him, sprang from the saddle, but didn't look too happy at finding his master, not so happy as the dogs; in fact not happy at all.

What ailed the man? Jethro carried himself with sober dignity most of the time; but now his sobriety lay on him with unusual heaviness. A man could say he looked downright sad on finding his master. Leslie heard other horses down the creek, but looked only at him. "Jethro, it certainly is good to see you, but how did you find me in this place?"

173

"I don't know exactly. Jimmy's people said you'd gone to French Lick; I got directions; the dogs helped a lot, but mostly it was him."

Whoever he was hadn't yet come into view. Leslie turned back to Jethro. He wasn't old; they were about the same age; but now he looked old, tired, scared, or something, like Armageddon was one hill over, coming his way. Jethro took off his hat and held it in both hands as if he wanted him to see it. Black silk; he didn't remember that particular hat, but it was the same as his father's coachmen wore; Jethro must have saved the hat from the time when he'd been an understudy to the head coachman.

Leslie looked at the hat again. He had seen something not ordinarily on a hat. No. He didn't need to look. He knew. That extra band was mourning crepe. Jethro was mourning for the man he respected and loved above all others. He found Jethro's eyes, but choked over his words: "My father?"

Jethro drew a long breath, took his glance from Leslie's face, brought it back as he said, "No. No, suh. Miss Sadie, she's the dead one. . . . You didn't read my letter to you, I left in your big Bible?"

"Miss Sadie? No, she couldn't be." He heard the relief in his voice and tried to change the tone. "And the boy?"

"Dead, suh."

"Indians?"

Jethro opened his mouth, stopped when a heavy sobbing sigh came from a clump of cedar brush.

That would be Rachel weeping for the sorrow he didn't feel, nothing but a cold heaviness within him.

"No, suh, it wasn't Indians. Some kind a lingeren fever. If you recollect, the little boy was punyen around when you went away. He was dead fore anybody knowed he was real sick. Miss Sadie lingered on maybe a fortnight or longer; she got better, then she got worse."

Leslie couldn't think of anything except: "Strong men don't weep." He had heard it somewhere and known it for a lie; he had seen strong men weep. The sad thing now was, it was too

174

damned easy not to weep. Beau was restless under the heavy saddle with what looked to be a bushel or more of corn slung on behind; with Jethro in the saddle, that extra load was too much for any horse, even Beau.

Jethro saw his disapproving glance and took off the corn, explaining as he did so: "He's not carried that corn and me but a little ways. He behaves better under a heavy load. He was meaner this mornen than common, and he's been one a the meanest horses I've ever handled all through the woods. If they was a tree close to our trace, he'd run smack into it tryen to break my leg or Jimmy's. And if he saw a big limb ahead, just high enough to catch a rider under his chin and break his neck, he'd try to run into it."

Leslie stepped over and began to unstrap the crupper. Beau hated a crupper even more than most horses, but now the brute sidestepped and snorted as if his master were a meddlesome stranger.

Jethro nodded, and began unbuckling a girth. "That's Beau's regular behavior. I can't think of no meanness he's not done; kicken back when a packhorse comes a shade close, bucken and rearen when he can't think up any other meanness. I'd better hobble him, don't you think? We've done it the whole trip, afraid he might run away."

Leslie shook his head; no wonder the proud beast was out of sorts. Hobbled every night! Jethro ought to know better.

"Howdy, Mr. Collins."

Leslie looked around, not certain he knew the voice, dressed in mourning as it was. He extended his hand. Jimmy Scott all right, but not the half-wild boy who'd slid off the house roof and jumped in front of him. There was still more fuzz than beard on his chin, but his eyes were those of a trouble-ridden man. Dead Sadie wouldn't have so changed him, even though he wore a mourning band around one sleeve and his voice was meetly sober as he said:

"I am sorry for your great loss. Granpa felt real sorry because he didn't know the Lord had already carried her and your little boy away when you come hunten them."

175

Leslie thanked him as he wondered. Did Jimmy and Jethro honestly think the dead child was his own, or were they pretending? Be nice if they didn't know the truth.

"I'm a courier," Jimmy was saying, "and a lot of my letters belong to you—but I don't reckon you feel like readen em now."

Jethro reached. "He will pretty soon. Some tells about Miss Sadie's sickness, and at least one's from the missus."

Death changed things. Jethro had never called Sadie "the missus." Leslie had reckoned he never would call anybody that except his mother, the mistress of the plantation where he was born.

Jimmy had thumbed the stack. "They're all here, been waiten a long time at Carter's store; that is some had. I hate to charge anything, but the man I got em from wanted a shilling and six pence; said he'd had to pay that to the man that left em there. And in hard money, no Continental. It's good for nothen but to chink the walls."

What good were letters. Never the ones you hoped to get. Want them or not, Jimmy must be paid well for his trouble. Leslie pulled out his purse, only to see Jethro paying Jimmy as he took the letters. He remembered his manners. "There are plenty of good dry rockhouses up there. Unpack and make yourselves at home, and I'll soon have breakfast."

"We've already had a hearty breakfast," Jimmy told him.

Leslie didn't urge him. His thoughts were on his dogs. They had stopped nosing his knees, and were now on the scent of something they wanted to tear to pieces; no barks, only angry snarls as they ran toward Rachel's rockhouse and down again. Cupid had found a hot trail; he bayed like a foxhound, then quieted, all his breath gone to the running.

He watched them until they disappeared in the brush along the creek. He figured they were after some varmint that had been around during the night, unless—where was Little Brother? Forever smelling of bear grease and the wolf skins he wore, they'd take him for a varmint and tear him to pieces.

He was running across the meadow, calling off the dogs,

when Jimmy yelled: "It's an Indian, a real brave they're after."
He reached for his rifle. "Less'n there's more around I won't
shoot. The dogs'ull kill him anyhow."

Leslie continued to run and call as Little Brother stepped
out of the willows by the creek a short distance from Beau. He
paid no heed to the oncoming dogs. His glance was fixed on the
stallion. Leslie cursed his dogs for not obeying him. He stopped;
they were maybe not hearing him through Jimmy's yelling and
the racket of two just-arrived mares exchanging loud greetings
with Kate and Cleo.

The boy noticed the dogs when it looked to be too late. He
jumped sidewise, glanced around as if he wanted a tree to
climb. There were none. He took a running leap for Beau and
landed on his back, sat for a moment astride, but with the dogs
leaping for his feet, he picked them up and stretched himself
full length on Beau. The stallion was rearing, whirling about,
screaming, but whether because of Little Brother on his back or
the snapping dogs, Leslie couldn't say.

Jimmy, come closer to watch, said with a sorrowful head
shake: "I remember now. He's the one that man told us not to
hurt. Now he'll be dead when Beau bucks him off and tramples
him to death like he's aimen to do."

It looked to Leslie that Beau was more interested in killing
the dogs than getting the boy off his back. He called again. This
time the dogs came with no looking back. They'd had enough
from Beau. He had quieted and was nibbling around as if he
enjoyed having an Indian on his back.

Leslie jerked off his hat and flung it on the ground. He'd
been a fool to believe that Spanish trader. Beau was "Spanish-
bred of exceptionally fine stock." Like hell he was. Well, maybe
ten or twelve generations back a fine Spanish stallion had wandered away into the plains. Beau had been stolen from a tribe of
Indians. Could be Little Brother's.

Ashamed of himself, he picked up his hat, aware of eyes
watching him in his grief. All politely looked at something else
when Jimmy said: "Well, I reckon it's good-bye, Mr. Collins. I'd
sure like to tarry with you awhile, but—I'm a courier now." He

177

swallowed; the squeak in his voice went away, and he continued: "I promised to take a letter to . . ."

Leslie had put his hand on Jimmy's saddle. "Wherever you're aimen to go, you oughtn't to go by yourself. Bide awhile and I'll go with you."

"I'd be much obliged, but I don't want to put you to any more trouble than you've already got. I'm not goen far, maybe no further than Boonesborough; it's a letter I got at Carter's store and promised to take to that yellow-headed woman that stopped at our place. She was headed for there."

"That's my missus. And she's here." Rachel, William David in her arms, came out of her hiding place behind a cedar.

Jimmy, already fishing in a saddlebag, swore as his horse shied and sidestepped. Leslie caught the rein. No wonder the beast had shied. The Mistress of the Mansion was running up, the usual cloud of pink and white topped with floating yellow. He wished she hadn't come. Sooner or later Sadie would hear he'd been living in the woods with a yellow-headed woman. He'd catch all kinds of hell, for he would never be able to make her believe he had no carnal knowledge of—Sadie was dead. He turned to the woman. "Maam, you're scaren this horse. Stand back."

She put on a pout, but stopped where she was. "Mr. Courier, the letter you have for a woman could be for me." She hesitated. "It would read, Mistress Charity Prudence Simons."

"Maam. Maam, excuse me but I think you're fergetten. Wasn't that your maiden name? Oh, I hope it's from the master." Rachel was so excited she had let William David kick off his red blanket to show a frill of lace.

The missus told Rachel to shut up, but didn't look around. She had eyes for nothing but the fat letter Jimmy was taking from a hog's-bladder pouch.

Jimmy studied the address on the letter, then looked at the woman, disregarding her outstretched hand. "You say your name is Simons? This letter belongs to—but let me read it; it's a long rigamarole." He read aloud: "To Madame Robert Barton Eversole, consort of . . ."

178

Rachel interrupted. "Thank the Lord. Oh, thank the Lord. It's from Captain Bob. That means he's still alive."

"Rachel, not another word." And with that the missus gave her a look that said: "The whipping post for you." She turned away and looked at nobody; her face now old, tired, all the bright eagerness gone.

"He's a colonel now, at least accorden to the letter," Jimmy said to Rachel. He looked at the woman, waited awhile, then said: "Maam, do you or don't you want this letter? It seems to be yours, and whether you take it or not, you owe me fourteen shillens six pence. I had to pay a good deal at Carter's store, because they'd had to pay the man who'd carried it all the way from Philadelphie where it had come from New York."

That was an outrageous price for one letter. Leslie watched the woman; it was plain this wasn't the letter she'd wanted, but . . .

"Your carriage is very dear," she said at last, "and anyway I have only guineas."

"I've got plenty a change for the little you'd get back." He took six shillings six pence from his purse, and waited while the woman stood, unable to make up her mind. At last with an angry jerk she flipped up a layer of petticoat to show a heavy-hanging reticule from which she extracted a guinea. Jimmy handed over the change, then held out the letter. She was slower in taking the letter than the change, but did at last accept it and carried it unopened toward her rockhouse.

Jimmy watched her going with a sorrowful headshake. "She sure has knocked me out of a nice trip to the northern Kentucky settlements."

"Bide awhile with us; then soon we'll all head for home," Leslie said without much heart. He had remembered he had no home.

"Wherever I head, it won't be home, but I would be proud to stay awhile with you, if you've got room for all the horsestock and the plunder we've brought."

"There's more room than anything else," Leslie told him. He didn't care; he didn't care about anything or anybody, but for the sake of politeness he asked: "Your grandfather and all your people well I hope."

"Liven the last I heared," Jimmy answered, and turned to his horse as if to shut off further questions.

"Suh, I'll show em the way to lead their horses." Rachel spoke to him, but she was smiling at Jethro.

He nodded. She was doing what he ought to have done. "I'll be up in a few minutes, soon as I finish what I was doen. Make yourselves at home." And what in hell had he been doing?

14

His world had changed. The world about him had not. The creek was still there. The hill across the creek no longer glittered in the morning sunlight; the frost was going, but the hill was still there. Leaves and nuts were still falling straight into their own eternities, no wind to carry them hither and yon to give them a make-believe life for a little while.

He saw the pot of honey he'd brought to the creek. Why? He shook his head. He'd brought the honey because he'd wanted to wash the bail, dirty from his honey-smeared hands. The bail was clean now. He'd been cleaning his knife with sand. Had he stuck it, smeared with sand and honey, back into its sheath and dirtied the sheath? No, he'd stuck it in his hunting shirt tie where it had done no harm.

And how could a lingering fever kill Sadie? He couldn't think of her getting sick enough to die any more than he could imagine a lusty young white oak keeling over in a light wind. There was no ague in the mountains; had the distemper been smallpox Jethro would have said so.

He held out his knife; it now shone clean and sharp. He would take the honey to his rockhouse, then go to work; but first he ought to round up the horses Jethro had brought and give them a good going-over. Rose had a tender back; she could have the beginnings of a saddle sore; Jethro had made a packhorse out of her. He shook his head and picked up the honey; the horses were somewhere up the hill close to his rockhouse.

Cupid whined and nosed his hand. He put down the kettle, ashamed of himself. The dogs had come so far, been happy to find him, and he hadn't spoken to either except to call them off Little Brother. He was comforting the dogs as they told him their troubles when Jethro came.

He had changed from his fancy dress but wore the same look of sorrow, dignified as the black clothing carried on his shoulders. His hands and arms were filled with other things, among them a steaming pot. He put down part of his load, carefully spread the clothing on a low-hanging sycamore limb, then turned to Leslie. "At a time like this you need to shave and shift. Rachel let me have some hot water." He took out the wicked-looking razor and, holding the strop with his teeth and left hand, began to play a tune as he stropped. "I won't be long. Over there's a nice rock. If you'll please sit on it. I'm aimen to shave you."

Leslie snorted. "Since when did you start shaven me? I'll do my own shaven."

Jethro's only answer was to work up a lather with a strange-smelling soap. Finished, he advanced brush in hand. Leslie sat on the rock indicated. Face lathered, he opened the door by asking in an offhand way how Jethro had come by the soap.

"It's a long sad story, suh. Please now hold real still. I'm not the best hand in the world at shaven and your whiskers are long and they look tough."

The whiskers were tough and in the sunlight the lather dried quickly. Jethro took his time both in the shaving and the story.

"First, about Miss Sadie; I reckon you'd like to know. Nobody can ever think she or the boy was ever neglected. The Weavers was mighty good to come and help tend Sadie. And lots a times they'd send their help. But, Lord, I didn't need em. We got along; and the old woman was there—most a the time.

"The boy took us by surprise. Like I said, he was dyen fore anybody thought he was real sick. Miss Sadie wanted her mama

182

and papa. Mr. Weaver sent Buck. And he sure took plenty a time on the way; the old woman never got there till more'n a week after the boy was dead and buried."

Leslie said: "Ouch."

Jethro apologized; the lather was dry. Making fresh, he sighed heavily. "Miss Sadie wasn't bad sick when the old woman got there. The day before she'd been out pullen flax; Angie wasn't shocken it the way she wanted. Then, suh, it looked like Miss Sadie had just been waiten for her mama to come. Her papa didn't want to leave his tavern.

"The old woman hadn't been there a day fore Miss Sadie took to her bed, throwen up, shaken and shiveren. I reckon the old woman doctored her the best she could; loaded her with castor oil, somethen she called calomel, and all kinds a tea, mostly black snakeroot I think. And she wouldn't let her have anything to eat but fresh milk.

"Mistress Weaver, or so Angie said—that girl was always slippen around eavesdroppen—told the old woman she didn't think Miss Sadie ought to have milk; seemed like it was maken her worse; and the cows sick. Flossie Bell was real sick, dyen you might say, when the boy died.

"Hold real still now. I'm a goen under your chin. Angie said she wasn't goen to drink milk or eat butter from a sick cow. And the triflen thing when she set out my victuals she'd never give me a smear a butter or a drop a milk. I didn't want it; Becky Sue was comen down when Flossie Bell died; and was too weak to travel when the old woman left. And was she ever mad. Can you hold your head a little higher, please, suh. Like I said I'm not used to this business."

Leslie studied the middle of the sky. If he were a praying man, he'd pray for his Adam's apple. Jethro, too carried away by his story to notice what he was doing, kept scraping toward it as if he meant to slice it off by mistake, thinking the projection a gob of lather. He wished he'd hush. Sadie was dead. That was that. Why must the man go on to tell of what happened after her death. It didn't matter.

"Miss Sadie wasn't cold under the sheet before her mama

183

was asken me about packsaddles and horses. She wasn't ready to bury yet when that old woman started hunten and rummagen, strippen quilts and blankets from the spare bed. She called me in soon as I'd finished diggen the grave to tie up a feather bed so a horse could pack it. I happened to see, squeezed down in that rolled-up feather bed, the silver candlesticks and salt dishes the missus sent with Angie when you married."

Jethro forgot it was a time for mourning and laughed. "I sneaked em out. Angie had the notion of fillen that big hole under the kitchen floor with dry flax and flax stalks. She told me why she was doen it and I helped her when I could. To save the flax until she could carry it off to her place, she told the old woman. Well, suh, one day when we had the hole about full, I was out by the wood block choppen wood—she used a terrible lot of wood—when I heard the awfulest scream comen out of that kitchen."

Leslie lowered his chin. Jethro wasn't doing anything now but talking while he made more lather, but when he lifted the brush, he made an upward motion. "I've got to go over your neck agin. I couldn't take that big crop off at the first mowen you might say. A body would think you kin of Esau and Samson, meanen no disrespect to the Bible."

"I've never found a Delilah, and as for my birth—" He shut his mouth. The razor was descending.

"Angie could be a Delilah except for her countenance. Anyhow, when I heared that awful scream, I got into the kitchen fast as I could carryen my ax. Angie was jumpen out a the kitchen hole and the old woman was runnen out the other door. 'Oh, Jethro,' Angie yelled at me. 'Go down in there and kill them two rattlesnakes that fell out a the flax shocks I just put in. I thought they was uncommon heavy.'

"The old woman stuck her head partway through the door. 'Don't you dare go down into that hole. They could bite you fore you'd see one. I ain't aimen to have you sick or dead on my hands. You have to holp me git my pore dead child's dower back home.'

184

"I was certain she was tryen to sneak out a good deal that hadn't been in Miss Sadie's dower, but I didn't say anything. Angie, though, she piped up: 'Them big snakes will be crawlen all over the house.'

"'You won't be in this house long. I'm taken you to where you won't be so sassy. Keep the kitchen doors tight shut, and do the cooken from now on.' She slammed the door.

"Pretty soon we heared her bawlen and quarrelen upstairs, and I whispered to Angie: 'You didn't have to make it so big. One little copperhead or even a big blacksnake would a been enough.' 'Quit quarrelen at me,' she says. 'Watch that door while I get Mr. Leslie's Bible from the bottom shelf of the safe where I put it. She's too old and fat to do much low stoopen, so I put it there after she told me to bring the Bible and his ink powder. I went and put it out a sight, then told her I couldn't find it. She's got no business writen in his Bible.'"

Jethro chuckled. "The old woman after that never so much as walked across the top a that hole. Then and there we put away the Bible, and after that any chance we had everything that belonged to you. The Bible was the only thing I took out on my trips back."

Leslie heard little of what Jethro told next. At mention of the Bible he was lost in wondering how many people knew he was a cuckold. His help must know, else they wouldn't have gone to all that trouble to hide the Bible. They'd been kind to him: Jethro leaving a letter which he hadn't seen; Angie going to the trouble of carrying flax stalks to that hole, then hiding his valuables and food for him. They hadn't done it out of love or respect, but pity. Pity was not for men, but for babies like William David.

"Suh, I said you don't have to cock your head to one side no more. I got that bad place kinda on the edge a your jaw bone."

The torture was ended. Jethro, still talking, was cleaning the razor. It appeared that somebody was trying to make tavern help out of him, and he wanted to be where he belonged, in the livery stable. Leslie listened a moment, nodded, thanked Jethro for the shave, then started for the creek crossing. He wanted to get to work; hard work like turning the log crusher would make him feel better.

"Please, Mr. Leslie, Rachel—she's a real obligen girl—said she'd have more hot water so you could wash before you shift to your mournen clothes."

Leslie turned back. His face was stiff as a green hide from all that soap. "I'll wash in the creek as usual, and I can mourn without special clothes."

"You asked about the soap; it come from the old woman's tavern, and will make you smell like roses for a week. She carried off better'n a bushel a yours, me and Angie had made from your hog grease. So, I took a little a hers. That creek water's too cold; I see ice in it; could give you a fever. Wait, please, while I run git some hot. Be nicer if you'd wash in your rockhouse."

Leslie, already stripped, left the soap, and ran on to his favorite pool. The last thing he wanted was to smell like roses. The creek water felt good, clean and cold. He scrubbed around with sand, taking his face first, then keeping all of him under water except his nose. It was only when his wet skin met the air that he felt the sharp cold. Running naked back to where he'd left his clothes was a cold business; his face cold as the rest of him; it was missing that nice warm growth of beard. He cursed himself for allowing Jethro to take it off.

He cursed more heartily when he reached the place where he'd left his clothes. Nothing he wanted, but a tow towel. Jethro had sneaked away his hunting shirt and other clothing when he brought the second pot of hot water. The good black suit with a frilled linen shirt and silk cravat, both white, were still hanging over the sycamore limb; nearby were black silk stockings and silver-buckled shoes that glittered like hoarfrost in the sun. He hadn't worn these clothes in months, and he didn't aim to now.

He took the towel and ran to his rockhouse where he found the clothes he'd been wearing, flung in a heap as if they were nothing. Jethro had gone too far; he'd give him a laying-down-the-law piece of his mind.

He was dressed and nearing the creek again when the black clothes on the white sycamore limb caught his glance. They chided him because he wore no mourning. His wife was dead. A length of black ribbon dangled across the shirt. He could tie that over the whang already holding his hair, make a small bow that Daniel wouldn't notice, and be in mourning. He tied the ribbon into a bow and walked on, more slowly than when he had started.

Yellow Eyes met him at the usual place, then conducted him to Daniel shoveling ashes from a newly burned pile into the sled. He was whistling some happy tune, and didn't see Leslie until he had reached the ash pile. One look, and Daniel flung down the shovel, anger in the action as in his voice: "Leslie, you know nobody expects you or any man to work at a time of great bereavement."

"I'd feel better worken."

"Didn't your help tell you I said to tell you not to think about comen to work today?"

"I was hopen for some hard work like diggen or crushen niter dirt to get my mind off my troubles, but if you don't want me I'll go," Leslie told him in the saddest voice he could summon.

"Moreover you're not able to work. You're pale as a ghost. Bide awhile by my saltpeter fire, and when you have recruited yourself enough to walk, go back and rest."

Leslie pushed back his hat and stuck out his face, chin leading.

Daniel stepped back. "Professor, why did you do it? You had the beginnens of a fine beard. Why, you might as well a been gelded. Have you looked at yourself since?"

"No."

"Don't. You wear your hat uncommon low, so your forehead is white as the heart of a turnip. Your nose and your ears with strips a cheek between is weathered brown and natural looken; the rest a your face shaded by your beard that was is pure white. Anybody strange comen on you in the woods would start runnen soon as he saw that face. Why ever did you do it?"

Leslie picked up the shovel. "I never thought how it would look. Jethro insisted on shaving me. That's all."

Daniel nodded. "Jethro sure is a fine man even if he is

nothen but a piece a property. I could hardly believe what I saw when my guard dogs barked and I looked down toward the creek mouth; from up here it looked like a great company was encampen on my place; and my rangers was haven trouble driven em off.

"I run and grabbed a firearm, already charged, and started runnen down siccen my rangers on loud as I could. It was getten late; I had to be close to see to shoot; I didn't want to hit any a the horses; it wasn't their fault somebody was trespassen. I was getten close when I saw Dalani—the one you call Yellow Eyes—maken for a black man's testes. That'll be about as good as a bullet, I was thinken, when the man so quick I could hardly see what was happenen, took Dalani by the scruff of the neck like he'd been a little kitten, and flung him into the creek water.

"The man saw me, and was real civil; called off his two dogs that had tangled with mine, and grabbed that big stallion that was doen his best to stomp and kick the life out of another'n. The man apologized; said he didn't know this was private property and they'd git off soon as they could. The boy— he's taller than most men but he's still a boy—stepped up, and told me where they was goen, then their names."

Daniel held out his hand. Leslie, not knowing what else to do, shook it. Daniel started up again. "Lord, Leslie, I'm ashamed a myself acten the fool when you're in great sorrow. But at least you cain't fault yourself or any man. She wasn't set upon and . . ." He jabbed the shovel into the ash pile with a quick angry thrust, and unmindful it was ashes he handled, flung a shovelful that fogged up into their faces.

Leslie wished he hadn't come. Daniel thought his sorrow for Sadie was as great as his for his dead Cherokee wife. He didn't want the anger, but he would be glad to take the sorrow. It would be good to have had a wife that no matter how far you had to go or how long your stay at work or war, she'd always been happy as a lark to see you, and just because you were you. Her children would be your children. You'd never think to doubt it.

He saw a shovel and went to work.

They were following Equo with the loaded sled before Daniel spoke again. "When I first learned about your wife and horsestock bein gone, I just reckoned she'd gone on a long visit to her people—there's no tellen what a white wife will do— and a bunch a horse thieves had got your horses. But I never did say nothen, be like scalden a fresh wound."

Leslie was surprised that Daniel had known Sadie was missing. How had he known? Nobody had been around to tell him. Yes, his Cherokee visitors. Jimmy and his grandfather had norated the word; the Overhill Cherokee knew everything the Overhill whites did.

They were shoveling ashes into the empty hopper before he could think to apologize for the disturbance caused by his help and ask if Daniel's dogs had been hurt in the fracas.

Daniel laughed. "You ought to a seen old Dalani when he come out of the creek. You'd never believe it but he just stood there and batted his eyes and watched; him too addled with surprise fer a minute to think to shake hissef. He didn't so much as try to git back into the fracas. And it was rough; that big black-and-tan cur you've got—he's bigger than any a mine —was on the way to maken mincemeat out a one a mine when Jethro called him off."

"I hope," Leslie said, "Jethro apologized, and they all went on with no more trouble."

"Went on?" Daniel was scandalized. "Why, soon as I learned who they was, I had them come to supper; too bad you was gone with the buffalo beef, but they had a good time. I brought out my peach brandy to celebrate. I thought the boy needed it; he looked kind a down in the mouth. Didn't they tell you anything about seein me?"

"They didn't have time. I left soon as Jethro finished shaven me when he was in the middle of tellen me how they got here." That wasn't exactly true, but Daniel was looking hurt because his hospitality hadn't been mentioned.

"That Jethro of yours is one slow teller. We'd been drinken, him playen his mouth organ and me singen mostly bawdy songs when I remembered to ask about your wife; looked like you had your horsestock back. Then they told me. I felt like a fool."

The sled was unloaded and Daniel had started to drag it out for another trip for ashes when he stopped with an oath. "You've not had a bite a breakfast, and don't say you have. I know, and here I've gone and fergot."

Leslie's protests couldn't dent Daniel's solicitude. If Leslie felt like work, he could go after another load of ashes, but he was going to cook him some breakfast; it was bad for a man to work on an empty stomach.

Leslie obeyed; hauled ashes; ate corn cakes, bacon, stewed dried peaches, and honey, and drank coffee, then after being asked if he felt able to do hard work, spent the remainder of his working day in digging, crushing, and shoveling niter dirt into the vat. The hard work lifted his spirits, but Daniel's continual solicitude irritated him. He hated the rest periods Daniel commanded him to take. He had nothing to do but aimless whittling until the notion came to him of making a toy for William David. He could whittle some kind of jangling toy to swing from the basket handle; he was too little for a jumping jack.

He decided bone would be best; good hard buffalo bone that wouldn't splinter. He'd cut several short rounded pieces and string them on a thong; they'd make a clicking sound when the string was jiggled. And when William David got older he could chew on one. *If* he got older?

He found some buffalo bone Little Brother hadn't taken and went to work. A slow job, he reckoned it would keep him busy through all the rest periods he would have to take. Working with his knife on the bone, he wished he'd made some kind of trinket for little Watts. He might have played with it and shown more life. He'd been a slow-moving, slow-witted child, but had learned a few words. One of these was *papa*. He would, with Sadie's coaching, say it over and over when Leslie was around; and always when Leslie heard it, he'd feel a thump of anger and pretend not to hear.

He wished he'd answered. No man ought to fault a child for coming from the wrong side of the bed, or for being ugly. He ought to have played with . . .

"Professor, it's none a my business, but you'll ruin your

whittlen knife tryen to cut a piece off that iron-hard bone. I'll go bring out my little cold chisel and hammer."

Leslie accepted the tools, thanked Daniel, and told him what he was trying to make.

Daniel was pleased with his thought for the baby, but continued to show no less concern for Leslie's grief. He had supper at a very early hour so that Leslie could go talk with Jethro and learn all about "your beloved wife's death."

He had heard all he wanted to hear of Sadie's death. Still, as soon as supper was cleared away, he hurried over the hill. He was ashamed of himself. He ought to have learned from Jethro what had happened to Angela. Jethro hadn't said a word of her fate. Was she being worked and beaten to death by his ex-mother-in-law? And he hadn't gone over his horses as he'd planned to do, but had walked off and left them with never a look at any save Beau.

He went first to Rachel's rockhouse. He wanted to see William David. It seemed a long time since he'd had a good look at him. In all the excitement of meeting Jethro and learning her master was alive Rachel might have neglected the baby.

He stepped under the overhang. William David was having the time of his life. Jethro, pretending to be a trotting horse, was going round and round with him on one shoulder. Jimmy stood in a corner and watched with a lonesome look. Little Brother, wearing his wolf skins but without quiver or bow, stood nearby, and was the first to see Leslie. He nodded, then looked overhead.

Whatever that meant, Leslie didn't know; he gave a quick nod in return, and after a long look at William David, considered Rachel. She seemed no kin of the woman he'd met down by the creek when he'd first come. No starving or mourning for her now. Her hair as always was tied up with the most of it under a cap, but now the cap was fashioned from a piece of pink ruffled cloth, fancy; more of the missus's torn-up underclothes he guessed. He saw with a feeling close to annoyance that the red woolen cloth he'd given her for a blanket had been made into a full-skirted petticoat. Also new were the spit curls by each ear.

She looked around, saw his glance, and lilted: "You've got some mighty fine help, Mr. Collins. He's cut wood fer us most a the day, and now he's taken care a your baby."

Jethro was looking at him; so was Jimmy. Leslie wished Rachel wouldn't say "your baby" when they were around. They might get notions.

Rachel gave a little gasp, for what he didn't know until she spoke, and he knew she'd forgotten what she'd planned to say first when she saw him. It was:

"Mr. Collins, I was terrible sorry to learn of the—untimely death of your wife and child. Nobody knows what the world will do to us next."

He thanked her, even though he was certain her words had come from Jethro and, in spite of trying, she hadn't been able to get the proper sorrow into her voice. "Your mistress and you must be happy hearen from your master."

"Lord, ain't it good to know he's not been killed, at least when he wrote. This letter must a been a long time finden us. The missus is so happy she's been cryen ever since she got it. He writes real often, but he's not seen the missus—been away off in New York—fer close to two years. I remember—I'd better be tenden to my victuals."

Leslie had backed to the overhang; Rachel would be telling him next the missus wanted to see him; she'd know he had more horses now. He reckoned he'd have to take her to Harrod's Station; from here the trip wouldn't be long or hard—provided the Indians let them through; but however easy the ride, the missus would be loudmouthed and quarrelsome; worse than usual. She'd be taking William David no matter what; she wouldn't like that. Worse, she'd heard from the wrong man.

He was past the overhang and out of the firelight. Only the dogs had noticed his going, and went with him to look over the horses. Twilight was thickening into darkness, but he could find them anyhow.

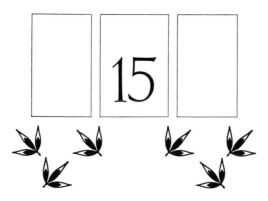

Jethro had fed the horses, but Leslie spent a long time with them, talking to each by turn as he felt hooves, shoes, backs, and mouths. Satisfied that all were well and in good spirits, he walked slowly back to his rockhouse with many stops to study the stars. He was in no hurry to read the letters Jimmy had brought.

Jethro had left the letters in a conspicuous place near the fire he'd built to give plenty of light. Leslie felt among the pile and took the three thin ones: two of these were from men claiming six square miles of land in the Blue Grass of Kentucky County, Virginia; they'd bought it from a land company, and now they wanted it surveyed. He shook his head; there wasn't any unclaimed, unsurveyed land in the Kentucky Blue Grass. The third wanted a survey made of twenty thousand acres "east of the Kentucky Trace and north of Cumberland River." He gave another head shake; insofar as he knew that land wasn't free of Indian title.

And anyhow, soon as he had all the powder he could get, he was heading for the South Carolina rebels. He remembered Little Brother. He reckoned he'd have to get him home. And what about William David?

He picked up two letters Jimmy had tied together. Each was sealed with what looked to be a thimble on tallow candle drip. The crabbed writing of his name with no Esquire gave certainty to his suspicion—the letters were from his mother-in-law. No, not any more.

He stood a moment and thought how good it would be to drop the letters unread into the fire and be done with the Hawkins crew forever. Reading didn't mean he'd answer; some of the "business" Jethro had mentioned might be in one.

He opened the first and waded through two pages of vilification: "Oh roo the day I let you cary off my darlen inosunt dauter.—alone, awl awl alone on her dethbed while you trapsed around the cuntry doen God knows what." He skipped several lines, but when he tried again, he read: "Alone awl awl alone to set by the dethbed of her sun."

He cursed, skipped everything until on the last page "100 lashes on her bear back" caught his eye. He struggled through the remainder of the letter without learning what had happened to Angela.

He flung the letter into the fire. An older anger tore through him. Slavery. It was a sin. He'd said so once to his brother Percy. That older brother was a toady, told their father. Leslie had been sent for; in the library his father had lectured him about how well slaves were treated, even the very old and the very young unable to work. Furthermore, slaves wouldn't be able to take care of themselves; their ancestors in their native land had been unable to do so and had been captured by other black tribes and sold to slave dealers.

His father had sent him from the room with no chance for rebuttal. He knew Leslie knew, as did everybody else know, of the piece of "gentry" two plantations down the river: that man bought green hands because they were cheap, then let his overseer beat some half to death because they didn't know how to strip tobacco either speedily or properly. What if Sadie had had a free hand with his help? He'd had to interfere more times than one and paid for it with hateful talk from her.

Forget it. Sadie was dead. Quit looking back. Reading this damned mail was looking back, and he had still another from that woman to be read. He needed a drink. The jug was in its accustomed place, but almost empty. It didn't matter. He had brought more than one jug.

The second letter from Mistress Hawkins was shorter than the other with the first pages taken up with a livery stable bill for nine horses for two weeks, plus what he took to be the copy of a farrier's bill for shoeing "said" nine horses, and also "without my cunsent 12 blank horse shues with nales."

He laid the bills aside and skimmed on, half his mind wondering where the horses had been the rest of the time, the other half hunting the names of his help. He only found: "I'm sartin your slave had somethin to do with stealen our horses and yurn. It cud ha been a shiffless bound boy I had. He run off the same nite yure horses was stole an my bound gal. I think yure man had a hand in that; he wuz oful sleepy nex day. I know he stole my horses; he wuz gone when they wuz gone with a sight a tavern guds."

He read on to learn she had the law after "yure man" and when found he would be burned alive. He flung letter and bills into the fire, and was cutting a whang for William David's beads when Jethro came.

"Mr. Collins, can we have our business talk now, if you please? I'll spread it all out by the fire so you can see."

Leslie nodded, then asked: "Where's Angela, and what's this about stolen horses?"

Jethro chuckled. "Suh, you must a been readen the old woman's letters. Angie and the horses are all right here." He began to pull from his pockets a multitude of folded papers and deerskin pouches. Finished, he picked up a pouch and handed it to Leslie. "Here's that wedden gift from your Uncle Percy; recollect the missus sent it along with Angie."

Leslie thanked him. "And how did you know I'd put this behind a rock in the kitchen chimney?"

"And so that's where it was. That triflen Angie never would tell me. She just handed it to me not long after Miss Sadie died and while the old woman was still poken and pryen to see what she could carry off."

Jethro touched a deerskin bag. "This here's the gold watch

your great-uncle Colonel William Leslie give you a long time ago. I wore the chain and kept the watch padded in tow. All your firearms, shot pouches, powder horns, ammunition, and bullet molds are over there with the rest a your goods. This little pouch is money—I hope you don't mind Spanish dollars. I was offered a good price for three kegs of your whiskey by a man taken off down river for the Salines. I sold the new. The old woman took considerable, but I got most a that back. The rest is buried."

He hesitated and looked at Leslie. "I hope you don't mind. I give away the whiskey I got back from the old woman —excuse me, I mean Mistress Hawkins. You see the men in my encampment hadn't had so much as their little old rum ration in weeks; they was mighty thirsty."

Leslie nodded in approval, and Jethro continued:

"I had to go about a good deal, and to do that a person like myself has to have a pass. So all these little chits are what I wrote out with the date, the business I was on, and I signed em with your name. And I wrote one for the whiskey."

Leslie admired the passes. Jethro's flourishing script made him think of a lusty young grapevine.

"Here's one I didn't write. You asked after her, and I meant to give it to you first, but forgot."

Leslie took the paper and read that Amos Andrew Weaver, "the undersigned," had in his custody a young black female known by the name of Angela and the property of William David Leslie Collins. The undersigned was taking said black female to French Lick on the Cumberland, and keeping her there until her owner the said William David Leslie Collins should want her returned. "And for the said Angela's services in house and kitchen the said . . ."

Jethro, thinking he had finished, interrupted. "Here's the eight shillens Mr. Weaver sent you for her first two months' work. And Mr. Weaver didn't take that triflen black girl by force. She started screechen and hollerin when the old woman said she was to come with her; she'd teach her what work meant, she said. Angie upt and run off to Weaver's so she wouldn't have to go with me and the old woman." Jethro's voice was beginning to tremble.

Leslie tried to comfort him. "You know Angie was always afraid of the woods, and it's a long lonesome trip to the Hawkins tavern."

Jethro snorted. "How long and how lonesome is the trip to French Lick? And a dangerous trace people say."

Leslie wished he could think of some comforting thing to say that wouldn't go wrong like his first try. He wondered if Jethro ever cried. The man looked ready to do so now. You couldn't blame him. Nobody could say he'd lost Angie. He'd never had her. That wasn't to say he hadn't tried. He'd had his eye on her since she was a child. Leslie reckoned his mother had sent Angela with the thought that she and Jethro would make a nice couple; the girl was just about old enough to take a mate.

There'd been hope for Jethro until Angela laid eyes on Weaver's Saul; young, with fine teeth, mighty shoulders and fists, bred to the ax and the plow, handsome, with a ready smile and a fine voice that could outsing a pipe organ.

Worse for Jethro, the Weavers gave their help considerable freedom and lived close enough Saul could come visiting quite often. Sometimes of summer evenings after the work was done, Leslie would hear a redbird call from the barn when all other redbirds were asleep. Angela would be off, a red ribbon in her hair; Jethro would sit on his doorstep and play mournful tunes on his French harp.

"Lord, I've let my mind go off my business. I've not brought out all my passes. Here's a chit I wrote for travelen to the old man's station with the spindly legs and silver shoe buckles and the scripture verses rollen off his tongue—only they're not rollen now—like beaten biscuit from the rollers."

"You mean Jimmy's father's station?"

"I wasn't exactly aimen to go there, but my pass had to say someplace. And a good thing it was I did go, otherwise I might never a found you."

"Jethro, you've done well, real well to do all that dangerous travelen, a good many miles alone. Weren't you scared?"

"Lord yes. There's no word big enough to tell how scared I was the night I lit out for good from the old woman's place. Seemed like everthing I touched made a racket—Cupid chewed up one of her dogs; the gelden I was riden nickered to the mares behind me as I was goen out the gate, and the saddles creaked and squeaked uncommon loud. I kept feelen she or her man could hear the whiskey gluggen in one half-keg. She'd sold considerable in the tavern was why it wasn't full. I was certain that if I got caught she'd have me whipped to death or burned alive for stealen when I was only tryen to git back what belonged to you."

"She'd have heard from me and the law," Leslie said.

"That wouldn't a brought me back from the dead or give me new skin . . . I just remembered I forgot a real important paper." He fished in a pocket and brought out a paper, folded and sealed with what felt to Leslie to be the tip of a powder horn in wax.

"Now, please suh, don't go losen that. It's for your plow horses and Dolly; she was so close to foalen time I didn't think she ought to come such a long rough way."

"Well, where is she?"

"Dolly and your plow horses are in good hands where I've been most a the time since Miss Sadie died—that is after I got away from the old woman." He got up and put more wood on the fire, then squatted again, arms around his drawn-up knees. "It's all part a the story about that sweet-smellen soap I never did get to finish this mornen.

"When we got to the old—Mistress Hawkins' place, all nine a your horses loaded to the gills—I could a cried for Dolly—her old man looked me over and said I'd make good tavern help.

"I tried to tell him I'd do better in his stables—he's got a little livery business—and he told me to shut up before he took an ax handle to me. So, there I was doen mostly woman's work in the tavern, bowen and scrapen to any white trash that wanted somethen to eat or drink.

"All the country round about there in South Carolina was

in Loyalist hands. I was certain of that. The old man and the old woman had the same persuasion, else they wouldn't have had all that wine and brandy to sell and a barn full a horses to hire. And in the tavern I'd hear people drink to the health of His Majesty King George. I was hardly ever by myself in that tavern; the old man watched me like a hawk, but he was in the kitchen given the cook hell when four men come in; two was wearen red coats, and one of them said to me: 'Where's that little herd a horses your master's put up for hire?'

"I was tellen him I reckoned he'd find them in the stables when the old man come runnen in like he had a hornet up his ass. 'Have a drink on the house, gentlemen,' said he, 'and we'll talk business.' Then he told me to go empty the tavern horse trough and fill it with fresh water.

"Soon as I got out a the tavern, I lit for the barn to find the stable boy. I found him cleanen out a stable with a black eye. I forgot to tell you about him. He's a bound boy they treat somehen awful, and him not full growed, strange to the ways a the country, but a fair hand with horses. He had to sleep in the stable loft the way I did was how I got to know him.

" 'Keep your ears pinned back when the old man comes with two redcoats and two men,' I told him. 'They'll go to the pasture where you cain't foller, but you might hear somethin. I think the old man's aimen to let him have my master's horse-stock.'

"He didn't say nothen, just nodded, then as I was leaven he asked: 'Do you know where is Moccasin Swamp?'

"I thought a minute. I know that country pretty well from haven been there for a good spell. I told him I didn't think it was more'n fifteen or twenty miles to the southeast.

"He looked all around, then said in a real low voice, 'They's good men in that swamp and they don't wear red.' Then he turned around and started raken up manure like I was no-where about.

"The old woman come to watch me in the tavern, and I couldn't git away till late; after a while the old man got back. And was he ever mean mad about somethen. I didn't find out what ailed him until it was bedtime and I saw the bound boy in the barn. First thing he said was:

" 'I don't reckon he got any bones broke, but he sure was roughed up; got mud on that fancy red coat. He shook his fist at that big stallion you rode here, and he sez, "I'm comen back in two, three days with a soldier that knows how to manage a horse like you. He'll ride you or kill you." '

" 'Two, three days,' I said. 'Beau must know what's up. He's not generally mean enough to throw a good rider.'

" 'Don't blame him,' the bound boy says. 'He let em catch him. And he let me saddle him. But when the man tried to mount him he reared and he bucked, and when that redcoat was on the ground he bit and he pawed, and would a killed that man if the others hadn't run up and grabbed his bridle and swung on.'

" 'Where's my master's other horses?' I asked.

" 'Out in the pasture eaten corn.'

" 'And where's Beau?'

" 'In a stable eaten oats.'

" 'If he quieted down enough you could get him into a stable,' I says, 'I reckon he'll let me ride him.'

" 'I reckon he will,' he says. 'He let me saddle and unsaddle him. I can do it again. This time I'll use a clean blanket. When I unsaddled him I found two cockleburs on his blanket next his skin close together right under the saddle seat. But his skin's all right.'

"I never did figure out how that boy got em in the blanket without one a the men noticen. Anyhow, I got my paper and ink powder, excuse me, suh, it was some a yours I took, and wrote me out a couple a passes while the boy saddled Beau.

" 'Don't leave no tracks,' he says, 'and don't git lost,' and I was off.

"That was the finest ride I ever had. The moon was just comen up, and there was a pretty good road part a the way. Beau went like the wind. He behaved. He knowed I was tryen to save him. He didn't like the dark swamp when we got to it, but he kept goen. And I don't think he liked my singen, for as soon as I got into that black desert, full a water moccasins I was certain, I started singen loud as I could that song about George Washington.

"I hadn't gone but a little way through the muck and the mire, singen, when I heared a low mean voice say:

"'Halt and shut up or else.'

"I stopped Beau, then the same voice said: 'What a you doen in this swamp?'

"'Hunten,' I said.

"'And what might you be hunten?' he says.

"'Foxes,' I told him.

"'Foxes don't live in swamps,' he says.

"'Red foxes don't, but there's another kind that does,' I told him. Beau was gitten mighty restless, and I wasn't certain the man was a rebel. At least I'd never seen him in the two years I was fighten in and around that part a the country. I could hear men whisperen together. The best I could tell they thought I was tryen to trick em by singen that rebel song. Then somebody asked me my name and my master.

"I told them, and was about to tell what was goen to happen to your horses, when they had me dismount and lead Beau to a shutaway camp. Some of the first ones knowed you, and at the camp one man remembered me.

"I didn't aim for daylight to catch me on the road back, so I didn't stay any longer than it took me to tell em the red-coats was aimen to take your horsestock. They offered me a fresh mount, but Beau wouldn't lead. A man rode back with me; said he'd scout the place, then bring back a bunch to meet me and get your horsestock the next night before moonrise.

"They come. Easiest piece a work you ever saw, only when we was in the stables the bound boy jumped out a the hay-loft. 'I'm comen, too,' says he. Well, they'd hardly agreed to take him before the bound girl jumped out a the hay. 'And take me, too,' she said.

"'A girl that runs from home and friend will come to some bad end,' one a the men said.

"'I've got no home and I've got no friend, and as for my

end it couldn't be no worse. I'll be a camp follower,' she says.

" 'And do you know what a camp follower does, little girl?' one of the men asked.

" 'Don't call me little girl. I'm nigh fifteen years old; I can wash clothes and tend the wounded like any other camp follower.'

" 'But that's not all they do,' one a the men said. 'And anyhow we've got no women with us down in the swamp.'

" 'All the more reason to take me. And quit rollen your eyes and take that smirky look off your face. I don't come here to lay in the hay with that boy, but I got out a that awful loft room, hot as blazes, because sleepen is better down here.'

" 'Could you sneak back?'

" 'Yes, but I'm not aimen to now.'

"The men looked at each other. 'She might come in handy with that sometime,' one said.

"Well, they took your saddles and anything else they needed, fixed your horsestock, laid down the fence in a good hard spot, and was off.

"The most a next day I couldn't work for laughen. First thing I heared next mornen was the old woman screamen for the girl to redden up the fires. Pretty soon the old man learned the boy was missen and rode off for bloodhounds. They was the meanest looken hounds I've ever seen, but no good; Cupid handled em both when they growled at him.

"They give the hounds a ragged dress belongen to the girl to smell; they trailed her to the let-down fence. The old man and woman went crazy; they'd jist learned your horses they was aimen to make some money on was gone.

"The hounds went crazy, runnen round and round, snarlen and carryen on, but pretty soon they started bayen fer all they was worth, but they took off in different directions. Like I said them hounds wasn't real bloodhounds else they wouldn't a gone after bear scent, and fox scent, and wolf; I almost forgot the wolf stockings; you know how to fix a horse you're aimen to—procure; you put stockings on his hooves so he won't leave no tracks; but they just smeared Beau's feet with bear oil.

"Them fool hounds followed that scent for miles—the rebels had rode off in the opposite direction from Moccasin Swamp till they got to a good-sized creek; they rode in the water aways and while they was still in the water they took off the horses' stockings and washed their hooves with turpentine to kill the smell."

Jethro got up. "I've wore you out with listenen and my tongue out with tellen."

"But how did you get away; you said you were scared to death."

"And scared I was. They come for me in two nights. The old man and woman was still hunten your horses when the rebels got back with the bound boy and girl and plenty a empty sacks. The boy showed the men the oats and corn bins, and while they sprung the locks, the bound girl snuck into the house and unbarred the tavern door so I could get your whiskey and some brandy and wine the men wanted—one was standen outside so I could reach stuff out to him.

"Then the girl got me into the larder and the smokehouse where we got all the ham and other victuals we thought the horses could take.

"By the time we got back to the stables, all the horsestock was saddled and ready to go, ever one but the ones for victuals had a bushel a shelled corn or two bushel of oats; and all wearen stockens or fixed with bear's grease. I rode ten miles or more before I could say a word. I was that scared."

"Jethro, are you sayen you took all the horses in the Hawkins' stables and feed into the bargain?"

"Naturally, Mr. Collins. And three belongen to redcoat cavalry officers that had half stoned themselves at supper that night from drinken toasts to King George."

"Jethro, don't you think taken all my ex-father-in-law's horses was—well, kind of raw?"

"Procurement, suh, is raw work. And recollect if we'd been Loyalists helpen ourselves to rebel goods, we'd a done worse, maybe burned the place. I'd better be gitten back to see if I can help Rachel. She's mighty busy with work and your pore little baby."

Leslie shook his head over the last words, but only said: "Stay long enough to pick up your money."

"My money?"

"Yes, you earned it, little enough for saven my horsestock. Go on. Pick it up."

Jethro hesitated. "I'm pretty well off. I got a fine Spanish cavalry saddle, provender, and ten shillings when I left to hunt you. I thought you'd read the letter in the Bible and learn I was goen to try to go back to the war; and then you'd come."

He squatted again, and one by one slowly picked up the coins. "I'll take it all but Angie's hire, and the sack of guineas from your father the missus sent with Angie." He looked at Leslie. "I've been kinda hopen you'd tell me somethen about back home. The master and the missus all right?"

"How would I know?"

"The missus must a sent you blank paper. It was a big fat letter. I put it in a special place over here by your whiskey jug where you'd be certain to see it." Jethro reached the letter ahead of Leslie, and picked it up. "Why, here it is, not so much as opened, and I told you first thing you had a letter from the missus."

Leslie looked at the letter: his father's seal, but addressed in his mother's hand. His father was dead, killed fighting for his king and England. He shivered as he broke the seal.

"My dear Son
I can only hope you receive this letter. We" . . . That meant his father was alive. How long ago? September 27 was the date. Did she know what he had done at the Battle of Camden? "have not had a line from you these two years. We wonder if you have received our letters. We wrote to the Illinois where we had heard you were, but lately we learned that you with other Valiant Men are defending our Western Frontiers."

His father must not be a Loyalist after all.

"My sorrow and sense of Bereavement are in no wise diminished, but you, if you be alive, are a source of comfort as well as Pride. It comes to my mind that you do not even know about your Brothers. My letter with that sad news never reached you, I fear. Their loss is not easily borne, but—"

Good God, his own brother Percy had died from the wound he'd given him, and somebody else had killed the other. He had no brothers left. He stared at nothing for a time before getting up courage to continue with the letter.

"In spite of the burning of Norfolk and other atrocities here in Virginia, Arnold's treachery, the mutiny of the Connecticut Line, the Cowardice of General Gates, the loss of Charles Town, and other Defeats, your Father's admiration for General Washington grows. He thinks a lesser man would long ago have given up in spite of many stout-hearted followers. Your Father scoffs at the notion held by many who ought to know better that General Washington plans to be our king when Victory is ours.

"Thus we continue to go deeply into our means to help outfit a regiment. He left me, his home, his plantation, and took the horses he holds so dear to go as a Colonel."

Leslie sprang up, ran halfway to Rachel's rockhouse, turned back; he reckoned he'd meant to tell Jethro; he didn't know; he ran back to his rockhouse, and stopped when the dogs reminded him he was cavorting around like a silly school boy. Thunder had jumped up, wanting to join in the play, but Cupid lay motionless and looked at him with more scorn than puzzlement. "You could at least get up and wag your tail for such a grand old boy," Leslie told him. "He ought to be a general. And my mother is worthy to be the squaw of a Cherokee chief."

Cupid answered with one flap of his tail. Leslie built up the fire to make more light and returned to the letter. Reading his mother's script was slow going; she'd never got over her education. Her penmanship had even more curlicues than Jethro's; the actual letters were often lost in the flourishes. She also wrote as if she had studied the art of circumlocution. He was not interested in the weather and the neighbors; he wanted to learn of his brothers. He stopped skipping around when he found:

". . . and though it happened years ago and I in time

wrote you the Sad News in a letter that came back to us, it is still fresh in my Mind and hence I write to you who do not know.

"I was walking one morning in the garden when Percy and Francis came to me. They were splendidly arrayed in officers' uniforms of the King's Army, but I considered their Happy Faces not their garments.

"Your Father came. He, too, was in military dress, but very different from that of his Sons. I cannot yet believe what followed. Your Father on seeing his Sons stopped on the other side of the fountain and looked, but with no smile or word of greeting. Rather, his Countenance was that of one who looks at an Enemy.

"Percy said 'Father' and ran toward him. Your Father only looked with that Terrible Look at Percy's uniform, but Percy continued on as if he would take his hand.

"Your Father gripped the Hilt of his Sword. 'I am no longer a Father to either of you, Traitors as you are to the Cause of Freedom. Greet your Mother, then go. You never more shall be my Sons.' He left us in the garden alone."

Leslie read on to learn he had struck their names from the family Bible. He next learned that the names of his two sisters, their husbands, and children had also been stricken because his brothers-in-law were Tories. "Alas, I have no little ones to visit me, no grandchildren to brighten my declining years."

He stopped to consider. Judging from the ages of his still-living grandparents, his father and mother had thirty or forty "declining years" left. His father, or so he had learned in stray remarks of the older help, had sown his wild oats thick, quick, and early, then married young. His mother would be younger, hardly fifty, young enough to bring up a grandchild and have great-grandchildren.

Hastily, with considerable skipping, he read an account of the troubles planters were having: tobacco waiting in casks to be shipped, but no shipping; shortages of help on the plantations because their masters, "as has your Father," had taken their cobblers, farriers, coachmen, saddlers, wheelwrights, coopers, and even stablemen because their work was needed in the war.

They were trying to grow hemp and cotton, but the land, she thought, was too worn out for either, and "your Father thinks our lands are too depleted by tobacco. He thinks there is a great future in Western Lands. As soon as we have won the War we plan to Emigrate with all our goods and chattels to some fair boundary of land in either what is now called Kentucky County, Virginia, or to a place in Western North Carolina known as the Great French Lick on the Cumberland. There is also Natchez where many are going, but your father as yet has acquired no land there.

"Your Father thinks that before too many Years have passed, our New Country will have by some means acquired all the Territory south to the Ocean and also that beyond the Illinois and on to the Western Ocean."

Leslie gave a low whistle as he looked beyond the rockhouse into the dark. That was his thought, and he had believed he held it alone. Did his father mean that in the years ahead settlers would cross the white-topped mountains that had held him back and settle in the valleys beyond? Well, he'd be there too, someday. First he'd help win the war. Then, after he had taken Little Brother home, he'd go on across the mountains and settle in some pleasant valley near the sea. Now, he'd soon be back with Marion's men; it was fine to know he would be fighting on the same side as his father.

He stared a long while before going back to the letter, and what he read next was only the small talk of a woman of wealth. She wondered if he dressed after the fashion of the "Overmountain Sharp Shooters" as described by his father. "These wonderful soldiers wear long-tailed shirts, somewhat in the style of a butcher's smock, but belted, with pockets, and made of coarse cloth or deerskin. Their footgear is made after the Indian fashion, and there is not among them a wig or even a properly styled head of hair. Each carries an uncommonly long and curiously made musket your father tells me is called a rifle. He sets great store by these men." He skipped the praise and the secondhand account of "unbelievably good marksmanship" with examples, but the next lines stopped him. "Your Father sends his Love with my Love for the only child left to us, wherever you may be. If God has yet spared you to the living, we would like very much to see you and your Baby. Surely you have one by now. In any case do come back to stay at least awhile. Your Father is eager to talk with you, and do bring the Baby we hope you have by now."

His mother didn't know he was a cuckold. And was his mother his father's mouthpiece, inviting him to become a prodigal son? Come home and go with them to a new plantation where he would become a great planter and horse breeder with more than two hundred slaves and an overseer or two to do the dirty work of getting the most work for the least cost? No thank you. He returned to the letter; he'd declined an offer that hadn't been made. Not a word was said about bringing his wife, and they didn't know she was dead.

His mother hoped Angela and Jethro were happy and serving him well, and last: "We hope you are in health, and will take all precautions possible in the dangerous Life you lead. Your Father feels that you and others who protect our borders and have wrested the Illinois from the British have done and are doing a Great Thing. He is indeed very proud of you."

He laughed so hard the last line blurred; it didn't matter, mostly begging him to write and a hope for God's blessing on him. So, for the first time in his life, except when he did well in school, his father was proud of him, actually proud. And he hadn't tried to please him.

He sat and stared at nothing until he felt the night chill and saw the fire had burned to nothing but embers pale under ashes. He refolded the letter, put it in a crevice in the stone, banked the fire, told Cupid and Thunder good night, then, carrying his bearskin and a blanket, went out to his sleeping rock. The night was cold and still with the creek fog thin and low; the waning moon had not yet risen so that the stars unsmirched by fog or cloud had the sky all to themselves.

He wished he could see the North Star, but whether he saw it or no, it was always there in the same place. And it was good to know that though the other stars moved, their roads were always the same so that on a clear, moonless night a man could tell the time and season from the stars.

People, the most of them, were not like the stars. Had his father been a star he would have stood high in the northeast one midnight; a year later you'd find him in another constellation southwest by south at midnight. How could he cast off his grown children because they had been true to England? That had been bred in them from birth: special prayers at church for the King's Majesty and the Royal Family; all that had gone into their minds and hearts had come from England along with their clothing, house furniture, books, money, law, and dainties for the table. Even their wines from other countries had traveled in English ships. The boys had been educated in England; the girls given long visits in London, all done to breed English ladies and gentlemen.

Now, because they had lived up to their teachings, they were cast out. And his mother grieved for a grandchild. It sure was one hell of a world; his mother wanting a grandchild and little William David with nobody to care whether he lived or died. Rachel did, but in the end she'd have no way out but to do the will of the missus. Right now the baby was doing real well on cow's milk.

Cow's milk? He sat up. Jethro thought milk from a sick cow had killed Sadie and little Watts. That seemed foolish to him, but there was no sense in taking a chance on William David's life. He ought to have given the cow a good going-over soon as he'd heard the news.

He put on his shoepacs, and, with the bearskin over his shoulders, felt his way through the dark to the calf pen where he thought the cow might be. At the lower corner of the pen he stopped to listen. How did a man know when a cow was sick? He knew nothing of cows; dairying was woman's work. Did a cow's nose get warm and dry like a dog's? He heard nothing, took a few more steps and stopped again. This time he heard the faint slurping grind of chewing. That meant she was chewing her cud. He'd heard no sound of grazing. A cow was a ruminant like a deer; she'd graze, then belch up her food and chew it while she rested. A cow couldn't be bad off if she ate so much during the day she had to spend half the night chewing it. The chewing stopped. He waited. He thought he heard a belch. Then, as if to oblige him, she started chewing again.

He'd heard Sadie say a cow was all right long as she chewed her cud. Still, he'd like to feel her nose. He was at the wrong end for that. He was moving closer when she gave him a hard slap across the face with her tail, and ran toward the creek. He rubbed his face and looked at the stars. A cow that could do that had nothing wrong with her, but from now on he'd give her a good going-over night and morning.

Except for Sadie it had been a lucky day. The stars said tomorrow's weather would be fine, a good day for work. He'd work like holy hell to make saltpeter to get a good deal for himself to make into powder to take to the rebels. And while he worked, he would think on a letter to his mother.

16

Early next morning he found the cow grazing. She let him get in a quick feel of her nose before running away, frisky as a pup. She was all right.

Daniel, though not exactly frisky, was in fine spirits, singing or whistling while he worked—until he remembered Leslie was a man of sorrow.

Leslie also found it difficult to think of himself as a grieving widower and father. Instead, he thought of his mother's letter and his father, a rebel like himself. Working with Daniel, he had little opportunity to think on his answer to the letter. Still, he was happy in the work, all of it done to make saltpeter for the hard-pressed French Lick settlers. Today even the dirty work of cleaning out, relining, and refilling the ash hopper didn't seem as bad as usual.

They were following Equo's zigzag course up from the creek when Daniel forgot again, and turned to Leslie to sing: "I'll sing you a song."

Leslie, glad of an excuse to sing the old song, sang the question: "And what will be your song?"

Daniel sang the answer; stopped; Leslie sang the question, and the two of them went singing up the hill. Daniel had reached: "Twelve of the twelve apostles, eleven of the eleven that went to heaven, ten of the ten commandments, nine oh nine how bright they shine, and eight of the Gabriel angels," when Leslie heard beyond the song a sound that always stirred his blood more than any music by mortal man.

Wild geese were going south; two long strings met to form a wavering V high in the sky. They brought back the unanswered questions of childhood; how did they know that in the north hard cold was on the way to freeze their lakes and rivers, and how had they learned the way; did the old ones remember and tell the young? And with his wonders on the how and why had been their commands, given in sorrow, but still commands, to get up and go as they were going, follow them.

He had followed, done more than follow; he'd been south, north, east, and west, but his going had never eased their sorrow or his restlessness—until now. He was old. The wild desire to see the world, measure himself against it was gone. Now, he wanted to turn back, go home, then back to the rebellion in South Carolina. His thoughts were interrupted by Daniel's blessings on the geese, then:

"Good luck on your long journey, my brave ones. And save your breath. No need to tell me to go. I'm goen south, but not so far as you; soon as I finish saltpeter maken, I'm goen."

He watched with Leslie until the geese were out of sight and sound. They had reached the saltpeter cave and Daniel had bent to unhitch the sled when he seemed to forget what he was about as he straightened to look in the direction of the vanished geese. He turned at last to Leslie. "You know what I've done. I've told them geese the wrong thing; and they believed me. I cain't leave this place and head south soon as I finish maken saltpeter. I've got to stay till Gideon Huccaby comes up from French Lick for saltpeter. I might have to wait here all winter."

"Maybe not," Leslie told him, "but supposen you do. There'll be other flocks passen by, and you can tell the leader of one to tell the leader of this flock when they meet that you told him you had misspoken."

Daniel nodded, happy again. "That I'll do." The geese and the press of work appeared to make him forget that Leslie was a man of sorrow to be treated with solicitude and cheered with conversation and song. It was not until they had emptied and refilled the ash hopper and were digging niter dirt for the next batch that Daniel's solicitude returned. It took the form of plans for an "extra-early supper, so you can look over your horses and get a good rest."

Leslie didn't feel the need of a rest; he'd looked over his horses; Jethro had done a good job taking care of them, and would keep on doing it. Still, he was pleased; he'd use the extra time alone to think on his letter—if he wrote one. He might visit instead.

He walked slowly back through the early twilight, thinking; by the time he'd reached the creek crossing, he had decided against the visit. It wasn't right to go larking over the country when the rebellion needed him in South Carolina. He'd make his visit when the war was won.

The letter was uppermost in his mind as he hunted the cow. It wouldn't be going to a happy place: his mother grieving for her lost children and grandchildren; sorrowing because she must leave Sea Winds, the place she had come to as a bride; but she could never weep, not before his father, stony-faced with anger at his children and some disgraced leaders of the rebellion. He'd have to write of the death of little Watts; more grief for his mother; she'd think of him as a grandchild, not a bastard.

He'd found the cow, and since she showed no sign of ill health, he hurried on to his rockhouse. Tonight, he'd make a first draft of the pleasant parts, tell of the country he'd seen.

He was settled in his rockhouse, quill flying to describe the country round about the Great French Lick, when he saw the dogs get up and start for the overhang. Now what?

A moment later he saw a flash of red, and Rachel called: "Can I speak to you a minute, Mr. Collins?"

"Come in." He told himself he'd given her the red cloth; she had the right to make a petticoat of it to wear whenever she wished. Still, the sight of it irritated him. Sadie had wanted a red cloak so long; he wished he'd bought the cloth when she'd first asked.

"Mr. Collins, the missus wants to see you real bad."

"Tell her I'll come as soon as I finish this letter. How's William David?"

"Fine as could be. Jethro, he's the nicest man, carries him when he cries and I'm busy."

She was gone and he looked at what he had just written: "many fine savannahs where" . . . Where what? He'd forgotten what he meant to say. He swore. The prospect of another talk with that damned woman had driven the letter out of his head. Now he couldn't plead a scarcity of horses as the reason for not taking her. The best thing might be to get her out of the way as soon as possible. He stopped. A Kentucky station short on everything except enemy Indians was no place for William David.

He took his time about going, and as usual stopped at the outside of her rockhouse to call.

This time, she came running. "Mr. Collins at last. I'm so glad you've come." She held out her hand. He took it, and she didn't let him loose until she had him sitting by the fire and she was spread out on a bedspread over a stack of featherbeds. Nearby on a jut of rock two wax candles flamed.

She ought, when somebody was around to see her, to stay away from strong light. The flaming candles brought out the wrinkles on her neck and around her mouth; they showed her pale eyes, ugly red and swollen from weeping. And why not? She'd had word from her husband instead of her lover. There was a quaver in her voice as she said:

"Please, come closer. I'm too weak to talk loud."

"I can hear you, maam."

She sat up, shook back her hair, and bent toward him, close enough to shower him with the smell of perfume. "Mr. Collins, I must get away from here at once, away from that Indian. I am certain from the way he looks at me he wants to violate me, then kill me."

"Maam, he's a good Indian. Don't you remember he helped save you and all of Weaver's party?"

"Fiddlesticks. The only good Indian is a dead Indian, as my father used to say. Why, he tried to kill me this forenoon. They're all against me; that's why you haven't heard." And with no question or encouragement from him, she launched into her tale.

First, several details on her own weak condition and the hardships she was undergoing: Rachel's cooking was killing her and she was getting feisty, not obeying as she ought; something would have to be done about "that black"; but Rachel was not threatening her life or worse like the Indian; each time he passed her rockhouse he'd never say a word, just stop and stare.

Leslie eventually managed to get in a word. "Maam, I reckon I could get you to a Kentucky settlement, maybe with our scalps, maybe not, but—"

"Don't talk to me of scalps and scalpings, just tales. I've heard them all my life, and never saw an Indian in Philadelphia. And that's the place I want to go to, not Kentucky.

"My husband," she went on when he said nothing, "will be home soon. I want to be there when he comes, but if"—her eyes had grown glassy with tears, and her next words were broken apart with sobs— "if . . . I don't get away . . . from this place . . . quick . . . I'll be dead."

Leslie pushed a fallen-away chunk into the fire. Well, one herring in the net was worth a whale in the sea. Lover lost, she'd go back to her husband. She could, he reckoned, ride partway with him and Jethro—if she kept quiet. "I can manage to get you through the mountains, I guess," he told her, and started to go.

She caught his arm. "But soon. It must be soon. I've not told you what they did to me this morning."

He swore under his breath as he squatted near the fire to listen. She was back on her bodily weakness when he noticed a short length of split poplar had fallen away from the fire. Jethro, he reckoned, had cut that; he ought to know better than to waste a pretty poplar on firewood; there was no heat in a poplar. He picked it up, scraped off the charcoal, and went to work on it with his knife. William David would soon be big enough for a jumping jack, and poplar was good wood for a baby; it didn't splinter.

He wondered how a woman with her kind of chopped,

quick-worded talk could take forever to tell a story that in the end was nothing but the horseplay of two boys feeling their oats. He wished he could have seen—and heard—it for: "I screamed, and I screamed when that monster jumped at me from the bushes. Rachel as always was fooling with that baby. I ran. I stumbled and fell; the monster was almost on top of me. I thought I'd faint. And all the time I could hear that young man, Jimmy, the heathen, laughing at a poor, pitiful, frightened woman. As I neared Rachel's kitchen in the rock, he yelled at me: 'Don't take it so hard, maam; it's Little Brother wearen a buffalo skull and a sheet.' Skulls don't have hair and horns, do they?"

"Depends on the buzzards," Leslie answered, and got up.

"And you will take me soon, real soon?"

"Soon as I can." He started outside.

She caught his arm. "And can we travel as fast as my strength will allow? The party coming out was awful slow. You know at night they'd stop early so they could round up their precious cows and milk. And they never went faster than a cow could go."

He pushed back his hat and looked at her. "You're forgetten we'll have a cow. The baby can't live without one."

She looked toward the front of the rockhouse, then drew closer, whispering: "There won't be any baby."

"And where will he be? You can't leave him here. He'd die."

"And whose business is that?" Angry again, she let her voice rise. "Don't look at me like that. You're not Jesus Christ. You've killed men, many men, haven't you?"

His voice didn't want to come, and when words came they were hoarse. "I've killed only men tryen to kill me or a mate."

She remembered to whisper. "If you hadn't come along when you did that baby would have been dead anyway in a few more days. How Rachel keeps it alive now I don't know. She pays no attention whatever to me when I tell her it's a waste of time to fool with it. Nobody can raise a baby without a wet nurse. And I'm not one."

She stopped as if expecting Leslie to speak. He didn't.

216

"Be sensible," she whispered. "It would die on the way anyhow, and I'm not asking you to do anything. Just leave it. Something could happen to it. Babies often die from accidents. You could—well—make one happen. Rachel trusts you. The bitch won't let me get close to the brat."

Leslie turned away, hands clenched, insides writhing into knots as he headed outdoors. Her voice followed:

"You're too chicken-livered, but I'll manage. I'll do it. . . . Don't you want ten guineas in advance to take me?"

"Not now, maam." Hard to get the words out. Hard to say anything.

He reached his rockhouse and saw the letter he had started to his mother. The words he'd had in his head were gone. He went to the jug of whiskey, but after a long drink he could think of nothing but his mother's sorrow when she learned he had no grandchild for her, and the yellow-headed woman eager to do away with her fine little son.

He was whittling an arm for the jumping jack when Jimmy came. Leslie apologized for not thanking him sooner for spreading word of his missing wife and horsestock.

"Oh, I had a good time riden over the country with Granpa. And he did, too. I thought I'd better tell you about Little Brother. It wasn't all him; part of it was my doen. We didn't mean any harm, but Lord if she'd had a gun she could shoot she'd a killed us on the spot."

"Just Little Brother, I reckon," Leslie said, then added: "I hope you've had word from your Uncle Matthew and your people are all well."

"Granpa's feisty as a young coon dog after he's caught his first coon. He's moven to down around Natchez—maybe already gone—and he took my little sister, but told me I belonged to stay with my dear, sick, flesh-and-blood father." Jimmy stopped, face turned aside, and when he again talked he had mastered the quaver in his voice.

"And nothen ails my dear, sick flesh and blood but he's had the Timothies a good many times too many. He fell on the floor and couldn't git up. That was on the day after the big victory celebration. Recollect, it was comen on when you

217

visited us. And he's not been out a bed since; there's about half a himself he cain't make work, but he can still holler for liquor and scream for somebody to come kill the rattlesnakes in his bed and drive out the bull buffalo that's got its head stuck through the door."

"His sickness makes it hard on Miss Nancy. You can't fault your granpa for feelen your place is with her at a time like this."

"Place. I've got no place. And as for Aunt-mama Nancy, she's never had it easier; nothen to do but set and knit lace if she wants to. Ever old bachelor and widow man for miles around flocked in soon as they learned the old man was on what looked to be his deathbed. 'Miss Nancy, that butter's too heavy fer you to carry to the springhouse. I'll take it and bring back some fresh water.' 'Miss Nancy, don't wear yourself out tenden the sick; that's a man's job anyhow; you're too weakly to turn him.' 'Miss Nancy, don't worry your head about victuals for me. The kitchen's full a your neighbors' pies and cakes—you've got mighty good neighbors—and I've brought a biled ham.'"

Each voice Jimmy mimicked had been different, the last a growling bass, and in none had there been a quaver, but it was back as he said: "It's Miss Nancy this and Miss Nancy that, all sayen they've come to help with the sick, but ever last one a them bucks is tryen to court her on the sly, and a hurryen Paw's end by given him whiskey ever time he asks. Miss Nancy don't need me. I'm in the way. There's no reason why I couldn't a gone with Granpa. Well, I don't mind losen him so much, but it's Granma and Cissy and Matthew."

Jimmy's quaver was worse and his eyes too bright. Leslie got up, said he needed more whittling wood and he'd have to look for it; just a length of poplar, but he'd forgotten where he put it.

The piece of poplar was by the jug of whiskey where he'd put it down to take a drink, but he rummaged around a bit. He didn't want to see Jimmy cry. The boy thought of himself as a man; he thought men never cried. He had a lot to learn. He thought he had no home, and had come to William David Leslie

Collins, a homeless son of a bitch getting old and tired of wandering over the world. He couldn't teach Jimmy anything. All he knew was that living could be a lonesome business even in a crowd, the way a wild goose sounded lonesome in the sky, going with others of its kind where it wanted to go. And a man had to learn that for himself.

Leslie's glance had happened upon a small kettle. "Jimmy, I think I feel a cold comen on. Would you drink a little hot toddy if I made some?"

"A little I reckon, thank you, but don't make much for me. I don't aim to start down that road Paw took."

"You won't," Leslie told him. "Sons don't often take after their fathers." Jimmy had sounded more like himself, and by the time Leslie had found the ginger and nutmeg Jethro had sneaked out to bring him, the boy wanted to talk.

"I hope I didn't give you the wrong notion about Granpa. He's not leaven his house and his land and the most of his kin just because he's come down with the moven fever." Anger appeared to have taken the place of sorrow when, after a long study of the fire, he said: "Two, three days after you visited us and Matthew was home, a party a men rode up; they called out for him to come to the gate, for some talk they said. Granpa wouldn't go; not fitten, he said; he'd listen to their talk in his own house, he sent word by me; I was there.

"So they all come into the house. Not a stranger amongst em, but they acted like they'd never seen Granpa before. They hemmed and they hawed awhile before they could get up the face to tell Granpa they'd heared he was harboren a Tory. One said that looked bad, real bad, so to clear hissef Granpa must take the Oath of Allegiance.

"Granpa wanted to know to who and to what. The oath I mean.

" 'To our new country,' one said. Accorden to that bastard, all Granpa had to do was swear on the Bible he'd never again have dealens with a Tory, but would be faithful to his country.

" 'What a you call faithful to a country?' Granpa wanted to know.

" 'Fighten in her wars,' one a them said.

" 'I've been fighten on her borders for close to forty years,' Granpa said.

" 'That kind a fighten don't count. You was just fighten for people, kin and neighbors mostly, I bet,' one a the blackguards said. I know. I was there.

" 'What is a country if it's not people?' Granpa wanted to know.

"They thought awhile and finally one said: 'A country is the government, the people that runs it.'

" 'George Washington send you?' Granpa wanted to know.

"They shook their heads at that and agin when Granpa asked if John Sevier had sent them. They kept tellen Granpa he'd have to take the oath.

"Granpa stood up. 'Taken this oath you want makes it look like that without the oath, I have been or will be a traitor.'

" 'You'll take that oath—or else,' one a the blackguards said.

" 'I'll take the else,' Granpa said. He was cutten a fresh chew. Granma never stopped runnen the little spinnen wheel in the back corner. It didn't make so much noise but she could hear. The men got up to go and she invited them to stay for dinner. I know. I was there."

Jimmy didn't know tears were running down his cheeks. Leslie got up to mix the toddy; the water was hot. Mixing, he swore the blackest oaths that would come to his tongue; the yellow-headed woman's "but there'll be no baby" had never left the top of his mind, and with her now were the bastards who'd driven Mr. Saufley out of the country, mostly he reckoned because the old man loved his son.

Jimmy took a sip or so of the toddy, then said with no tears: "I wish we was in a place where I could do target practice. I need to be the best shot in the country."

"It'll take some doen to beat Michael Stoner," Leslie told him, and looked at the fire so as not to see Jimmy's eyes. They looked the way Daniel's did sometimes.

"Leslie?"

"Yes."

"Do you think Matthew's a coward because he didn't fight

at Kings Mountain—or anyplace else insofar as I know? Well, if you do think it, don't. Nobody knows but Granpa and Granma and me that he's got a Tory sweetheart on the other side a the mountains. Her people are Tories, or Loyalists, I mean."

"I never thought Matthew a coward. I fought with him when your station was attacked."

"And you don't think Granpa was a coward for not stayen and taken the else? He wanted to, but Granma and Matthew was both after him to go. Matthew has been down there, and said he was goen with or without Granpa. I think his sweetheart and her people are goen. Lord, I'd sure like to be at the wedden."

"You know, I know, and everybody knows your grandfather is no coward. You oughtn't to ask such foolish questions," Leslie told him with some heat. He had started to catalogue, with the hope of destroying Jimmy's doubt, some of the many exploits of his grandfather, when the dogs ran out, tails wagging.

They returned with Jethro. Leslie offered him toddy and a seat by the fire. Jethro thanked him and declined both. "I just come," he explained, "to see if there was anything you wanted me to do. Rachel said you was doen mighty hard work over the ridge maken saltpeter. Couldn't I come, too? I cut enough wood today to last a spell."

"We're about finished maken saltpeter and the hard work is all done, but there's plenty to do here," Leslie told him. He mentioned several of his jobs: feed and curry the horses, tend the fires, help Rachel with the calf at milking time, and anything else she had trouble in doing. "But the most important thing is watch over Rachel and the baby. There are varmints all around —I saw wild hog sign not long ago—and when Rachel has to go tend her missus, you stay close to the baby. And when her missus takes a walk, keep her in sight. One more thing. When the cow doesn't come at milken time, you go hunt her, not Rachel."

Jethro smiled. "Be kind a nice to be a cowboy agin."

"I didn't know you'd ever been a cowboy. Tell us about it," Leslie suggested.

Jethro folded his long legs into squatting position near the fire. "I'll have to begin with Mistress Haggard. She, like a lot a the wives, would ride over real often, mostly at night so no Tory would see where they was goen. Well, she was riden along by herself one moonlit night, and when she was ten, twelve miles from our camp, she run into a drove a beeves taken up the whole road. She couldn't do nothen but slow down and amble along. One a the drovers come up to her. He took off his hat, and was real polite when he said: 'Maam, me and my buddy here and these beeves we're all from Pennsylvanie. So we don't know this country. The owner of these beeves told us to deliver them to Tarleton's camp, or a bunch of his men.' "

Jethro rocked back and forth laughing so hard, it was difficult to follow his story. Mistress Haggard told the drovers Tarleton's men were camped close, maybe no more than ten or twelve miles; all they had to do was keep on this road till they got to a thicket of live oaks, and then turn right. She'd ride with them, at least partway, but she was in a hurry to get to her sick mother-in-law.

" 'The old lady's mighty sick,' she told them drovers. 'Wouldn't you men like a snack from these victuals I'm carryen? She's too sick to cook and not much on eaten. I've got a lot more here than she'll need.'

"The drovers was mighty glad to get some victuals. They let her through, and as she was riden away, she told them, 'Now, there might be somebody from Tarleton's camp at my mother-in-law's. If there is, I'll send him to get help for you. You must be tired walken so far.'

"When she'd got a little way ahead—the drovers had stopped to eat her victuals—she turned left and rode like hell.

"A party a scouts had just got in, and I was rubben down their horses when I heared a curious noise back on the edge a the swamp. I offered to go see what it was, but Captain Haggard said it was his wife tryen to sound like a loon, that was the signal for a friend or member; and he said that if that woman didn't learn to make a loon call better than that, she'd have to quit visiten him.

"Captain Haggard sounded mad when he left, but he sure didn't sound that way when he come runnen back. 'Beeves, boys,' he said. 'Two or three a you get into some red coats.

They're all too skimpy for me. Recollect these beeves had started to Tarleton's gang.'

"The bound boy and me rode with em. The drovers was real glad to see us. Most a the talken was done by one man in a red coat. 'And,' he finished off, 'I presume the payment for these beeves is between somebody in the British Army and the owner?'

" 'All you have to do is sign a paper that says you have the beeves,' one a the drovers said. 'If we don't have the paper we won't git paid when we git back.' He held out a paper with some writen on it.

"Captain Haggard was already holden out a quill and some ready-mixed ink he'd brought along. A rebel in a red coat signed, and hoped the drovers, they was nothen but boys, got good pay fer driven the beeves so far.

"One a the drovers cussed and said they'd get hardly nothen and none till they got back. It had never come into their mind South Carolina was so far from Pennsylvanie. The man had said it would be about a week's drive, and they'd been on the way since June, and now they had to walk all that way back to get their pay.

"Captain Haggard said that was a kind of low way to treat a man. The redcoat pulled out some Spanish dollars, said he'd take up a little collection. And he did. You know, that little out-fit had a good deal a English hard money amongst em. I don't know how they come by it. Anyhow, the drovers was tickled to death with all that money.

"The redcoat, I oughtn't to call him that, he was just wearen one, told em to stop at a tavern, and if they didn't feel like walken back in a hurry, they could send the bill of receipt for the cattle by somebody goen to Pennsylvanie. The redcoat put the man's name and where he lived on the outside a the paper, told em to get it sealed at a tavern, and we all drove the beeves —they was in good shape—back to our camp in the swamp. And after that the bound boy and myself watched over em after we got em to a pretty little meadow deep in that swamp. We didn't have to stay with em all the time, just go count em—we started out with thirty—once a day, and salt em sometimes."

"I'll bet Captain Haggard wasn't mad at his wife any more," Jimmy said.

"Lord, no." Jethro laughed. "She was just leaven when we got back. The last I saw of her that time, Captain Haggard had her half out a the torchlight, squeezen her and beggen her to come back real soon. 'Honey,' he said, 'I don't mind if you do sound like a screech owl with the ague when you give your loon call, you're still my darlen sugar dumplin.'"

Jethro got up. "If there's nothen else you want me to do, I'd better be getten back to help Rachel."

Leslie was still curious. "Did you learn how the drovers got cattle for the Loyalists through rebel country like Virginia?"

"Captain Haggard asked em that. Kind a risky, they said, except when a redcoat asked, they could tell the truth and say the beeves were headed for Tarleton's camp. And when they thought it was a rebel asked, like in Virginia, why they'd say the beeves were goen to the Continental Line in North Carolina. Good night to both a you."

Jimmy followed Jethro. Leslie looked at the beginnings of his letter. Not enough to call a beginning. It would please his father to learn Jethro had been with the partisans under Marion. He'd remember to put that in, and tomorrow at Daniel's place he'd get it all in his head; there wouldn't be much to do until this batch of saltpeter was cooked.

Cresting the hill next morning, Leslie heard Daniel singing down in the valley and stopped to listen. He soon decided it was a prayer song, something like the one he'd sung before going to hunt the buffalo. No different from other Cherokee warriors, Daniel prayed a good deal. Leslie wished he'd pray for William David; the little bastard needed all the help he could get.

The rangers met him in their usual place, and after a few suspicious sniffs led him across the horse pasture to within sight of Daniel on the hillside above the bigger creek. Unwilling to interrupt the prayer, Leslie stopped a few feet away.

Bareheaded, facing the east, Daniel stood several paces from a good-sized poplar, hands lifted, head moving slowly up and down as he looked from base to top, and sang his prayer as if the poplar were listening and could understand.

The prayer finished, another voice spoke from the other side of the poplar: "That was real nice. I know now she'll go through the water like a swan." The speaker came around the tree to show himself to be a lanky woodsman dressed in worn buckskins and with dark hair swinging below a black hat. He and Daniel were consulting on where the tree should fall and never noticed Leslie.

Daniel, he remembered, had said not long ago that a Gideon Huccaby was coming from French Lick for powder. He walked up, hand extended, and when he had caught the man's glance, said: "I'm glad to see you. Gideon Huccaby, I believe."

The man backed off, fright in his eyes, as he whispered: "Don't put me in a dead man's shoes."

Daniel muttered something in Cherokee, then turned to the stranger. "He meant no harm. He never knowed poor Gideon Huccaby them evil Shawnee got. He's the Professor I was tellen you about, the man that can figure out how wide a river is without crossen it, or how tall a tree with no climben." He turned to Leslie. "The man is Samuel McGee, walked all the way up from French Lick, and is aimen to make a pirogue to take our saltpeter back in. You feel like helpen him cut this poplar for the pirogue? I ought to go hurry up that cooken saltpeter."

Leslie took the ax, and Daniel hurried away. He was no sooner out of sight than Samuel stopped, ax lifted, to whisper: "It was a party a Draggen Canoe's braves got Gideon, not the Shawnee. They've not been around."

Samuel sent the ax into the wood. Leslie soon discovered that, though a good hand with an ax, the man was not much on talk. Yes, a man named Weaver had got through with his party. No, none of the stations had run out of powder yet, but they were "dangerous low." Yes, they had sulphur, some, and he reckoned maybe there were niter caves fairly close, but the Creeks and Draggen Canoe's braves killed most all the men that ventured into the woods. No, they couldn't hunt; that is if they wanted to keep their scalps.

The forenoon was gone before Leslie learned that much. Already hating himself for asking questions, he stopped trying.

However, during the nooning he learned from Daniel's conversation with McGee that John Sawyer had promised to meet McGee here with a load of sulphur so that McGee could take back gunpowder instead of saltpeter. A French Lick settler going into the woods for dogwood stood a good chance of losing his scalp; McGee was thinking John Sawyer might have lost his.

"He'll come, never you fear," Daniel comforted. "You don't know how far he's had to go on the hunt of sulphur. Maybe past the Watauga settlements and clean across the mountains. Recollect, Leslie, he's the man that brought the yellow-headed woman. I'm so certain he'll come with sulphur, I'm aimen to ask one a you to hunt dogwood for charcoal while I take your place maken the pirogue."

Leslie suggested McGee take the easy job of hunting dogwood.

McGee shook his head. "I'd ruther swing the foot adze with never a stop till dark than do any more walken. Walken up from French Lick was enough."

As Leslie was leaving for the dogwood hunt, McGee told him to be on guard against wild hogs, and if he saw a drove, run. "I'm not ashamed to tell it. Comen up here I walked smack into a drove. And when I saw what I had done, I went up the closest tree."

Daniel nodded. Leslie laughed as he left. A wandering hunt in fine weather would be pleasant. Alone, he could think on his letter.

Dogwood, dead but still standing and sound, were easily found on the limestone hillside above the bigger creek, but more words for his letter could not be found. He shied from giving the false birth date of Sadie's bastard as written in the Bible. Yet, he'd have to give his mother some such date, otherwise she'd think ill of him for not marrying the mother of his child as soon as he ought. She'd never believe he'd stooped so low as to take a wife whose child, born after marriage, had been fathered by another man.

His thoughts went off as they often did to William David. Last night the woman had left no doubt that she was going without him. He couldn't leave the child to die. And his mother hoping to see his baby. And William David with nobody wanting him. He stopped. What had he smelled? His nose was going. He should have known at the first whiff it was witch hazel.

He saw that in pushing his way through a tangle of grapevine he had broken a twig from a witch-hazel bush. The dangling twig held three small yellow-white flowers. The leaves had fallen; wild geese were going south; the harvest moon was in the wane; but more than any of these, the blooming witch hazel betokened the coming of winter. Its flowers were the last to bloom before winter.

Winter. He wished it were farther away. Why? He had never feared travel in winter, not even here where winter weather was apt to be cold rains, wet snow, and worst of all, ice on the trace.

He saw a dogwood, not quite but almost dead; cut and barked it, and went on to hunt others. He tried to plan his route of travel for the trip east. He'd stop at Sadie's place long enough to rest the horses and collect the gunpowder, what whiskey the horses could carry, and anything else that would be useful to the partisans, and then go on with Jethro and Little Brother to the first group of partisans he could . . .

He swore and hurried on to hunt more dogwood. He had forgotten the yellow-headed woman, Rachel, and William David.

Daniel's valley was filling with twilight by the time he got back to it. He'd left two likely piles of cut and peeled dogwood on the bank of the big creek. Looking up the hillside, he saw three men outlined around the fire. John Sawyer had come. He hurried to meet him. John, about his age, was a likable man, uncommonly brave, but never foolhardy.

John must have heard a rock roll or a twig snap, for he came running. Their whispered talk turned almost at once to the war. This trip finished, John would not make another one into the back parts until the war was ended. "No, I'm not goen back home because I think the British with their Hessians and Loyalists are about ready to take Virginia. They may do a lot of damage, but they'll never take her."

"Is there still talk of given the command Gates had to General Nathanael Greene?" Leslie wanted to know.

John nodded. "It's more than just talk. After runnen away and leaven his men to be killed on Camden battlefield that Gates will never give another command as long as he lives. He's not worth the brine it would take to pickle him."

Leslie nodded, but said nothing. He was trying not to think what could happen to his parents if there should be another Camden; this time in Virginia.

John glanced in the direction of Daniel who appeared to be busy over the cookhole. "You haven a hard go with Daniel?" he asked, then added: "He's a good man, but I reckon right now he's fractious tryen to make up his mind which he loves the best—his beard or a pretty Cherokee girl he's set to marry. His mournen days for his first wife are about over I'd say."

"We've been worken together all right. Times he has been ill favored, but I had reckoned he was thinken on his dead wife, rememberen maybe how she was killed, or that we are on different sides in the rebellion. Then I'd think he had just changed from the way he used to be."

John was shaking his head. "No, the way I had it from a trader to the Cherokee, nothen much ails Daniel now except he wants to marry again and his beard's in the way. Accorden to this trader, when Daniel lost his first wife and children, he swore to let his beard grow as a token of his sorrow and never shave until he had avenged his wife's death."

Leslie glanced toward the fire. Daniel, from the best he could make out, was looking their way. "We'd better move on," he told John. "And no Cherokee girl will have a man with all that hair. . . . He's had vengeance for his wife?"

John nodded. "Speaken of females, I learned from Daniel with no askin that woman I brought out is still around. She oughtn't to be. Back in September—she'd said she wanted no more travelen till the weather was cooler—I asked a packhorse man goen her way to take her. He was goen with empty packhorses from French Lick to Harrod's Station to pick up a woman with two children that had lost her man to the Indians. He could have put this woman at least closer to Detroit."

"She's changed directions," Leslie told him. "Wants to get back to Philadelphia in a hurry."

"That woman couldn't hurry if her life depended on it. She's hard on a horse, setten like a deadweight, sawen on the reins, confusen the horse, ruinen its mouth, and all the while quarrelen, screechen, maken more noise than a flock a crows." He sighed. "But I reckon I can take her. I'll have empty horses."

"John, I don't want to put her off on you. You've carried

her once. Anyhow . . ." Daniel was calling: if they didn't get a move on his supper would be ruined, and it would be too dark for Leslie to see his horses.

Leslie, his mind taken up with the rebellion, his parents, and William David, had little thought for his horses on the other side of the hill. Jethro would look after the horses; Rachel would take care of William David, but she might not notice whether the cow was sick or well. And he would like to see William David for himself. He ate supper, left at Daniel's bidding, and walked over the hill.

He found the cow chewing her cud. William David had eaten a big supper, Rachel said, and was getting bigger and livelier every day. Jimmy, Jethro, and Little Brother were also in the rockhouse awaiting supper. The buffalo beef had been slow to tender was why supper was so late, Rachel explained.

Satisfied that all was well, Leslie went to his rockhouse to work on his letters. He got little work done for thinking of the war. Jethro had brought about twenty pounds of powder. The kegs he hadn't been able to find were in Jethro's cabin loft, he'd lately learned from Jethro. It might be the best thing to forget what Daniel might let him have, and start back tomorrow. He didn't know: the rebels might need the powder he'd got from Daniel more than they'd need him to come a few days sooner without that extra powder.

He had by next morning made up his mind to stay and get all the powder he could.

Another day came, and then another; warm sunlight, only light frosts of morning, the kind of fall weather women around New River called Indian Summer. A foolish name from a foolish notion. Indians would strike most any time except during deep snow or when some festival like the corn dance was on.

Both valleys were peaceful: in Daniel's the pirogue was taking shape; closely stacked circles of dogwood, cut into short lengths and split, were slowly burning into charcoal; and the saltpeter business was going strong. Things in the other valley were also going well: Little Brother and Jimmy were thick as thieves; Rachel and Jethro were taking to each other like ducks to water; the yellow-headed woman had recovered from her fright and, according to Jethro, was walking about a good deal.

Leslie had finished his business letters; one a short note to his ex-mother-in-law with a bill for horse hire and Jethro's wages; that, he figured, would quiet her down about Jethro's "evil ways." And though it galled him, he had also written Sadie's parents of his sorrow at not being home when she and the boy died. He had made a first draft of the pleasant part of his letter to his parents, but had yet to write of the deaths in his family.

Tending a charcoal fire away from the sound and sight of human kind left time and mind for writing, at least making a rough draft. He was staring at: "I am sorry to add my sorrow to your sorrow," and not liking it. He was taking for granted his parents would be sorrowful at the loss of a daughter-in-law they'd never wanted; furthermore *sorry* was the wrong word; a man would use that for the loss of an old, worthless hound or . . .

He lifted his head. Somebody was coming around the creek bluff, mumbling to himself like a man with woods fever. He soon made out John Sawyer's voice, not mumbling senseless words, but spitting out black, dirty oaths. Now what? Something was bad wrong or John, ordinarily good-natured, wouldn't carry on so.

John, on seeing him, laughed. "Leslie, is it manly virtue or beauty that makes our great lady choose you above all others?"

"What great lady? Nobody loves me."

"Miss Charity Prudence Simons, and I didn't say a word about love."

"You left off the *née* and Madame Robert Barton Eversole."

John gave a low whistle. "Some of the women whispered around she wasn't goen to a husband but runnen away from one. Anyhow, she means for you to take her. And I'm sorry for you. I went to her sweet-mouthed and polite, never letten on— at first—that I wanted the money she owed me. But she was already mad when I got there. And do you know why she was mad at me? You know or at least have heard of Andrew Dunagan?"

231

Leslie nodded. "You couldn't find a better scout or braver man."

"Kindhearted, too. He's the man I persuaded at French Lick to go out of his way to take this poor lone woman to Harrod's Station. 'And do you think,' she said to me, 'I'm low enough to ride with a piece of stinking trash like that? I can't bear men who chew tobacco; and his beard was brown with tobacco juice. Why, he spit once right in front of me.'

"I could a strangled her on the spot. I hope Little Brother takes her scalp. Andrew's a clean man; that's the color of his beard. And he don't stink. She does. Said she was in a hurry. Well, I could a taught her what hurry is."

His glance happened upon Leslie's writing materials. "If you have any letters you want to send, I'll be glad to get em close as I can to where they're goen. I'm headen for home, close to Spotsylvania, but I could go out a my way some, and I'll be leaven here in four or five more days."

Leslie thanked him for the offer he was glad to accept, then suggested John do the easy work of burning charcoal while he went to help McGee on the pirogue, or work with Daniel.

John shook his head. "I feel like hitten somethin real hard." He looked at Leslie. "And I oughtn't to feel that way. I didn't tell you that comen past Daniel, he told me I could take at least two hundredweight of powder back with me. I couldn't have done that if the woman had picked me over you. But I do feel sorry for you."

"I'll manage," Leslie told him.

They went together to the pirogue where they found McGee more than glad to change jobs. He'd been swinging the foot adze or using the gouge most of the time since daylight.

Leslie worked later than common, and went straight to his rockhouse after finding the cow and waiting for her to chew her cud. If the missus had sent word by Rachel for him to come see her, he hadn't got the message. He wanted to think awhile before tackling her again. He also wanted to work on the letters he must write.

The evening was peaceful, though he thought more than he wrote. Next day was also peaceful with the work going at a good clip. During another very early supper, Leslie decided that in addition to the cow he would also look over his horses and William David.

He was walking by the canebrake looking for horse sign when he thought he heard, from around the hillside, somebody shoveling dirt. He hurried on to see, a little above the bend of the creek, Jethro digging a gravelike hole. Closer, he saw it was a grave with the corpse nearby, a wild boar, big but headless.

Jethro saw him. "Lord, Lord, Mr. Leslie, was there ever such a day. I hope to God I never have another'n like this. . . . No, nobody was hurt, at least not bad in their bodies. Their feelens are you might say wounded."

"William David all right?"

"Oh, I wouldn't let your little chap get hurt."

"What did happen? The dogs all right?"

"Thunder got a nick from this old boar's tusks, that's about all, except Little Brother's cut, and she didn't get at him good. . . . I never seen anybody dig a hole with an ax; now, I've got to put down this shovel—you made Rachel a real nice shovel, but no wooden shovel like this can be used like a spade in this hard ground, so I chop the dirt loose and shovel it out." He picked up the ax.

"Jethro, will you please leave off that work—we'll drag this carcass to the closest sinkhole—and tell me what did happen. Who cut Little Brother? Was the fight between you all and the hogs or among yourselves?"

Jethro dropped the ax. "Now, you don't think Rachel would take a long kitchen knife and try to cut out Little Brother's eye after he'd saved her, or helped save her, from a ragen wild boar, do you, suh?"

"Just tell me what did happen."

"It was the missus done the cutten. You know, if she wasn't so behindhand when it comes to worken, the missus, judgen from her looks, would make a fine camp follower."

"Jethro. Watch your tongue. You don't know anything about camp followers. Get on with the news."

"Beggen your pardon, suh, I do know about camp followers. I reckon Captain Haggard had had word; he got all the visiten

wives out and the little bound girl, just before some kind body
sent us a wagon load a camp followers. They got there early in
the forenoon, and you ought to a seen them women work. Said
we all stunk and was liven like pigs. We shaved and shifted;
they washed our clothes, cleaned up everthing in sight before
there was any goen to bed. And you know that kindhearted soul
that sent em; he didn't forget the persons like myself; I had the
prettiest, nicest-mannered coffee-with-cream-skinned girl."

"Jethro. Please, what happened here, this day?"

"Sorry, suh. I got carried away looken back. Let me see.
It's a long tale. This mornen early Rachel said it was such a
pretty day, she'd like to do the clothes washen she had to do
for the missus down by the creek. I told her I'd bring up wood
to heat the water, carry water, and watch William David. He
ought to be outdoors on these pretty days.

"It was comen on to dinner time, everbody haven a good
time and getten the work done. Little Brother and Jim—'Jimmy
is for little boys, so please call me Jim or James,' he said to me
one day, and when I remember I call him Jim—anyhow, he was
haven a lesson in target practice from Little Brother with a bow
and arrow; Little Brother hitten a sycamore limb so far up the
creek I could hardly see it, and Jim just tryen.

"Like I said, it was a good time when I saw the missus
walken down the hill. Rachel looked at me, then rolled her eyes
toward William David. I picked him up, basket and all, and
had carried him a little way, just foolen along, when I heared the
woman say: 'What a pretty little pig. I'll bet he'd be good
roasted.'

"I was already runnen back fore she finished, and I think I
was callen, tryen to tell her and that fool Rachel to leave the pig
alone and go to their rockhouses. Jimmy was yellen, too, for her
to leave it alone. She must a hit it or somethen; it squealed
enough to wake the dead. And Rachel just standen there, wet
clothes in her hand, grinnen like a fool.

"I looked down the creek, and saw an army of wild hogs.
They'd heared that pig squeal. This big old boar was in the
lead, gallopen faster than a horse. Look at what long legs he's
got.

"I started runnen back to Rachel, little William David jouncen around somethen terrible. I didn't have to tell that Rachel a second time to run with the baby to a safe place. She met me. She'd seen the hogs. They was right on us; and the missus still beaten that pig.

"I don't hardly know what happened next. The missus started screamen and tryen to run; Little Brother was given his Indian war whoop, leastways I reckon that's what it was.

"I thought this big boar had the missus for sure—Little Brother grabbed his war club and was doen good; but that wasn't stoppen em. Jimmy and me was beaten em with anything we could find, rocks and chunks a wood, tryen to make em move on up the creek.

"Lord, I thought that boar would kill the missus for sure. We couldn't get close to him for that sea a hogs. A big old sow knocked Jimmy down, but Little Brother helped me drag him free. He wasn't hurt, but his wind was gone.

"It was Thunder and Cupid saved us. They grabbed this big boar, each taken an ear, holden on the way you've trained em so he couldn't turn his head and slash their bellies wide open with his tusks. Little Brother got to him first, I think; Jimmy if he wasn't first was close; two or three cracks over the head with that war club knocked him senseless, then one or the other slit his throat. I reckon it must a been Little Brother; Jimmy was pretty woozy, but he kept goen."

"And everybody's all right?"

"You might say that. Well, the missus is feelen kind a, well, not so good. She's wanten to see you, real bad."

Leslie had expected that. "You've done well, real well. I'm proud of you, Jethro." He turned to go, eager to see for himself that William David was all right.

"Oh, that's not all, suh. In a way not the worst part. I think I ought to tell it."

"If you must, but you're all alive, nobody bad hurt after a fight with a drove of wild hogs. That's all that matters."

"Beggen your pardon, suh, I'm not so certain this matters and I'm not certain I saw it all. Like I said when she finally got it into her head that wild hogs was wild, after everbody tellen her half a dozen times, the missus started runnen. She was late. An old sow tore off a petticoat or two while pigs was runnen between her legs tangling in her skirt tails. She kept beaten about her and screamen while she tried to run.

"We got the hogs off enough she could run up the hill aways. By that time it was about over. The dogs had the boar, Little Brother had bashed his head in and slit his throat. She, the missus I mean, must a looked back, else she wouldn't a fainted dead away, back down on a soft mossy spot.

"First thing I knowed Little Brother was on top a her; up above Rachel was runnen and yellen: 'Put water on her face till I can git her smellen salts.' I run and got Little Brother by the shoulder, tryen to pull him off her. She was screamen worse than a catamount.

"Then she was half setten up, poken under her petticoats and bringen out a long kitchen knife quick as a flash and slashen at Little Brother. It was about then Jimmy run up. You can't blame the boy; he was flustered when he grabbed one a Rachel's piggins, dipped it in some dirty, hot, soapy wash water, and run up and flung it full into her face and hair. The water was hot, not scalden hot, but from the way she screamed a body would think so. And it brought her right out of that faint. She jumped up and started runnen."

Leslie pushed back his hat. "Little Brother hurt?"

"Got a little cut on one arm. Not bad."

"Did he have his knife out?"

"Naturally. He'd just stuck the boar. I remember his knife was drippen blood."

"Did he try for her scalp?"

Jethro hesitated. "I'd say he was just tryen to help her up by the hair of her head. If I remember right, he had it pulled up in one hand."

Leslie gave Jethro what he hoped was a Terrible Look. "You believe the boy was just tryen to help her up?"

"Suh, it's what I like to think. . . . What is laud-a-num?"

"You must mean laudanum. If you do it's a kind of opium. How does it happen you know about the stuff?"

"Well, when I was putten a little a your whiskey on Cupid's

cut—it don't amount to much—Rachel heared him cryen and come runnen with a little box. She said the missus had give it to her when William David was born, and told her to give him considerable in his gruel and it would make him go to sleep. But Rachel is afraid of strange medicines for babies, so she didn't use it. I didn't try to get any down Cupid."

"What makes you think it's laudanum?"

"I figured it was either that or law-dan-um from the spellen on the box. I reckon the missus forgot Rachel can spell out words."

"The first was right," Leslie said, and tried to think of something to tell Jethro about the medical uses of laudanum, some kind of pretty tale, but he didn't feel up to talking, let alone trying a lie that wouldn't change what the man was thinking.

"Mr. Collins."

"Yes." Jethro with neither ax nor spade in his hand looked uncommonly tall.

"Mr. Collins, I've never told you once in my whole life what I thought you ought to do. Have I?"

"No. What have I done now?"

"It's not, suh, what you've done, but what you have failed to do, if I may say so."

"Go on."

"Well, after things had quieted down after the wild hogs, I got to thinken. What if I'd been off up the hill getten wood to warm water, or the hogs had come to Rachel's rockhouse when she was out and William David was in. That baby would a been dead by now. Dead and not baptized." He hesitated. "An you could baptize him. You're not a priest or vicar, but you've got a prayer book and you can read the service. I've heared you say you'd had to read services for the dead. That baby ought to be christened proper and baptized."

Leslie figured Rachel had been working on Jethro. It didn't matter. Jethro was no fool. He'd been around enough to know that laudanum was dangerous; it wouldn't take much to kill a baby. He looked up the valley. He had come early; now it was late with the dusk thickening.

What was it old man Scott had told him and Weaver when

they were with him during that Indian scare before the attack? "A light from on high was comen into this dark valley and a deep voice like thunder called me to preach."

No light from on high was coming into this dark valley, and the voice telling William David Leslie Collins what to do came from the nether regions. And he would obey the voice, gladly, gladly.

"And you will baptize your baby, won't you please, suh?"

He had forgotten Jethro. "Yes. The day after tomorrow in the forenoon."

He started for his rockhouse, but stopped when he had gone only a few paces. "Jethro, there's no use to wear yourself out buryen that boar. We'll drag it to a sinkhole in the mornen. Go back now and watch the baby, and keep Little Brother away from the missus. . . . Jethro, do you remember where you put that sweet-smellen soap?"

Leslie had washed all of himself, including his hair, in the sweet-smelling soap, and now whistled softly as he pulled on fresh nankeen drawers. He stopped the tune when he studied the fit of the drawers; too loose; that extra cloth would fold and wrinkle to make humps and bulges in his pantaloons. The weather was too warm for skintight knitted woolen drawers; they'd itch him to death; but his skintight breeches ought to be over tight drawers.

Whistling again, he found the woolen drawers, and in spite of the itchy wool nodded with satisfaction when he'd got himself into them. They fit with never a wrinkle. He got into his fanciest shirt, white linen with ruffles and lace.

He sat on a rock to pull on black silk stockings, and was standing again to get inside the broadcloth breeches when he became uncomfortably aware that both Cupid and Thunder had awakened and were watching him with a kind of wonder in their eyes. They continued to watch as he buttoned the back flap of his breeches to the front then the leg buttons; both dogs arose as one when, instead of tying on the strips of red cloth he ordinarily used for garters, he strapped on silver knee buckles. Thunder came to investigate the brightness. "You can sniff," Leslie told him. "But that's all; no licken, no jumpen on my fancy breeches; as you can see they're pale cream, practically white."

Sometime or other Jethro had given the clothing Leslie almost never wore a good brushing and polishing. The twinkle of the silver knee buckles was nothing compared to the fiery glitter in the firelight of the gold-buckled shoes he next put on. Cupid came to sniff each shoe buckle, but Thunder drew away as if he'd sooner sniff a chunk of fire. Both dogs watched in wondering silence as he swore himself into a white silk stock that made him feel he was choking.

The waistcoat of embroidered crimson silk gave no trouble except he had to shush Cupid when he barked at it. He couldn't fault the dog for barking at such a garment. The coat he next put on was lined with the same bright silk, so he must be careful not to flip the tails around, might give her the notion he didn't take fine clothes for granted, and was trying to show off. Keeping his tails quiet didn't matter; the coat itself was a show-off; viewed from the rear it was a decent dove gray except for the collar; but the front was wilder than the waistcoat with sleeves widely banded with the crimson silk, and more of the same in facings that formed the collar and ran down the front to call even more attention to the overly fancy buttons.

He'd had the suit made in New Orleans not long before he'd gone on Clark's first campaign to the Illinois. Down in New Orleans the outfit hadn't seemed so fancy, but after leaving the place, he had stored it and other clothing with a friend on New River until a good while after his marriage. In spite of Sadie's pleadings he had never had the guts to wear it in these parts until now.

He had cursed when he saw with what junk Jethro had burdened the horses: clothing a man would never wear in the woods, utensils and dishes he didn't need, like the pink and gold china teapot. Now, he was wearing some of the clothing, and the teapot, filled with hot water, was waiting by the fire for the hot toddy spiced with ginger and nutmeg.

Satisfied there were no wrinkles in the breeches, he buttoned himself into the coat, emptied the teapot, then poured in what he estimated as six gills of whiskey. The pot was big enough to take that much liquor and still have room for the spiced water steeping over the fire to make the toddy hot and spicy. And plenty of sugar; she'd like it sweet, but he did wish he had white loaf instead of only maple.

Drink mixed and keeping warm under a clean towel that had to serve for a cozy, he flung a cape, also from New Orleans, about his shoulders, put on the beaver from London, and, with the dogs sniffing the cape, went for his dressing case, a gift from his mother sometime or other.

He carried the case into the firelight, opened the mirrored cover, and looked at the face of William David Leslie Collins, Esquire. Take a long look now; after this night's work and that on the day after tomorrow, you'll never be able to look at your face again. He wished he had a wig; then, the face might seem strange to him.

He put the case away; then, mindful of the toddy pot, and cursing the slick-soled fancy shoes that made walking over the rocks difficult, and keeping his voice low as he ordered the whining dogs not to follow, he went to the woman's rockhouse.

He stopped under the sandstone overhang and called, but not so loudly as to risk Rachel or Jethro's hearing: "Madam, I heard you wanted to see me, or do you feel like talken to me now?"

"Oh, Mr. Collins, do come in. I can't get up. What they done to me this day has near killed me. Please, please can't you get me away from here?" She was sobbing and hiccuping as if from a long crying.

"I know, maam, I know," Leslie said, walking up to the fire, remembering to take off his hat. "You've had a bad day. I got here as soon as I could." He gave a silent sniff. Brandy.

"Oh, Mr. Collins, if only you could have been here, they wouldn't have done what they done to me. . . . Won't you join me in a small brandy. I'm taken it to settle my nerves."

Leslie set the pot of toddy by the fire, then turned to the woman. She was half lying, half sitting on the feather bed, and from the best he could tell was too lost in self-pity to do anything but stare at her brandy glass. She hadn't looked at him. "I thank you, maam, a brandy would be agreeable. You need something. I didn't know you had anything of that nature, so I brought you some hot, spiced toddy I've just made."

Mention of toddy brought her sitting straight up. She appeared to forget his gift on seeing him. "Oh, Mr. Collins, how beautiful. I didn't know you were so handsome." She drank him in; shining shoes to his clubbed hair tied with a satin ribbon.

Lost in him, she didn't seem to know she was one godawful mess; unkempt hair all over, eyes ugly red and swollen from crying, or maybe it was the lye-soap wash water Jimmy had flung on her face, but lye-soap water or none didn't have anything to do with the once-fancy, now rundown slippers over torn stockings, or the food stains on her wrinkled dressing gown.

"Your liken this outfit makes me feel better," he said. "I thought it a shade too fancy for a mournen husband and in the backwoods to boot, but it was about all my man brought in the way of decent clothes; and I like to get out of my worken rags now and then, especially when callen on a pretty lady."

She sighed. "I wish all men out here felt that way. They don't care how they look—or smell. That awful Indian. I can still see and smell him. Why you don't kill him is a wonder to me." Unmindful of her weak condition, she got up for toddy glasses, then insisted on doing the honors of pouring and serving.

She praised the toddy, praised Leslie for being a good mixer of drinks as well as a kind and thoughtful man. "And you will take me soon, real soon. It wouldn't be so bad if you would stay around, but ever day you go off and leave this help-less woman with these wild beasts. And today that Indian tried to violate me again."

He wished she'd wipe her snot-dripping nose. He'd like to tell her that all Little Brother had wanted was her scalp—if he wanted that. The boy had thought her dead. Instead, he lifted his glass. "Here's to fine travelen, maam. A safe trip to Philadelphia and your loved ones."

"You are so very thoughtful," she said, and drank.

The toddy and the prospect of Philadelphia did not, as Leslie had hoped, make her forget, or at least shut up about, Little Brother and his attempted "violation" of her. She had started off with: "Oh, you don't know. No man can ever know what a horrible, horrible thing that Indian . . ." when she stopped and patted the feather bed. "You'll ruin those beautiful breeches sitting on that rock, and anyhow the bed's more comfortable."

Leslie went to sit beside her, then was sorry. Over on the clean rock his woolen underdrawers had only felt a bit scratchy, but here near the fire with his bottom buried in feathers, sitting was a torture. And a long one. The tale of what had happened to *her* with never a word of how the others had saved her life after she'd brought the hogs by making the pig squeal, nor with any mention of her knife, seemed to go on forever.

He didn't remind her of what she was leaving out but confined his remarks to soft sounds of sympathy, except when the itch from his underdrawers became unbearable; he would then spring up and walk about, muttering "Begad" or some such.

She finished with a hand on his knee, and: "Mr. Collins, I hope you can see from this why I must get away from here, and soon. Very soon. I'll pay you well, even more than the ten gold guineas I've already offered to get me out of this place."

He swallowed. "Yes, maam. That price is all right, and I'll go soon as I can."

"That won't be long I hope. You know that awful John Sawyer come back a little while ago, but I wouldn't travel with a beast like that." She launched into a vilification of John Sawyer such as Leslie had never heard poured out on any mortal. He'd come to her in worn-out dirty clothes that stunk to high heaven of God knew what. He'd even tried to get money out of her, claimed she'd owed him.

And would "Mr. Collins" believe it, John had had the nerve to fault her for not going with that awful man he'd sent?

Leslie listened in teeth-gritted silence. He didn't remind her that she did owe John money, or "that awful man" he'd sent was one of the best guides in all the backwoods. He didn't explain that John's stink had come from mixing gunpowder and burning charcoal. He would of course have smelled of bear's grease; like any smart man, a stranger to Daniel's dogs, he had rubbed his lower parts with bear's grease.

She had finished. The sobs were gone, though there was a

slight hiccup, when after a refill of her toddy glass, she patted his knee and said: "You're such a gentleman, and this lady travels only with gentlemen. You know that awful John Sawyer had the gall to curse in my presence. Shitfire, don't he know a lady when he meets one? I'd liked to a kicked his balls clean through his asshole, teach him how to treat a lady."

Leslie blinked.

She gave his knee a soft squeeze, drew closer, and whispered: "Oh, I'm so glad you're going to take me, and soon. But," she stopped and looked around, "you haven't done the—you know—the other business."

"What other, maam?"

"Don't pretend. You know. We're not taking that baby. And we can't just leave it. That fool Rachel might try to get back to it—do anything."

She waited for an answer. None came. She continued: "Anyhow, it's dying all the time. You can't raise a baby on cow's milk. Everybody knows that. Why it'll soon be dead anyhow."

He nodded. "Liven for all of us is nothen but the road to dyen."

She squeezed his knee. "At long last you agree. It's such a little thing. Thousands and thousands of unwed mothers have done the same thing. Always. Why, there's lots of sad old songs about girls doing—you know—to young babies."

He nodded, and waited for his throat to loosen enough to let out words, the right words. Soon, he could speak. "It would come high. He's not newborn, but a little child. I've never done anything like that."

"Quit trying to act like Jesus Christ. You've killed many men. I can see it in your eyes. You won't be doing anything, but maybe hurrying up its end a little. That's all. And anyway the baby is nothing to you."

"Almost nobody is. But I want to do what's best for you. And I reckon it would plague you to go home with the little chap when your lawful husband had been gone from you considerably longer than it takes to make a baby."

She was hissing like a snake for him to hush.

He stood up.

"Don't leave me. You will do it, won't you? Promise?"

"I'll promise—if the price is right."

She sprang up, her weakness forgotten. "When can we start? Tomorrow?"

"You've not heard the price yet."

"I'm sure I can pay it."

"First, the taken you. Ten guineas, hard money, like you offered."

One hand went under her dressing gown to return, open, extended, bright with the gleam of gold.

He picked up a piece, hefted it on one finger, rang it on a rock, bit it, and nodded as he laid it back in her hand.

"You thought it was lead or iron coated with gold? Is that why you didn't take it?"

"We must first write out our agreement."

She drew back. "Not all. Not about the baby."

"This agreement I aim to write is just for taken you to Abingdon or someplace where you can get carriage to Philadelphia."

"Yes, yes. I know you won't take me all the way. But the other. I must be certain. Are you charging extra for a little thing like that?"

"Is Rachel your property?"

"That's none of your business."

He turned and started outdoors. She ran after him. "I own Rachel, but why must you pry into my affairs?"

"You sure you own her? Not your husband?"

"Shit." She flounced off, but after some rummaging around her bed, came back with a folded paper, the seal broken. She handed it to him with an angry: "Read it for yourself."

The writing was less flourishing than his mother's; the language long-winded legal, but he soon had the gist of it: a deed of conveyance by William Braxton Eversole in which he gave to Charity Prudence Eversole, consort of said conveyee's son Robert Barton Eversole . . . etc., etc., "one black female, twelve years of age, known as Rachel, born on the plantation

245

of the said conveyer . . ." he skipped the rest and was looking at the date, but hadn't learned the day in October 1767 when she snatched the paper from him.

He smiled. She was afraid he might get some notion of her age. "Keep that handy," he told her. "You have materials for writing out our agreement?"

"You'd have to mix the ink powder." She was whispering again. "And you can't, you must not write all our agreement."

"You know I wouldn't put anything on paper that could be held against you. Read what I write and you'll see."

It seemed forever that she fiddled around hunting ink powder, paper, and a quill; but once the materials were at hand, the agreement to take Madame Robert Barton Eversole to Abingdon, one mount, one packhorse, and provender furnished for the sum of ten gold guineas was soon finished. He signed his name, handed it to her with the request she read and sign.

She glanced at the paper, signed, then lay back on the bed and smiled at him. "Now, as soon as you tend to that other business we can start. Couldn't you do it tonight?"

"Do what?"

"You know perfectly well what I mean. Doesn't this paper mean you'll, well—just hasten the passing of a dying baby?"

"Read it. Our agreement means what it says."

She read, this time with care, and when she lifted her head, not all the bright color in her face came from liquor. "You dirty b-b-b . . ." She was so mad she stuttered, and seemed unable to think of words foul enough for him. She was able within a few seconds to come up with: "You're a coward, a yellow-livered coward. You've tricked me and chickened out on the baby."

"Last time I thought you said you'd do it."

"I said no such thing. Anyway, Rachel won't let me get close to it, or its milk."

He thought of Jethro's story of laudanum, and felt the cold sweat on his hands. He wondered if sweat gleamed on his forehead, but would not lift a hand to feel. "We've not said anything about the price."

"You're far from poor, but you certainly don't mind taking a lone woman's money, a lone woman far from home and husband. Well, speak up. What is your price?"

"Rachel."

"Don't joke with me. Name your price."

"Rachel."

"I'll do it myself before I'll give you Rachel for such a little thing."

Leslie lifted his hand to push back his hat; remembered his hat was not on his head. That was cold sweat he felt on his head. He went over to the bed, sat down, and put an arm around her bare shoulder, gave the shoulder a little squeeze. "Honey, I was just plannen to save you trouble."

She didn't draw away, but cocked her head around to look at him. "Trouble? You know, I think that if you'd leave off your sly tricks you could be kind. If the right woman came along."

"Maybe she has," he said, and gave the soft shoulder a bigger squeeze.

"It would be no trouble," she went on, kind of snuggling against him. "I expect he's half dead anyway. I could send Rachel off for something, get some laudanum down him, slip it into his milk or something."

His encircling arm reached around her shoulder and one finger gently stroked her throat. He looked at the soft throat, beginning to wrinkle. He could with his two hands choke her to death. Quickly. Soundlessly. Nobody would know. Think she'd died in one of her faints. He would then have to write a letter of condolence to her husband. No, he would offer no condolence; tell him only that she was dead. Would that help? She'd still own Rachel. And what would happen to young William David? A foundling home?

"You're making a mountain out of a turd. I can manage with no trouble."

He played with a strand of her hair. "I thought you said a minute ago you couldn't do it. Howsomever, I wasn't thinken of that kind a trouble for you."

"What other kind could there be?"

He had himself in hand and could speak more easily. "You

know your help better than I do, but I've seen enough of Rachel to believe she'll cry and carry on, and keep it up after that baby's gone. She'd talk. Sooner or later your husband would learn what you don't want him to know."

"There are ways of keeping her quiet. But suppose she does talk on the sly. Nobody believes slaves. They can't testify in court."

"But they whisper among themselves. Your husband might hear enough to get suspicious."

She laughed and emptied the toddy pot into her glass. "That wouldn't be anything new."

"And anyhow," he went on after another squeeze, "you'd have all your help prayen for you behind your back or maken jokes in the stable."

"Prayer and jokes never hurt anybody. But it won't come to that. I'll see to it that Rachel doesn't talk. If she acts up I'll sell her on the way home or have her tongue cut out."

He blinked. His planned words flew away. "I could," he managed in a moment, "sell her for a little somethen to the Creeks or Spaniards. Maybe a Cherokee would take her off my hands."

"If I sell her to a backwoods settler there'd still be a good chance of her ending up with the Indians. Then, nobody would know what tales she told."

"There would be differences."

"What differences?"

"The overmountain men don't hobnob with the British, so there's no British gold or silver, only Continental. You would for all your risk and trouble get nothen but that, and Continental money is hardly worth the paper it's printed on. You could maybe get Spanish gold for her in Natchez or New Orleans; that is if anybody will buy a bawlen wench like she'll be."

"Bawlen or tongueless, she could still work."

He got up.

"Don't go," she commanded.

He didn't answer. He wanted to do something with his hands. He reached for his whittling knife before remembering there'd been no place for it in these tight pants or the fancy coat. The fire was a gome; Daniel would have called it that. He was pushing the fallen-apart chunks together when she asked: "Why build up the fire? It's warm enough in here."

"I thought I'd better redden it up a little before I go to check on the horses with Jethro, find out if an Indian has slipped off one or two since sundown. They'd come in the early dark."

"Indians?" She stood up. "There's no Indians around here but that horrible one you won't kill."

"This is Indian hunten territory. It's hardly six months since they killed a guide and captured his party less than a mile from here. We've been lucky, that's all."

"Don't go. Stay longer. I'm not afraid when you're around."

"You'd better be—but that does remind me. Since we've got ink ready-mixed, and you're set on taken Rachel, I'd better write out another agreement for us to sign; be the same as for you, just fifteen guineas extra." She didn't hit him, but for a minute he thought she was going to.

She contented herself with calling him a vile name. "You don't mean you're charging more for taking Rachel than me? Why, the agreement I signed included both of us."

"Send me to Bedlam if it does. I've got but the one side-saddle with me, and one mount broken to a sidesaddle. I'll have to go somewhere and pay the hire on mount and saddle in order to take Rachel."

"Let her walk if you won't live up to our agreement."

He nodded. "I thought you said you wanted to hurry. After the first hundred miles or so she'd come along mighty slow, and each extra hour we spend in Indian territory adds to the danger."

She was reading the paper they had signed. She was a slow reader. It seemed a long while before she looked up from the paper. He read her look. She was so mad she'd kill him if she could. He stood silent under the hail of vile names and accusations of lying trickery that followed. She stopped when she had only enough breath left to say: "I hope they make a hotter spot in hell where a lying, cheating, son-of-a-bitching bastard like you can burn forever."

He reached into a pocket, took out the coins she had given him, and laid them on the bed. "Here's your money, maam. Now, please hand over the agreement we signed. I'll throw it in the fire and go on about my business. I've already wasted too much time tryen to get you out of a mess."

She flopped down on the bed and beat the pillows like a child in a mad fit. He oughtn't to have made that toddy so strong with a good taste into the bargain; she'd drunk it as if it were tea; but how was he to know she was already having brandy?

He walked about until she had quieted a bit. "I'm sorry to have upset you, maam, when you've already had a most terrible day. I thought I was doen you a favor, not asken for more to take you than you offered." He made a quick guess. "And that's not a third as much as you gave the man who promised to take you north, then ran away, or tried to, when Indians attacked."

She called the dead coward a vile name, then lifted her head to look at Leslie. "That was different. I had plenty then, I thought, to get me to—to Detroit."

She said the last word as if it were paradise lost to her forever. Next came brokenhearted sobs. He looked at her heaving shoulders. Not much longer now. She was going to let him have Rachel.

He wiped the sweat from his face and went to the mouth of the rockhouse. The air back there was dirty with his lies and her foul language. He'd hardly had two deep breaths of clean, pine-smelling air before she came to grab his arm. He led her back sobbing on his shoulder.

There were no sobs, more like contented smiles, when he left her, the old conveyance and a new one for "the black female known as Rachel" in a coat pocket. She had cost considerably less than he had been prepared to pay—at least in hard cash. He had agreed to take the woman and do "the other" for only five guineas and Rachel.

A few paces from the rockhouse, he stopped to look at the moon. There was no moon. He stared in puzzlement at the sky with only stars. The waning moon was rising late, long past the early dark, but seemed like he'd been with that woman long enough for the moon to be in the western side of the sky.

He heard laughter and looked ahead. The light from Rachel's fire cut a path of brightness across trees and rocks. Nobody had gone to bed. The night was not far gone. Time to go tell Rachel who owned her now.

He started toward the light and laughter; stopped again. He couldn't go as he was and they'd see him if he crossed the band of light.

Finished with his long circuit through the dark, he paused to make certain he had everything: Rachel's deed of conveyance was still in his pocket; his hat on his head; the teapot safe in the towel; his itchy underdrawers over one arm; silver knee buckles wrapped with the pot.

He had everything except warmth and light. His rockhouse fire was either dead or lost in the ashes. He wanted light. Why, he didn't know. He could change clothes in the dark. And light wouldn't warm a man's insides. He had got what he wanted and more. He ought to be happy, feel proud, not dirty as he felt now with coldness like a sickness inside him.

He remembered Jethro's laughter, warm sounding and happy. He'd go to the light and the laughter.

Where was the whiskey jug? A long drink would help warm him.

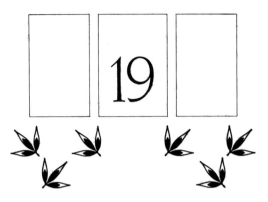

He'd heard his mother use the word. What was the word to describe this upcoming business? Sacrilegious? Profane? Neither
was strong enough. Sinful? That was taken for granted as was
desecration.

"Suh, I don't know where your mind is, but it's not on
getten ready. I've begged you three times to get into your slippers, but there you stand in your stocken feet."

"Jethro, I aim to wear my second-best boots, and not the
gold-buckled shoes; they're dancen pumps, I think."

Jethro, dressed in the sober outfit he'd worn when he
brought news of Sadie's death, was scandalized. "Now, Mr.
Collins, whoever saw a bishop or a priest christenen a baby in
boots? Please, suh, won't you put on these decent shoes? They're
fitten. It's late and about all you've done is scrub off that smell
a saltpeter and brimstone."

"I helped mix gunpowder till late last night is why I smelled
so. All right, I'll wear the damned shoes, gold buckles and all."
He was tired of the argument. He'd better be studying the prayer
book to get the christening service straight in his head. He'd
planned to read it last night; instead, after getting home late, he
had worked on the letter to his parents; wasted time; the letter
was no further along than it had been, which was nowhere.

"Now, suh, if you'll just hold still I'll get you into a plain stock like a clergyman wears, and then put on your waistcoat hindside fore, you'll look the way you ought."

Leslie nodded without listening as he thumbed the prayer book. He'd just found the end of the christening service and was leafing back to the beginning when a doleful voice said:

"Mr. Collins, I've tried and I've tried and I cain't get Little Brother to put on the pants you loaned him."

Jimmy was looking at him as if the bottom of the world had dropped out. "He knows it's some kind a ceremony, and it looks like he's aimen to wear that buffalo skull or maybe the wild boar's; he's been tryen em on turn by turn. What'll I do?"

"Nothen." He'd found the beginning, only a page over. Thank God it was short. Careful not to lose the christening service, he tried to console Jimmy. "No matter what his nation or how long his people have traded with white men, it's a rare Indian that'll wear breeches of any kind. They'll wear our kind of hats, shirts, and most anything else except breeches. Quit worryen, and think how nice you look with your hair combed and . . ." He wasn't certain. Jimmy as yet had nothing much but fuzz; still he added, "a fresh shave."

Jimmy flushed with pleasure, then hurried away. Leslie returned to his reading while Jethro went on with his work. *To take away all scruple concerning the use of the sign of the Cross in Baptism; the* . . .

There came a hushed and tearful: "Don't he make you think a heaven and the angels?"

"He sure shines. A bishop couldn't look finer."

Leslie closed the prayer book. He'd been mistaken. Jethro and Rachel were not speaking of young William David, but of him. Rachel looked away from him, flustered, remembering he was her master now. She'd seemed pleased when he told her, though she had said only: "Yes, suh." A short time later she had asked: "And can I keep on taken care a your baby?"

"Naturally," he had answered. She was too forehanded when she used that *your,* but he had said nothing about it.

Now he said: "You look very nice yourself, Rachel."

"Thank you, suh, but I'd look nicer if I could a done a better job on my cap. It's not all it ought to be, but the best I could do with just somethen the hogs got into. When I helped the missus out of her clothes that day, she said she never wanted to see a stitch a them never no more. They come in mighty handy for William David. I made him a cap, but he don't like to wear it too well."

Leslie couldn't blame him. No man would want that concoction of lace and ruffles on his head. He appeared to know something was up, looking around him with curiosity in his wide gray eyes. He was as yet behaving, not even trying to kick off Leslie's best hunting shirt, which Jethro had without asking loaned Rachel.

Jimmy came hurrying past with Leslie's shaving mug, its silver holder freshly shined. "It's the christenen water," he explained. "Jethro told me you used it in your church. Fresh caught from a rockhouse drip; that's cleaner than creek water. I'm goen to set it on the altar."

Leslie hadn't known there was an altar. He was following Jimmy when Rachel said behind him, "But this baby ain't about to die."

He turned around and looked at her. "Who said he was?"

"Why, you've forgot, suh, you just sprinkle with holy water the ones that are weakly and about to die, so bad off dippen em all the way in would hurry their passen."

"Rachel," Jethro spoke with authority, "the priest don't have to dip a baby all the way under. Sprinklen's enough. And anyhow, I don't think that copper wash kittle is big enough to take all a William David."

Leslie wished he had more closely watched infant baptisms in the church he had attended as a child; and he ought to have studied the prayer book; it should have something on how the ceremony was performed. He walked on past the rockhouse he'd had Rachel move to so as to be farther from the missus. The argument continued behind him. Weary of it, he promised to do the baptism both ways.

Silence for several more steps until Jethro said in a hushed voice: "Here's the church, suh."

Leslie went into the indicated rockhouse, then stopped to look around. In spite of a low fire, the back was still shadowy, looked to be mostly rock walls and more rock fallen from the roof. One of the rocks was paler than the others with two glimmering objects on top of it. The altar, he reckoned; below it, set on a pile of rocks and surrounded by fern leaves, the copper wash kettle, belonging to the missus, gleamed from its long scouring. Everybody, except himself, must have worked all day yesterday to change a rockhouse into a church.

Jethro walking in solemn dignity went to lay the Bible on the altar. And what was he supposed to do with it; he hadn't noticed the man was bringing it. He watched while Jethro lighted a splinter in the fire, then returned to the altar to light the three candles in each holder. The silver candlesticks belonged to him, a gift from some relative or other; but he wondered on the candles and hoped Rachel hadn't snitched them from the missus. He wanted no part of her here.

He forgot to sniff the candles when he went to stand behind the altar with the Bible open in front of him and the prayer book on top. He was hunting "Baptism of Infants" when Jethro's mouth-organ music rolled out from some recess behind him. Cupid, who had with Thunder followed him to the altar, howled when the music hit his ears. Leslie shushed him, and he followed Thunder away.

Leslie looked out and up at the rockhouse roof. He was reminded of a church he'd been in sometime, somewhere; a country church of stone, big, but plain; maybe in England, not Wales, the stone would be gray; could be Scotland or France. The nave high and all red-brown stone like this, and past it a great sweep of world, but different; no trees like the ones he could see from here, and beyond, the hill across the creek with the pines on top, black-seeming against the blue sky. And while he looked a great bird, too big for a hawk, had to be a golden eagle, cut a trail across the sky with never a wing beat.

He looked down. Rachel was standing a few feet away. "Mr.—Reverend Collins, I mean," she whispered, "I forgot to tell you. Mr. Jimmy said he had too much sin on his soul to be a godfather and carry up the baby because we've got no godmother, so Little Brother is the godfather. And he ought to be. Recollect, he helped save our lives."

Leslie nodded. "He'll be fine," he told her. Rachel went to sit down; Leslie thumbed the prayer book, found the baptismal service. *Then the priest shall take the child into his hands, and shall say to the Godfathers and Godmothers,* Name this Child. *And then naming it after them (if they shall certify him that the Child may well endure it) he shall dip it in the Water discreetly and warily. . . .*

Inwardly he groaned. Little Brother couldn't say William David's name; he wouldn't know he was supposed to. Rachel was right about the dipping, but why hadn't he seen it when he'd read part of the service the first time. He looked at the top of the page: "Publick Baptism of Infants."

He turned pages and found the service he had read; that was only for infants in houses; there were two services; one for the home and one for the church; that was "Publick Baptism," and ungodly long, pages and pages of fine print difficult to read in the uncertain candlelight. The book was new when his mother sent it, but she liked to keep things; maybe it had been printed a hundred years ago and the service had been changed since. No hope; he'd found the date: Cambridge 1770.

He looked up and drew a deep breath. He wished he were on the other side of this business out there with Jimmy and Little Brother. They had stopped in full sunlight under the outer edge of the overhang, heads craned, lost in looking at something in the sky he couldn't see from where he stood. The big bird, he reckoned.

The two of them whispered together until they stepped out of the sunlight into the shadow of the rockhouse, then came silently on to sit on rocks behind Rachel. Little Brother had decided on the boar's skull, and a fearsome thing it was, tushes looked to be a handspan long. He'd had sense enough to leave his war club behind, but showing behind the shoulder of the white shirt Leslie had loaned him was the top of his arrow-filled quiver. His face was painted in shades of red, brown, and black; until the coming of Jimmy he had used only soot and pokeberry juice, but Jimmy had introduced him to the red juice of puccoon and the dark brown dye of black walnut hulls.

The mouth organ hushed. Jethro tiptoed across the rock-house to sit near Rachel.

Leslie felt the four pairs of eyes on him, waiting. No, there were six. Music gone, the dogs had returned. Worried by the awful stillness, they stood with lifted heads to look at him.

He knew christenings took place immediately after the morning or evening service. Was he supposed to preach a sermon? God, if the white man had a god, ought to strike him dead for what he was about to do. He'd suffered a lot in God's name; even getting the catechism had brought on several beatings. He'd been beaten a hell of a lot in God's name; the creed to be memorized in Latin he at first had not always understood had been the hardest; but he had learned it; at times it still rolled through his head. It was beginning to roll now, but what in hell did the creed have to do with a christening? Nothing. But let it roll.

He lifted his arms. The congregation stood up. All except Cupid and Thunder listened with bowed heads as the Latin rolled over them. The dogs listened, heads lifted, ears cocked. Taking advantage of the bowed heads, he glanced at the prayer book. The words *that Baptism be ministered in the Vulgar Tongue* leaped at him. Here, that meant English, and Baptism was to be on a Sunday *and other Holy-days;* he felt somewhat better when he saw that if necessary it could be administered on any day.

The creed was running out; before going down to the font and reading the service as directed, he ought to say something. "Suffer. . . ." That was the way it began. He was going to use that word in writing to his mother of Sadie's death. He always remembered the spelling—now. Early, when out in the real world of men, he'd got the reputation of a good scribe. His fellow sailors, and now and then a hunter or chain carrier, would ask him to write a letter. If a love letter, he'd plan to write something like, "My heart suffers for thee," but for the first time or two he'd been unable to make up his mind whether suffer had one or two f's. He'd borrowed a Bible and found the word in Luke, and the rest he wanted was somewhere in St. Matthew.

He stopped the creed and indicated the congregation should

sit. He gave chapter and verses then read: "Suffer little children to come unto me," and continued for four verses. Meanwhile, he'd found what he wanted in St. Matthew. He read four verses and ended with a fifth: "But whoso shall offend one of these little ones which believe in me, it were better for him that a millstone were hanged about his neck, and that he were drowned in the depths of the sea."

Finished, he looked at the congregation, then beyond them to the hill. "Let us hope that the little one here today may know only kindness from the world and grow into an honest man with courage and a heart that knows no evil. May he follow in the footsteps . . ." No, he must not say ancestors, not for a child born of a harlot and sired by a blackguard who didn't look after his bastards. ". . . of the many who have gone before him and made themselves worthy of this Earth loaned to them for a little space. And when times of trouble come to him as to all mortal men, may he be able to look up and say: 'My help cometh from the hills.'"

He couldn't think of anything else to say; he thought he'd done all right; he could make out the glitter of tears on Rachel's cheeks. The hard part was still ahead.

Carrying the shaving mug of water in one hand and the prayer book in the other, he walked down and around to the copper wash kettle on its waist-high mound of stones. That damned boar's skull was so in the way, he couldn't tell whether Little Brother was looking at him or not. He motioned him forward anyway, then said, hands extended: "Will the godfather please bring the infant to be Christened."

Rachel got up and laid William David across Little Brother's slightly crooked arms. He then walked slowly toward the "Font," holding the baby on his forearms away from him as if his burden were a lighted keg of powder.

Leslie watched, fighting an impulse to go for the child; Little Brother was carrying him so low the long-tailed outfit he wore was dragging on the ground. Suppose Little Brother tripped over it and fell on top of the child; the tushes in that skull could give him a mortal wound. And if he didn't watch out, the baby would see that skull, start kicking and screaming, then roll off onto the rocky floor.

Nothing happened. William David was almost touching his chest, and at peace with the world as he sucked the necklace of buffalo bones Leslie had made. Nothing to do but read the service, and hope Jethro or Jimmy would make the responses Little Brother as godfather was supposed to make. He began: "Hath this Child been already baptized, or no?"

Little Brother answered with a resounding: "No."

The service moved on: the congregation knelt and arose at the proper time. Little Brother renounced the devil; Leslie skipped the affirmation of beliefs for Little Brother; he had his own religion; instead he affirmed the beliefs of an uncle, the other godfather *in absentia.* Maybe that wasn't legal, but better than having Little Brother add more lies to this false ceremony.

Time to take the child. He hesitated. God ought to strike you dead, William David Leslie Collins, for what you've already done this day. Finish.

He reached for the baby, looked at Little Brother and said: "Name this Child."

He was wondering who would answer when Little Brother said with unaccustomed loudness: "William David Leslie Collins, second."

Leslie repeated the name, slowly; William David looked at him, trusting, unsuspecting, with no notion he was to be dipped into a kettle of what was no doubt very cold water. He lowered him in as he reached the last part of his name, held him there while he said the words in the prayer book: "I baptize thee in the Name of the Father, and of the Son, and of the Holy Ghost. Amen."

Somebody had thought to warm the water. William David never screamed until he had him out, and was sprinkling water from the shaving mug; he thought a drop had hit him in the eye until Little Brother reached over and put a piece of the buffalo bone necklace back into his mouth.

Leslie read again, and as directed made the sign of the cross on the child's forehead.

259

Not knowing what else to do, he continued to hold the baby as he hurried through the remainder of the service; William David, wet through, could get a chill. The congregation knelt to say the Lord's Prayer, and in spite of his haste, all finished at the same time.

He finished with the admonitions concerning the instruction of the child in religious matters, then gave him back to Little Brother, who needed no prompting to take his burden to Rachel.

Now what? All continued to sit, eyes fixed on him. Time to dismiss the congregation. But how? He returned to the altar, said: "Amen," lifted his head, and waved his arms forward to indicate the congregation was dismissed.

Jethro tiptoed past to make more music. Leslie looked at the Bible before him. He ought to write in Family History what he aimed to write; the longer he put it off the harder it would be. He had everything in his head.

He needed fresh air, a lot of air. He hadn't reached the outdoors before Rachel stopped him, tears dripping off her chin. "Oh, Reverend, it was wonderful, just wonderful. And wasn't William David good? Seemed like he knowed he was wearen your fine christenen dress Jethro brought, and was tryen to live up to it."

He nodded, about all he could do. He wished he could take a running jump and land in cold creek water where he'd scrub himself with sand. And he wished she wouldn't call him reverend. She and nobody else knew what he was up to.

Jimmy was looking at him with wonder. "I didn't know you had it in you to preach so fine."

"I didn't exactly preach. Mostly I read the service."

"Whatever it was, it was fine. Your baby's goen to grow up to be a great man. That big eagle swoopen round while he was bein baptized was a fine token. You see him?"

Leslie nodded.

"That eagle come so low over Little Brother and me, I think I could a killed him with a bow and arrow. And I know Little Brother could have. He didn't try, though. He just lifted his arms to him and said somethen I couldn't make out."

"I'm glad he let him live," Leslie said, and didn't add to spoil

Jimmy's token that Daniel talked much of the eagle he'd seen. In spite of his eagerness to be out of his churchly garb, he went for a handshake of congratulations when he saw Little Brother alone down by the creek. Leslie thought the boy understood he was being congratulated for his part in the service; he let go his dignity long enough to clap Leslie on the shoulder.

He was in his rockhouse putting on his leggings when Jethro came with the Bible, prayer book, and shaving mug. Leslie cut short his praise for the fine service by thanking him for the work he'd done in arranging a church. "And Little Brother did so well, you must have coached him."

"I didn't do it all," Jethro told him. "Mr. Jim and me, we took turns readen the services out a your prayer book to him. I think he liked the sound of it. . . . Suh, it's close to dinner time. Recollect, when you told Rachel to move you said she was to keep the baby out a sight a her missus, and I was to take her meals, but Rachel must keep on doen her cooken and washen."

Leslie nodded.

"Well, oughtn't I to go now and tell her dinner will be a little late on account of the christenen, otherwise she'll come hunten Rachel and see William David."

"No. You're never to say one word about William David around her, better to act like he's dead. It would be a good thing for you to tell her dinner will be late, except today I'll go by and tell her on my way to work."

"But how'll we keep her from seein that baby when we travel along together?" Jethro wanted to know.

"We won't stay together, at least not close," Leslie told him. He hadn't yet planned their order of travel. It would be a tricky business, but he didn't worry about it as he finished getting into his working clothes, then started for the woman's quarters. He hadn't seen her since the night he'd bargained with her. He dreaded it now. She'd be in a passion, accusing him of rape and trickery.

"Why, Mr. Collins it's nice to see you when I was expecting Jethro with my dinner." She smiled at him from the sunny rock on which she sat, several feet down the path from her rockhouse.

He stopped, and hoped his smile hid his surprise. She was

neatly dressed in a dark outfit sprigged with little rosebuds, and her hair was up, brushed and shining. Stranger still, she was busy with some kind of embroidery. He told her that Rachel was late with dinner, but Jethro would be bringing it soon.

She shook her head over Rachel. "That wench is doing no better for you than she did for me. But then I ought not to have brought her. She was bred to the loom and the needle, and is no cook or lady's maid."

"Maam, the sad soul's tears make slow work of her cooken today."

"I thought she might hate to leave me."

He nodded. "Naturally, maam. That and the baby together are about to kill her."

She sprang up, looked around before whispering: "You've done it?" She seemed surprised.

"I promised, didn't I?"

"How?"

"Water."

"You dropped him in the creek by accident?"

"Maam, I don't like to talk about it, and I try not to think on it. You can go back to your husband with a light heart."

She didn't look lighthearted as she said: "There was no way to save him."

"You could have taken him back to your home, and claimed his parents had been killed in the war. Nobody would have suspicioned anything; not in these times. He isn't—wasn't goen to favor you, but his father. He'd have been tall, spare built, gray-eyed with—"

"Hush." Her eyes were filling with tears that seemed to come from sorrow instead of anger.

Leslie was ashamed of having made her cry over a man she'd have to forget. "Don't shed any tears over the worthless blackguard that fathered the child. Decent . . ."

"How dare you say such a thing of Colonel Littleton? He didn't know I was . . . We were to be married as soon as . . ."

He patted her shoulder. "Sorry, maam. Chirk up. You'll soon be home and out of the woods. And if you want to walk about in this fine weather, tell Jethro; he is to stay with you so you won't be afraid. He's a good guard."

Her sobbed-out "Thank you, Mr. Collins. You are most kind" didn't make him feel any better.

He wished her good day, and left for work. The burden of her faith in him and belief in the lies he'd told her so weighed on him, he was halfway to Daniel's before he thought of the writing materials he'd left behind. He swore and walked on; it would have been a good time to work on the first draft of the letter to his parents.

20

Daniel was waiting dinner for Leslie when he got there, so he had to sit around, pretend to eat, and listen to the talk of the other three. He didn't mind; it was good to let other men do the talking.

Nooning finished, he and John Sawyer put charcoal through the crusher while Daniel dug niter dirt and McGee worked on the pirogue. Daniel stopped for a rest and a look at the crushed charcoal. He decided it wasn't fine as it ought to be, and went into his private quarters to return with a corn pounder.

Pounding charcoal was a one-man job. He and John took turns, but the turns were so short there wouldn't have been enough time to work on his letter, if he had remembered to bring paper and ink.

The pounder was heavy, and with charcoal dust flying up in the pounder's face, it was a nasty job. He was glad when Daniel dragged up a mixing trough, and said they could start measuring and mixing. A little more than a keg of saltpeter, crushed and pounded, plus half a keg each of sulphur and charcoal were put into the shallow trough, then shoveled and raked until there was an evenly colored mixture that Daniel said he would have to try before he'd call it gunpowder.

He put a greased thread into a short length of dry cane closed at one end, poured in powder until it was almost filled, added priming powder, then stuck it under a good-sized rock, and lighted the thread.

The men ran a short distance away, but not quite far enough to be completely out of the shower of dirt after the high-flying rock. "She's powder all right," Daniel said as he untangled a cane splinter from his beard.

He was happy, singing in Cherokee or whistling as he helped with two more mixings of powder. During supper he told them: "Boys, we've got the saltpeter and sulphur, so with the charcoal comen along all right, in two more days we'll have better than eight hundredweight of gunpowder. No later than sunup two days from tomorrow mornen, John ought to be headed east with at least two hundredweight, and you, McGee, could be pushen off with most a the rest. The Professor has got some sulphur, and his powder can come out a the last cookens."

McGee nodded.

John looked at Leslie.

He knew the look meant the letters John was to take would have to be finished in two more nights after this one.

Walking back to his rockhouse, guilt for his trickery of the missus topped off with the false baptism and dread of the lies he must tell his parents, left no room for planning the letter.

Back in his rockhouse with a good fire going and more light coming from a flambeau, Leslie decided to copy what he had already written, and so begin the final draft. Time was running out. He mixed ink, cut a fresh quill, and settled himself, fresh paper and smudged first draft under his hand, Bible and prayer book within arm's reach.

He read what he had already written in bits and pieces at odd times. It would do, he reckoned, after a little rearranging, and some of the words had a strange look. He'd have to check their spellings with the Bible and the prayer book as usual—unless he called on Jethro; he didn't aim to do that.

His mother's rule was that all household help must be able to read and write a joining hand. This meant they had to learn to spell. Jethro had taken to spelling like a duck to water while Leslie was less readily taking to Greek and Latin. Jethro had never got past Dilworth's Grammar, but he could just about spell every word in Entick's Dictionary. Leslie wished he'd bought one the last time he was in Richmond.

He thought of Dr. Johnson's Dictionary in the library at Sea Winds. His mother had consulted it more often than his father. In a way female education made more sense than that for boys with a father like his. Schools for young ladies maybe wasted time on needlework, but the most of what they taught, even the Social Graces, could be used in later life. Females were incapable of learning Greek and Latin. Instead, they were taught French, music, needlework, and above all English spelling and proper usage. Finished off they could, in his mother's words: "speak with propriety and compose with ease."

He couldn't. He shook his head over his woolgathering ways, dipped quill into ink, and wrote:

"My Dear Mother,

I was much pleased to hear from you. Yet I am" . . . He reached for the Bible. He had written *greved* in the first draft; it didn't look right. The word would be in Job. He found it. . . . "grieved to learn of the great Sorrow that has befallen you and Father. I can offer no words of" . . . Yes, he was certain; by rights comfort should begin with *cu*, but it didn't. . . . "comfort if comfort there be. I can only add my Sorrow to your own. I learned of the Defection of my Brothers late in the fall of 1777 when on my way to go with Gen. Clark on his first Illinois Campaign."

He stopped. He'd finished his first big lie. He'd known nothing of Percy until he'd shot him at Camden. Nobody, not Percy who hadn't seen him, knew he'd shot his brother. He wondered as he had wondered many times what his shot had done to Percy. How would it be to go through life with one arm? Kinder to have killed him. At least in shooting him, he had saved the life of the rebel Percy was about to kill. The man he'd saved was a stranger; could be some son of a bitch not worth the powder to blow him to hell.

He next copied a repeat of his letter thanking her for the wedding gifts; she hadn't received the first one.

Now for war and western lands. He could spell words relating to horsestock and land as he could for travel, surveying,

266

and war. He thus had no difficulty in copying what he had written of Clark's campaigns in the Illinois. His father would be interested.

Both parents would be interested in a first-hand account of the country around Natchez, the Great French Lick on the Cumberland, and the Blue Grass region of Kentucky County, Virginia; according to his mother, his father expected to migrate to one of the three. There was a good deal of fine land in each locality, and he suspected his father knew of the western lands only through hearsay. The stories traveling east would make each place into a Paradise on earth, and say nothing of the forted life all settlers had to endure because of constant Indian harassment.

He wrote of what he had seen on his travels and while surveying in each place; he didn't want his parents to think he was just passing on information got from others. He next wrote of Indian attacks on forts and the ambushing of travelers, but, because of his mother, left out the grisly parts. Still, the smootheddown tales with mention of the miseries of a forted life ought to be enough to make the old boy think twice before leaving Sea Winds to settle in any one of the three.

Finished with the western lands, he stopped to stare into the fire at nothing. It was now time for the first part of his big lie. In order to give him time to marry again soon enough for his second wife to bear a child now the age of William David, he would have to do away with Sadie and little Watts shortly after that false birth date in the family Bible.

Might as well begin. He had it all in his head. He cut a fresh quill, inked it, and wrote:

"I must now add yet more to your Sorrow. The Seventh Day of May early in the Morning of 1779 my former Wife was delivered of a Boy. I thought of writing you the News, but had I told you All, it would only have added to your Sorrow. The Birth was a hard one. The Child's Life was in doubt from the first."

He hurried on to get the baby dead at "five Days of Age" with Sadie following a day later. She had died from what "a neighbor Lady said was Childbed Fever."

He must put in some grief, but considering that he was to remarry within less than six months, he ought not to lay it on too thick. He thought a while, then wrote: "Death in the Spring seems uncommon cruel. At first the shock of my Loss seemed too great to" . . . This bear was spelled the same as a bear in the woods. . . . "bear. I gave myself up to Grief until I remembered I was needed in South Carolina.

"A neighbor Lady, wife of a Good Man, wanted to hire Angela. I let her go. Jethro wanted to get back to the War. We went."

He next wrote of Jethro's activities in South Carolina after the Loyalists burned his master's livery stable. "Jethro was soon a" . . . The word ought to be spelled *pahtizan,* but there was an *r* and an *s* in it. Why did people in the South have to spell the way New Englanders like the missus talked? He wrote again: "partisan under Brig. Gen. Pickens."

He gave Jethro high praise, then wrote briefly of his own soldiering under Marion, taking care not to mention the Battle of Camden or his work as scout.

He wrote only enough of warfare to introduce the women who "—no matter how dark the night or wild the weather slipped into the swamps with provender for their men. They are a plucky lot."

He laid the final draft aside. The business coming up was ticklish; he'd better do a first draft of his introduction to the girl who was to be the mother of William David. The meeting would have to be by happenchance. His mother would think it outrageous for a newly made, still grieving widower to go courting a maid.

He'd meet his future second wife on some night when she slipped into camp with provender for the partisans; and always he'd have to have an older married woman with her. War or no war, the proprieties must be observed for his mother.

He inked his quill, and wrote of the two women he had seen several times in camp, and of whom he had thought the younger was the daughter of the older, Mistress Snowden, wife to Lieutenant Snowden.

He stopped to stare into the darkness beyond the fire.

Sooner or later he'd have to say a bit about her carriage and her countenance. He'd have to take care to make her different from any of the many pretty girls he'd ever known. She'd have to match William David in hair and eyes. Or did she? A light bay mare bred to a black stallion always dropped foals more black than bay. And a black mare bred . . .

William David's mother could have any color eyes and hair she wanted—except pale blue eyes and red or yellow hair.

He wrote again: "he had soon become better acquainted with the girl and the older woman when night after night they rode into camp with all manner of provender; he learned the girl was no kin of the older woman, Mistress Snowden. She was an orphan with no close kin in the world. Her mother was long since dead; and her father" . . .

What name should he give her? He couldn't name her till he'd named her father. Lydia Ann would be her given name; it suited her and had a pleasant sound. That didn't matter; her last name was the one that would matter to his parents.

Her surname ought not to be that of a well-known First Family such as Byrd or Beverly, Lee or Carter; but she must belong to the gentry with a gentleman for her father. He had to be careful; his mother had relatives in South Carolina. Come to think of it, one or the other of his parents, sometimes both, had kin and friends over most of the English South.

He stared unseeing into the dying fire. He found no name, and roused to learn he could scarcely see the paper before him. The fire was down to one feeble blue flame, and his flambeau burned to nothing.

He went to bed. Tomorrow he'd think up the right name and write more on the first draft; there were still charcoal fires to tend. Moreover, he had two more days and two more nights before the letter was to go; time enough and more.

Next day at work there was no sitting alone to tend a charcoal fire. Instead, somebody would look to the fires as he made a round with Equo and the sled to collect what charcoal was ready, then hurry back to help with the work: grind and pound charcoal and saltpeter, mix gunpowder, whittle on paddles and poles for the pirogue, get ready for another run of saltpeter.

Daniel was in a great bustle of work that did not hold back his talk. The cloudy day instead of damping his spirits served as an excuse to foretell the weather. These clouds would bring only a light fall rain, warmish with no snow. This time last year winter had already come; why late last fall when the braves were coming home from their fall hunts, they'd walked across the Cumberland; it was frozen that hard. The hard cold had killed many birds and beasts. He'd picked up dead redbirds and peckerwoods too weak to fly. But the pitifulest things had been the deer; they'd starved and froze by the dozen.

Daniel stopped his story of the hard winter to study the sky, then said he thought he'd better go hunt a sled load or two of dry hickory—he knew where there was a dead tree—for cook wood.

Leslie and John Sawyer were left alone together to crush and pound saltpeter for the upcoming batch of gunpowder. Leslie looked forward to such moments; alone, the two of them could talk of the country to be when the rebellion was won, and other matters unmentionable around Daniel. He was disappointed now when John, instead of starting on the war, asked: "You notice Daniel's good spirits this mornen?"

Leslie nodded. "Today's one of his up days. I'll wager that in the mornen we'll find him way down."

"Most likely you'd lose your wager. It'll be up all the way now for Daniel. At least he thinks it'll be. You know what a time he's been haven to make up his mind which he loves the most, that outlandish beard or a pretty Cherokee gal. Well, he's made up his mind."

"And which do you think he loves the most?"

"The gal. This mornen before you got here, he said to me: 'Well, John, reckon you'll know me when you see me agin and I don't have this beard?' I was certain what he meant and congratulated him. He seemed real pleased and wished I could come to the wedden. . . . Here, it's past time for my turn on the pounder."

They had finished the pounding and measuring and were mixing a batch of powder when John asked: "Leslie, have you ever seen our flag?"

Leslie considered: Gates had most likely had flags around him at Camden, but he hadn't seen Gates. He shook his head. "Not that I know of, but I did read in the fall a 1777, I think it was, that the Congress had specified how our flag was to be made. General Clark put up a flag at Kaskaskia soon as the place was in our hands, but it was our flag, Virginia's blue and yellow like sulphur."

John laughed. "Gold, not sulphur-yellow. Anyhow I saw our national flag for the first time when I visited home not long ago. My sisters had made one in the same way they'd piece a quilt, except they'd sewed the white stars on top of the blue field. It was real handsome."

They continued to talk of the new country. Their opinions were much the same. John believed the country would grow and travel on to greatness. He was wondering if west of the Illinois wouldn't be a good place to live after he married and settled down, when they heard Daniel's whistling as he came up from the creek.

John had only time enough to say he was sorry to leave this part of the country where all the stations needed men, but he thought he was needed worse in the Continental Line. "I aim to fight under General Greene to break the hold of the British and Loyalists on the Carolinas; else they'll take Virginia." Leslie shook his head. The British might invade, but they'd never conquer all of Virginia.

Daniel was upon them, explaining he had come back sooner than he'd aimed. He hadn't gone for cook wood; he'd stopped with McGee to try out the dugout. She was taking to the water like a swan; all she needed now was oars and oarlocks. McGee had argued he could get along with a pole and paddle, but McGee was wrong: a boat that size needed oars on the Cumberland. Later on, would Leslie mind going to hunt a good white oak to make oars for *Queen of the May*? "That's McGee's name for her, not mine."

Leslie found a suitable white oak with less looking than he had hoped. It was good to be alone in the woods. Back with Daniel, he wished he'd stayed longer when he learned he was to make the oars. A foolish job, and a tedious one. Made of unseasoned oak, the oars would warp, and furthermore, McGee declared he'd never use one.

Full dark had come before he could start back to his rock-house. It was in the dark, while he wondered on his parents and the prospect of the war coming back to Virginia, that the name he had forgotten to hunt came out of nowhere. Carlyle would be her surname. He knew of at least one great family of that name; it didn't matter; his second wife could be either a very distant relative or no kin at all. Better yet, he'd never when in his father's house heard of kinships or visits between his parents and the Carlyles.

His letter, he saw, had stopped at "her father." . . . He wrote: "Andrew H. Carlyle, an Officer under Col. Pickens, had been killed at the Battle of Kettle Creek. Her name was Lydia Ann Carlyle."

He hated to kill her father, but he couldn't risk close kin, certainly not another grandfather for William David.

His quill leaped from acquaintance to love and on to marriage, not forgetting to apologize for remarrying so soon after his "great loss." "I think we were drawn together because each of us had lately lost a loved one."

He drank from the jug of whiskey, then continued: "The Church Building was in Loyalist hands, but the stouthearted Priest, a good rebel who had served the Church before this War, published our Banns and Married us. We became Man and Wife October 12, 1779 in the home of my wife's motherly companion, Mistress Snowden.

"The War kept us often apart, but in our Hearts we were still one.

"Early Spring came. I was very happy. Lydia Ann was in the family way. My sorrow was that I would have to leave her for several weeks. I had to go over the Mountains and on into the limestone valleys where back in the caves niter dirt needed for gunpowder can be found in great plenty. Marion's men and the other Partisans appear to get little of the gunpowder made east of the Mountains.

"I had planned to go alone with only packhorses, some carrying sulphur. Lydia Ann was to stay with friends while I was gone. I would return long before she was brought to bed."

He wrote of the miscarriage of his plan. He hadn't had the heart to ride off and leave a little bunch of rebels, "mostly older couples and war widows with children. They wanted to flee South Carolina, overrun as it was with British and Loyalists. They wanted me to guide them to French Lick on the Cumberland.

"Lydia Ann wanted to go, too. She declared she'd never felt better in her life, and looked it. I was a fool. I let her come. I ought to have brought her to you or left her with Mistress Snowden. Worse for her, the departing families were slow in preparing for their journey. It was June before we could start.

"Travel, as you know, is wearisome over first the Hunter's Trace then the Kentucky Trace, but we had no trouble until we reached a narrow creek valley better than a day's travel north of the Cumberland River."

He studied what he had just written, then decided to make a final copy of it instead of writing more.

Finished with the final draft that went slowly because of the several words he checked with the Bible or prayer book, he realized the night was growing old. Daniel had said come early; there was a big day's work ahead.

Next morning when Leslie reached the saltpeter works, he soon learned Daniel had meant what he said. His first job was to help clean out, reline, and refill the ash hopper. Next, Daniel brought out a small gouge and suggested Leslie take it and go down to the dugout where with help from his whittling knife he could cut and gouge out oarlocks. Leslie knew how to make them, didn't he? Just be certain to get them in the right place. He'd do the work himself, but he had to tend the saltpeter and do a deal of cooking; neither John nor McGee could cook much of anything while they traveled.

He had the oarlocks roughed out in time for the brief nooning. Next, he helped McGee mix another batch of powder, thinking as he stirred and shoveled how the bright sulphur lost its brightness when mixed with black charcoal and pale saltpeter; on the other hand the sulphur made the gunpowder lighter-colored than . . .

He was roused from his thoughts on sulphur by the sound of a lame horse coming up the hill. The horse led by John wasn't lame; he'd cast a shoe. There was nothing to do but help John set up a smithy of sorts with the small anvil and hand bellows Daniel brought out. Leslie turned blacksmith and shaped and fitted a blank shoe while John worked the bellows on a fire of uncrushed charcoal.

Shoe on the packhorse, he helped mix another batch of powder, fill and head kegs for the boat, load the boat, then fill sacks for John.

Leslie was glad Daniel served an early supper; he wanted to get back to his letter. He swore under his breath when Daniel brought out better than a peck of hickory nuts he'd gathered and seasoned. The men were to crack and get out the kernels for the hickory-nut–honey cakes he'd bake while he cooked saltpeter tonight. There was nothing so good, he told them, for a man to travel on as hickory-nut–honey cakes made mostly of nuts and maple sugar.

Leslie figured he found the tedious job no more irksome than John and McGee found it, and worked with them until the last kernel was out.

Back in his rockhouse with plenty of light from a flambeau and the fire Jethro had built shortly before, Leslie remembered his letter was ready for the Indian ambush. His account of the attack was pretty much the same version of the one he'd lately heard except he and Lydia Ann were there, and he had no coward to run away and be killed.

Ink dripped off his quill as he hesitated. He shook his head, redipped, and hastily wrote: "It gives me great pain to tell what I must tell. A bullet struck Lydia Ann at the point where her right underarm went into her shoulder. I didn't know she had been hurt until the skirmish was over and the Indians defeated. She had not made a sound but had lost considerable blood.

"It was my fault. I had wanted her to run hide in the big hollow sycamore with the children. There wasn't time to argue. She grabbed one of my rifles and said she'd reload one rifle while I fired the other one; the rest of the women were doing the same. None of them got hurt."

274

He stopped. He'd done a sinful thing in wounding his good and beautiful Lydia Ann, a mother-to-be. Kinder to have killed her on the spot than have her suffer so. No, she had to stay alive long enough to bear William David Leslie Collins II, grandson of Wyatt Collins III, Esquire, of Sea Winds. No man ought to have two wives die of childbed fever.

A drink, and he was able to write of how his party had headed across country for Price's Station to avoid Indians; no trail for the roughest going he had ever seen. Lydia Ann grew paler and paler. "But weak as she was she sat straight in the saddle and never a word of complaint."

The night was long. The night was short. He stopped to make a pot of toddy when: "She got so weak and her time getting close, I thought we ought to go into camp. The other women in the party agreed Lydia Ann was in no shape to go on to Price's Station."

The toddy gave out after William David was born. "I began to understand. My Lydia Ann was on her deathbed. She didn't have childbed fever. She just got weaker and weaker."

He needed another drink to get her dead and buried. "I got a man I knew well to read the burial service. I could not."

And with no need to go hunting in Job or the prayer book for expressions of sorrow, he wrote of his. "I'll be a son of a bitch," he whispered, and sprang up. A drop of water had smeared "woe." There was no drip from the roof above him. His sweat? He rubbed his forehead. Only clammy damp; no drip there. His eyes; they were watering from the smoke and bad light like an old man's eyes.

The rockhouse was cold and lonesome with darkness creeping in from the night. Fire and flambeau were dying together; just about enough coals left to steep a pot of coffee. He put on a pot of coffee, then took two tallow dips from the store of goods Jethro had brought. He hated the smell of the things, but with his last flambeau about burned out, he'd have to write by candlelight and firelight.

He went outdoors for a look at the sky. He could see nothing beyond the thickening clouds; there was no wind. The world was still and dark as a dead world until he caught the low murmur of pines on the ridge top talking among themselves. He shook his head and returned to the rockhouse. The pines had told him nothing that would help in his next and last big lie—the christening.

He built up the fire and drank coffee cooled with whiskey before tackling the letter again. The christening went smoothly; he had it all in his head; first, the lateness of the date must be explained by the scarcity of "adherents to our Church and hence Clergy," and for this same reason, William David's god-mother and one of his godfathers had had to be *in absentia*. He gave the names of older relatives he hoped were good rebels.

The godfather who made the responses was "Monsieur L. B. Lapeer LeGrand, a worthy gentleman and friend met years ago on my travels." The name looked fine on paper. His mother couldn't know L. B. stood for Little Brother, or that Lapeer was leaper with an e out of place—Little Brother, the great leaper. A pity his mother knew French; otherwise one of the boy's names could have been *Poisson*.

Next came the pride-swallowing part. He begged her "for the sake of my small son" to give the child a home at Sea Winds "until such time as I can somehow make a place for him. I have no home, no one in whose trust I dare place him save you. My own future is uncertain. I must now return to do my part with Marion. It is for this reason I send you Jethro, Rachel who has taken care of my son, fifty guineas for the upkeep of my son, the Family Bible you so kindly sent, the three head of horsestock, and sundry deeds for land I earned through surveying."

The letter was finished except for expressions of love and good wishes, but most of it would have to be recopied for his mother. There must also be one whole copy for Jethro who was to read it until the dates and names were fixed in his head well enough he could teach it all to Rachel.

He was melting wax for the seal when he lifted his head to listen. The ducks were telling him it was time to get up.

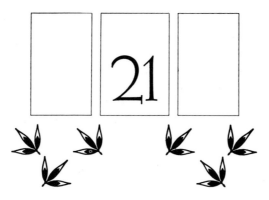

He stood near the saltpeter cooker and watched John Sawyer cross the creek and start up the hill. His mother would get the letter if John got through alive. Would she believe what he had written and accept William David as her grandson? He shook his head. No use in looking back at the letter. It was finished and gone. There was worse ahead.

He'd rather write that letter twice over than travel the Kentucky Trace with a divided party; more like two small parties. They'd have to be far enough apart that the damned yellow-headed shrew wouldn't learn William David was still alive. There was a man named Daniel Boone. He'd divided his party. Cherokee got the one that had his son. The poor boy's mother, safe in Daniel's party, had to sit still in her hideout and listen all night to the screams of her lad as he died by slow torture. Leslie shivered.

This Daniel had been happy as a June bug all morning. Now, he stopped whistling to chide: "Professor, you know better than to watch a lone man out of sight. You'll bring him bad luck."

Leslie saw no reason to answer. He had stopped watching John. He turned slightly so that John and his two packhorses were no longer in his line of vision. He would ride in front with Rachel, carrying William David, close behind him; no, Cleo might give trouble, if she couldn't travel next to him and Kate. Rachel would have to ride behind Cleo, and next to her, Little Brother on Beau.

Jethro and Jimmy with the yellow-headed woman would have to ride far enough behind, she couldn't hear William David when he cried. And he would cry. But that would give the yellow-headed woman the protection of two gunmen with only himself for William David. Well, Little Brother could be counted on for some help. Jethro and Jimmy would be close enough to hear a rifle shot. No, they wouldn't be. How far behind would they have to be so the yellow-headed woman couldn't hear the cow bawl? He'd forgotten the cow. If she heard the cow she'd know William David was along.

Furthermore—Daniel had said something. Leslie turned and said by way of apology: "Sorry, I must have been woolgatheren and didn't hear exactly what you said."

Daniel came out of his world with the new wife he'd been whistling about to give him a long disapproving look. "Leslie, I didn't say a word you could answer. Call it woolgatheren if you will, but that's not what ails you." He shoved a stick of wood under the saltpeter kettle. "You're homesick, sick a the woods. You'd like to a gone with McGee when he left at daylight in his *Queen a the May*. Now, you're wanten to ride off with John. That's what ails you. You look like the wrath of God."

Leslie nodded. It would be strange if he didn't look like a man on whom God had wreaked his vengeance. He'd spent most of the night in killing his second wife; the rest had gone to getting a pack of lies in shape for his parents to read. He'd slept none, eaten too little, and drunk too much.

Daniel's look had changed from disapproval to pity. "Leslie, my boy, when a man gits in the shape you're in, he's liable to come down with woods fever."

Leslie laughed, and pointed to the sun just clearing the ridge top. "Why, Daniel, I'm all right. I know that's due west where the sun is risen."

"Woods fever is nothen to joke about, boy."

Leslie didn't answer. His glance had happened on an empty peck measure, yellow as gold inside. It had been used to measure

sulphur. Everything touched by sulphur changed color. . . .
The packhorses loaded with gunpowder ought to be up front
with him. That would make them close to William David.
Cherokee, Chickasaw, Wyandot, or Shawnee, it didn't matter;
all would kill for gunpowder. . . . "Daniel, will sulphur poison
a person?"

"Leslie, if you hadn't lost your wits you'd recollect that
sulphur and molasses is good medicine in the spring when a
person's blood is weak; and that sulphur mixed with salty grease
and turpentine is mighty good for open sores on man or horse.
Your mind is wanderen around worse than a lost sheep. There's
nothen much to do here till this saltpeter's finished. That won't
be till late in the day. Stead a mopen around here all that time
with nothen to do, and driven me out a my mind, you could be
at your place at work getten ready to go. Then come back to help
mix the last hundredweight a your gunpowder. You ought to
bring two horses, else you'll have to make two, three trips to
carry it all."

Leslie nodded. Daniel could be expecting Cherokee visitors, but the main thing was he wanted to be rid of William
David Leslie Collins; and said Collins was just as eager to get
away for a while. A plan was building in his head. Daniel had
started up again:

"The sooner you start back across the mountains, the less
liable you'll be to come down with woods fever. And when you
come back, you could bring your sulphur. We may need some
of it for this last batch."

"I won't forget the sulphur. And I'm much obliged to you
for letten me go." His last word finished, Leslie ran past the
cooker to begin a climb up the steep, pathless ridge side above
Daniel's private quarters.

He laughed to himself at Daniel's gawping. He doubted
if the man had ever seen a case of woods fever. At least he had
not seen that poor soul in the Barrens on his way home from
the Illinois. He'd been lost in the Barrens and lost in his head.
He was hunting a tree, a big tree to climb and sleep in so as to
be safe from Indians. Indians had scalped and killed his buddy,
stolen their horses and provender, but he had got away.

No, just because the sun had risen over yonder didn't mean it was east and the way back home. Armageddon was at hand. The sun could rise anyplace because the world was split apart, turned upside down. The hosts of Beelzebub and Satan were laying waste the land. Flee, brothers, flee. Find a tree.

You couldn't rightly say the man had woods fever, but the contrary. He'd grown up in the tall timber. There, he'd felt at home and safe from Indians; but in the Barrens with never a tree, not even brush, he'd been scared to death.

He'd wager, too, the poor man when a child had been made to sit through too many "eternal damnation in the flaming pits of Hell" sermons. He'd heard one the time he'd gone to Sadie's church; that one alone was enough to give grown men daytime nightmares, and ruin children for life.

He crested the ridge, but instead of going straight over to reach the creek below, followed the ridge top until he reached the place where ridge and creek turned together. Now, with the leaves off, the yellow-headed woman when she stood or sat in the mouth of her high-up rockhouse could see anybody on the path he'd made to Daniel's and watch any movement on the remainder of the ridge side above the creek bend. Well, for this business he didn't want to be seen by anybody—not now.

He had crossed the creek and was searching out cover for the trip up the valley to his rockhouse when he gave a start of surprise. His glance had happened upon a grave, so new the mound of earth was raw red. Who had died? Not William David. The mound was long and wide enough for a man, but the gravestone was only a loose slab of limestone. Nobody around him could have sickened and died without his knowing. Who?

He swore, and walked on. That mound of earth was over the hole Jethro had dug for the dead boar. He had told the man to drag the carcass to a sinkhole, instead of bothering with a grave. Jethro had done that, then filled up the partly dug grave.

The mound reminded him of a thing he'd forgotten to put in his letter. He should have written: "My Lydia Ann lies buried in a lonesome grave over the mountains in a faraway valley. I marked the mound with a great gravestone, but marked or no,

I will know it the rest of my mortal life." Or something like that. Anyhow, if his mother came looking for a grave, there'd be one for her to see. Tonight after dark he'd roll down a big gravestone.

Careful to walk behind cedars and brush on the lower levels with pine and brush on the higher side for a screen, he angled up to his rockhouse without being seen by anybody except Thunder and Cupid, who'd heard and smelled, he figured, before they saw. They came quietly for which he was thankful; and to keep them quiet, he gave each a handful of smoke-dried buffalo meat, tough as groundhog hide.

He looked over each dog until he found on Cupid a patch of dark brown hair that seemed a good match for the color he wanted. Cupid, busy with the tough meat, didn't mind while he dusted the brown patch with flour. The hair became grizzly like an old man's hair. He dusted on more flour, then swore; the hair was too white for any human being he'd ever seen.

He went for the sulphur and sprinkled a pinch on another brown patch; that was more like what he wanted, a pale brown shading to gold where he'd let too much sulphur fall. He'd be more careful with the hair that counted.

He went to the load of plunder he had faulted Jethro for bringing. First, he found a flimsy silk handkerchief, just the thing for dusting. He next took the old tow shirt of Sadie's making, clean and almost white from its many scrubbings in strong lye soap.

He cut and tore out the sleeves with pleasure. He'd always considered tow shirts were for field hands and other hardworking men. Sadie had thought all men who had "to get ahead in the world" ought to be hard workers.

Ashamed of himself for quarreling with the dead, he cut with his knife and tore until the sleeves were reduced to strips of cloth, two wide, the remainder narrow. He next cut and tore out the back, folded it, made a slit in the center of the fold, then a short lengthwise cut from the slit down one side. He cut and tore three squares from the front of the shirt, and stuffed the unused remainder into a rock crevice where it wouldn't be noticed.

He found the worn and stained spare saddle blanket Jethro had brought. Fit for nothing but to bed down a sick dog, he'd use it this once. Nobody save Jethro had ever seen it.

He took the smallest square of shirt cloth and folded it over a little chunk of hard maple sugar. He put a handful of flour into the next, then laid the silk handkerchief on top of the other and put on a good handful of sulphur. He secured all of them by gathering up the corners and tying each with a string of cloth. Careful to keep the sugar sack separate from the sulphur, he put them into his hunting shirt pockets. He folded the other material he had torn into the horse blanket. This, he put into the big middle foldover of his hunting shirt.

Cupid and Thunder at his heels, he hurried to Rachel's rockhouse, but stopped to listen a pace or two from the overhang. The sounds he heard and didn't hear were right for him. Nobody was talking to Rachel. William David's cry was the angry squalling he always gave when he wanted to be taken out of his basket. That meant Rachel was busy and nobody else around to pick him up.

Leslie went to the overhang, and called Rachel, softly so as not to be heard by any ears he didn't want to hear. Only William David answered with a louder scream.

He walked in. The place was a mess such as he had never seen around Rachel's quarters: smoking fire, unwashed dishes, pots and pans scattered about. He could make out Rachel's shape in the back of the rockhouse. It was unlike the wench to stand idle while work waited and William David cried.

He called more loudly.

This time she heard, and started toward him with a sobbing bleat of: "Oh, Mr. Collins."

Now what? He picked up William David; he at least was clean and didn't need "changing." The little devil at once hushed. Leslie wished he hadn't. Rachel's sobbed-out words came more clearly.

"Oh, Mr. Collins how did you" *sob, sob* "bear up under it all?" More sobs and a hiccup. "The good Lord has been with you" *sob, sob, sob* "else you couldn't a stood up under it all." *Sob, sob, hiccup, sob.*

She didn't seem able to stop either crying or talking. As she repeated her words of commiseration, he forced himself to look at her. Worse than he had expected. Her eyes were bloodshot from weeping; two lines of lighter skin marked the saltwatery course of her tears. He couldn't tell whether the water that dripped unheeded from her chin was tears or tears mixed with nose drippings. "It's the pitifulest saddest thing that ever happened to mortal man."

Choked with sobs, she couldn't go on. He asked his question: "Where are the boys and Jethro?"

"Jethro kept readen that letter to me over and over till I thought I'd die. 'Listen and quit cryen,' he'd say. I couldn't. It was killen me. I sure was glad when him and the boys went up the creek to hunt white-oak crotches for packsaddles—whatever that means." Whatever else she tried to say was lost in sobs and hiccups.

Luck was with him. He planned to go down the creek—at first. "I think I'll take William David for a little stroll. The weather's uncommon warm for this time a year."

"Please be careful, suh. You don't want to let nothen happen to the last human you've got left. Oh Lord, I'd better try to git to work. Dinner's goen to be awful late."

He was sorry he'd caused the woman to suffer so, but she was regaining at least some of her wits. She remembered to bring William David's red blanket. He told her to cheer up, then fled to the bend in the creek, careful to keep well covered by cedar and brush on the way. He stopped behind a thick growth of willows to take the cloth-wrapped lump of maple sugar from his pocket and dip it into creek water. William David could now taste the sweetness as soon as he put it in his mouth. William David, as usual when being carried, was quiet, and he meant for him to stay that way until the right time came.

Leslie walked on, shaking his head over Rachel. She knew the last part of the letter was a lie; she'd been at the borning of William David; she knew his mother wasn't dead. Jethro knew the whole letter was a lie; he knew when and how Sadie and little Watts had died. His mother didn't know the truth; she maybe would believe.

It could be he had written an exceptionally fine tale. Rachel's tears didn't mean anything. Some women could get so wrapped up in a novel they'd cry and carry on bad as Rachel and all the time they knew the tale was a lie from one end to the other. Men could be just as bad. Two or three years back, he'd taken a copy of *Robinson Crusoe* with him on a surveying trip. One of his chain carriers had got so wrapped up in the tale, he'd look for the print of a big bare foot whenever he happened upon a bit of bare sandy creek bank.

He stopped when he saw, a short distance up the hillside, a little nook under a limestone ledge half covered with wild grapevines. He doubted anybody would be wandering in such an out-of-the-way rough place, but a man ought not to take a chance on being seen at the devilish work he had to do.

He tucked William David under his elbow in order to use both hands. The baby started the beginnings of a yowl. Leslie stuck the sack of maple sugar into his mouth. The cry was never finished. The maple sugar sack had to be held, else the greedy little fool would suck down cloth and all to choke himself to death.

He fished in a pocket until he found a narrow strip of cloth torn from the shirt. He tied one end to the string around the maple sugar sack, the other to a conveniently close grapevine. He brought out the saddle blanket, laid it in a leafy spot behind the grapevine, and put William David down. The maple sugar kept him quiet.

Taking off the wrapper and dress Rachel had put on him, then redressing in the makeshift outfit cut from the shirt went quickly and soundlessly, except for one short yowl. This came because in slipping the tow-shirt dress over his head, Leslie had to take away the sugar sack. He got it back into the baby's mouth as quickly as he could.

Now to dress his hair. He took a strip of cloth torn from a shirt sleeve, folded it, then tied the cloth around William David's forehead to protect his eyes from a chance sprinkle of sulphur. William David didn't mind: he could still peep from under the edge of the cloth, nor did he appear to notice anything except the good taste of the maple sugar as Leslie began the slow work of shaking sulphur through the silk handkerchief onto his hair.

Finished at last, Leslie considered the job. He thought he might have used too much sulphur; the hair was more yellow than the light chestnut he'd aimed at. Worse, though William David's hair was about the same dark brown as that patch on Cupid, the dog's hair was thick and coarse where his was thin and fine. You didn't have to hunt to see his scalp. Now, several spots on his scalp were sulphur-yellow, and there was no way of getting them off without rubbing sulphur off his hair.

Leslie dipped the tip of his little finger in the flour he'd brought and rubbed the yellowed spots. Soon, the scalp was spotted with sickly white. Well, let him look sickly. He rubbed on flour until the scalp was a fairly even white.

That pale scalp didn't match his face. He was beginning to get color in his cheeks, and his lips were pink from all the work they were doing. Leslie lightly floured his face. He wished he hadn't. The child was the color of a corpse.

He dusted off considerable, but not all. William David continued to look sickly, and with that white bandage around his forehead, half hiding his eyes, a person would think he was half dead from a wound.

Well, wound him, make a good, bleeding wound—if he could find the right thing for wounding on the way back to his regular path home from the saltpeter works.

He crossed the creek, and, careful to keep under cover, angled up the ridge side toward the path home. Halfway there, he stopped when he saw, among a bed of brown curled leaves, a brown leaf with faintly rounded lobes and a stem in the middle. Puccoon. He gouged here and there in the soft leaf mold near the leaf until he felt a thickish root.

He pulled out a goodly length of root, already with a bead of bloody juice at either end. He wiped the root clean with a handful of leaves, then went to work on William David.

Finished, he had a red wound on William David's forehead, still bleeding; the white cloth had a big red patch above the wound with a streak across his cheek and onto his chin where it had dripped off to make a spot on his makeshift dress. Leslie returned the root to its bed, covered it, and hurried on.

He maybe ought not to have wounded William David. Anybody with any sense knew blood dried more black than red; puccoon juice stayed red.

He stopped when, high up on the ridge side, he neared his regular path. Hidden behind a brushy pine, he studied the sky. The even gray cloud covering, though thick enough to hide the shape of the sun, was too thin to hide its glow completely; that bright patch in the clouds high in the southern half of the sky, was the sun, about as high as it would go in early November. The missus would be expecting her dinner about now. At such times when the weather was agreeable, she either sat in the mouth of her rockhouse or walked slowly about while waiting for dinner.

He scanned the valley without finding sign of her. She'd surely come out on a warmish, windless day like this. If he had to wait too long, William David might go to sleep, or eat so much maple sugar he'd be sick.

Leslie walked slowly down the path, pausing now and then to look and listen for the woman. He had about given up hope when he stopped again on a limestone ledge near the creek. This time he saw, half hidden in the brush, a pink blur moving toward the yellow-headed woman's rockhouse. He'd come too late; she had finished her walk, and was returning to her rockhouse where she might not hear William David's crying.

Give it a try. He sprang down the ledge, and behind the screen of willows by the creek, took William David from his shoulder where he liked to be, then jerked the sugar sack from his mouth, whispering as he flung it into the creek: "I'm sorry to treat you so, but it's the only way I know to make you scream without hurten you. Scream, honey, scream."

William David obliged. He screamed more loudly and kicked for all he was worth when Leslie laid him on his back. He hated to lie flat on his back, and Leslie knew it. The woman would surely hear him now.

She did, and came in a rush to meet him, her face red with anger. She didn't glance at the baby, caterwauling for all he was worth, but fixed her glare on Leslie. "Why you dirty, lying son-of-a-bitchen bastard, you tricked me when you took my money and told me that—"

She either wouldn't mention aloud that she'd hired him to kill her woodscolt or she'd been stopped by a glimpse of that bright yellow hair—out in the open like this it sure looked bright; he'd overdone the sulphur.

"Maam, it hurts that you should think so ill of me, callen me a trickster when thrust upon me is one a the pitifulest cases mortal man has ever seen."

She took a step closer to glance at the pale sickly face and bloody head, then fix her stare on the golden hair.

"I know, maam, you don't want babies around when you're travelen, but I won't let the cow slow us up. I'll make a muzzle for the calf out a willow twigs"—Jethro had long since made one and was trying to train the calf to lead, but without much success—"and somebody can lead the calf from horseback. That'll bring the cow right along. I couldn't help but agree to get this child to his grandmother over the mountains."

"Where did he come from? No, with all that golden hair it must be a girl; be a shame to waste such hair on a boy."

Now, that was good to hear. She was believing what she saw. Still, Leslie began to walk as he talked. He wanted to get William David out of her sight; if he were sweating as much as this man spinning lies over him, his sweat would wash that "golden hair" to dark brown right before her eyes, and turn the flour on his cheeks to biscuit dough.

"The last thing in the world I wanted to do was this, but while I was mixen gunpowder at the works, a man rode up with this child. He begged me to take it to its grandmother somewhere past Abingdon. The man that brought it—her—said he was on his way to French Lick, and he didn't seem to care whether it lived or died. He'd dropped her. And from the look of its head, she landed on a rock."

"But its parents? Why don't they—?"

"Oh Lord. Oh Lord."

He had reckoned without Rachel, but here she was running to see what he'd done to William David. Anger at him, terror for the baby, had dried her tears. He held up his hand, palm outward, and gave her what he hoped was a mean look.

She returned his mean look as she came on to get a closer look at what had been William David.

Let her look. "Her parents. That bastard—excuse me, maam, I've let my feelens get the better of my tongue—anyhow, he said the father had been ambushed and scalped while out cutten firewood with two other men. His widowed wife was nothen more than a young and foolish girl and had her baby daughter here, her first, comen along fine until one day—" He stopped the oath that wanted to come out when he felt a warm wetness spread over one hand. You'd think the little devil could have waited a little longer.

Instead of swearing, he shook his head at Rachel, moaning again as she came up and jerked William David from him.

The missus turned her stare on the black woman instead of the baby. "Rachel, what ails you? You look like somebody had beat you half to death."

Rachel turned her mean look on the missus: "Nobody beats me—now."

"She's never got over losen that little chap. Still cries a lot."

"That's no excuse for such a late dinner."

"I'll wager the rabbits brought in by the boys are slow in cooken tender," Leslie said to the missus, then to Rachel: "You may have to give the lady somethen else; maybe she'll send down some ham or somethen."

He hurried to finish his tale. "As I said, this baby's mother was young and foolish. Indians kept that station in northern Kentucky under such close watch, water had to be brought from the spring by men under guard, and then only enough for cooken and drinken. Well, a few days ago this baby's mother told another woman she wasn't goen to let the Indians force her baby to wear dirty clothes.

"The other woman thought she was just talken, but lo and behold next mornen real early she slipped out a the fort—the guards must a been asleep. They wakened in a hurry when they heard this child's mother scream—just once as the Indians tore off her scalp."

He managed a doleful sigh with a head shake to match.

The missus said: "What a fool, forcen us to travel with her poor little girl. But, shitfire, from her looks she won't be with us long." She turned and headed for her rockhouse.

Leslie started to his quarters; he wanted to wash his hand with soap. He wished he could sing or whistle, but felt he ought not in the middle of such a sad business. He gave his hands a quick scrub, then hurried toward Rachel's rockhouse. He ought to have gone there first. In her present mean humor, she might put what she thought was a strange baby into the basket and let him cry his heart out.

Coming up to her overhang, he heard a soft giggle. Rachel was rubbing sulphur out of William David's hair. She saw him and smiled. "Suh, it was mighty good a you to take so much trouble with William David here so we can all travel together without the missus suspicionen. I was skeered she'd notice them pretty pink toes kicken around that you fergot to put flour on. But all her mind went to that pretty hair. She's never seen him, but once when he was real little, she asked me if he didn't have real dark hair. I told her he did, and she started bawlen."

"In that case, you ought to keep the sulphur in his hair, and not rub it off," Leslie told her, annoyed because she was ruining his work.

Rachel gave another giggle. "That sulphur keeps rubben off. Anyhow, from now on when he's outside, he'll have to wear one a his caps to keep dirt out a that wound you made in his head. What I aim to do is crop off enough hair from that sulphur colored patch on the calf to make a few little sprigs to stick out from under each cap. I'll sew em on the edges of his caps, real tight with fine stitches goen back and forth. The missus won't notice him much nohow."

Leslie laughed. "You're a smart girl, Rachel."

She burst out bawling. "Oh, Mastah Collins, it's so good to see you still able to laugh after all the trouble the good Lord has sent on you."

He swore under his breath, and left to hunt Cleo. He'd forgotten he'd need a packhorse or two to bring his powder over the ridge; and whoever did the work should have a good bait of corn with plenty of time to eat it.

A note about the author

Harriette Simpson Arnow was born in Wayne County, Kentucky, and received her education at Berea College and the University of Louisville. She taught for four years in public schools, but gave up teaching to devote more time to writing. After her move to Cincinnati, between working on short stories and her first novel, she held odd jobs until her marriage in 1939. A few months later, she and her husband, Harold Arnow, a former Chicago newspaperman, bought a farm of sorts in the Cumberland National Forest on the Big South Fork of Cumberland River in Kentucky. Here, they planned to write and practice subsistence farming. The struggle for subsistence from the worn-out land left no energy for writing; after five years of trying, they moved to Detroit during the Second World War. Mr. Arnow returned to newspaper work while Mrs. Arnow settled into crowded, wartime housing. They lived here a few years, then with their two children moved in 1950 to a place in the country near Ann Arbor, Michigan. Mr. Arnow commuted to his work in Detroit; save for flowers and a vegetable garden, there was to be no more farming.

Her first novel, *Mountain Path*, was published in 1936, and is still available in paperback. It is set in her native mountains, as is *Hunter's Horn*, which was published in 1949 with considerable success. Her third novel, *The Dollmaker*, published in 1954, became a best seller. She has also done two works of social history, *Seedtime on the Cumberland* (1960) and *The Flowering of the Cumberland* (1963). Her most recent novel is *The Weedkiller's Daughter* (1970). Her books have received several awards, among them a prize from The Friends of American Writers for *The Dollmaker*, and in 1961 an Award of Merit from the Association for State and Local Historians for *Seedtime on the Cumberland*.

A Note on the Type

The text of this book was set in Caledonia, a type face designed by W(illiam) A(ddison) Dwiggins for the Mergenthaler Linotype Company in 1939. Dwiggins chose to call his new type face Caledonia, the Roman name for Scotland, because it was inspired by the Scotch types cast about 1833 by Alexander Wilson & Son, Glasgow type founders. However, there is a calligraphic quality about Caledonia that is totally lacking in the Wilson types. Dwiggins referred to an even earlier type face for this "liveliness of action"—one cut around 1790 by William Martin for the printer William Bulmer. Caledonia has more weight than the Martin letters, and the bottom finishing strokes (serifs) of the letters are cut straight across, without brackets, to make sharp angles with the upright stems, thus giving a "modern face" appearance.

W. A. Dwiggins (1880–1956) began an association with the Mergenthaler Linotype Company in 1929 and over the next twenty-seven years designed a number of book types, the most interesting of which are the Metro series, Electra, Caledonia, Eldorado, and Falcon.

The book was composed, printed and bound by Kingsport Press, Inc., Kingsport, Tennessee. Typography and binding design by Anthea Lingeman.